Magda's Daughter

ALSO BY CATRIN COLLIER

Historical

Hearts of Gold
One Blue Moon
A Silver Lining
All That Glitters
Such Sweet Sorrow
Past Remembering
Broken Rainbows
Spoils of War
Swansea Girls
Swansea Summer
Homecoming
Beggars & Choosers
Winners & Losers
Sinners & Shadows
Finders & Keepers
Tiger Bay Blues
Tiger Ragtime
One Last Summer

Crime

(as Katherine John)
Without Trace
Six Foot Under
Murder of a Dead Man
By Any Other Name
The Corpse's Tale
The Amber Knight
Black Daffodil

Modern Fiction

(as Caro French)
The Farcreek Trilogy

Magda's Daughter

CATRIN COLLIER

First published in Great Britain in 2008 by Orion Books,
an imprint of The Orion Publishing Group Ltd
Orion House, 5 Upper Saint Martin's Lane
London, WC2H 9EA

An Hachette Livre UK Company

3 5 7 9 10 8 6 4 2

A CIP catalogue record for this book is
available from the British Library.

ISBN (hardback): 978 0 7528 8585 8
ISBN (trade paperback): 978 0 7528 8586 5

Typeset by Deltatype Ltd, Birkenhead, Merseyside

Printed and bound in the UK by CPI Mackays, Chatham ME5 8TD

The Orion Publishing Group's policy is to use papers that are natural,
renewable and recyclable products and made from wood grown in sustainable
forests. The logging and manufacturing processes are expected to
conform to the environmental regulations of the country of origin.

www.orionbooks.co.uk

For the dedicated postmistress of Upper Killay,
Ivy, and her husband Erich Ubischek,
with many thanks
for their help in reading my translations and taking
such care of my manuscripts.

Chapter 1

NED JOHN picked up a blue inflatable chair from the centre of the threadbare rug in his bed-sit and walked down the passageway to the communal kitchen. Helena Janek was leaning on the ironing board, her back to him. Her tartan mini-kilt swung high, revealing tantalizing expanses of slim, white, tight-clad thighs, as she pushed the iron over her long blonde hair.

'One day you're going to burn yourself doing that, shunshine,' he warned.

She looked sideways at him. 'Showing my legs or ironing my hair?'

'Ironing your hair. I think you've already been burned for showing your legs.'

'Only by you, and I'd say warmed rather than burned. As for my head – better a minor burn than curly hair.' She pushed the iron aside and studied the results of her handiwork in the blotched mirror that hung over the sink. Satisfied there wasn't a hint of wave left, she unplugged the iron and folded away the board.

'You wouldn't be quite so cavalier if you have to wait hours in Casualty for treatment.' He pulled her towards him before remembering why he'd come looking for her. 'I take it everything that's left in our room is rubbish?'

'Not everything.'

'The car is full.'

'I only want to keep one or two small things. I'll slip them into my suitcases.'

'Your suitcases are already in the boot. And given the job I had closing them, it seems you don't understand the concept of full. The car has room for two more items – me and you. Although after

1

seeing what you've stacked on the passenger seat to carry on your lap, I'm not too sure about you. So this,' Ned batted the plastic chair towards her, 'has reached the end of its life.'

'No!' Helena wrapped her arms protectively around it. 'It's the first thing we bought together.'

'You mean it was the first mistake we made – and you talked me into it,' Ned teased.

'Ned John—'

'Go on, admit it. It's more comfortable to sprawl on the floor, especially when we sprawl together.' He winked at her.

'But it's such a pretty blue.' She led the way back to their bed-sit.

Ned unclipped a safety pin from his sweater. 'Time for a ceremonial bursting.'

'Don't you dare.' Helena backed towards the window. 'I'll de-flate it. It will fold down to practically nothing.'

'There's no room in the car for "practically nothing". And the quickest way to deflate it is with this.'

'Over my dead body.'

'It's only a chair, and a useless one at that.' Ned leaned against the door and looked around. 'This room looks weird without your mess.'

'*My* mess?'

'All right. *Our* mess. These, I take, are full of rubbish?' He pointed to two cardboard boxes packed with newspapers and magazines.

'Yes.' She frowned. 'Although there's an article on pop art in last week's *Observer* that I meant to save, and one on Byron—'

'They'll print them again.' He picked up the boxes and carried them out before she could start rummaging.

Helena dropped the inflatable chair in front of the window and balanced carefully on it. She had learned from experience that if she didn't get her weight distribution just right, it tipped over. She looked around. Ned was right. Stripped of the embroidered tablecloths, hangings and posters, which she had used to cover the grubby wallpaper, the rickety bed, stained sofa and chipped table, the room did look weird. Bare, shabby and unwelcoming, yet it had been home to both of them for eighteen months. Now, it was just another nondescript bed-sit waiting for the next tenant.

She opened the window, leaned out and watched Ned stack the boxes next to the bins. Even after two years of what her mother quaintly called 'courtship', eighteen months of living with Ned and six months of engagement, she still couldn't believe he was hers. She recalled all the times she had sat just where she was now, ostensibly studying, but really watching and waiting for him to return from the interminable shifts he had worked in the hospital. She recalled the thrill she'd felt whenever she had seen his tall, well-built figure striding along the pavement beneath her, his auburn hair shining. She would wait in anticipation for his tread on the uncarpeted stairs . . .

'If I'd known how reluctant you'd be to leave, I'd never have suggested moving to Pontypridd a month before our wedding.' He was back already.

'I was miles away.' She swallowed hard before turning around in the hope that he wouldn't realize she was close to tears. 'We've been happy here.'

'Slum that it is, we have,' Ned agreed. 'But I hope we'll never have to live in anything quite so awful again.'

'It's not a slum.'

'I suppose the place had its good points. Along with a shared bathroom and kitchen, I had you.' He held out his arms and she went to him, leaning her head against his chest.

'Love you.'

'Love you, too. Just think, six weeks from now we'll be in our new house with a bathroom and kitchen of our very own. And there won't be any marauding law students to steal our food.'

'That's six weeks away. I hate the thought of losing you.'

'You're hardly doing that, when we'll be married in four, and honeymooning for two,' he observed in amusement.

'After living apart for a month.'

'The house is ready. You could move in there with me now. You were the one who didn't want to shock your mother,' he reminded her.

'She'd never talk to me again if she knew we'd lived in sin.'

3

He suppressed the urge to say, 'That would be a plus.'

'We could have another go at trying to persuade her that this is the 1960s not the 1930s?'

'You know my mother. When it comes to morality, she's behind the times.'

'And very Catholic.' Ned's refusal to convert to Catholicism had caused the deepest of several rifts between him and Helena's widowed mother, Magda, who'd wanted her only child to celebrate her marriage with a full mass, not the ceremony reserved for 'mixed marriages'. Even now he wasn't sure why he'd held out. Not when he'd conceded that any children they had would be brought up in Helena's faith.

'I thought we'd agreed not to discuss religion, or my mother, any more.' One of the side effects of Helena's strict upbringing was a loathing of arguments. Especially with people she loved.

'We did. I only wish I could understand the Catholic preoccupation with morality and guilt. Before I met you I used to think all you Papists had to do was nip down to the confessional, tell the priest a few titillating stories to brighten his day, say a couple of Hail Marys, and hey presto – absolution and a clean slate, all ready to blot again. But you haven't been to confession once since we moved in together.'

'And I won't while we continue to sin.' She fell serious, as she always did whenever they discussed her Church.

'What sin?' He wrapped his arms around her and kissed her neck. 'Practically every couple we know is shacked up together.'

'But none of them has told their parents. You haven't even told yours.'

'Not officially, but they're not stupid.'

'Are you saying my mother is?' she bristled.

'Of course not, sunshine,' he said hastily. 'But she is a little naive if she expects me to keep my hands off you until our wedding night. Talking of which . . .' He pulled the sleeveless, black-ribbed, polo-necked sweater she was wearing free from the waistband of her kilt and slid his hands beneath it.

'Ned, we've stripped the bed . . .'

'And now it's time to strip something else.' He silenced her with a kiss. Kicking the door shut with his heel, he pulled up her sweater. 'Promise me you'll never wear a bra.' He kissed each of her breasts in turn before unclipping her skirt and tugging at her tights.

'You're insatiable.'

'So are you, and it wouldn't be the first time we've made love on this floor.' He swung her off her feet and dropped her gently onto the carpet.

'But it will be the last.'

'No more nostalgia until we get in the car,' he pleaded. 'Not while we've one more memory to make inside these walls.'

'You two finally off?' Alan, who lived in one of the ground floor bed-sits, eyed the two bulging plastic bags that Ned was carrying down the stairs.

'As soon as I've dumped this rubbish and Helena's cried her last goodbye.'

'I heard that,' Helena called after him.

'You were meant to. The time you're taking, it will be midnight before we reach Pontypridd.' Ned dropped the bags, pulled out his keyring, slipped the front door and room keys from it, setting them on the table that held the mail.

'Lucky sods,' Alan murmured. 'I'd move if I could afford a better place. Living on the first floor you've never had to share a kitchen or bathroom with the terrible twins. It took Angela half an hour to scrub the bath free from mud pack last night before she could use it.'

The terrible twins were two Mods from Reading who looked, talked and dressed exactly alike in Mary Quant mini-dresses and black kiss curls, which they stuck to their cheeks with false eyelash glue.

Helena carried the inflatable chair down the stairs. Propping it behind her, out of Ned's reach, she took her keys from her handbag and handed them to Alan. 'Apart from raiding our food cupboard when they come back from the pub, the boys on our floor aren't too bad. You and Angie could move into our room.'

'We could, couldn't we?' Alan took her keys and scooped up Ned's from the table. 'Thanks, I wouldn't have thought of that.'

'And thanks for letting us know about this place.' Ned held out his hand and Alan shook it. 'It was all you said it would be: cheap, friendly, close to the university and the hospital. Noisy, unsanitary and infested with two-legged rats.'

'You referring to me and Angie?' Alan asked.

'The boys on our floor, who enjoy nibbling what doesn't belong to them,' Ned replied.

'Look forward to seeing you and Angie at the wedding.' Helena kissed Alan's cheek.

'And the bachelor party.' Alan clapped Ned on the back. 'My first in Wales. Should I bring a leek?'

'Just your passport,' Ned joked. 'Without it, they may not allow you across the border.'

Alan threw a playful punch at the chair. 'I remember the night I tried to balance my beer on that and got soaked.'

Ned unclipped the pin from his sweater again. 'Helena wants to take it. There's no room in the car and I don't fancy wasting time trying to squash all the air out of it.'

'Could you use it, Alan?' Helena asked.

'Given the state of the furniture in this place, all donations will be gratefully received.'

Helena handed it over. 'I like to think of it staying in our room.'

'A monument to our lost love – except our love isn't lost. And it's our room no longer.' Ned went outside and dumped the bags by the dustbins. 'As for Helena's chair, Alan, make sure it has plenty of fresh air. Bath it once a week and sing lullabies to it every night, or Helena will come back and haunt you.'

'The only promise I'll make is that I'll christen it again in beer from time to time.' Alan wolf-whistled when Helena's kilt rode up as she climbed into Ned's MG.

'Stop ogling my girl,' Ned warned, not entirely humorously.

'You're one lucky sod,' Alan said. 'Long blonde hair, innocent blue eyes and legs up to her neck. Do me a favour, Helena, tell Angie how you grew them?'

'I'm more likely to advise her to look for another boyfriend.'

'I'm free anytime in the next month if you want to leave Ned and elope with me. Law pays more than medicine in the long run.'

'Thanks, but no thanks, Alan,' she blew him a kiss as Ned drove away.

'You've hardly said a word since we left Bristol.' Ned slipped his hand onto Helena's knee as they drove out of the Cardiff suburbs and headed north. 'I hope you're not considering Alan's offer.'

'He's besotted with Angie; he'd run a mile if I took him seriously.'

'I'd rather you didn't put him to the test.'

'I've no intention of trying. I was just thinking how much has happened to us in the last two years.'

'And more good things will happen to us in the next few years.' He glanced across at her. 'Stop worrying. You'll get the job.'

'And if I don't?'

'We'll survive on my salary and start that family we talked about sooner rather than later. And then you won't have to wrestle with your conscience about the Pope's edict on the contraceptive pill. As if any priest has the right to tell anyone how to live their personal life.'

'You're starting another argument.'

'Sorry,' he apologized, 'but it makes my blood boil to think that anyone, let alone a sworn celibate, whatever his rank in the Church, believes that they have the right to meddle in people's sex lives.'

'I've told you that I don't want to be just a housewife.' Helena deliberately changed the subject.

'You agreed you'd want to stay at home and look after our children when the time came.'

'Only after I've established my career so I can return to it when they're old enough.'

'Perhaps by then we'll be able to afford a nanny to look after our eleven children while you work.'

'Eleven? Last week it was twelve.' She switched on the car radio.

'I've decided twelve would be excessive.' The seductive sound of Danny Williams singing 'Moon River' filled the car. 'They're playing our song. That has to be a good omen.'

Not wanting to think about good or bad omens lest she hex her chances of getting her dream job, she ignored his comment. 'I won-der how my mother will take to being a grandmother.'

'Judging by the way she fusses over babies when they're brought into the shop, I predict she'll love them until they're old enough to answer back.'

'I wish you two got along better.'

'And I wish she'd stop bullying you,' he retorted.

'It's not bullying. She simply pushes me to do my best so I can——'

'Achieve your full potential,' he finished. 'I've heard it all from her, sunshine. And it's more like your mother has manipulated you into living the life she wanted for herself before the war got in the way. Only you refuse to see it.'

'My mother had a dreadful time before she came to Pontypridd. Seeing my father murdered when I was only three weeks old. Forced to work as a slave labourer for the Nazis. Trying to make a home for us in a Displaced Person's camp before she was able to get the papers she needed to come to Wales. And it hasn't been that easy since. Managing the shop and bringing me up single-handed. Always having to worry if there'd be enough money to pay our bills and educate me.'

'Magda's tough and she does have her good points,' he conceded. 'They say look at your girlfriend's mother and you see her in twenty years' time. I'll count myself a lucky man if you resemble Magda. But that only goes as far as resilience and looks,' he qualified.

'That's not likely given our very different colouring.' She laid her hand over his. 'Does that saying apply to men and their fathers?'

'Not in my case, because I'm much better-looking than my father ever was.' Ned squeezed her fingers lightly, before lifting his hand and brushing his hair back from his forehead.

'I'll tell him you said so.'

'If you do, I'll say you made it up. Just look at this!' He braked when they hit a traffic jam on the Treforest Trading Estate. 'You and your endless goodbyes. We've caught the five o'clock factory rush hour.'

'I was ready to leave when I finished ironing my hair. You were the one who insisted on delaying.'

'So I did.' He couldn't resist a smile. 'Where do you want to go first – my parents' house or your mother's flat?'

'My mother's, to drop off my things.'

'You don't want my parents to see how much junk you've accumulated in Bristol.'

'That's right.' Helena leaned back in her seat and closed her eyes. She couldn't stop thinking about the teaching post she'd been interviewed for. She'd longed to emulate her much-loved English teacher, Miss Addis, ever since she'd taken her first English lesson in the Girls' Grammar School after passing her eleven-plus. That examination had seemed an insurmountable obstacle at the time, and there'd been so many others since.

For over ten years she'd dreamed of realizing her ambition to teach. She'd frequently pictured herself in the same classrooms she'd sat in as a pupil, inspiring a love of English literature and poetry in generations of young girls, just as her beloved mentor had done. But despite Ned's optimism, she now felt she'd been over-ambitious, and should have set her sights on a lesser position in a primary school.

'Are you going to stay in the car all night?'

Helena reluctantly abandoned her fantasy of a procession of highly-acclaimed female authors who'd returned to the Grammar School to thank her for her encouragment. She opened her eyes and discovered Ned had parked outside the cooked meat and pie shop that her mother managed.

Ned climbed out. 'I'll carry your cases upstairs. We'll take the boxes of books and other things straight up to the new house to save me humping them twice.'

'That's sensible.' Helena moved a box of long-playing records onto the driving seat, and reached for her handbag.

'Hello, Magda, you spotted us.' Ned dutifully kissed Helena's mother's cheek, as she stepped out of the side door that led up to the flat above the shop.

'I expected you two hours ago,' she reprimanded.

'We would have arrived at the crack of dawn if Helena hadn't got all maudlin. She had to say goodbye to every hole in the carpet and stain on the wall of . . .' he paused, only just stopping himself from saying 'our', 'her bed-sit.'

'That's not true, Mama.' Helena hugged and kissed her mother.

'It would be understandable. A part of your life is over. Your student days are behind you. Now you're a young lady who has to earn her own living.' Magda frowned at her daughter before returning her embrace. 'Is that a skirt or a belt you are wearing?'

'Mama, mini-skirts are fashionable.'

'In my day a girl would have been horsewhipped for showing so much leg. A letter has arrived for you. From the council. It's on the sideboard,' she shouted after Helena when her daughter raced up the stairs.

'Good news?' Ned asked, knowing how much Helena's heart was set on the post she'd applied for.

'I think you should wait for Helena to tell you.'

'You opened the letter?' Ned hoped to embarrass Magda. One of the few things Helena was prepared to argue with Magda about was her mother's insistence on opening all the mail addressed to her daughter.

'A mother's right,' she snapped. 'Is that all you're bringing in?' She watched Ned lift two suitcases out of the car and set them on the pavement.

'We decided to take Helena's books and other things straight up to the new house in Graigwen.'

'I suppose that's sensible,' Magda said in a tone that brought a sharp reminder of all the evenings Ned had spent during the Christmas and Easter holidays listening to his future mother-in-law argue as to why he and Helena should postpone their wedding for two years.

Ned could remember all Magda's reasons: setting up home was expensive – it would take at least that long to save the money they'd need to buy essentials; Helena was too young to go straight from college into married life; he'd need time to adjust to working as a GP without the distraction of a wife; and most annoying of all, if he took weekly instruction from Father O'Brien for two years he wouldn't have any qualms about making the commitment to convert to Catholicism.

Hampered by the suitcases, Ned followed Magda up the stairs. Helena was standing in the middle of the room holding the letter.

'You've read it?' Magda asked.

'So have you.'

Ned refrained from cheering when he detected reproach in Helena's voice.

'A mother's right,' Magda repeated.

'You always say that, but the letter was personal, addressed to me,' Helena emphasized.

'If you haven't got the job, you can always apply for something else,' Ned cut in. He couldn't bear to wait a moment longer to find out if Helena had been successful.

'I've got it.' Helena eyed Ned. 'Your father . . .'

'Has absolutely no influence with the governors of the Girls' Grammar School,' he interrupted, knowing what she was about to ask. 'But you're an ex-pupil. Everyone who has had anything to do with the school knows you and what you're capable of. You did this one all by yourself, sunshine.'

'The headmistress and governors know an intelligent girl when they see one. A girl who will work hard and take her work very seriously.' Magda opened the sideboard door and took out a tray of tiny glasses and a bottle. 'A drink to celebrate.' She poured three minute measures of Polish vodka, and lifted one to the framed photograph on the wall. A prettier, younger version of herself, holding a bouquet of roses, stood arm in arm with a young, fair-haired man. She was dressed in a long white dress, he a well-tailored dark suit, white shirt, collar and tie. Behind them a distinctive redbrick church loomed over a graveyard. 'Your papa is looking down on us, Helena. He is very proud of you and what you have accomplished.'

Helena raised her glass to the photograph, wishing yet again that she had one memory of the man who had fathered her.

Ned took the glass Magda offered him. 'To the best English teacher the Girls' Grammar School will ever have.'

'To Helena Janek, BA and teacher,' Magda toasted formally and proudly.

'Soon to be Helena *John*.' Ned slipped his arm around Helena's shoulders. 'Congratulations, sunshine.'

11

Magda touched her glass to Helena's. 'To your future. May you always be as blessed as you are today. And now we must lay the table. I invited your mother and father to supper, Eddie. They'll be here in an hour and I haven't even mixed the dough for *pierogi*. I thought I'd stuff them with raspberries and strawberries. They were very good on the market today.'

Helena gave Ned a sympathetic smile. Named and christened Edward after his mother's brother, who had been killed fighting in the war, he had been called Eddie for the first eighteen years of his life by his family and everyone in Pontypridd. But as soon as he left his home town for Bristol University he changed it to Ned. Even his parents had capitulated and accepted the change he had engineered, but Magda stubbornly clung to Eddie.

'I'll put Helena's suitcases in her bedroom.' Ned replaced his glass on the tray.

'No, you will not, young man.' Magda wagged her finger at him. 'You will leave them outside the door because it is not proper for a man to go into a young girl's bedroom. And, after you've left them, you will come back here, extend the table and slot in the extra leaf. We'll need it. Mrs Raschenko will be here as well.'

'Auntie Alma is coming?' Helena beamed. Alma Raschenko – a widow who owned a chain of cooked meat and pie shops that existed on the high streets of every town and village in South Wales – was not only her mother's employer but also a close friend and her godmother. As Magda frequently said, she was the nearest person they had to a relative.

'Helena, you arrange the flowers and check the silver is clean while Eddie sorts the table. I'll see to the food.'

Ned gave Helena a surreptitious wink before picking up the suitcases. Happy, as her momentous news finally begin to sink in, she kissed him.

'Helena, we have work to do,' Magda rebuked. 'The time for kissing will be after the wedding. There are too many things to do first.'

'I've made the most important arrangements, Magda.' Ned couldn't resist irritating his future mother-in-law. 'Train tickets to Venice and two weeks in a hotel overlooking the Grand Canal.'

'I was talking about the hundred and one things that need doing *before* the ceremony. The cake, the reception, the food for the guests, the dresses for your sisters and the other bridesmaids, the flowers, Helena's gown . . .'

'Has it come?' Helena asked.

'It's in your room, which is why I wouldn't let Eddie go in there.' Magda lowered her voice and pointed to Ned, who'd returned to the living room and was opening the dining table ready to insert the extra leaf. 'You can see it after you've arranged the flowers and I've finished making the *pierogi*.'

'It's beautiful, Helena. You'll be a fairy tale bride,' Alma Raschenko predicted when Magda proudly showed off the wedding dress and lace veil that had been made for her daughter.

The minute they'd finished eating Magda's excellent supper, Helena, Alma and Ned's mother, Bethan, had left Ned and his father, and closeted themselves in Helena's bedroom to admire the gown, tiara and wedding finery Magda had bought.

'Won't she just.' Magda lifted the crystal-ornamented bodice of the white silk gown so the beads caught the light.

'Now,' Alma smiled conspiratorially, 'what about your trousseau, Helena? Have you bought your lingerie?'

'We're going to Cardiff on Thursday after I've closed the shop for half-day.' Magda looked as excited as if she were about to buy her own trousseau.

'Why don't I meet you there? We'll make a day of it,' Alma suggested. 'You'll have to come too, Beth, to make sure that your future daughter-in-law doesn't skimp on lace négligés, silk knickers and French perfume.'

'I do have a budget,' Helena warned, knowing how embarrassingly generous her future mother-in-law and godmother could be when it came to presents.

'That's why we need to come, to make sure you exceed it. And we'll lunch in The Angel, my treat. It's ages since I've given myself a day off from the business. You might be Magda's daughter, but, having two boys, I like to think that a little bit of you belongs to me.' Alma hugged Helena. 'The girl I always wanted and never had.'

'The best godmother ever,' Helena said sincerely.

'The best godmother you could have had to spoil you,' Magda amended. 'Whenever I wouldn't give you something when you were little, you used to pout and say, "I'll ask Auntie Alma instead."'

Their laughter echoed down the passage to the living room where Ned and his father, Andrew, were sitting at the table nursing two small brandies.

'Your mother is in her element helping to organize the wedding.' Andrew heaped a spoonful of sugar into his coffee. 'Much as she didn't approve of Rachel's choice of a fiancé, she was disappointed when your sister broke off her engagement.'

'Rachel's very young.'

Andrew suppressed a smile. 'I wouldn't let Rachel catch you saying that. She would take it as an insult coming from a brother two years younger than her.'

'I feel older.'

'I hope so, given the responsibility you're about to take on.' Andrew eyed his son. 'Nervous?'

'Not about the wedding or the responsibility. Helena's the most mature person I know.' Even if he had been nervous, his father was the last person Ned would confide in. Andrew John had always seemed a remote figure to his eldest son, possibly because he had spent the first five years of Ned's life – the war years – in a German POW camp. By the time Andrew returned, Ned had forged such a strong bond with his mother that he'd regarded his father as an interloper. When his eldest sister Rachel had enthusiastically assumed the role of 'Daddy's girl', Ned had been only too happy to relinquish his share of their father's attention to her.

'So you're expecting Helena to look after you?' Andrew didn't conceal his amusement at the thought.

'We'll look after one another, with more than a little help from you and Granddad. We'd be renting not buying a house if he hadn't left me a trust fund. And it would have taken me years to buy into a partnership in a General practice, if you hadn't offered me a place in yours.'

'That's down to pure selfishness. Aside from the fact that I could do with your professional help, with Rachel intent on working

14

abroad next year, your foster-sisters all married, and Evan and Penny heading for university in the next couple of years, your mother and I appreciate you settling close to home.'

The foster-sisters were four orphaned sisters Bethan had adopted during the war. Evan and Penny were Ned's younger brother and sister.

'Helena wouldn't consider living anywhere except Pontypridd.'

'She's a marvellous girl. We're proud to have her in the family and look forward to eating Sunday lunch with you at least once a month – your place, of course,' Andrew joked.

'I didn't know Evan was intent on going to university. Penny, possibly, once she calmed down, but Evan?' Ned looked quizzically at his father. Evan was his least academic sibling, and Penny had earned herself the reputation of being the wild one. Keener on boys, dances and parties than studying for her GCE examinations, she had been forced to repeat her fifth year in the Grammar School.

'Penny has discovered art and decided to make a career of it. I haven't dared ask in what branch. But the school seems to think that if she works, which your mother and I are realistic enough to know is a big if, she might get a place at art college.'

'And Evan?'

'You know Evan. All he's interested in is music, or what passes for music these days.' Andrew offered Ned a cigar.

Ned shook his head. 'Last I heard, the Royal Academy of Music wasn't taking pop or rock musicians.'

'He's not aiming that high. But he's taken up the violin again. Although that hasn't prevented him and his friends from making an almighty din in the barn behind the house every evening with their electric guitars. They call it practice. I call it cruelty to all living creatures within earshot.'

'I can't wait to see him, Penny and Rachel.'

'Magda invited them to supper, but Saturday nights are sacrosanct. The management of the Regent Ballroom wouldn't bother to open if the Johns ceased to patronize the place.'

'It seems a million years since I was there,' Ned mused.

'Spoken like an old man. You ready for General Practice after the excitement of a hospital?'

'Coughs, colds and minor injuries will be a welcome relief after two years in a city Casualty.'

'More like miners' chests, rheumatism, arthritis, emphysema, housemaid's knee, and the bugbear of a GP's life – the hypochondriacs.' Andrew lit his cigar.

'You get many of those?'

'Our fair share,' Andrew replied evasively. 'When do you want to start?'

'How soon do you want me?'

'A week Monday? That will give you time to buy a few things for your new house and get it sorted the way you and Helena want it, as well as do last-minute things for the wedding. If the lists Alma, Magda and your mother were compiling over supper are anything to go by it will take you and Helena a week to run all the errands they've earmarked for you two. By the way, your mother and I thought you might need a bit extra to furnish the house. It would be false economy to dip any more into your trust fund, so we put five hundred pounds into your bank account to cover it.'

Ned was overwhelmed by his father's unexpected generosity. 'Five hundred pounds, Dad . . .'

'You've your grandparents to thank for it. You weren't the only one they left money to, and we've done no more for you than we will for your sisters and brother. You haven't too heavy an overdraft, I hope?'

'Nothing I can't handle.'

'Good.' Andrew knew better than to probe deeper. 'Just remember to buy quality not quantity when it comes to carpets and furniture.'

'Helena has very definite ideas. She prefers old to new.'

'Wise girl.' Andrew looked up as Helena returned with the other women. 'We were talking about your house. Ned said you prefer old furniture to new.'

'He's right, Doctor John,' Helena smiled shyly. Despite the warm welcome Ned's parents had given her, and their friendliness towards her, she was still slightly over-awed by them.

'How about calling us Andrew and Bethan instead of Doctor and Mrs John?' Bethan suggested.

'I'll try if you want me to.'

'That's not an order, Helena.' Andrew left the table. 'Marvellous meal, Magda, thank you, but I'm afraid we have to go. I've an early meeting with the Welsh Regional Hospital Board tomorrow.'

'On a Sunday?' she asked in surprise.

'It's the only day that suits all of us.'

Bethan reached for the cardigan she'd draped on the back of the chair. 'Thank you for a lovely dinner, Magda. I'll look forward to seeing you on Thursday. You too, Alma.' Bethan hugged and kissed both of them. 'I've had a sudden thought. The farmer sent us two legs of lamb yesterday to thank Andrew for curing his gout. Why don't you all come for lunch tomorrow, to help us eat them?'

'I'd like to but if I do, I'll have to leave early. I promised Father O'Brien I'd help out at the church. We've organized a tea party and prize-giving for the Sunday school.'

'Of course I don't mind you dashing off, Magda. We're family now,' Bethan answered.

'In that case, Helena and I would love to come.' Magda returned Bethan's kiss.

'Thank you, Beth,' said Alma. 'I've been looking for an excuse to postpone a meeting with my accountant.'

'You work Sundays, too?' Andrew asked.

'It's the only day when the telephone doesn't ring. Apart from Theo, that is.'

'He's coming home from Oxford for the summer?' Bethan asked.

Alma's son, Theo, was a favourite with all his mother's friends.

'Soon, no doubt with a mountain of washing.' Alma looked happy at the prospect. 'Thank you for a lovely evening, Magda. See you tomorrow and on Thursday.'

Ned opened the door for his parents and Alma. 'I'll be home after I've given Helena and Magda a hand to clear up.'

'Nice try, a young man, but it won't take us a minute to clear the table and put away the leftover food,' Magda said firmly. 'And you need your sleep after driving all that way today.'

Ned knew when he was beaten. 'Pick you both up tomorrow morning, to drive you up for lunch? We'll go on up to the house in the afternoon, Helena, and measure for curtains and carpets.'

'And make a list of what we need to buy,' she added.

'Don't forget I promised you a fridge and cooker as wedding presents.'

'We remember, Mama,' Helena assured her mother.

'You will choose good ones, not rubbish? And don't turn up too early in the morning, Ned. Helena and I are going to mass.' Magda gave Ned a perfunctory kiss on the cheek.

'I won't.' Ned led the way down the stairs and out to the street. He lingered, while everyone said goodbye, then waved his parents and Alma off. 'Tomorrow,' he whispered to Helena, kissing her goodnight after Magda went indoors. 'It's going to be a long cold night without you.'

'Don't remind me.'

Magda's voice wafted down the stairs. 'Helena, don't stand around out there. It might be summer but it's cold. You'll catch a chill.'

'Coming, Mama.'

'Sweet dreams.' Ned gave Helena one last kiss, jumped into his car, started the engine and drove away.

Chapter 2

ANDREW JOHN sat back in his chair at the head of the table set up in his garden. He looked around at those of his family and friends who hadn't disappeared into the barn after lunch to hear his younger son's pop group, breathed in deeply and smiled.

'Feeling just a little bit smug, darling?' Bethan teased. She set a tray of coffee, strawberries and cream on the table.

'Why shouldn't I?' He refused to rise to her bait. 'I've just eaten an excellent Sunday lunch, my compliments to the chef,' he nodded to his wife, 'and I haven't a blessed thing to do before tomorrow morning. My garden is looking its best, my roses are blooming, and Evan has shut the barn doors so we can still hear the birdsong.'

'I hate to disappoint you but you promised to pick Penny up from the stables later on this afternoon.' Bethan lifted the bowls from the tray.

'That's hours and a pleasant drive away.'

'Thank you.' Magda took the coffee cup Bethan handed her. 'I love eating outdoors in summer. It reminds me of home, although your garden is much prettier than my family's farmyard. And there aren't any animals to be seen.'

'Not since Andrew built a fence to screen the chickens.' Bethan handed Magda the milk jug and Alma the sugar bowl.

'My father and brothers used to carry the big old table out of the barn every spring and leave it on the veranda until autumn. We used to eat all our meals there in the warm weather, and we children especially liked eating there in the evening, because our parents would drink one or two glasses of wine or beer, which would make them mellow, and then they would allow us to stay up past our bedtime. My mother would light the lanterns and place them on the table, and all the farm workers and any neighbours who called in would join us. After we'd eaten, the grown-ups would play music and sing . . .' Magda glanced self-consciously at her fellow guests and coloured in embarrassment. 'I'm sorry. I always get carried away whenever I talk of home.'

'Home?' repeated Ronnie Ronconi, Bethan's brother-in-law. 'You left Poland – what, twenty-odd years ago? And it's still home? Magda, we'd like you to think of Pontypridd as your home and us as your family now.'

Everyone around the table laughed.

'Do *you* think of Pontypridd as your home, Ronnie?' Magda asked seriously.

'She has a point.' Bethan passed Ronnie the bowl of strawberries and jug of cream. 'You were born in Italy.'

'I left there when I was five,' Ronnie reminded her.

'But you went back when you were in your twenties,' Andrew said thoughtlessly. 'I'm sorry,' he apologized when Bethan gave him a reproachful look.

'No need to be sorry. As you all know, I spent some of the happiest years of my life there.'

Everyone fell silent. Ronnie had returned to Italy with Bethan's younger sister, Maud, after they'd married in the 1930s. He had returned to Pontypridd after she had died of consumption during the war.

Bethan broke the silence. 'If Maud's letters were anything to go by they were the happiest years of her life as well.'

'But neither of us thought of Italy as home when we were living there, any more than I do now.'

'You visit the country often enough.' Andrew passed the coffee pot down the table. Ronnie and his ten brothers and sisters hadn't sold their grandparents' farmhouse after their death, and the extended family frequently returned to Bardi for their summer holidays.

Ronnie thought for a moment. 'It's like having two homes. But Italy is definitely the second or holiday home. Whenever I'm there I think of Pontypridd and the house in Tyfica Road as home. It's where Diana and I brought up Billy and Catrina.' He smiled absently when he mentioned his second wife, who had died unexpectedly six months before following a brain haemorrhage. 'I can't imagine moving away from here, even if Billy and Catrina do torment the life out of me by trying to run my life as well as the business. Do you think there's any chance of Evan's pop group breaking into the big time and the younger generation embarking on a world-wide tour?'

'Not much if that din is anything to go by,' Ned remarked.

Ronnie glanced at the barn where the sound of off-key guitars and Catrina's voice vied for supremacy. 'I am so glad you have a barn, Bethan, otherwise that lot might be tempted to practise in my attic.' He turned to Alma's stepson, Peter, who had arrived in Pontypridd as a teenage refugee after the war. 'What about you? Do you think of Russia or Wales as your home?'

Peter lifted his youngest daughter, who was only three and prone to falling asleep after every meal, from her chair and onto his lap. 'Pontypridd is the first home I had.' He glanced at his wife, Liza, the eldest of Bethan and Andrew's four foster-daughters. 'Before I came here my entire life had been spent in camps. First Stalin's then Hitler's. So, yes, Pontypridd is definitely my home because here, I have a family, and I've been able to make my own decisions as to how I want to live my life.'

'So, there you have it, Magda.' Ronnie poured cream over his strawberries. 'Peter and I are both of the opinion that it is where you live, not where you were born, that dictates the place you should think of as home.'

Peter stroked his daughter's hair as she snuggled against his shirt. 'You wouldn't want to go back to Poland, would you, Magda? Not while the Communists are in power.'

'No, I wouldn't. But I have to disagree with both of you. For me, the place where I grew up will always be home.'

'We have been happy here in Pontypridd for seventeen years, Mama.' Helena tapped Ned's hand playfully when he stole a strawberry from her bowl.

'Yes, we have been happy here, very happy,' Magda agreed, 'but I think in Polish, and when I dream I roam the countryside surrounding my father's farm, not the hills around Pontypridd. And in my best dreams your father is with me once more. So, in my opinion that makes Poland my home, not Pontypridd.'

'The best dreams are always those in which our dead are alive again.' Ronnie held out his coffee cup to Bethan for a re-fill.

'I think everyone our age would agree with that.' Alma looked at Peter. Although he was her stepson, she was as close to him as she was to the son she had given birth to. And one of the reasons she loved him so much was his strong resemblance to her husband.

Magda glanced at her watch. 'But now I am very much in Pontypridd and I have to leave if I am going to help Father O'Brien with the Sunday school tea party.'

Ned rose from his chair. 'We'll drop you back at the shop, collect the things you need for the party, and drive you to the church, Magda.'

'There's no need to take me to the church. Father O'Brien is picking me up in half an hour, and the trays of sausage rolls and pastries are all ready to load into his car. He told me to thank you for selling them to the church at cost price,' Magda said to Alma.

'As he always does, and I've no doubt he'll want the same for the next party.'

Magda hugged and kissed everyone. 'Thank you for a lovely lunch, Bethan, Andrew.'

'Don't forget we're all meeting on Thursday to buy Helena's trousseau.' Alma returned Magda's hug.

'We won't,' Magda assured her.

'Go on, admit it,' Andrew grimaced as an unearthly wail issued from the barn, 'there is no Sunday school tea party, and you two don't need to measure for curtains. You just want to escape that screeching.'

'I'll tell my daughter what you said about her singing, Andrew.' Ronnie blew a kiss to Magda. 'Any time you want to visit the Regent Ballroom on a Saturday night, Magda, give me a call? We mature people can't let the young ones have all the fun, now can we?'

'I'll think about it, Ronnie, but it would mean you staying up past your bedtime,' she joked.

'For you, Magda, I'll make an exception,' he called after her as she climbed into Ned's car.

*

Ned unlocked the door of their new house and stepped inside. 'Just look at this place! All spotless, waiting for us to mess it up.'

'You call this spotless?' Helena followed Ned into the living room of their house, which, given it had only one small bedroom upstairs and one large downstairs, was more like a bungalow. 'It's filthy. Can't you see the dust on the mantelpiece and skirting boards, or the plaster and paint marks on the floor? You'd think that the builders would have been more careful given that it's costing us over two thousand pounds. As for the window, to quote one of my mother's favourite expressions, you could grow potatoes on the glass.'

'It's nothing a good clean won't cure. I'll give you a hand, if you agree to move in with me, right now, this minute.' Ned put down the box of books he'd brought in, and took the carton of linen Helena was carrying from her, dropping it onto the floor. Then he danced her around the room before kissing her slowly and thoroughly.

'Aside from the dirt, I prefer real to imaginary furniture,' she murmured when he released her.

'Who needs furniture?'

'Have you forgotten the night we slept on the floor of your sister's flat in London? You didn't stop complaining about your back for a month.' Helena studied the parquet wood-block floor. In between the scuff marks were deeper scars, which she suspected no amount of polishing would remove.

'We'll use our imaginations and improvise.'

'A bed?'

'Let's start with the small things. This will be our coffee table,' he pointed to the box of books, 'and I spy a telephone.' Ned fetched a white plastic telephone from the corner of the room and set it on the box.

'Does it work?'

He lifted the receiver. 'I have a dialling tone.'

'That was quick.'

'Doctors have priority over mere mortals when it comes to connecting a line, and I told my father that I might move in here before the wedding. Although, after the early hours of this morning, "might" is becoming a certainty. You should have heard Evan bumping around when he came in at two o'clock. Everyone within five miles of Penycoedcae knew he was drunk, even before my father started shouting.'

'Poor Evan.'

'Inconsiderate Evan,' he contradicted. 'Now all we need to finish this room is a television.'

'Before a sofa, chairs, carpet, curtains, lamps and bookshelves?' she asked in amusement.

'I've spent the last six years studying. It's time to catch up on the rubbish that's broadcast every night so I can join the people who complain about it in the pub.'

'So that's where you intend to spend every evening after we're married.' She grabbed him and began tickling.

'Mercy!' he shouted.

'No mercy.'

He retaliated by imprisoning both of her hands in one of his and holding them fast. 'If I want to spend every evening in the pub after we're married, I will, woman. And I'll expect you to wait up for me with my supper on the table and my slippers warming in front of the fire.'

'Been having dreams of living in Victorian times lately?' she retorted, knowing he was goading her.

'Roll on a return to the good old days when females knew their place, that's what I say.'

'Let me go and I'll show you where a woman's place is.' She shrieked when he responded by tickling her with his free hand.

'Not until you promise you won't nag me after we're married.'

'That will depend entirely on what sort of a husband you become.'

'I was nice to you in Bristol, wasn't I?'

'We weren't married in Bristol.'

'How about you move in with me now, so we can carry on pretending?' He dropped his bantering tone.

'Aside from my mother, there's still the question of furniture. And we might not even have electricity and running water.'

He went to the light switch. 'Damn, no bulb.' He walked down the passage to the airing cupboard, opened it and switched on the immersion heater. 'It's glowing red.'

Helena went into the kitchen and turned on the tap. 'And we have water. Switch off the heater or we'll run up a bill before you've even moved in.'

Ned returned to the living room, picked up the carton she'd brought in, and hauled it into the downstairs bedroom.

She followed him and watched him open it. 'What are you doing?'

'Making us a bed.' He lifted out the hangings, towels and cheap Indian bedspreads they'd brought from Bristol, and spread them over the floor.

'There are no curtains. Anyone can see in.'

'Not here, at the back. The houses behind us are too low down the hill.'

'We're supposed to be making a list of what we need and measuring for curtains and carpets.' Her protest was half-hearted, even before he kissed her again.

'We haven't celebrated your new job yet.' He caressed the sensitive skin below her ear, something she'd never been able to resist.

'We have so much to do . . .'

'None of it can be done on a Sunday afternoon when the shops are closed.'

'The cleaning and measuring can.'

'I'd prefer to measure these.' He slid his hands along her legs, moving gently upwards to her thighs, over her tights and under her skirt.

'You're seducing me.' She allowed him to unbutton the jacket of the suit she'd worn to church.

'Now that I no longer have to work shifts in the hospital, it's a new John tradition. Sunday love-ins.' He unzipped her skirt and it fell in a puddle at her feet. He slipped the pearl buttons of her blouse from their loops. 'Will you take your tights off, or shall I?'

'I will. You always ladder them.'

He watched her wriggle out of them as he unbuckled the belt on his jeans. 'I love seeing you in knickers and nothing else, especially green ones.'

'I know you do.' She dropped her tights on top of her skirt.

'So you wore them in the hope that I'd undress you?'

'You bought me twelve pairs for my birthday, remember? And threw all my others out.'

'So I did.' He tugged her silk panties downwards. 'You look fabulous in them, but even more fabulous out.'

'At this rate we'll never get the house finished.'

He tossed the last of his clothes on top of hers. 'What house?'

Then he pulled her to the floor on top of him.

'This is the last, Father O'Brien.' Magda carried a large flat box of sausage rolls from the shop.

'I'm glad to hear it. The car is full, as the Sunday school scholars will be after eating all these baked goods.' The priest loaded the box carefully on top of the others on the back seat of his car.

'I'll see to the doors then I'll be with you.' Magda took her keys from the pocket of her cardigan, then found herself struggling with the lock. The keyhole suddenly seemed to be too small for the key. And even after she managed to insert it she found it difficult to turn. She checked and double-checked the door, as well as the separate entrance to the flat, while Father O'Brien sat waiting for her in his Morris 1000. Finally, sensing his impatience, she opened the passenger door and sank down beside him.

'Are you all right, Magda?' the priest asked in concern when she held her head in her hands.

'It's just a headache. I get them from time to time. I'll be fine once I take a pill.'

'It's the stress you've been under lately, on top of working in the shop. Getting in a state over Helena's examinations, when everyone said she'd graduate with honours, which is exactly what the girl did. Not to mention panicking as to whether or not she'd get a job – and look how well she's done for herself there. Now you've her wedding to fret about. And I haven't exactly helped, asking you to organize this Sunday school tea party.'

'I enjoyed it, Father. It gave me something to think about besides Helena. And you were right telling me not to worry. Everything

26

couldn't have turned out better.' Magda opened her handbag and looked for the bottle of aspirins she carried.

'You've done a brilliant job of bringing her up, Magda. Helena has turned out to be a fine girl, a credit to you and herself. And she's got herself a good man, even if he isn't Catholic. But take my advice, slow down. The world will keep turning if your shop runs out of pies and pastries an hour before closing time, and there's only two sausage rolls for every three children at the Sunday school tea parties.'

Magda made a face as she dry-swallowed two aspirins. She knew from experience that the sooner she took the pain-killers, the sooner the stabbing pains would stop. But Father O'Brien was wrong about one thing. Her headache had nothing to do with stress and everything to do with the war. Just one more bitter souvenir.

She sat back in the seat, closed her eyes, and waited for the foul taste of the pills to subside along with the pain.

'I know you wanted Helena to be married with a full celebratory mass, but the mixed marriage ceremony is a splendid one in its own right, Magda. And who knows? When the children start coming along, Helena's young man might change his mind about being received into the Church. And then there'll be another cause for celebration.'

Magda could hear Father O'Brien's soft, musical Irish lilt, but the pain in her head had intensified, closing out the world around her. She'd had many headaches before, but never one like this. It was as though everything was conspiring to make it worse. The lurching movement of the car. The heat of the sun burning her face through the windscreen. The discordant blast of a car horn behind them . . .

'Magda . . . Magda . . . Mother of God . . .'

She heard Father O'Brien's voice rise in panic. She tried to open her eyes, but the pain prevented her. She gradually became aware that the car was no longer moving. A pleasant draught of cool air blew across her body as the passenger door opened. She sensed the touch of the priest's hand on her forehead.

She heard Father O'Brien shout to someone to telephone for an ambulance, then she heard him recite words she had last heard in another time, another language, another country. But the rhythm and the sombre tones were unmistakable.

'Through this holy anointing, may the Lord in his love and mercy help you with the grace of the Holy Spirit . . .'

Father O'Brien was administering the Last Rites. Suddenly it was the end. She thought of all the things she'd left undone, unsaid.

'Helena . . . forgive me, Father, for I have sinned . . .' she whispered. She gripped the priest's hand with all the strength that remained. 'Helena,' she repeated urgently. 'Tell her . . . I'm sorry . . .'

The priest broke off mid-sentence. 'To be sure, Magda, you've nothing to be sorry about. And this is only a precaution. The ambulance is on its way.'

Magda knew she had no time left for lies, even kind ones. 'It was a sin to keep the truth from her. I knew it was a sin . . . but I loved her . . .'

'What was a sin, Magda?' A tear fell from the priest's eye onto Magda's cheek. It splashed close to her mouth.

'I was afraid she'd blame me . . . hate me . . .'

'No one, least of all Helena, could hate you, Magda.' The priest knew he was speaking to a corpse, but he continued to hold Magda's hand. 'May the Lord who frees you from sin save you and raise you up . . .'

Father O'Brien didn't release Magda until he had completed the ritual. Not even when the ambulance came and Andrew John stopped his car and ran to see if he could help.

Helena was half sitting, half lying against Ned's chest, her arms entwined in his. She felt sleepy, contented and just a tiny bit smug as she surveyed the bare room. Their first home and she was about to earn enough money to furnish it exactly the way she wanted.

'White walls and paintwork, two simple Art Deco his and her wardrobes, an equally simple dressing table,' she said decisively, 'and a headboard to match. In beech if we can find it, but almost any light wood would look good. We'll put the bed against that wall. We'll buy two matching bedside cabinets and a writing table. A bookcase and an upholstered Queen's chair . . .'

'And I'll have to call the builder back to knock down all the walls, to accommodate madam's wishes for this one room. It only looks big at the moment because it's empty,' he warned. 'A king-size bed will fill it.'

'We can't have a king-size bed. They're modern. We'll never find an antique headboard large enough to fit.'

'I like to sprawl.'

'And I prefer cuddling.' She snuggled even closer to him.

'Temptress. I can see you're determined to get your own way as soon as I put the ring on your finger.' He dropped a kiss onto her neck. 'Who on earth can that be?' he said irritably when the telephone shrilled in the living room.

'Answer it and you'll find out.' She rolled away from him and lay back with her head on her arms.

'Not likely. I'm not dressed and, unlike the back, the front of the house is overlooked. Besides, it's bound to be a wrong number. No one knows our number or that we're here.'

'Your father would know it; he arranged to have the telephone installed.'

'He's picking my sister up from the stables. See, I told you,' he said when the phone stopped ringing.

'It could be him,' Helena suggested when it started up again. 'Perhaps it's an emergency and he needs help.'

'One of his partners is on duty this weekend. You answer it.'

'If it is your father, he'd hardly be ringing me,' she pointed out.

'It could be your mother.'

'She doesn't know the number. Here, wrap yourself in this.' She handed him a beach towel.

'And if anyone sees me?'

'They'll think you've had a bath.'

'When we haven't even moved in?'

'You could have got dirty scrubbing out the place.'

'It's stopped again. It has to be a wrong number.' He pulled her towards him, but as they settled back on the bedspread it started again.

'Damn!' Ned reached for the towel, wrapped it around his waist and padded on bare feet into the living room. Crouching beside the box of books, he picked up the receiver and barked, 'Hello.'

'Ned?'

'Dad?'

'Meet me at home as soon as you can.'

'What's the problem?'

'Just get here, and bring Helena.'

'Dad—'

'It's not urgent, so don't break the speed limit.'

'But it is bad news?' Ned fished.

There was resignation and something Ned couldn't quite decipher in his father's voice. 'Just come home, Ned, please.'

The line went dead. Ned hung up and turned to see Helena standing behind the door, cloaked in the bedspread.

'What's the matter?' she asked.

'I'm not sure. You were right, it was my father. He wants us to go home but he said it's not urgent so it can't be anything serious.'

'Perhaps it's something to do with the wedding.'

'Perhaps.' He glanced down at the towel he was wearing. 'I suppose we'd better look for your green knickers.'

Helena sat beside Ned on the sofa in Andrew and Bethan John's drawing room. She was so still, so quiet, that neither Father O'Brien nor Andrew was sure she'd understood a word they'd said. She simply continued to stare out of the window. She didn't even look up when Bethan brought in a tray of tea and set it on the table.

'Magda was taken quickly, Helena. From what I saw, there was very little pain. Just one of her headaches, or so she said. During the war I saw more deaths than any man should in a single lifetime, and you can take it from me that your mother's was peaceful. In the end, that's what we all want for our loved ones and ourselves. To slip away quietly to the Lord's kingdom.'

Helena turned to the priest. 'Did my mother say anything?'

'That she loved you and was sorry.'

'Sorry?' Helena repeated in a dull, cold voice. Ned and his father both saw she was in deep shock.

30

'I think she was sorry she didn't have time to say goodbye to you.'

'Why?' Helena asked Andrew. 'Why did she die? She was fine at lunch. You all saw her. She was fine.' She looked to Ned and Andrew for an explanation.

'Your mother's death was so unexpected, Helena, that there will have to be a post-mortem.' Andrew broke the news as gently as he knew how.

'You're a doctor. You were with her just after it happened. You must have some idea what caused it.'

'From what Father O'Brien said about Magda complaining of a headache and the suddenness, it's possible she suffered a brain haemorrhage,' Andrew diagnosed. 'But that is only a possibility. I could be wrong.'

Bethan poured the tea into a cup, sweetened it and handed it to Helena. 'You must move in with us, darling. Ned will take you down to the flat to get your things.'

'Thank you, Mrs John, you're very kind, but I should go back. I have things to organize. Mama's funeral ...' As Helena said the word funeral, the finality of her mother's death hit her.

Ned saw her lips quiver. He reached for her hand. 'My mother's right, Helena. You must move in here.'

'I have too much to do.' Her hand shook, and Ned took the cup from her.

'You can arrange everything from here. We'll help you as much as we can.' Ned looked to his father for support.

'You won't be able to arrange the funeral until your mother's body is released after the post-mortem, Helena,' Andrew warned. 'Bethan is right; you can't stay in the flat by yourself. You're part of this family and your place is here, with Ned and us.'

'In the meantime there are people who have to be told.' Father O'Brien rose to his feet. 'Mrs Raschenko and Magda's family in Poland.'

'I telephoned Alma just after she reached home. She's on her way back here.' Bethan took the empty cup the priest handed her.

'I wish I could stay, Helena. But I have to deliver the food to the church hall. The women can manage the Sunday school tea without me. I'll be back as soon as I can.'

'There's no need, Father. I'll be fine,' Helen replied unconvincingly.

'I'll see you out, Father.' Andrew followed the priest to the door.

'It's a sad day, Doctor John.' The old man shook his head. 'I met Magda Janek the week she and Helena came to Pontypridd. Magda wasn't one for complaining, so she didn't say much, but I could tell that she'd had a bad time of it during the war. And although Mrs Raschenko did all she could to help her and Helena, Magda didn't have an easy life, even here. Not with a child to bring up on her own in a strange country, so far from her family. But Magda just got on with things. She was one of the best. We'll miss her at the church, but it's selfish of me to think of anyone besides Helena now she's all on her own.'

'Helena's not alone, Father.' Andrew opened the door. 'She's part of our family. She has my son and all of us.'

'So she does. But I'll be back later to see how she's getting on, if that's all right with you, Doctor John.'

'You'll be very welcome any time, Father O'Brien.' Bethan joined them in the hall. 'I heard a car pull up in the drive. I was hoping it would be Alma.'

'It is.' Andrew walked out to meet her.

'Mrs Raschenko.' The priest shook Alma's hand. 'I'll say hello and goodbye, but I'll come back to pay my respects on the loss of your dear friend.'

'Thank you, Father.' Alma shook the priest's hand and hugged Bethan. 'Where's Helena?'

'In the drawing room with Ned.'

'She's in shock,' Andrew warned.

Alma looked from Andrew to Bethan. 'As we all are.' She went inside and took off her coat.

'Auntie Alma. It's kind of you to come back here straight away.' Fighting tears, Helena left the sofa and hugged Alma as soon as she walked in.

'It was the least I could do. Your mother was one of my closest friends as well as my employee. I'm so sorry. I know how much you two meant to one another.' Alma returned Helena's hug before they both sat down.

'The shop,' Helena began. 'You're going to have to put someone else in to manage it, and there's the flat—'

'I'll close the shop for the time being out of respect for your mother,' Alma said decisively.

'For how long?' Helena asked.

'As long as it takes me to find someone to run it, but I have no intention of looking until after the funeral. As for the flat, you're welcome to stay there rent-free for as long as you like.'

'We're hoping Helena will move in here with us,' Bethan said.

'Do you want to, Helena?' Alma asked.

'I'm not sure what I want,' Helena replied.

Recalling the numbness that had beset her after she'd lost her husband, Alma knew exactly how Helena felt. 'I agree with Bethan. You shouldn't be alone at a time like this. But there's no hurry to make any decisions, or move your own or your mother's things out of the flat.'

'We have to cancel the wedding,' Helena said suddenly.

'Postpone it,' Ned amended.

She looked at him. 'I couldn't go ahead with it. Not the way my mother planned it.'

'Of course you couldn't,' Alma agreed, 'Everyone will understand you not wanting to think about it at the moment, Helena, and you must leave the re-organization to us. But there are some things you can't postpone. You have to write to or telephone your grandmother and your mother's brother and sister.'

'I doubt anyone in Magda's family will be allowed to leave Poland to attend her funeral,' Andrew cautioned.

'That's a shame.' Alma gripped Helena's hand. 'I know Magda wrote to her mother, brother and sister every week, and sent them regular parcels of food and clothes.'

Helena suddenly realized that although her mother had told her many stories about growing up on the farm in Poland, and read her several extracts from the letters her family had sent them over the

33

years, she didn't even know if her mother's family had remained in the same village where Magda had been born. 'I don't know any of their addresses.'

'They will be in Magda's writing case,' Alma reassured her.

'I have to go back to the flat.' Helena stood.

'You should rest first,' Ned protested.

'I can't just sit here, Ned. I need to do something.'

'I'll come with you.' He rose to his feet.

'No.' Helena knew her refusal was too curt, too sharp, but she couldn't bear to be near Ned, or be reminded that, while her mother had been dying at the side of the road in Father O'Brien's car, they had been making love. It would have horrified her mother. She tried to soften the blow. 'I need to be alone for a while.'

'I can't let you go to the flat by yourself,' Ned insisted.

'She won't be alone. I'll drive her down. If that's all right with you, Helena, Bethan?' Alma checked.

Helena nodded. Bethan and Andrew were too wise to protest. It had been Alma who had first befriended Magda when she had arrived almost penniless in Wales. And it had been Alma who had found Magda and Helena a room before they had moved into the flat, and subsequently given Magda a job as well as helped her solve all her practical problems.

'Are you sure you don't want me to come with you?' Ned pleaded.

'Absolutely sure.' Helena avoided his gaze. 'I'll see you later. Thank you for the tea and everything, Mrs John – Bethan.' Unable to stay in the same room as Ned a moment longer, Helena went into the hall and lifted her jacket from the stand.

'I'll telephone you from the shop, Beth, Ned.' Alma followed Helena.

'Alma, wait.' Andrew handed her a small envelope. 'Tranquilisers. Just in case. Helena's too calm, too controlled. It won't last.'

Chapter 3

THE FINE SUNDAY summer afternoon had attracted crowds into Pontypridd, but most people were either heading into or leaving the enormous park that covered the floor of the valley behind Taff Street. The women were carrying picnic baskets; the children rolled-up towels that contained their bathers. The smaller ones hurried to the free pool in the playground; the teenagers to the Lido, where sixpence would gain them admission to the larger, deeper pool with its paved suntrap for sunbathing – and flirting.

Helena recalled all the warm summer evenings she'd spent with her mother there after Magda had shut up the shop. They had picnicked on the lawns, Magda reading library books to improve her English, while she'd studied for her examinations. She remembered the swimming lessons her mother had given her in the 'grown-up' pool, the tennis lessons Magda had scrimped to pay for on the public courts, the Sunday afternoons when they had sat around the bandstand listening to brass bands. She couldn't bear the thought that they would never go there together again.

Throughout her childhood, her mother had constantly searched for new ways to introduce her to all that the world had to offer, always encouraging her to watch, listen and learn. Praising every effort she made, rewarding her with 'treats' of visits to theatres and cinemas, and consoling her whenever she was disappointed, with the assurance that next time she *would* be successful.

'*So you failed your geometry mock GCE, Helena. So what?*'

Helena recalled the indignant shrug Magda gave whenever she dismissed criticism directed at her daughter.

'*Teachers always make the mock examinations impossible, and mark them down to make their pupils work harder. But you don't need to work any harder, Helena, because you always do your best. Now forget all about your geometry mark and look at what came in the post this morning. It's the programme for the New Theatre in Cardiff.* Rebecca *is playing there on Saturday. I will telephone them and book tickets for the evening perform-ance, and on the way home we'll buy fish and chips in Rabaiotti's cafe.'*

She heard her own voice echoing back. *'Mama, you can't always make everything come right.'*

'No, I can't. But if you stop worrying about things that don't matter, you will make everything come right for yourself, Helena.' She could almost feel the touch of her mother's hand stroking her hair away from her face. *'You are intelligent, pretty and have so much good sense. You will lead a charmed life, my daughter. I promise you.'*

But how could it be a charmed life when her mother was no longer there to share it with her?

'Would you like me to come into the flat with you, Helena?' Alma switched off the ignition after parking outside the shop.

Lost in memories of her mother, Helena looked at Alma in surprise before collecting her thoughts. 'Please, Auntie Alma.' She glanced at the shop, unsure what she should do next.

'You have your key?' Alma asked.

'To the flat.'

'I have a master key for the shop.' Alma left the car, locked it and followed Helena.

Helena opened the door to the flat and stepped inside. The air was close, warm and still. Whatever the weather, Magda always locked all the doors and windows against burglars whenever she left the building.

Helena walked up the stairs and into the living room. She only just stopped herself from calling out, 'Mama, I'm home.' Even then, she half expected her mother to walk out of the kitchen to meet her, dishcloth or duster in hand, because Magda never could bear to sit still for a minute. Whenever she watched television or listened to the radio there was always wool or cotton thread, a pair of knitting needles or a crochet hook in her hands.

'Do you want to pack a few things, Helena?' Alma said when she saw Helena hesitate.

'As I only returned from Bristol yesterday, most of my things are in the wash. It really would be easier if I remained here.'

'Would you like me to stay with you?' Alma asked tactfully. 'Theo—'

'Telephoned this morning to tell me that he is visiting friends in Devon next week.'

'Don't you have to run the businesses?'

'I can do that just as well from here as I can from Cardiff. I have to go there tomorrow morning. I'll pick up some clothes then. You can lend me a nightdress and a toothbrush, can't you?'

'Of course. Mama keeps a packet of spare toothbrushes in case of visitors . . .' Helena looked gratefully at her. 'This is very kind of you, Auntie Alma.'

'At times like this I always find it easiest to concentrate on practical things. Can I make you a cup of tea and a sandwich?'

'Tea would be nice, but I'm not hungry.'

Alma didn't press her. 'Your mother often showed me photographs and letters. Didn't she keep them in the bottom drawer of the sideboard?'

'She did. And all her important papers are in a box file in her wardrobe. She tried talking to me about them but I wouldn't listen. I couldn't bear the thought of her dying, or being without her . . .' Helena didn't cry but her dry-eyed anguish was almost more than Alma could bear.

'I'll make the tea. You get the box, letters, pen and paper. We'll start by making a list of things to do.'

Helena squared her shoulders and went to the sideboard. Alma watched her before going into the kitchen. She made the tea, and despite Helena's assurance that she wasn't hungry, buttered four rolls, placed cheese and tomatoes on them, and set out a tray. When she had finished she carried everything into the living room.

Helena had found her mother's writing case, photographs, letters and box file, and was looking through the letters.

'These are all from Mama's friends in Cardiff and Pontypridd. I can't find any from Poland. But I know she was worried that we would get burgled and her family's letters would fall into the wrong

37

hands. She was terrified that the Communists would punish her relatives because she had fled to the West.'

'Have you found your mother's address book?' Alma poured the tea.

Helena flicked through the pages. 'There are only local and Cardiff addresses in here. Yours, Doctor and Mrs John's, friends and customers.'

'The foreign addresses will probably be in another book or the box file.' Alma handed her the tea, placed a roll on a plate and gave it to her without asking if she wanted it.

'Would you help me to go through these papers, please, Auntie Alma? I've found Mama's insurance policies but I haven't a clue what to do with them.'

Two hours later, Alma and Helena had composed a paragraph to be placed in the 'Family Notices' sections of the weekly *Pontypridd Observer* and daily *South Wales Echo*. They had set the insurance policies aside until the formal issuing of Magda's death certificate, and made a list of Magda's friends who were on the telephone. But, Helena was reluctant to speak to anyone, and insisted they wait until the morning before contacting any of them. Neither of them had been able to find an address for Magda's family in Poland.

Helena looked through the photographs. The earliest baby picture of her had been taken when she was about one year old. She was outside what looked like a mansion. Magda had told her it was in Germany. Another had been snapped among the wooden huts of the Displaced Persons' camp, where she and her mother had lived before they had arrived in Pontypridd. There was one of her grandparents, uncles, aunt and mother standing outside the family farmhouse in Poland, and a photograph of the stone cross memorial that had been erected on her father's grave. In some that she couldn't remember seeing before, her mother looked like a schoolgirl. Two other young girls smiled alongside her. Friends or relatives? Given how often her mother had spoken of her pre-war life in Poland, she thought it odd that Magda had never mentioned them.

She went to the sideboard and lifted down the photograph of her parents that had been taken on their wedding day. 'You know, my mother always spoke of my father as if he were still alive.'

'And I understood why,' Alma said. 'I speak to my husband all the time.'

Helena wasn't sure what had happened to Alma's husband, but she knew he was Russian and had been forced to return there after the war, against his will. 'Mama regarded herself as still married to my father.'

'That too I can understand,' Alma said.

'Which is why I have to bury my mother in my father's grave.'

'In Poland!' Alma exclaimed. 'Darling, the Polish government would never let you.'

'I have to try,' Helena said emphatically. She sat down at the table, still clutching the photograph.

'Supposing they did, by some miracle, give you permission. The cost would be prohibitive. Can you imagine trying to ship a coffin all that way? You'd need official papers. That could take weeks to organize.'

'I could ask Father O'Brien for a dispensation to cremate Mama. I know it's not usual for Catholics, but I'm sure he wouldn't refuse if I explained that I wanted to return my mother's ashes to Poland. She loved my father, Auntie Alma. She would want to be with him for eternity. I know she would.'

Alma laid her hand over Helena's. 'And she is, darling. You can be sure of that.'

Helena refused to be so easily placated. 'You know how much she missed Poland and my father. She would have never come to Britain after the war if she'd had a choice. She would have returned to Poland.'

Alma knew more than Helena about the choices Magda Janek had made after the war, but she also knew that this was not the time to discuss them with Helena. Perhaps that would come later, when Magda's death wasn't quite so raw. 'Your mother wanted a better life for you and for herself, Helena.'

'If I carry Mama's ashes back to Poland, the only cost would be my travelling expenses,' Helena continued stubbornly. 'Papa is buried in the graveyard of the Catholic church they were married

39

in. If the priest knew Mama – or even just heard her story – I'm sure he and the Church authorities wouldn't refuse me permission to bury my parents together. Or prevent me from adding Mama's name to his gravestone.'

'The Catholic Church is outlawed in Communist countries,' Alma reminded Helena. 'Even if they allowed you to travel there, I doubt you'll find a priest.'

'Father O'Brien will be able to find out if there is one. If there isn't, some kind of government authority must care for churchyards and cemeteries. I'll write to the Polish Embassy and ask. And there are my relatives. Mama helped her mother, brother and sister in every way she could think of for years. They can't refuse to help me with this.'

'If we find their addresses,' Alma qualified.

'We know the name of the village where Mama was born and grew up in. Mama's maiden name was Niklas. Her mother's name was Maria, her brother was called Wiktor and her sister Julianna. There was another, older brother, Augustyn, but he was killed by the Nazis alongside my father and grandfather. Thanks to Mama, I can speak, read and write Polish. I'll write to the village church before I go, and put on the envelope "to be opened by an official in the absence of a priest". There's bound to be a council, shop or a post office of sorts. Someone will know where my grandmother, uncle and aunt are, even if they've moved.'

As Helena continued to outline her plans, Alma realized she was channelling her grief into a crusade to return her mother's body to Poland. She wondered if it was the result of something Magda had said, or simply displacement activity.

'Did your mother ever talk about wanting to be buried with your father?' she asked eventually.

'Not in so many words, no.' Helena paused, recalling the only conversation she'd had with Magda that had touched on the subject, albeit indirectly. It had occurred shortly after she had met Ned. And they had been talking about love, not death.

'*All men and women wait for true love without even knowing that is why God put them on this earth,*' Magda had said. '*We have to be watchful lest we miss the person. But when a man and a woman recognize their destiny,*

40

nothing else exists for either of them. It is as though there is no earth, no sky, no time, no past, no future. Your papa is with me, Helena. He has never left me. We are separated only by a mist. One day that mist will clear and we will be together for ever. When that day comes, do not shed tears. Your papa and I will know perfect happiness again.'

'Helena . . . Helena?'

'Sorry, Auntie Alma. I was miles away.'

'Have you forgotten how frightened your mother was of the Communists?'

'No, but they can't do anything to me. I am a naturalized citizen. I hold a British passport.' Helena continued to stare at her parents' wedding photograph.

'But you were born in Poland. How do you think your mother would react if she were here now, listening to your plans?'

'I don't know, Auntie Alma. I only know that I have to do this one last thing for her.'

Alma realized it was useless to continue the argument. 'We'll talk to Father O'Brien in the morning, darling.'

'He knew and respected my mother; he will help me.' Helena exhibited the first signs of animation she had shown since she had learned of her mother's death. 'I'll telephone the church now, and ask him to call here in the morning.'

'You'd better telephone Ned, too,' Alma suggested, 'and tell him that I am staying here with you tonight.'

If Helena heard her, as she made her way to the hallway, she didn't reply. Alma picked up the grainy black-and-white wedding photograph. It was one of the few possessions Magda had owned when they'd first met.

'You weren't supposed to die young, Magda,' Alma reproached. 'Not when your daughter still needs you. I'll try to look after her for you. But it's going to be quite a task. I think the last thing you would have wanted Helena to do was postpone her wedding and go haring off to Poland with your ashes.'

Alma stared at the photograph for a few more seconds. Was it her imagination, or had a chill draught cut through the warm, still air of the living room?

*

'It's the craziest idea I've ever heard.' Andrew paced to the window before turning. Alma, Father O'Brien and Bethan were watching him intently, but his attention remained riveted on Ned and Helena. 'Forgive me for stating the obvious, but Poland is a Communist country!'

'We know, Dad.' Unlike his father, Ned had spent all morning listening to Helena, and had come to terms with her stubborn resolve to return her mother's remains to Poland so they could be interred in the grave of the father she had never known. He, Alma, his mother and the priest had already wasted over an hour trying to persuade Helena that it would be foolhardy to attempt the trip, before his father had returned home from morning surgery.

Father O'Brien had concurred with Alma. He had told Helena point-blank that, given the political climate and Arctic state of the Cold War between Eastern and Western Europe, it could take years for her to obtain permission to transport Magdalena Janek's body to Poland; that's if she ultimately succeeded. But she might, just might, with help from him and the Catholic Church, be able to take her mother's ashes to Poland, unless an officious bureaucrat or customs officer took it into his head to search her suitcase or ask questions that would land her in trouble – or jail.

To Ned and Alma's relief, Helena had listened to the priest. But now his father was threatening to destroy what little headway they had made.

Ned searched for something positive he could say in favour of the proposed journey. 'A couple of friends of mine from university drove across Europe last summer in their old van, Dad. They crossed from West Germany into East, and went on to Poland and Russia. They reached Minsk before they turned back. They said it was comparatively simple. All they had to do was pay for the relevant visas for the countries they intended to visit behind the Iron Curtain, and buy enough local currency to cover the cost of their food and lodging for the length of their stay. The authorities fixed the amount. They did say that the youth hostels and restaurants weren't up to much, but apart from the grim state of the roads and the low quality of the food, they enjoyed the experience. Everyone they met was friendly and very helpful.' Ned realized from the expression on his father's face that Andrew remained unconvinced.

'Obviously your friends survived because they returned to tell the tale,' Andrew allowed grudgingly. 'But that doesn't mean Helena should emulate them. No young girl should contemplate travelling alone to police states that are renowned for their hostility to Westerners. And that's without bringing the "friendly" locals into it. You know as well as I do that Western students have been murdered in the Eastern bloc for their jeans.'

'The papers exaggerate—' Ned began.

'They'd have a job to exaggerate murder. Either someone is killed or they're not! Helena, I'm sorry, but you'd be an obvious target for every thug looking to make easy money,' Andrew declared.

'I wouldn't drive there, Doctor John. I'd take the train.' Helena lifted her chin and met Andrew's steady gaze.

'And when you reach the other end? How far is your mother's home village from the nearest railway station?' he asked.

'I don't know,' she admitted, 'but I sent a letter there this morning. Auntie Alma and I couldn't find any family addresses in the flat, so I wrote to them care of the village shop or post office.'

Andrew took a deep breath, and Bethan knew he was making an effort to control his irritation. 'With all due respect to your mother's family, Helena, you've never met them. You don't know the first thing about any of them.' Andrew steeled himself to play a trump card, although he was wary it would be taken the wrong way. 'Magda must have had sound reasons for not returning to Poland and her family after the war. Did she ever discuss them with you?'

'Other than to say that she was afraid of the Communists and couldn't bear to return to the village where she had seen my father murdered.' Helena bit her lip to stop it from trembling. Every mention of her mother's name brought a painful reminder of her death and the agonizing realization that she would never ever see her again.

'Both sound reasons, Dad,' Ned observed, but Andrew ignored him.

'Can you imagine what your mother would say if she were here and knew that you were contemplating travelling to Poland alone?' he asked.

'Helena won't be travelling alone. I'm going with her.'

Andrew turned to his son. 'You're *what?*'

'Ned and Helena won't be able to do anything right away,' Bethan reminded Andrew. 'Arrangements have to be made for Magda's funeral and, as the formal identification won't take place until tomorrow morning and the post-mortem is to be held after that, we've plenty of time to talk this over.'

'Helena and Ned won't be able to book tickets until after Helena has heard from her family,' Alma added.

'And in the meantime we've a lot to do here in Pontypridd.' Bethan looked meaningfully from her husband to the chair he'd vacated.

'Magda Janek touched so many people's lives,' Father O'Brien murmured. 'Not just her friends and customers in the shop but fellow worshippers she met at church. She was a warm and loving woman, God rest her soul. I predict a hundred or more will want to pay their respects at the funeral mass. This morning I received delegations from the Union of Catholic Mothers, the Legion of Mary, the Sunday school teachers, and the altar flower ladies' committee. They all want to fund and host Magda's funeral tea in the church hall as their contribution to mark and honour her life.' The priest turned to Helena. 'I know you would like to hold it in the flat, because it was your and your mother's home, Helena. But it simply won't be big enough to hold all the mourners.'

'You're welcome to have it here,' Andrew offered as he sat down.

'Thank you, Doctor John. What did you tell the ladies, Father O'Brien?' Helena asked.

'That I'd talk to you and give them your decision as soon as possible.'

'The church hall isn't far from the crematorium in Glyntaff. It will be easy for the mourners to walk there from the church and back down the hill for the tea afterwards,' Alma commented.

'Yes, it will,' Helena agreed. 'Please tell the ladies that it is very kind of them to offer to host the funeral tea and that I accept, grate-fully and gladly, Father.'

'Then that's settled.' Father O'Brien rose to his feet. 'I'll tell the ladies to go ahead with the planning but to hold off buying the food until we are in a position to set a date.'

'And in the meantime, you don't have to worry about Helena. We'll take good care of her, Father.' Alma reached for Helena's hand.

'And help her with the practical things, as they arise. Living one day at a time, as the saying goes.' Bethan gave Helena a reassuring smile.

'While I wait for a letter from Poland,' Helena murmured, more to herself than the others.

'While you wait for a letter from Poland,' Alma echoed, avoid-ing Andrew's eye.

'Have you thought what you'll do if a letter doesn't come from Poland?' Andrew asked Ned after Alma, Bethan and Helena left for the florists to choose wreaths and flowers.

Ned set aside the copy of the *Pontypridd Observer* he'd been pre-tending to read. It was only when he folded it that he realized he hadn't taken in a single word, not even the headlines. Disturbed and preoccupied by Helena's reaction to Magda's death, he was unable to think about anything else. 'Auntie Alma warned Helena that mail from the West is routinely opened by the Polish authorities, so on that basis it's possible Helena's letter might not even reach her rela-tives.'

'As I said, even if it has, she knows nothing about them.'

'I realize you think it's foolhardy of us to go to Poland, Dad. But you saw Helena when she was talking about reuniting her parents. That's all she can think about right now – doing this one last thing for her mother.'

Andrew clenched his fists impotently. 'I'm aware of how close Helena was to Magda.'

'It's not just that they were close,' Ned commented perceptively. 'Helena also feels that her mother sacrificed a great deal for her.'

'That's stuff and nonsense. Any parent will do whatever they can

45

for their child. As I hope you two will find out for yourselves one day.'

'Magda suffered during the war——'

'As did many others.'

'She left her country, her family and her friends. She brought Helena here when she didn't know a soul, and risked everything to give her a better life.'

'She did,' Andrew agreed, 'but she wasn't the only one who took risks or made sacrifices. You only have to look as far as your name-sake, your mother's brother, Eddie. He paid the ultimate price at Dunkirk when he was barely out of his teens.'

'Do you know something about Helena's mother I don't?' Ned asked.

'I doubt it,' Andrew answered evasively. 'I don't know how much Magda told Helena about her background or why she came to Wales, but I am certain that no one here knows anything about Magda's life in Poland before the Germans invaded the country, or what happened to her during the war.'

'Helena told me that the Nazis used Magda as a slave labourer.'

'That's what Magda told Alma, and I have no reason to doubt it.' Andrew pulled his cigar case from the inside pocket of his suit and reached for an ashtray.

'For all the propaganda, my friends – the ones who drove to Minsk – said that the poeple behind the Iron Curtain are just the same as us,' Ned said defensively.

'No, they're not,' Andrew contradicted.

'They may be poorer——'

'There's no maybe, Ned. They *are* poorer. They're also cowed by officialdom and terrorized by the State, and that's a dangerous combination. Life is cheap there, a lot cheaper than in Britain, and I would hate to see you or Helena get hurt – or worse.'

'The papers here are always looking for horror stories to fuel the Cold War. When they can't find any they make them up.'

'It's not just the papers. You were only a toddler when Alma's husband, Charlie, was deported back to Russia. We never found out what happened to him but it's a fair bet that he was either sent to Siberia or shot.'

Loath to cause his mother or Auntie Alma pain, Ned had never asked questions about 'Uncle Charlie', whom he could barely remember. 'Mam told me that you and Uncle Charlie were close.'

'We were. Feodor Raschenko, or Charlie as everyone in Pontypridd called him, was your grandfather's closest friend and became one of mine after I married your mother. I was privileged to know him,' Andrew said. 'He rarely spoke of his early life in Russia during and just after the revolution, but what little he said terrified me. I couldn't imagine anyone living through half of the privations and horrors he had, and remaining sane. Like his father, Peter has seldom mentioned what he went through in Russia, especially during his childhood in the camps and never mentions the time he spent in Auschwitz during the war. It's understandable. He makes a good living from the garages, dotes on Liza and their girls, and lives very much in the present.' Liza had married Peter within months of his arrival in Pontypridd just after the war. 'But he did open up to me once about his early life in Russia shortly after Charlie was forced to return there. And it sent shivers down my spine. So forgive me for trying to prevent you and Helena from travelling to the region. If anything happened to either of you, I would never forgive myself.'

'Nothing will happen to either of us, Dad,' Ned said forcefully. 'We're both over age and sensible enough to make and take responsibility for our own decisions. Besides, Poland isn't Russia.'

'Hard-line Soviet Communists rule both countries. Peter and his father said people are so frightened by the regime that, guilty or innocent, they would report their own family members, friends or neighbours for any crime or misdemeanour if they thought it would keep them out of danger, prison or a camp. They have also been taught to be suspicious and envious of Westerners. The propaganda isn't one-sided, or only in the Western press. Many Communists believe what they are told in their newspapers – that we all live like degenerate millionaires. If Helena takes Magda's ashes back to Poland, I suspect she's going to have a great deal of trouble persuading the authorities to open her father's grave. And, if she succeeds, she may well find herself facing even more problems with her relatives.' Andrew finally lit his cigar.

'In what way?' Ned asked.

'Either they will want nothing to do with her or . . .'

'Or?' Ned pressed when his father fell silent.

'Or they will see her and you, if you accompany her, as wealthy benefactors. Given Helena's precarious mental state, that could prove disastrous. Emotionally for her, and financially for you both.'

'Surely you can see why I have to go with her if she insists on this trip?'

Andrew left his chair and laid his hand on his son's shoulder. 'I can. But in the meantime, as your mother and Alma keep saying, we must take life one day at a time. First the formal identification of Magda, then the post-mortem, then the funeral.'

'Followed by Poland,' Ned said.

'Yes,' Andrew muttered, grim-faced. 'If Helena is intent on going there.'

Apart from the raised bed in the centre, the room was bare. Painted a bland cream and white, it was no better and no worse than the room set aside for the same purpose in the Bristol hospital where Ned had worked. But Ned had only ever accompanied strangers to visit their recently deceased loved ones. Now it was the girl he loved.

Helena leaned over Magda and gently touched her cheek. 'She looks peaceful, doesn't she?'

Choked by emotion, Ned nodded. He had driven Helena and Alma to East Glamorgan Hospital, so Helena could formally identify Magda's body. Given his chosen profession, he had seen many corpses, but he hadn't as yet become accustomed to the sight of death. Despite his tutors' assurances to the contrary, he was beginning to doubt he ever would.

Helena kissed Magda's forehead.

'She does look peaceful,' Alma agreed. 'She's lost that worried look that she so often wore in life.'

'Do you think I could cut a lock of her hair?'

Helena glanced at Ned, but the nurse who had shown them into the room produced a pair of scissors from her apron pocket. Ned sensed that she had heard the request many times before. Alma stepped forward to help Helena. He left the room and went into the ante-chamber where an official was waiting to record the formal identification of Magda's body.

'My condolences at this sad and difficult time, Doctor John.'

Although the man must have uttered those same words a thousand times, he sounded sincere.

'Thank you.'

'I have had the pleasure of meeting your parents many times.'

'Have you?' The question was inane, but Ned couldn't think of another response.

'And, like everyone else in Pontypridd, I knew Magda Janek. A wonderful lady. She had a kind word for every customer, no matter who they were.' He glanced through the open door into the room where Alma was wrapping a lock of Magda's hair in a handkerchief. 'It's a terrible loss for her daughter. There are no other relatives?'

'None in this country,' Ned confirmed.

'I'll prepare the papers right away.' He opened a file and unscrewed the top of his fountain pen.

Ned leaned against the wall and waited patiently for Helena and Alma to join them. They came out ten minutes later. The only tears Ned saw were in Alma's eyes.

The official explained the post-mortem procedure to Helena. As Ned and his father had already told Helena what to expect, she didn't seem to pay much attention. The official read the papers to her; Helena signed them. Then the nurse entered the ante-room, closing the door behind her. She handed Helena a parcel wrapped in brown paper, and a brown leather handbag.

'Mrs Janek's clothes and effects.'

Helena took them from her. Ned felt suddenly upset by the sight of Magda's handbag although he couldn't have quantified why.

'Mrs Janek's jewellery is in a box in her handbag.'

Helena handed the parcel of clothes to Alma, opened the handbag and removed a white box. She lifted the lid. It contained Magda's tortoiseshell hairpins, plain, stainless-steel watch, and two pieces of jewellery: a distinctive embossed gold wedding band, and a gold locket.

'I've never seen Magda wear that,' Ned commented when Helena lifted out the locket.

'She always wore it tucked beneath her collar.' Helena touched a catch at the side. The locket flew open, revealing a grainy sepia image of a young man holding a baby. She held it out to show Ned and Alma.

'You with your father?' Alma guessed.

'It was taken when I was a week old. My mother used to say that she was lucky the Nazis never discovered she was wearing it. If they had, they would have taken it from her.' Helena looked at the picture for a moment before closing the locket and returning it to the box.

'Time to go home for lunch, sunshine.' Ned wrapped his arm around Helena's shoulders.

Helena turned to the official. 'The post-mortem . . .'

'You will be sent a copy of the report, Miss Janek. As soon as it has been typed.'

'Thank you.' Helena looked at the official and the nurse. 'You have both been very kind.'

'Our condolences, Miss Janek.' The nurse opened the door for them.

Ned was beginning to feel that society's way of coping with bereavement and the bereaved was by resorting to well-worn platitudes.

But as he walked Alma and Helena to his car, and saw the droop of Helena's shoulders and the heart-rending expression of bewilderment on her face, he could think of nothing more original than, 'I am so sorry, sunshine.'

The post-mortem report was delivered to the flat two days before the funeral. Ned was sitting with Alma and Helena, who were discussing the final arrangements with Father O'Brien. He went downstairs, picked up the post, and waited for the priest to leave before giving the envelope to Helena. She saw the address on the outside and handed it back to him.

'Please read it for me.'

'If you want me to.' He opened the envelope with his thumb.

Alma stood to leave.

'Don't go, Auntie Alma,' Helena pleaded.

Alma sat down again.

Ned scanned the report as quickly as he could. 'The cause of death was, as my father suspected, a massive cerebral haemorrhage.' He frowned. 'What *is* surprising is the number of healed fractures the pathologist found on Magda's body. Three on her skull, one on her arm, and two on her legs.'

'I can't recall Magda ever breaking a bone,' Alma said.

'The pathologist has stated that they were all old fractures.' Ned looked at Helena. 'Could they be a result of war wounds?'

'I have no idea.' Helena frowned.

'Magda didn't like talking about the war,' Alma reminded them. 'But she did say that she was forced to work for the Nazis. They were notorious for beating their prisoners of war and slave labourers.'

'They were.' But the thought of Magda's injuries troubled Ned when he considered Helena's resolve to travel to Poland. What if they *weren't* the result of wartime beatings?

His father was right. Helena knew nothing about her mother's family other than the few snippets Magda had read to her from the occasional letters, which must have been destroyed because neither Alma nor Helena had found any trace of them in the flat. In fact, there was nothing in the flat to connect Magda with Poland except a few photographs, the handwritten Polish recipes in her cookery book, and the selection of dried herbs and spices in the food cupboard.

He recalled conversations with Magda in which she'd told him that if she ever dared to return to Poland, even as a naturalized Briton and the holder of a British passport, she would be severely punished for 'defecting' to the West after the war. She had certainly lived in constant fear of the Communist regime tracking her and Helena down, and taking reprisals against the family she had left behind. But he still thought it extreme of Magda to destroy every scrap of evidence that linked her to her Polish family.

Had Magda's memories of her life in Poland been so painful she hadn't been able to bring herself to talk about them, even to Helena? Or had there been other, more sinister reasons that had driven Magda to keep the knowledge of her family to herself? Were they vicious criminals? Were they in prison?

Was that why none of them had yet replied to the letter Helena had sent to the village enquiring about her grandmother, uncle and aunt's whereabouts? Should he take his father's advice and do more to dissuade Helena from making the trip? But even if he did, would Helena take any notice?

Chapter 4

NED HAD BEEN christened and confirmed into the Anglican Church
– to be precise, St John's on the Graig – but he, like many teenagers
busy with their social life and, to a lesser extent, studies, gradually
stopped attending services. On the rare occasions someone asked
him why he no longer went to church, his stock answer was that he
regarded religion as 'a personal thing', but in truth he scarcely gave
it a thought. Aside from weddings, funerals and christenings, he
hadn't set foot in a chapel or church of any denomination for over
ten years, and Magda's funeral was the first full Catholic mass he had
attended. Not only did it seem interminable but it also emphasized
the chasm that had suddenly opened between him and Helena. Or
perhaps it had always been there and he had simply chosen to ignore
it.

Everything Helena treated so familiarly was alien to him: the
smell of incense wafting from the burners; the multi-coloured
crucifix above the altar that bore the broken and bleeding body of
Christ; the plaster Madonna and saints in the niches in the walls; the
garish biblical scenes that hung on the walls; the text of the service;
the litany, the hymns, the rehearsed tones of the choir; the way
Helena used her rosary . . .

Watching her during the service as she stood beside him – physically close, yet emotionally distant – he felt as though she were
a stranger, or worse. Strangers could be introduced. There was
a chance that they might strike up a conversation. But the most
Helena had said to him in days was 'yes', 'no' and 'thank you'.

She had become self-contained in her grief. No matter what he
said, or did, to try to reach her, she pushed him away and retreated
into a world from which she had excluded him. It was as though

someone who didn't want to know him had taken possession of the body of the girl he passionately loved and wanted to spend the rest of his life with.

The congregation finished singing a hymn, and Father O'Brien led them in prayer. Ned knelt beside Helena. Time was passing so slowly. It seemed as if days, not hours, had passed since they had entered the church. Under cover of his clasped hands he glanced sideways at Helena.

Dressed in funereal black, her colourful mini-skirts abandoned for a new black knee-length one, her legs encased in black stockings, a black lace veil covering her hair, she looked pale and ill. He knew she had lost weight in the ten days that had elapsed since Magda had died, but he hadn't been aware just how much, until he had seen her in mourning.

Her face was drawn and there were dark circles beneath her eyes. Sleeplessness? Or the result of crying at night, away from his and other prying eyes? His father was right; she was too calm, too controlled. But he sensed that behind her dry-eyed composure, Helena was racked by illogical guilt as well as grief. He only wished he could think of some way to coax her into discussing her feelings.

If Helena was aware that he was watching her, she gave no sign of it. She closed her eyes and rested her forehead on her hands. Her lips moved in silent prayer until, a few minutes later, at a signal from Father O'Brien that Ned failed to interpret, the congregation rose. Throughout the ceremony people had stood, sat and knelt at the correct time, intoning responses, while he floundered, constantly watching the priest and Helena before making a move, and consequently always making it seconds too late.

The final Amen was uttered, the organist began to play Mozart's *Requiem*, and Ned looked to Helena again. She stared at Magda's coffin as the bearers – Alma's son Theo and his half-brother Peter among them – carried Magda shoulder-high out of her beloved church for the last time.

Ned offered Helena his arm but she ignored it. He walked with her out of the door, through the porch and into the brilliant sunshine where the funeral cars were waiting, then stood beside her as Magda's coffin was loaded in the hearse. Father O'Brien slipped between them and helped Helena into the chief mourners' car.

Ned felt like a useless appendage as he followed Alma into the car. They sat in silence, Helena gazing at her mother's coffin as it lay in the back of the hearse in front of them. A few minutes later they reached the crematorium. It was packed to capacity, and the doors had been left open so that those who had failed to get inside could hear the committal.

Helena didn't look away from the coffin until it finally sank from view. Only then did Ned dare touch her hand. It was icy. At the priest's prompting, Helena led the way outside. It was only when Ned followed her into the covered walkway that he realized just how many people had made the effort to attend Magda's funeral.

For a woman who had arrived in Wales after the war, penniless and knowing no one, Magda had certainly made a lot of acquaintances. And, judging by the number of people clutching damp handkerchiefs to their eyes, friends.

'She was a lovely person, Helena,' said an old lady. 'She would do anything for anyone if she thought she could help them. I'm going to miss her. Truth be told, I can't believe she's gone.' She pulled a black handkerchief from her sleeve.

'Thank you, Mrs Morris.' Helena clasped the woman's hand. 'My mother was very fond of you. She said no one could bake a scone as light as you, or play the piano with so much feeling.'

Ned stood behind Helena. She was making a point of speaking to everyone who had returned to the church hall for the funeral tea the church ladies had provided, but her voice was clipped and her gestures so nervous that he expected her to break down at any moment.

'Mrs Albright, how kind of you to come. How is your leg?' Helena crouched down besides an ancient woman in a wheelchair.

Ned knew all about Mrs Albright. She was his father's oldest patient and, according to his father and all the partners in the practice, had absolutely no right to be alive.

'Can't complain, dear.' He clasped Helena's hand between her bony claws. 'After all, I'm still here, when your poor mother isn't.'

'So sorry, Helena. We all loved Magda. Pontypridd won't be the same without her running the shop in Taff Street.' Ronnie Ronconi kissed her cheek.

'Thank you for coming, Mr Ronconi, and for your condolences and the wreath your family sent Mama. It was beautiful.'

'I know what you're going through, Helena, and all I can say is that nothing, not even the first scorch of grief, lasts for ever. It will get less painful in time.' He gripped her hand briefly before moving on.

Helena didn't doubt his sincerity. The sudden loss of Ronnie's beloved second wife, Diana, had taken most of the light from his life.

'Helena, we're all thinking of you. If there's anything, anything at all that we can do, just ask and we'll be there.' One of Ronnie's many younger brothers, Angelo, hugged her.

As Ned moved back to make more room for the extended Ronconi clan to talk to Helena, he noticed a middle-aged man staring at her. He didn't know him and was fairly certain he hadn't seen him before. But, from the way the man was watching every move Helena made, he obviously knew her. There was something about him that made Ned uneasy, although he looked unremarkable. The shiny elbows of his dark-blue, three-piece suit suggested it had seen better days. But it was clean and well pressed, as were his white shirt and black tie. He was of medium height, with nondescript features and brown eyes. His thinning mouse-brown hair was slicked back with an overdose of Brylcreem. He had the work-roughened, coal-pitted hands and broken black nails of a miner, and looked no different from a hundred other working-class men in Pontypridd.

Ned waited until the crowd around Helena thinned before walking across the hall to him, but the man met Ned halfway.

'Doctor John Junior?'

'Yes.' Ned shook his offered hand.

'Father O'Brien mentioned in the service that you're engaged to Helena Janek.'

'He did.' Father O'Brien had told the congregation how happy Magda was with her daughter's choice of future husband.

'I wanted to give Helena my condolences and tell her how sorry

56

I was that things didn't work out between Magda and me. But there was nothing I could do about it at the time.' The man shrugged. 'The housing shortage after the war was cruel. The only place we could have lived was Mam's front room, and she went up in the air when I came back from Germany and told her I wanted to marry a foreigner. I thought I could talk her round. As it turned out, I couldn't. Mam went on and on at me – drove me mad. She said that after my gallivanting all over the world I'd grown too big for my boots, that I thought Welsh girls weren't good enough for me any more. As if fighting a war was gallivanting! But that was my mam for you.'

'Do you know Helena?' Ned cut in impatiently, not understanding the relevance of the man's ramblings.

'Last time I saw her she was a tiny nipper. But I knew Magda well enough. That's why I came here, to say how sorry I was that things didn't go as planned between her mother and me.' He looked across the hall; Helena was still talking to the Ronconis. 'When Helena was a kid she was as pretty as a picture. I always knew she'd grow up into a right looker. And didn't she just?'

'So you knew Magda?' Ned prompted, his temper rising. He didn't like the way the man was eyeing Helena.

'As I said, well enough, if you get my meaning.' He nudged Ned. 'To cut a long story short, I worked on Mam, but just as she was coming round to the idea of me and Magda getting married when I could get her over from Germany, I had a letter from Magda. In it was a photograph of Magda with Helena. Well, *that* was *that* as far as Mam went. She wasn't happy with the idea of me marrying a foreigner in the first place, but a foreigner with a kid was out of the question. That's when she started inviting Betty round for tea. Well, one thing led to another,' he appealed to Ned, 'you know how it is. I wrote to Magda and told her not to come, but I guess she never got my letter.'

'What letter?' Helena heard the final word as she joined them.

'Not from Poland, sunshine,' Ned explained, knowing that was the only kind of letter Helena could think about.

'The letter I sent your mother before she left the Displaced Persons' camp in Germany, telling her not to come to Wales.'

57

Helena looked from the man to Ned. 'I don't understand.'

'Neither do I. Let's sit down over here.' Ned spotted an empty table in the corner furthest from the buffet, and steered Helena and the stranger towards it.

'Don't you remember me?' the man said as they all sat.

'No,' Helena answered.

'And Magda never talked about me? Robert? She, Magda that is, used to call me Bobby. Well, everyone did in those days. Bobby Parsons?'

'She never mentioned you.' Helena eyed the man with suspicion.

'I met her when you were living in the Displaced Persons' camp outside Munich after the war. It was horrible, just a collection of wooden huts that leaked. Whole place was falling apart. Some said it was an old army barracks, others that it had been one of those camps where the Nazis worked prisoners to death. Either way, it was no place for a young woman with a child. And your mother wasn't the only woman there. There were loads of them. The Germans had shipped people in from all over the place to do their dirty work for them during the war – from Poland, Czechoslovakia, Latvia, Lithuania, Russia, even Greece. You name it. And I'm talking about ordinary people, not Jews – everyone knows what the Nazis did to *them*.'

'I have no memory of it, but I knew we were in a Displaced Persons' camp,' Helena said.

'Not many of the women had kids. Most of those who did had lost them to disease or starvation, which wasn't surprising in a place like that. But Magda would have starved herself to death to feed you.'

'You were working in the camp?' Ned asked.

'Not me. I was a driver. I used to drive truckloads of people from other camps that were being closed to that one. Anyway, I sort of fell for Magda the first time I saw her.'

'You *loved* her?' Helena was shocked that this nondescript, middle-aged man could have had a relationship with her mother.

'No one could blame me for it. In fact, most of my mates envied me. Even skinny as a rake, Magda was pretty with that long black

58

hair and those dark eyes. And she carried you around with her everywhere. Wouldn't let you out of her sight. I remember thinking it was odd. There you were, a white-blonde kid with a mother as dark as a gypsy. I had some chocolate in my bag and I gave it to you. Magda took it away. I knew she wanted to use it for barter. A small square of chocolate would buy a loaf of bread in those days. But I told her I'd get her food, all that she and you could eat. After that, every time I went to the camp, I'd look for her and give her something. That went on for six months or so.'

'Six months,' Helena repeated in bewilderment. 'How long were we in the camp?'

'I don't know how long Magda was there before I met her, but she was there for four months after I was demobbed. It wasn't easy getting permission for her to come here. I had to fill in hundreds of forms in Germany, and more after I came home. And my CO in Germany wasn't keen to help, I can tell you. He didn't approve of Welsh boys marrying foreigners. And even after we were given permission for Magda to travel, I had to pay her fare in advance from this end, to prove that I wanted her over here. They wouldn't take any money from Magda, not that she had any to give them,' he added illogically.

'So you wanted to marry my mother?' Helena sat back in her chair.

'I can't understand her not telling you about me.' The man pulled a packet of Woodbines from his pocket, offering it to Ned and Helena.

Helena shook her head. 'Didn't Mama want to return home, to Poland?' She tried to put herself in her mother's position. If she had been left in Germany, a widow with a young child in a camp like the one she'd just heard Bob Parsons describe, all she would have wanted to do was go back to whatever family she had left, Communist country or not.

'If she did, she never told me about it, and I never asked. Everyone in the camps wanted to go somewhere in those days. And with the roads and railways bombed, and hardly anyone having any papers to prove who they were, and Nazi big knobs hiding among the camp inmates and prisoners, it was a nightmare. But after I asked your mother to marry me, the question of her returning to Poland didn't come up. I applied for permission to marry her and, eventually, after a lot of argy-bargy, it was approved. She was placed on the list of refugees waiting to be given travel warrants to come to Britain.'

'You were formally engaged to my mother?' Helena couldn't have been more stunned. After all Magda had said about her husband being the one great love of her life, to discover that she had considered marrying someone else was devastating.

'I suppose we were. I gave her a ring; swapped a couple of tins of ham for it. I often wondered what would have happened if I'd asked for permission to marry Magda in Germany. That would have been more difficult. You had to prove special circumstances, and I never found out what they were. Officers were different. They knew people who could pull strings. A lieutenant married an Estonian girl who lived in Magda's barracks. The girls organized a bit of a do for them. But even if we had married in Germany, Magda wouldn't have been able to come home to Wales with me when I was demobbed. It would have been done and dusted, though. Mam wouldn't have been able to argue with a wedding certificate, would she?'

When neither Ned nor Helena commented, Bob continued. 'Well, it's all water down the Taff now. I came back, started courting Betty. We'd been married a week when your mother turned up on the doorstep with you in her arms. Mam wouldn't let her in the house, so I took her into town—'

'Pontypridd?' Helena asked.

'Mam's house was in Trallwn so we didn't have far to walk. I carried you and Magda's suitcase. I couldn't swear to it, of course, but I think you remembered me and the chocolate I'd given you in the camp. I took your mother to Ronconi's – the restaurant not the café. It cost more, but Magda had come all that way and I wanted to give her a treat, so I bought her fish and chips. While she was eating them, I told her that I was sorry but I couldn't do anything for her. She didn't take it too well, but as luck would have it I had my Post Office book in my pocket. So I nipped out and drew out a fiver – that was a lot of money in those days – and gave it to Magda. Next time I saw her she was working in Charlie's shop. She nodded to me but we never spoke another word.' He shook his head at the memory. 'I often wondered what would have happened if she hadn't had you. But when Mam kicked up a fuss about bringing another man's kid in the house I knew there was no point asking Magda to leave you in the camp or have you adopted. She wouldn't have done it. She thought the world of you back then. And looking at you now, I don't doubt until her dying day.'

Helena was too dumbfounded to speak.

Bob left the table. 'Betty, my missus, doesn't know I'm here. She thinks I've nipped down the billiards hall for a game with the boys. She knows about me and your mother because she opened the door to Magda all those years ago. What little she didn't guess or know for sure, Mam told her. Betty didn't like it, and she didn't like Magda staying on in Ponty. In fact, she never went near Charlie's shop after your mam started running it. Even crossed the road to avoid walking past the door. But I felt I had to pay my respects and explain what happened. I was never sure what your mother told you about me, so I wanted to give you my side of the story. It wasn't my fault that Magda didn't get my letter telling her not to leave the Displaced Person's camp. I did all I could for her when she turned up. Gave her a fiver, bought her a meal. If I could have done more at the time I would have. Oh – I almost forgot.' He slipped his hand into the inside pocket of his suit and brought out an envelope. 'I kept the photographs Magda gave me in Germany, as well as the ones she sent me after I came home. My missus would crucify me if she knew I'd hung on to them. I told her I burned them years ago. But there's no point in my keeping them now.' He laid the envelope on the table; Helena took it.

'Mr Parsons?'

'Bob.' He smiled.

Ned reflected that if Bob Parsons knew Helena better he might have been put off by the stony expression in her eyes.

'Did you love my mother?'

'I suppose I did – at least, I thought so back in Germany. I got her that ring – and a tin of ham could buy a lot in those days. And I gave two for it. But it's funny how time makes you see things more clearly. Magda and I were chalk and cheese. She was ambitious.

Always talking about making a better life, especially for you. And she did that all right, working her way up until she became manageress of a shop. Me, I like the quiet life. I do enough work to bring home a wage that keeps me and the missus, and buys us a couple of drinks down the club on a weekend and a fortnight in Porthcawl every end of July and beginning of August. And that suits me and Betty fine.' He rammed his hat on his head and gazed at Helena for a moment. 'Course, it might have been different if I'd had kids to think about and plan for. Me and Betty never had any. And you were a lovely little nipper. Two years old, and so quick to learn. Magda had plans to teach you all languages – Polish, German, French, Russian. Do you speak them now?'

'Polish, French and German, not Russian,' she said shortly.

'Clever girl. I can just about manage English. Good spread, by the way.'

'Pardon?' Helena asked in confusion.

'Good spread.' He waved his arm in the direction of the buffet table. 'You did Magda proud and saw her off in style, fair play.'

'Mr Parsons, can I ask you a question?'

'You can ask,' he said warily, 'but I don't have to answer it.'

'It's nothing personal,' Helena said. 'Did my mother pay you back the five pounds you gave her?'

'Oh aye. I received a postal order from her a month after I drew it out of the bank. She paid it back all right. In full, and the money it had cost me to pay her fare here.' He hesitated and smiled. 'Betty never found out that I took that fiver from the bank.' He placed his cap on his head. 'I'm sorry about Magda. I really am.'

Ned slipped his hand around Helena's shoulders and, for the first time since Magda's death, she didn't move away. They watched Robert Parsons walk out of the hall.

'Magda never told you that she came to Wales expecting to marry a British soldier?'

Helena shook her head.

For all his protestations to the contrary, it was obvious that Robert Parsons had treated Magda shabbily. Ned could understand Magda not wanting to tell anyone that she had travelled halfway across Europe only to be jilted at the other end. But he couldn't help wondering if there were any other secrets that Magda had kept from her daughter.

'I knew your mother had come to Pontypridd to marry a British soldier who changed his mind when she arrived. But she never mentioned his name, and I never asked who he was.' Alma set fresh cups of tea on the table in front of Helena and Ned.

The wake was coming to an end, the church ladies were packing away the remaining cakes – there were no savouries left – and the clatter of dishes being washed in the kitchen could be heard in the background above the conversation of the remaining mourners.

'Do you know Robert Parsons?' Ned passed Alma the milk jug.

'I never even heard the name.' Alma looked up as Ronnie Ronconi pulled a chair out from their table.

'Alma told me what happened. Do you mind if I join you?'

'Not at all. Did you know Robert Parsons, Mr Ronconi?'

'No, Helena,' Ronnie answered.

Helena laid out the photographs Robert Parsons had given her. They were a series of snapshots, some blurred. Most were just of her and her mother, but there were other women and servicemen in some of them, none of whom she recognized. 'I simply don't understand how Robert Parsons could have asked my mother to marry him, made all the arrangements for us to come to this country after the war, and then changed his mind.'

'It's difficult to explain wartime to people who didn't live through it,' Alma mused. 'It's back to the cliché – live for today, for tomorrow you may die. Every week we seemed to hear news of someone, family or friend, who'd been killed. Most of us honestly believed that we didn't have a tomorrow, so we did all sorts of crazy things we never would have considered under normal circumstances.'

'I'll agree with you there,' Ronnie echoed.

'But the war was over when Robert Parsons met my mother,' Helena emphasized.

'Only just, from what he told you,' Alma reminded her. 'And he was overseas, far from home. The fighting had stopped and with it the excitement. He was probably lonely, most certainly bored, and your mother was a beautiful young woman who had been treated appallingly while mourning the loss of her husband, her home and her country. He paid her attention and I imagine she was glad to receive it. I know she had you, but it's difficult to have a meaningful conversation with a baby.'

'How did you meet Magda?' Ned asked Alma and Ronnie.

'I met her in the restaurant.' Ronnie poured milk into his tea. 'Peter and I had come into town on business for the garage and stopped for a meal. One perk of being family, probably the only one, is free food in the Ronconi restaurant and cafés. Magda was sitting at a table with you,' He smiled at Helena. 'Being a sucker for children, something that happens when you're the oldest of eleven – and you were gorgeous, not that you aren't now – I started playing with you. Then Peter realized Magda was crying. She told us that she'd arrived in London docks that morning expecting her fiancé to meet her boat. When he didn't turn up, she asked a Red Cross official for advice. As she had her fiancé's address in Pontypridd, he arranged an instant loan from the hardship fund so that she could buy train tickets to Pontypridd.'

'That much I know, because as soon as Magda had saved enough money from her shop wages, she went to the library to find out the address of the Red Cross in London so she could send them a postal order to repay the loan,' Alma confirmed.

'That's my mother,' Helena commented, thinking of the money she had sent Bob Parsons.

'When Magda arrived at Pontypridd station she showed someone her fiancé's address. They directed her to the house, and his wife opened the door. It must have been a dreadful shock. When your mother told me and Peter what had happened, we decided that, as the man was already married and in no position to do anything for your mother or you, it wasn't worth looking for him.'

'A wise decision,' Alma endorsed. 'Given your temper and attitude towards men who mistreat women and children, Ronnie, you probably would have thumped him.'

She picked up the story. 'As luck would have it, I was visiting the Pontypridd shop that day, and Peter fetched me. Liza was managing the shop at the time, but she was pregnant and I was looking for someone to help her. Peter and Liza gave Magda a room in their house, and one of the young girls in the shop looked after you,' she nodded to Helena, 'during the busy times. I realized Magda was capable of running the shop by herself the first week she worked there. So, when Liza gave up work to have her baby, your mother took over. When the flat upstairs became vacant, you and Magda moved in and the rest you know.'

'One of my earliest memories is of moving into the flat above the shop, although I can't remember Peter's house,' Helena said slowly. 'I remembering carrying my doll up the stairs and following Mama around the rooms. She was so happy, especially with the furniture. She kept on repeating, "Look, Helena, our very first home."'

'I often wondered how you and Magda ended up in Pontypridd. But I never liked to ask,' Ned pushed his empty cup away from him.

'Why didn't you tell me that my mother had come here to marry someone?' Helena asked Alma and Ronnie.

'Because if anyone should have told you it was Magda. And before you blame her for not telling you, consider how she must have felt. To have travelled halfway across Europe carrying a small child and all her worldly possessions in one small bag, only to discover that her fiancé had married someone else. She must have been morti-fied. When I first set eyes on her in Ronconi's restaurant she was devastated. She honestly believed her entire future had been taken away. She thought you would both be sent back to the Displaced Persons' camp.' Ronnie pushed his chair back from the table.

'She was lucky to have found you.' Helena looked from Ronnie to Alma. 'Why did you help us?'

'Because we – all of us, Peter, Ronnie, me – felt sorry for your mother. And because she'd been forced to leave her country during the war, just as Peter had. It was obvious that she was afraid to go back there. Something Peter understood only too well.'

Helena looked across the hall to where Peter Raschenko, his white-blond hair shining like a beacon, was sitting, surrounded by his wife and four daughters.

'Peter has made a good life for himself in Pontypridd, just as your mother did. But like his father – and this is something I found difficult to accept when I was living with Charlie ...' Alma fell silent for a moment as she searched for the right words to express her feelings. 'You only ever get to know a part of them,' she said finally. 'People who have been forced to leave their homeland – and I don't count you among them, Ronnie, because you left Italy of your own free will – seem to leave something of themselves behind. And I don't mean material things. A side to their nature that, no matter how much you love them, or think you know them, you can't begin to understand.'

'Shared memories of childhood,' Ned suggested.

'No,' Alma contradicted. 'It's deeper than that. It's something in the blood. A bond between a person and their birth country that transcends logic. I can't explain it better than that. But what I do know is that no matter how hard an exile works to build a new life, how good that life is, or how cruel or hateful the government in their native country, people born behind the Iron Curtain will always feel as though they belong there and nowhere else.'

Ned looked at Helena. 'Perhaps it's just as well that your first memory is of moving into the flat above the shop.'

'Perhaps, but I still sensed that my mother was never really at home here,' she answered.

Ned didn't disagree. He too felt that Magda hadn't really belonged in Wales. Or ever been truly happy in Pontypridd.

After talking it over with Alma and Bethan, Helena had decided that she would move in with Ned and his parents while she cleared the flat and made arrangements to take her mother's ashes to Poland. But when Ned drove Helena into the town centre after the funeral to pack her clothes, he sensed that she was having second thoughts about living with his family. He parked outside the shop and switched off the ignition.

'I'll come up and help you,' he offered.

'There's no need.' Helena opened the passenger door and stepped onto the pavement. Ned followed her. 'I think I'll stay in the flat tonight so I can sort through a few things. I'll ring you tomorrow . . .'

For all of Ned's resolve not to put any extra pressure on Helena, he snapped. 'I know you're grieving for your mother, I know you're distraught, and I can't begin to imagine what you are feeling right now, but don't keep shutting me out.'

'I'm not,' she protested unconvincingly. 'It's just that I have so much to do. I have to go through all Mama's possessions . . .'

'I thought Alma spent the last week helping you.'

'With the insurance papers and the business side, but not Mama's clothes and personal things. Apart from the bed, which I changed so Auntie Alma could sleep in it, Mama's bedroom is just as she left it.'

He could see her visibly tensing at the thought of sifting through Magda's belongings. 'You don't have to do anything, sunshine, especially on your own. Why don't I come upstairs with you and pack everything in the flat that belonged to your mother into boxes and put them in the car? We can take them up to the new house and they can stay in the spare bedroom for as long as it takes you to get around to sorting through them.'

'My mother would be horrified. You know how spotless and tidy she kept the house. Everything neat and in its place. If something had happened to me she would have gone through everything at once . . . she wouldn't have . . . wouldn't have . . .'

The moment Ned had been waiting for arrived. Helena sank her head in her hands and sobbed. Harsh cries tore from her throat, savage and rasping. Ned held her tight.

'Your key?'

She fumbled blindly in her handbag and handed him the key. He opened the door and closed it behind them as he led her inside. She sank down on the stairs and he wrapped his arms around her.

They sat there for over an hour. Helena rested her head on Ned's shoulder, her tears soaking through his shirtsleeves to his skin. When she finally grew quiet, Ned moved away and held her at arm's length.

'I'll drive you up to my parents' house. You can go to bed. I'll bring you your supper on a tray. You won't have to talk to anyone.'

'No.' Helena shook her head fiercely. 'It's bad enough that *you've* seen me like this. Besides, I haven't packed any clothes.'

'If you want privacy we could stay here, or go up to the new house.'

When she didn't answer, he released her, and rose to his feet. 'Let's go upstairs.'

She led the way into the living room. He followed, opened the sideboard and took out the bottle of brandy Magda kept there. She bought one every Christmas, and it invariably lasted until the next. He poured a small glass and handed it to Helena.

'There's no urgency to clear the flat,' he reminded her. 'Alma said that you can keep it for as long as you like, rent-free.'

'I know, but every day the shop is closed, it's losing money. And whoever runs it will need the flat. It wouldn't be fair to leave our things here.' She looked feverishly around the room. 'Auntie Alma arranged to have half a dozen tea chests delivered from the grocer's yesterday as well as some cardboard boxes. And we scavenged a pile of newspapers to wrap the china. They're in the kitchen. It's a good idea of yours to take everything up to the new house. That's if you're sure you don't mind cluttering up the place,' she qualified.

'Why would I mind? It's your house as much as mine. And we're not likely to need the spare bedroom often. If we do, we can always pile the boxes into a corner.' He breathed a heady sigh of relief. Helena was talking to him – granted only about practical matters, but it was conversation of a sort.

'I'll get the boxes.' She put the untouched glass of brandy down on the table.

'Not now. Just pack a bag with what you need for tonight. We'll come back tomorrow—'

'No!' She glanced at the clock. 'It's only half past five. We could get a lot done this evening. But you don't have to help—'

'I want to,' he interrupted, realizing that grief had made her ir-rational. 'And later on, I'll go out and get us fish and chips.'

'I'm not hungry.'

'You haven't eaten for days, and that's your doctor talking. Keep it up and you'll be too ill to go to Poland,' he warned, knowing this was the only threat that would work. 'Where do you want to start? Here or Magda's bedroom?'

Helena couldn't bear the thought of taking her mother's clothes out of her wardrobe, but she disliked the idea of someone else doing it even more, which was why she had refused Alma's offers of help.

'In here, please,' she said decisively. 'We'll start by emptying the sideboard and packing the crockery and cutlery.'

'I'll get a chest and newspaper.'

'And I'll stack everything on the table.'

Chapter 5

WHEN NED RETURNED to the living room with a tea chest, he was amazed by the height of the piles of china and silverware on the table, and Helena was still stacking them.

'I had no idea one sideboard could hold so much.' He opened a newspaper and began wrapping pieces of Magda's cherished porcelain dinner service.

'This is only one cupboard. We've the tea service, glasses and everyday sets to do next. As well as the silver.' Helena lifted out the butler's tray that held the silver cutlery Magda had bought, one place setting at a time, from the jeweller on the corner of Mill Street. She picked up one of the forks and looked at the hallmark on the back.

'Your mother had good taste and always bought the best.' Ned was anxious to keep the conversation flowing.

'She used to say that no matter how dismal the room, or how bad the situation, you could always lay a festive table. And a clean, embroidered, well-ironed tablecloth and a few wild flowers could make bread and jam taste like a banquet fit for a king.'

'She was right, although Magda never served me anything as ordinary as bread and jam.' Ned placed the heaviest meat and dinner plates in the bottom of the chest.

'That's because you were never here for breakfast.'

He steeled himself to ask the question that had been bothering him for days. 'Have you decided what you're going to do if you don't hear from your relatives in Poland?'

'Yes.' She busied herself lifting Magda's prized cut glasses from the sideboard so she wouldn't have to look him in the eye. 'The undertaker will fetch Mama's ashes from Glyntaff tomorrow. He

70

offered to bring them to me here, but, as I wasn't sure whether I would be staying here tonight, I told him that I would collect them. He suggested I choose an urn, but Father O'brien told me to pick out a plain box casket as it would be easier to transport.'

'And?' Ned pressed when she didn't volunteer any more information.

'My passport arrived yesterday and I have the forms to apply for the visas I'll need for East Germany and Poland. As soon as they come I'll book the train and ferry tickets.'

He took a deep breath and mentally counted to ten. 'I'm going with you, remember?'

'You don't have to.'

'How many times must I remind you that I love you? If it was up to me I'd marry you tomorrow.'

'No!' Her voice pitched high in hysteria.

'I don't mean the lavish white wedding in the Catholic church that Magda planned for us, but a quiet ceremony in the register office.'

'Mama would have been horrified.'

'We could ask Father O'Brien to bless our union afterwards.'

'No, Ned.' She saw that she'd hurt him again and whispered. 'Please, give me time.'

Sensing she would shrink from a more intimate embrace, he wrapped his arms around her shoulders and dropped a kiss on top of her head. 'You can have all the time in the world, sunshine, on one condition.'

She looked up at him.

'Come back to me, when we return from Poland, Helena. Because without you, I'm lost.'

'As you see from the number of tickets, you have to make a lot of changes, but I've booked seats for you on all the trains, and berths on the overnight ferry.' The clerk in Pontypridd's only travel agency laid the tickets on the desk in front of Ned and Helena. 'You take the train from here to Cardiff, change at Cardiff for London Paddington. At London Paddington you take the underground to Victoria – they have maps showing you where to go on the station walls—'

'We *have* been to London.' Ned resented the man's patronizing tone.

'Sorry, but not many people in Pontypridd go there. Not often anyway,' the clerk amended defensively. 'You'll have four hours to kill there if you want to do some sightseeing. But you'll have your luggage.'

'There is a left luggage at Victoria.' Ned sat back and crossed his arms.

'Yes, there is.' The man coughed in an unsuccessful attempt to conceal his embarrassment. 'From Victoria you get the boat train to Harwich,' he continued hastily. 'You take the overnight ferry from Harwich to the Hook of Holland. At five in the morning you disembark and catch the train to Germany. It will stop at the East German border – you have applied for visas?'

'They came this morning,' Helena informed him. 'For East Germany and Poland.'

'Good, because without them you'd be turned back.' The clerk traced their journey on an imaginary map on his desk. 'In Berlin, you change trains for Warsaw. It's about an eighteen-hour journey from the Hook of Holland to Warsaw. I can't be more precise because the train has to go through four customs' checks, and there could be a delay on any one of them, depending on what the officials find. The first will be at the Dutch port, the second at the Dutch–German border, the third at the West–East German border, and the last at the border between East Germany and Poland. I can't book you into a hotel in Warsaw but I can give you a list of hotels that are reasonably close to the railway station.'

'That might be useful.' Ned said dryly.

'I have booked you on the nine a.m. train from Warsaw to Zamosc, and that's as far as I can help you. You'll have to make enquiries in Zamosc for a local bus or train to take you to this ... this ...' He squinted at the destination Helena had written out for him on a piece of paper. 'This unpronounceable village,' he finished lamely.

'Thank you. You have booked us open return tickets?' Ned asked.

'I have, and they are valid for three months, but don't forget to call into the local travel agency and ask them to reserve seats for you on the trains, and berths on the ferry, before you journey back. It shouldn't cost very much and it will be well worth it. The trains can get crowded, particularly in summer, and you don't want to stand all the way from deepest darkest Poland back to Pontypridd, now do you?' he joked.

'That would be good advice if such a thing as a travel agency exists in deepest darkest Poland.' Ned studied the dates on the tickets before pocketing them. 'I don't believe the Poles have much call for them.'

'Every town needs a good travel agency,' the man retorted indignantly.

'When was the last time you saw a Russian or Polish tourist in Wales?' Ned asked.

'I take your point,' the clerk replied sheepishly.

'Tourism isn't something the Eastern bloc governments encourage. Either way.' Ned rose to his feet.

Helena stood too, and offered her hand to the clerk. 'Thank you for making the arrangements.'

'My pleasure, Miss Janek. I was sorry to hear about your mother. She was a lovely woman. Lovely. Had a smile and a kind word for everyone. I always bought my lunchtime sausage rolls and pasties from her. I'm going to miss her and our little chats.'

'Thank you.' Helena almost ran from the shop.

'Everyone loved your mother, even travel clerks who can't see further than the nose on their face. Travel agency in Poland my—' Ned saw a policeman standing close to them in Taff Street and amended what he was about to say, 'eye.'

'He meant well,' Helena said absently.

'I suppose so, and he did take pains over booking the journey. Where do you want to go now?' he asked. 'Back to the flat for a last look around, or up to the new house?'

'Back to the flat, so I can telephone Auntie Alma. I need to tell her we've finished emptying it, and ask her what she wants me to do with the keys.'

'And tonight?'

'Our suitcases are at your house, so we'll have to sleep there.'

'I thought we'd go for a meal first,' he suggested. 'Just the two of us. We haven't spent a quiet minute alone together since . . . well . . .' He lapsed into silence, remembering the phone call from his father in their new house.

'I know, Ned, and when we return from Poland I'll make it up to you.'

'There's nothing to make up. I just want to spend some time with you *alone* – and I don't mean making love,' he added conscious of how she shrank from his slightest touch since learning of Magda's death.

'We've an early start and a long day tomorrow. Do you mind if I just look round the flat, leave the keys and then go back to your parents' house so I can get a good night's sleep?'

Ned did mind. But he thought of his own large and supportive family and how devastated Helena had been by the loss of Magda, the only relative she had ever known.

'Do you want to look around the flat by yourself?' he asked.

'Please.'

'I'll wait for you in Ronconi's restaurant. We'll eat there when you've finished – even if you're not hungry,' he said firmly. 'That way you can go straight to bed when we go in.'

She didn't look at him again until he left her at the door to the flat. Then, to his amazement, she kissed his cheek and hugged him.

'Thank you for being understanding. See you shortly.'

'I'll be waiting,' he promised.

Helena closed the front door behind her, walked up the jute-carpeted stairs and onto the landing. She stared at the row of hooks on the wall at the top of the stairs, and recalled all the times she had hung her county school blazer on one of the wooden coat hangers there.

Magda's voice echoed, lecturing her from the past. *'Don't you dare hang that blazer by the hook sewn into the back, Helena. The weight will pull it out of shape and then what will it look like on you? Like it's not fit for the rag-bag. Look after it, Helena. It cost a great deal of money.'*

Her own voice rang back. *'I know it did, Mama, but I hang it on a peg in school. All the girls do the same.'*

'All the girls! Phoo! I don't care what "all the girls" do. You are not "all the girls." Take a hanger to school, Helena. People judge you by the pride you take in yourself and the care you bestow on your clothes. Never leave the house with a dirty face, hands or nails. Your hair should always be brushed, your clothes neatly pressed and mended, your shoes polished. And remember, a real lady is never, ever seen in public without her hat and gloves, no matter how warm the weather.'

'Poor Mama,' Helena murmured to the silence. 'You saw so many changes in your life, so many conventions overthrown.'

She walked down the passage into the living room, which over-looked Taff Street. She had cleaned the window panes, dusted the furniture and hoovered the carpet, but the room looked forlorn, as though it sensed the flat had been abandoned. There were lighter squares on the wallpaper where her mother's mirror and wedding photograph had hung. The sideboard looked bare, bereft of the other photographs Magda had displayed.

Helena as a small blonde toddler dressed in white for Sunday out-ings to Pontypridd Park. Aged four in a homemade knitted swimsuit. Almost five, forcing a nervous smile, dressed in a sensible navy-blue pinafore dress and white blouse for her first day at primary school. Aged six, surrounded by her classmates in the backyard behind the shop, all of them dressed in their best summer cotton print frocks and cardigans, chattering excitedly, as they waited for Magda to snap a memento of her birthday party. Her subsequent birthday parties until the age of eleven. The momentous photograph her mother had taken outside the front of the shop when she had left for her first day at the Girls' Grammar School, proudly wearing the braided blazer, gymslip, tie and girdle that had cost her mother the enormous sum of twenty pounds.

Holiday snaps of her in Porthcawl and Barry Island on day trips, and the annual two-week holiday Magda had booked every year to coincide with 'miners' fortnight' because it was the shop's quietest two weeks of the year. They invariably spent it in a caravan, once in Devon but more usually Porthcawl. Pictures Magda had taken of her on the days she had received her O- and A-level results. A posed shot of her standing next to her suitcase on Pontypridd station before she'd left for Bristol University.

When she'd taken them down she'd realized that every photograph on display had been of her, because Magda had always been behind the camera. Unlike her college friends, who'd possessed any number of photographs of both parents, she had very few of her mother. The only ones that existed had been taken by their friends, and Magda had left them in folders and envelopes. There had been half a dozen of her on church outings and Holy days, taken either by Father O'Brien or one of the other ladies on the church committees, and a couple of Magda and the rest of Alma's staff at the annual staff dinner and dance.

Helena had collected all the photographs and put them, together with the framed photograph of her parents on their wedding day, into a box in her suitcase, hoping that she'd soon be able to show them to her mother's family.

Although she and Ned had checked every inch of the room, she opened the doors of the sideboard again, pulled out the drawers and ran her fingers underneath them and over the back. She searched beneath the cushions on the three-piece suite but found no more pennies and halfpennies. She moved the sofa and chairs to see clean, unblemished carpet.

Then she went to the door, her mother's voice still echoing in her mind. *'A part of your life is over. Your student days are behind you. Now you're a young lady . . .'*

'A young lady without a family, Mama.' She took one last look at the living room and closed the door behind her.

The kitchen smelled strongly of bleach and ammonia. She had scrubbed out the cupboards and bin ready for the next occupant. Was it her imagination, or could she smell faint traces of cinnamon and paprika, which her mother had used so lavishly. She could see Magda standing at the table, rolling pastry, and shaking sugar onto the fruit pies she had baked most Thursday afternoons after closing the shop.

Helena walked down the passage to the bedrooms and bathroom. She didn't know why, but she had to double-check everything, even though she and Ned had checked the flat a dozen times already. Alma's offer to allow her to stay there rent-free for as long as she liked had been a kind one, but she knew she had made the right decision to leave. Her mother's ghost met her in every room.

The last thing Helena did was look at her watch before picking up the telephone and dialling Alma's number. It was answered on the fourth ring.

'Hello, Auntie Alma, it's Helena. I've finished emptying and cleaning the flat. Where do you want me to leave the keys?'

'You can hold on to them until you return from Poland, if you like, darling.'

'No.' Helena said firmly. 'It's ready for the next occupant.'

'In that case, leave the keys next to the telephone. I'll pick them up sometime in the next couple of days. Are you all ready to go?'

'As I'll ever be.'

'Good luck, darling. I'll be thinking of you.'

'Thank you. And thank you for everything you've done to help me since Mama died.'

'It was nothing, Helena. You'll write to let me know how you're getting on?'

'If I can.'

'Let me know the minute you get back so I can come and see you. Love you.'

'Love you, too, Auntie Alma.' A tear fell from Helena's eye when she replaced the receiver. She took her mother's keys and set them beside the telephone before unclipping her keyring and slipping the keys to the flat and shop from it. She placed them beside the others and looked back at the closed doors on the landing.

'Time to move on.' She laid her hand on Magda's bedroom door but made no attempt to open it. 'I'll never, never forget you, or stop loving you, Mama.'

Helena walked down the stairs and out of the flat, slamming the door behind her. She tested the Yale lock to make sure it was secure before crossing the road to Ronconi's restaurant. Ned was sitting in the back room with Peter Raschenko.

'Hello, sunshine.' Ned left his chair and gave her a chaste peck on her cheek. 'Peter's been giving me some more tips on how to behave in Poland.'

'As it's nearly twenty years since I left Europe, all I can tell you is what I've heard from the Russian and Polish sailors I've talked to down in Cardiff Docks.' Peter rose when Helena entered the restaurant, and didn't return to his seat until Helena sat.

'You go down Tiger Bay?' Helena was shocked. Given its reputation, she assumed that no respectable man or woman would go near the place.

'My father had friends down there, and I look them up from time to time. It's the only chance I get to practise my native tongue.'

'Tongues, from what I've heard,' Ned amended. 'Liza told me you speak dozens of languages.'

'Not quite dozens,' Peter corrected. 'Only the ones I had to learn in order to survive. Occasionally I like to remind myself that I haven't forgotten them.'

There was an expression in his eyes that Helena hadn't seen before, and she recalled what Alma had said about the ties between a person and the country of their birth. 'Have you any idea what we can expect when we get to Poland?' she asked.

'Behind the Iron Curtain you'll see poverty, food shortages and queues outside the few shops for the most basic of essentials. You and Ned are wise to travel by train. Aside from the fact that a car would be a target, there are very few petrol stations, and the ones that do exist are tucked away in back streets. A Polish sailor I know bought a car and took it back on a cargo ship. Last time I saw him he said he wished he'd never set eyes on it. He can never buy enough petrol to drive it anywhere worthwhile. No one he knows has enough money to buy it from him, and if he tried to sell it to someone he didn't know, he'd run the risk of the authorities investigating him and asking what else he's smuggled into the country over the years.'

'Is Poland dangerous? I mean, are we likely to get attacked?' Ned asked.

'In daylight, probably no more than you are in Taff Street on a Saturday night when the pubs throw out the drunks,' Peter said lightly. 'But be sensible. Don't wear expensive jewellery, watches or clothes.'

'As if we have any after finishing university.' Ned waved to the waitress to attract her attention.

'I'm serious, Ned.' Peter tapped the gold watch on Ned's wrist. 'Isn't that your twenty-first birthday present?'

'You know it is. From my parents.'

'Leave it at home and buy the cheapest Timex you can find, one you won't mind losing or swapping if you need a favour. The same goes for you, Helena.' He glanced at the watch that had been last year's Christmas present from Magda. 'You were given guidelines on how much food and lodging is likely to cost?'

'We were.' Ned drew the waitress aside. 'I'll have sausage and mash, please. Helena, what would you like?'

Helena felt that food would choke her, but the last thing she wanted was another argument with Ned, who was concerned about the amount of weight she'd lost in the last few days. 'The same, please.'

'Eat with us, Peter?' Ned invited.

'No, thank you. Liza will have my supper waiting. But I will have another coffee, please,' he said to the waitress. 'Black—'

'And strong, and I'll refill the sugar bowl when I come back with the sausage and mash.' She knew Peter's penchant for sugar cubes, which he never dissolved in his coffee but ate separately, the Russian way.

'Add ten per cent to the embassy guidelines if you want decent food and a clean room; twenty if you want luxury. But I warn you, Polish luxury and ours are poles apart. Forgive the very bad and unintentional pun.'

'Perhaps we should take a few Timex watches with us. We have a couple of hours to kill in London. We could spend it shopping.' Ned glanced at Helena.

'That's not a bad idea,' Peter said. 'You could also take a couple of pairs of extra jeans. The Eastern European sailors always stock up on watches, jeans, chocolates, tinned ham, tights, lipsticks, perfumes, face creams – in short, any and every luxury good you can think of. Oh, and Western music records, especially the Beatles and Elvis Presley.'

'Can you buy *anything* in Poland?' Ned asked.

'Wood carvings, embroidered tablecloths – items that can be made cheaply at home. I've bought the girls a few wooden toys and handmade dresses from the sailors over the years, but the locals will want foreign currency, preferably dollars not zlotys. Are you taking travellers' cheques?'

'Of course,' Ned confirmed. 'They are the safest way of taking money abroad. If they are lost or stolen, we'll get the money back.'

'They may be the safest, but you run the risk of not being able to cash them. Do yourself a favour, buy some dollars, marks − West German of course − or francs on the boat tomorrow. Keep the cash on you at all times. And a couple more tips: try not to draw attention to yourselves, treat everyone who approaches you in a friendly manner, as if they are secret police − they will be − and never, *ever* give a beggar money or goods, no matter how pathetic or persuasive they are. Give to one and you'll be bludgeoned by ten others for whatever's left in your pockets. And invest in a money belt big enough to carry your spare cash and passports around your waist.'

'I already have.' Not for the first time, Ned wished he'd succeeded in talking Helena out of making the trip.

'Any suggestions on presents for my mother's family?' Helena asked.

'You still haven't heard from them?' Peter started emptying the sugar bowl of cubes and heaping them on to the saucer of his empty cup in anticipation of the fresh one.

'No.'

'Then take the standard universal presents of food, chocolate, wine, whisky, brandy, tea, coffee and perfume. If you find Magda's family and they don't use what you give them, they can barter the gifts for other goods. And take extra if you can. If the customs officials realize that you are carrying luxuries they will want a share. Don't try to argue with them. If you do, they'll take the lot and you won't be able to do a thing about it. Cheer up, Ned.' Peter dug him in the ribs, as the waitress brought their food and Peter's sugar. 'It will be a new experience and, like all new experiences, a mixed bag − some good, some not. Just be careful, very careful,' he added seriously, 'and trust no one.'

'Not even my family?' Helena asked.

'Especially your family. You have to ask yourself: if they are such great people, how come Magda didn't tell you more about them?'

'You've been talking to Ned's father?' Helena eyed him keenly.

'No,' Peter answered, 'but he's a sensible man who can see the wood for the trees. And one good thing *will* come out this trip.'

'Reuniting my parents, if only in death,' Helena said.

'No.' Peter took the fresh coffee the waitress handed him. 'A better appreciation of Pontypridd when you return. I guarantee that after Poland, you'll look at this place in a new light. It may not be Paradise, but compared to Russia and Poland, it's almost Utopia.'

Andrew helped Ned carry the suitcases up the steps of Pontypridd railway station and on to the platform. He glanced behind him to check that Bethan and Helen were out of earshot before clasping Ned on the shoulder and drawing him aside.

'I have many misgivings about this trip, but what worries me most is that if anything goes wrong, you may not be able to get in touch with us – or anyone who can help you. Helena's experience suggests the mail is unreliable. Peter told me that the telephone system is not too hot in the towns and virtually non-existent in the villages. You might not even be able to contact the British embassy in Warsaw—'

Uneasy because his father was voicing his own fears, Ned cut in. 'We'll be fine, Dad, stop worrying.'

'Father O'Brien said there isn't even an official priest in that village that you can go to—'

Ned caught sight of his mother and Helena approaching. 'Everything will work out perfectly,' he insisted loudly, for Helena and Bethan's benefit. 'I promise we'll write, and telephone, if and when we can.'

'Look after one another, take care and good luck.' Tight-lipped, Bethan hugged them fiercely. 'No heroics. We want you both back in Pontypridd safe and sound as soon as possible.'

Ned raised his hand as if he were taking an oath. 'I promise not to argue with any secret policemen and, if they arrest us, to sit quietly in my cell until rescued by embassy staff.'

'Not funny, Ned,' Andrew reproached.

'Sorry.' Ned slipped his arm around Helena's shoulders. 'We'll be all right. We've had enough good advice to fill an encyclopaedia.'

'Never drop your guard for an instant, and remember that money and things, including passports, can be replaced. You two can't.' Andrew paused, looking awkward. 'I never thought I'd be saying this to a son of mine before he married, but if Magda hadn't died you'd be man and wife by now, so to hell with reputations. I know you've made separate bookings on the overnight ferry, because it would have been the talk of the town if you hadn't, but don't leave Helena alone for longer than you can help it once you're in Poland, especially at night.' He saw the signal fall and waved to a porter. 'I wish you'd let me drive you to Cardiff station.'

'No point, Dad. We have so many changes to make; one more or less is neither here nor there.'

'All our love and good wishes go with you.' Bethan embraced Helena as the train roared deafeningly towards the platform.

Ned showed the porter their tickets and reservations, and he took their cases. Glad there wasn't time for more than a quick handshake with his father, Ned followed the porter on to the train and watched him stow the cases on the rack in their carriage. Then he joined Helena in the corridor. The guard slammed the doors, blew his whistle, and the train began to move. Ned pulled down the window to wave. 'We'll be back before you know it.'

'Take care, darlings,' his mother shouted. 'Come back safely.'

'We will.' Ned wrapped his arm around Helena's shoulders again, and held her until the train rounded the corner and his parents were no longer in sight. 'Well,' he looked at her, 'we're on our way.'

'At last.'

'Long journeys are exhausting, although I have absolutely no idea why when all you have to do is sit on a train or boat and watch your luggage doesn't go astray.' He led her down the corridor to their carriage.

'The longest journeys I've ever made were to Devon and London with my mother, and they only took half a day.'

'My father insisted that all of us went on as many student exchanges as we could fit in. He said it broadened the mind. After about a dozen of them, I came to the conclusion that all I'd learned was how to drink dubious European brews and swear in half a dozen languages.'

'Perhaps it's just as well that my mother could never afford to send me.'

'I remember the first time I went to France when I was thirteen. After a day on a train and a night on a boat, followed by another half-day on a train, all I wanted to do for the first three days in my host home was sleep.' He sat next to her and opened his duffle bag. 'Presents for you.' He handed her the lastest copies of *Studio* and *Scene*.

'How thoughtful. I'm sorry, I have nothing for you.'

'You're forgiven. I packed a few James Bond books for myself.' He pulled out a copy of *Thunderball*. 'Thinking about what Peter said – perhaps we should make a list of things to buy in London. On the other hand, we could always buy them on the boat. How much room do you have in your suitcase?'

'Not much. But I have packed a few things for my relatives.'

'A few things?' He lifted his eyebrows.

'Chocolates, tights, cosmetics, tinned ham, salmon . . . I didn't need Peter to tell me what to pack. My mother has been sending parcels to Poland for years.'

'So that's why your case weighs a ton.'

'I didn't buy perfume, wine or spirits, because I knew they would be cheaper on the boat.'

'From what I remember of the duty free shops on the ferries, chocolate might be, too. Perhaps we ought to buy another bag as well?' he suggested.

'We already have a duffle bag and a suitcase each.'

He recalled what Peter had said about the customs' officials in East Germany and Poland. 'I can manage another bag.' He glanced out of the window. 'Taff's Well already. We'll soon be at Cardiff Central. But after that, we won't need to make another change for two and half hours. Do you want to have an early lunch on the train or a later one in London?' When she hesitated, he added, 'Tell me you're not hungry and I'll make you eat two lunches. One on the train, and another in London.'

'Can't we make do with a sandwich?'

'No, we can't. I'm already hungry and I ate six times as much at breakfast as you.'

'I suppose it would save time in London if we ate on the train,' she conceded.

'Let's hope it's edible. Train food always tastes slightly odd to me, but I admit I haven't eaten much of it since I started driving.' He looked out of the window again. 'Another ten minutes and we'll be there. Perhaps I should have let my father take us to Cardiff after all. We no sooner seem to have climbed on this train that we have to get off.'

When they reached Paddington, Ned brushed aside Helena's protests and insisted on summoning a porter and taking a taxi to Victoria.

'Ned's rules. Number one: carry your own cases as seldom as possible, to minimize the risk of pulling a muscle, not to mention wearing yourself out. Number two: take taxis. They save time and effort. You can walk for miles on the tube, so taxis are a cost-effective necessity, not a luxury. Besides, it will give us more time to shop.'

'We won't have much money left to shop,' Helena warned.

'I had a bit put by for a rainy day.' He dug into his pocket and tipped the porter who had carried their cases from the train to the taxi rank.

'The way you're spending, anyone would think we're million-aires.' Helena stepped into the back of the cab after their cases had been loaded. 'And London is expensive. When Mama and I came here for a weekend so I could go round the museums, we couldn't find a room in a decent hotel for less than twenty-five shillings a night. Or a restaurant that served a meal for less than four and sixpence.'

Ned climbed in beside her. 'When we return to Pontypridd, we'll cut the housekeeping allowance by five bob a week to make up for the dip in our savings.'

Helena lifted her duffle bag on to her lap, conscious of her mother's ashes safely tucked into the bottom beneath her toilet bag and spare sweater. 'There'll be no housekeeping until we marry.'

'If there was, the headmistress of the Girls' Grammar School would have a fit. Don't worry, sunshine, I have no intention of ruining your reputation.' He smiled wickedly. 'Or mine.' He leaned forward and spoke to the driver. 'Could you take us to Victoria station, please, so we can leave our luggage there, and then on to Carnaby Street?'

'Be glad to, sir.'

'Carnaby Street?' Helena repeated in surprise.

'You need to buy a new, non-student wardrobe. You have a grown-up job that starts in September, remember?'

'I doubt I'll find anything in Carnaby Street that the governers and headmistress of Pontypridd Girls' Grammar School will approve of. It'll be knee-length skirt suits, shirt blouses and sensible shoes, not mini-kilts, skinny rib sweaters, trouser suits and stilettos.'

'Then we'll buy you things that you can wear in private.' He adopted an excruciating French accent. 'When we're alone.'

'I think we'd be better off buying the things Peter suggested.'

'We can pick those up anywhere. If you want grown-up clothes we could go to Liberty's, or just sit, take the air and have coffee somewhere.' A truck in front of the cab belched out a cloud of diesel fumes. 'Forget what I said about air. Let's just have fun.'

Chapter 6

GIVEN THE FREQUENT visits his family had made to London to shop and see the sights, Ned knew the city well. At first, Helena resented his determined efforts to keep her entertained, but by reminding her that they had four hours to kill and may as well use the time profitably, Ned succeeded in coaxing her into shops. And once she was in them, he insisted she try on a few outfits.

When he tried to persuade her to buy a psychedelic smock dress that skimmed the top of her thighs, she smiled. But afterwards, when she caught herself laughing at the antics of a street clown, she thought of her mother and felt horribly guilty. Ned sensed her mood, caught her hand and bullied her into entering a teashop where he ordered coffee and a plate of cream cakes.

'Magda wouldn't want you to spend the rest of your life crying for her.' He took her duffle bag and set it on the chair between them.

'I know, but she's not even buried ...' She reached for her handkerchief.

'She soon will be. And after we've done all we can for Magda, we'll return to Pontypridd and marry quietly in a register office, as I suggested.'

Helena nodded. 'But we will have our union blessed in church.'

'Of course. I think we should just invite Alma, Theo, Peter and his family, and my parents, brother and sisters to the wedding and blessing, and everyone who was invited to the wedding your mother planned to a party afterwards. We'll hold it in the New Inn.'

'Wouldn't that be extravagant?'

'Not as extravagant as a wedding.' He was relieved that he'd finally managed to draw her attention from her mother, but he could see that she knew exactly what he was trying to do.

'Thank you for being patient with me. Your father was right,' she conceded, 'Mama would have been horrified at the thought of me racing off to Poland with her ashes.'

Ned glanced at his watch. 'Time we found another taxi and headed back to Victoria to catch the boat train.'

'So soon?'

'We might not find a taxi straight away. Besides, we've been here for two and a half hours. And that's something we might regret later. The only thing more tiring than travelling is shopping.'

'But we did manage to buy some things on our list, and a few that weren't.' She picked up her duffle bag and the carrier bags of clothes he'd persuaded her to buy.

'There's one thing I really do regret,' Ned said when they were waiting on the pavement for a taxi to appear.

'What's that?'

'I didn't haul you into a register office before we left. If I had, we could have shared a cabin tonight. I've missed sleeping with you, sunshine.'

Again, Helena tried to suppress the thought that she and Ned had been making love when her mother had been dying. It wasn't all right – not yet. But perhaps after she had done all she could for her parents in Poland, it might be.

It was ten-thirty before Ned and Helena walked up the gangplank of their ferry at Harwich. As Ned had predicted, they were exhausted. Helena had fallen asleep half an hour before they had reached the port. Ned had pulled her head down on to his shoulder and wrapped his arms around her in a way he knew he would never have succeeded in doing if she had been awake. He had enjoyed the intimacy, even though Helena had been unaware of it, and hoped it heralded a return to the close, loving relationship they had shared when they'd lived together in Bristol.

A porter carried their cases to their cabins. Ned wasn't pleased when he discovered that not only were he and Helena sharing with three complete strangers, but their cabins were in different corridors.

'We should have booked first class, and called ourselves Mr and Mrs John.'

'With different names on our passports?' she questioned.

'They would be different if we had married last weekend because you wouldn't have had time to apply for a new one. I had hoped that we would at least be reasonably close to one another,' he complained when they reached her cabin door.

'I'm so tired I could sleep standing up,' she yawned.

He saw the stewardess staring pointedly at the 'Ladies Only' sign. 'I'll look round the duty free shop. It won't open until we're at sea, but at least I'll be able to earmark what we need. You go to bed.'

'Do you mind?' She blinked in an effort to keep her eyes open.

'Better you fall on a bunk than on the floor, sunshine. Meet you here in the morning?'

'OK,' she mumbled.

'Don't make a move until I get here, or we'll risk missing one another,' he warned.

'We could meet on the train.'

He lowered his voice. 'We should go through customs together.'

Helena knew that Ned was thinking of her mother's ashes. They were in an oak casket, which Ned's father had placed inside a secure, airtight container used to transport medical suplies. He and Ned had tried to persuade her to pack them in her suitcase instead of the duffle bag, but she couldn't bear the thought of her case going astray.

Andrew John had checked all the regulations he could find on the import and export of human ashes between Britain, Europe and the Soviet bloc, and, as far as he could ascertain, there were no health or agricultural restrictions. But that didn't mean the customs officers of all the countries they were travelling through would be sympathetic.

Helena left Ned and went into her cabin. She was amazed at how much had been shoehorned into a tiny space. The cabin held four bunks, two on either side, the bottom ones four feet below the top ones, which were too close to the ceiling for comfort. The narrow gangway between them led to a minute washroom, which was barely eighteen inches wide. Above the sink and lavatory was a sign – 'DO NOT DRINK THE WATER' – printed in such large red letters that she wondered if it was safe to use it to wash her face.

The air was stuffy and stale with a chemical taste. She looked around for a porthole she could open but there wasn't one; the cabin was obviously in the centre of the ship.

She was too tired to do more than take her toilet bag and pyjamas from her duffle bag, wash her hands and face, clean her teeth, and change. Taking the bag with her, she climbed into one of the top bunks without even bothering to look for the light switch. The sheets were cold, coarse and stiff with starch. There was only a thin grey blanket, but given the stifling atmosphere, she doubted she'd need more. The other bunks were still empty when she wrapped her arms around her bag and closed her eyes. Within seconds she plunged into a deep and dreamless sleep.

It could have been minutes or hours later when she awoke in pitch darkness to the sound of snoring. She lay tense and fearful until she recalled where she was. Muscles aching, she turned over on the hard narrow bunk and cracked her head on the ceiling.

'What was that?' a stranger demanded in a harsh Scottish accent.

'Sorry,' she whispered, blinking hard in an attempt to adjust her eyes in the gloom.

Her companion grunted, and the sounds of heavy breathing and snoring reigned once more. Helena lifted her arm and tried to look at her watch, but she had taken Peter's advice and left the expensive one with fluorescent numbers in Ned's house. And she couldn't read the face of the cheap replacement she had bought.

The noise and vibration of the ship's engines resounded through the metal walls, a dull, persistent drone that made her feel as if she'd been locked inside a giant cement-mixer. And as if that weren't enough, she could hear an irregular swooshing and swishing. She turned her head gingerly and saw the outline of a light-coloured garment hanging on the back of the cabin door. It swung alarmingly towards her then receded, and she realized the boat was rocking from side to side.

Nauseous, she swallowed hard and closed her eyes. She knew

she'd never find her way to the bathroom in the dark. The only thing she could do was lie still and try to sleep until the ship berthed at five o'clock.

She tried everything she could think of – counting the novels she had read for her degree work, and the ones she had read simply for enjoyment; furnishing the new house in various colour schemes – but it was no use. She couldn't sleep. What was worse, her mother's image persisted in intruding into her mind.

Magda standing in front of the sideboard in their living room, lifting one of the small glasses of Polish vodka that she had poured. Helena felt she only had to reach out to touch her. *'Your papa is looking down on us, Helena. He is very proud of you and what you have accomplished.'*

Papa, whose absent presence had ruled their lives ever since she could remember, and not only when she had done something praise-worthy. Whenever she'd misbehaved, or disappointed her mother, Magda had looked mournful and said, *'You have made your papa in heaven very unhappy.'*

Helena tried to recollect every crumb of information Magda had given her about the man who had fathered her. She knew that Adam Janek and her mother had both been born in the village where they had grown up, that they had attended the same small school, and that he had been her mother's childhood sweetheart – the only man who had ever kissed her, according to Magda. And even then he had waited until her sixteenth birthday. But was that true?

Wouldn't Robert Parsons have wanted more than a few kisses before incurring the expense of bringing her and Magda over from Germany at the end of the war? Or had relationships between men and women really been so different in the 1940s, as Magda had always insisted?

According to Ned, times changed, people didn't, and the number of unmarried mothers who had been incarcerated in workhouses during the last century proved it. But for all his belief in timeless and universal morality – or rather the lack of it – Ned had never dared argue the point with her mother whenever Magda had voiced disapproval of the 'swinging sixties'. And whenever she and Ned had returned home from college, she had always been very careful to hide the packs of birth control pills that the college doctor had prescribed for her.

But whatever Robert Parsons had or hadn't been to her mother, Magda's life after the war had been very different from her childhood and early life in Poland. Helena knew that much because of the wonderful stories she had related of the idyllic rural life she, her two brothers and sister had led on their parents' farm while they were growing up.

Magda's descriptions had been so vivid that Helena was certain she would not only recognize the large wooden house set in fruit orchards – if it was still standing – but also be able to find her way around it; from the back door in the yard that opened into the enormous farmhouse kitchen, to the dining room, twin parlours, downstairs bathroom, and up the stairs to the six bedrooms and attics.

She knew the house was on the outskirts of the village, half-hidden by trees, and surrounded by family fields that had been tilled for crops and grazed by her grandfather's cows and horses. Her mother had 'walked' her around the outbuildings; the stables, barns, poultry sheds, pigsties and enormous cowsheds, which housed over a hundred cows and calves. She knew how eagerly the entire Janek family had waited for spring and summer because the warm weather meant forays into the woods for horse-riding, picnics, and berry- and mushroom-gathering.

Her mouth had watered when Magda had waxed lyrical about the mammoth cooking sessions that her grandmother, Maria, had supervised at harvest time. Every female member of the family, including the maid – Magda had been at pains to stress that the maid was not paid to do the dirty work, but the daughter of another farmer sent for training, who lived in as one of the family – had pickled, preserved, smoked and dried the surplus fruit, vegetables and meat that would see the family through the winter.

Magda had taught her to cook and bake in the small kitchen of their flat, painstakingly passing on Polish family recipes. Together they had made the Eastern European Easter and Christmas delicacies: home-made marzipan and cinnamon cakes; savoury and sweet dumplings; pancakes; sausages; and fruit-flavoured custards, which the Janek family had enjoyed on high days and holidays. Magda had stressed, between mixing, beating and kneading, that when the time came, it would be Helena's duty to pass on the knowledge of her Polish heritage to her own daughters.

There had been tales of uniquely Polish celebrations, saints' days, family weddings, christenings and funerals. And the best story of all, which she had never tired of hearing, was her mother and father's wedding. Magda's account never varied, so Helena knew it by heart. How it had taken Magda, her mother, grandmother and aunts an entire month to stitch Magda's wedding dress, which was made with real white silk bought in the best store Cracow had to offer. That it had taken Magda and her grandmother two days to travel to the city, and two days to travel back. And that had been without the two days spent shopping for the wedding finery. She could even remember the first time Magda had told her the story. It was a freezing November evening during her first year at the Girls' Grammar School. She had finished her homework early and they had been sitting in easy chairs on either side of the fire.

'We were away six whole days, and for two of us to be away from the farm for so long put a strain on those left behind. My father, brothers and sister had to work many extra hours to make up for our absence.' Magda's dark eyes had glowed in the firelight as her knitting lay forgotten on her lap. 'How my father complained when we returned! But not for long. He was so proud of me when he saw me in that white silk dress with the lace veil. And he loved my Adam. He knew that I had caught the best husband a woman could hope to have. The strongest, most God-fearing, hardest-working man, who was not only kind, but also handsome and rich . . .'

Magda's most treasured possession had been the wedding photograph, which her sister, Julianna, had sent to her in the Displaced Persons' camp after the war. The look of love that had been etched in Adam Janek's eyes when he had turned to watch her mother walk down the aisle of the church, had been captured in that picture.

The entire village had feasted and danced for three days and nights to celebrate their wedding. She had also seen the light fade from her mother's eyes when she had told her how the lives of everyone in the village, indeed the whole of Poland, had been blighted when the

Germans and Russians had invaded the country less than a year later in September 1939.

The Russians were bad, but when the Germans declared war on the Soviet Union in the summer of 1941, the Poles discovered that the Germans were even worse. Secondary schools were closed, and the only education open to Poles was rudimentary primary, which ended at the age of twelve. According to Magda, even that was designed to make the Polish people nothing more than good servants for Germans. German soldiers had constantly raided her father's farm for produce and the village for healthy young men and women they could deport to Germany as slave labourers. Jews, Communists and old people were rounded up and never heard of again. The food rations allocated to Poles were set at below subsistence level, and everyone starved.

'*Starved in a land of plenty!*' Magda had railed, still emotional about the injustice after more than twenty years. '*Our food, the food we had worked so hard to produce, was stolen from us by those monsters.*'

Magda had told her of the German raids on all the farms in the village. How breeding animals, stores and even seed corn and potatoes, which were needed to see people and livestock through the winter, were stolen by the Nazis.

Decree after decree and raid after raid made daily life gradually worse until the fateful morning in June 1943 when a unit of German soldiers rolled into the village with a tank and armoured cars. The soldiers rounded up all the villagers, selected the young, healthy men and women, and ordered them to march out.

As the major landowner in the district, Adam Janek had been elected spokesperson for the Poles in the area. He had been nursing Helena, a three-week-old sleeping baby, when the Germans arrived, but that hadn't stopped him from approaching the senior officer. He had dared to ask where his neighbours were being taken. The officer had listened, then pulled out his gun and shot him.

The shot was a signal for the rest of the Germans to open fire. Adam Janek had been standing next to other men, women and children, including her grandfather and her mother's eldest brother. Both had died in the hail of bullets, along with several of their friends and neighbours.

Magda hadn't even been allowed to bury her husband, but her grandmother and surviving aunt and uncle had done it for her. Helena knew because Magda had read her extracts from a letter that enclosed a bill and a description of the memorial that had been erected on Adam Janek's grave with money her mother had sent for the purpose.

If only she had been able to find those letters, she thought. There might have been an address, which would have been helpful now, when she was on her way to her mother's home village.

She knew what her father had looked like, what a kind, generous and loving husband he had been, and how he had died. But she had no idea of his education or how he'd earned a living, only that he had been 'a rich landowner'. Had he owned more than one farm? Had he and her mother lived on a farm after the fairytale wedding that was her mother's happiest and most treasured memory? Had her paternal grandparents been farmers, too? Had many people in the village survived the massacre? Was her mother the only woman from the village to be sent to labour in Germany? What kind of work had her mother done? Factory work? Munitions? And who had looked after her while her mother had worked?

So many unanswered questions. If only she had thought to ask her mother more about the past when she'd had the chance. Now it was too late.

When Helena woke for the second time, the noise of the engines had softened to a dull hum, and the coat on the back of the door was hanging straight and still. She picked up her duffle bag and climbed down from her bunk, closeted herself in the tiny bathroom, changed out of her pyjamas, washed and dressed in the same jeans she had worn the day before, but changed her navy-blue T-shirt for a grey one. Slipping on her cardigan, she opened the door and stepped back into the cabin.

'About time, too!' a woman with dyed blonde hair complained. She threw back the bedclothes on the bunk beneath Helena's, and dived into the bathroom before either of the other occupants of the cabin could move.

Helena muttered 'good morning' as she squeezed past her and

the tousled heads of their companions, checked her bunk to make sure that she hadn't forgotten anything and left the cabin. Ned was outside, talking to the stewardess.

'Good morning. Did you sleep well?' he asked her.

'Fine.'

'Liar.' He dropped two shillings into the saucer the stewardess had placed on a narrow shelf at the top of the corridor, and picked up Helena's suitcase from the rack. 'We've berthed. Want to come up on deck and see what Holland looks like?'

'My first foreign country.'

'It looks better on deck than through a porthole.' Ned led the way up the stairs.

'We didn't have one to look out of. Where's your case and the carrier bags from yesterday?' she asked.

'Safe, on deck. I bought a holdall in the shop for the carrier bags and duty free goods I stocked up on last night. I left them with a steward; he's arranging for a porter to take our luggage to the train.'

They walked to the ship's rail and looked down on the dock below. Helena wasn't sure what she'd been expecting from her first glimpse of foreign soil, but it certainly hadn't been a grey concrete platform filled with goods' sheds. Yet logic told her that any port would look the same. She shivered, and Ned slipped off his jacet.

'Here.' He draped it over her shoulders.

'You'll freeze.' She tried to hand it back to him.

'You know me, I'm always warm. Besides, the temperature will rise when the sun comes up.' A loud bang echoed along the quayside. 'That's the gangplank going down. Time to find our porter and follow him to customs.'

'You're expecting problems, aren't you?'

'Not in Holland,' he reassured. 'But I've never liked going through customs. All those grim-faced, staring, uniformed men are enough to make you feel guilty, even when you're innocent. And before you ask, I bought well within our spirits, tobacco and perfume allowance on the boat. Only an idiot would do otherwise.'

'You think the duty free shop would tip off the customs' officers if you'd bought more?'

'I'm sure they would,' he answered flatly.

Helena and Ned followed the porter the steward had engaged for them off the boat and into the customs' shed. Helena's heart sank when she saw the contents of a middle-aged woman's case strewn across a trestle table, and cringed in embarrassment when she saw an officer thumb through the woman's underclothes. But the official their porter led them to looked at their passports, checked their visas, asked them a few perfunctory questions about cigarettes and spirits, and waved them through.

'That wasn't so bad,' she said to Ned when they approached the train.

'I've a feeling that it won't be quite so simple when we reach the East German border.' He reached into his pocket for the Dutch guilders he'd acquired on the boat. 'But look on the bright side: we won't have to make any changes for the next eighteen hours.' He stepped on to the train ahead of her and held out his hand to help her up. 'Do you want to play snap or read after breakfast?'

'The last thing I want is breakfast.' Her stomach heaved at the thought.

'You felt the boat rocking last night?'

'I thought it would never stop.'

'Were you sick?'

'No, but I thought I was going to be.'

'Then I prescribe a real Continental breakfast. Plenty of warm, fresh, stodgy bread rolls with lashings of butter, jam, cheese, cold meat, orange juice and coffee.'

She entered the carriage, smelled the coffee and realized Ned was right. She was hungry.

'You go ahead to the dining-car and get a table. I'll see our luggage into the carriage. Order two of everything and cheer up. Tonight, if we don't get held up at the borders, we'll sleep in Poland.'

'Poland,' she repeated, instinctively clutching the duffle bag that contained her mother's ashes. She walked down the train, breathing in the scents of food and freshly ground coffee. Most of the tables were already full, but she found an empty one and took a window seat. She set her bag carefully on the bench beside her.

'Not long before you're home, Mama,' she whispered. 'Not long now.'

Helena pushed the remains of her cheese roll to the side of her plate, leaned back in her seat and gazed out of the window.

'What do you think of your first glimpse of Holland?' Ned asked, as the manicured Dutch fields and neat, doll-like houses rolled past.

'I've never seen so many flowers. And the countryside is beautiful, so clean and tidy. It looks as though everything has just been polished.'

'Unlike poor old dusty, coal-smudged Pontypridd.'

'You have to admit that, by comparison, this country positively sparkles.'

'Especially in early-morning sunshine. But, as I don't speak Dutch, I won't be moving here this week.' Ned reached for his orange juice. 'I'd miss Pontypridd too much, even the slag heaps and coal tips.'

'So would I.'

Ned looked into her eyes. 'Would you?'

'What a strange question. It's home.'

'You were born in Poland.'

'But I don't remember it.'

'I've always thought that Magda brought you up as a Pole.'

'She was proud of her upbringing and her country, but she was grateful to Britain for taking us in and allowing us to live there after the war. I think she tried to give me the best of both worlds: a British education with extra lessons in Polish culture.'

'I remember seeing you when you were small. You were always dressed differently from the other girls. Your clothes were more colourful and heavily embroidered. And they were clearly not bought in any shop in town. They were too well made.'

'You noticed me when I was a child?' she asked in surprise.

'Even when I was in short trousers, I knew a pretty face when I saw one,' he joked.

'When you asked me to dance at the Freshers' ball in university, you said you'd never seen me around Ponty.'

'I lied.' He took an apple from the bowl of fruit on the table and cut it into wedges.

'Why?'

'Because I couldn't think of any plausible explanation as to why I'd ignored you all the times I'd seen you in the Regent Ballroom and the New Inn dances. Not that you were there often. The other boys used to say your mother kept you locked up.'

'That's rubbish.'

'You hardly ever went out with the girls.'

'Only because I liked to spend time with my mother. We both loved going to the theatre, opera and ballet. And after they turned the Town Hall in Pontypridd into a bingo parlour, we had to travel to Cardiff or Bristol to see plays and shows. So when did you start noticing me?' she demanded.

'When did I not?' He turned the question back on her. 'But something certainly clicked that night I saw you at the Freshers' pyjama dance.'

She raised her eyebrows. 'My pink baby doll pyjamas?'

'It wasn't the first time I'd seen your legs. I'd seen you diving into the pool in the park.'

'So you noticed me there, too?'

'Guilty as charged.'

'But you never said a word to me.'

'It was Ponty. Speak to a girl and three-quarters of the town has you walking up the aisle with her.'

'And the other quarter has you getting her pregnant.'

'You know the place so well.' He fell serious. 'I used to call in at the shop almost every day when I was in the Boys' Grammar School. Town was out of bounds in the lunch hour so naturally we all descended on it, and our first shop was always Charlie's cooked meat and pie shop. Your mother used to talk about you all the time—'

'I know. It was embarrassing,' she interrupted.

'I thought you were lucky to have a mother who thought so much of you.'

'As if you don't.'

'My father could have been more understanding when I was younger.'

'He might have been if you'd given him half a chance.'

Ned thought about this for a moment. 'Let's just say that we didn't see eye to eye for a long time.'

'What's important is that you do now.'

He gave her a wry smile. 'Sometimes I think you're fonder of my family than me.'

'Mama adored your mother and father. They made us – both of us – feel like family from the very first time we visited.'

'That's my mother. She's the nice one.'

'Your whole family is.'

'*You're* the nice one if you think that of my sisters.'

'If they're horrible to you, it's only because you tease them unmercifully.'

'You're talking like Rachel already. But to get back to the Freshers' ball, I wasn't entirely lying about seeing you for the first time. Because that's just what it felt like. I might have known who you were but it was just like seeing you for the very first time. And it wasn't just your legs – although they are rather wonderful. It was your eyes, your deep blue come-to-bed eyes. I looked into them and saw my future – and I hoped yours, too. I'll wait as long as it takes you to do whatever you have to in Poland, sunshine, and I'll help you in any way I can. But you'll have to forgive me for being impatient to get back to Pontypridd so we can marry and start our life together.'

'Our life together,' Helena repeated slowly. She rested her chin on her hand and looked out of the window in the hope he wouldn't see her tears. 'I love being part of your family. I just never thought I wouldn't have anyone left of my own.'

'No one will ever replace your mother, but you do have relatives in Poland.'

'If we find them.' She looked at a windmill. She had been excited when she had seen the first one, but that was before she realized just how many there were in Holland. 'Do you think it's as dangerous as my mother thought it was to travel behind the Iron Curtain?'

'Not on a British passport,' he reassured.

'My mother applied for a passport after she was naturalized. I think she only did it to prove to herself that she really was a British citizen. She never used it because she was convinced that

99

the Communists were watching her every move, and that if she'd travelled abroad they would have pounced on her.'

'And done what exactly?' Ned pushed his plate away from him.

'Dragged her back to Poland and put her in prison. Or killed her.'

'You're not really worried about going there, are you?'

'A little,' Helena admitted. 'As you just reminded me, I was born in Poland.'

'But you've been a British citizen since you were what? Four years old?'

'About then. What I can't understand is why no one in Mama's family has replied to my letter.'

'It's possible they didn't get it.' Ned opened the coffee jug and looked inside to make sure there was enough there for both of them before topping up their cups.

'So everyone keeps saying.'

'But you're not convinced.'

'A letter addressed to the village post office or shop should have been opened by *someone*.'

'Perhaps no one felt that they had enough authority to open it. Or maybe they thought it looked suspicious and set it aside to be opened by the police. It might have been waylaid by officialdom before it even reached the village. It could be lying unopened in some office in-tray right now.' He spooned sugar into his coffee and stirred it.

'I'm sorry I dragged you into this. You would never have considered travelling to Poland if I hadn't insisted on taking Mama's ashes back.'

'No, I wouldn't,' he agreed. 'Because I'd have no reason to go there. But,' he lowered his voice and reached for her hand, 'I love you, and if you can stand it, so can I.'

'Stand what?' she said nervously.

'Whatever we find there. Shall I ask the waiter to bring more coffee?' He deliberately changed the subject.

'No thank you.'

'Then let's go to the carriage. You look as though you could do with a catnap.'

Their carriage was full of British servicemen returning from leave. Arms crossed, legs stretched out in front of them, they seemed to fill every available inch of space. Ned led the way to their corner seats. He gave Helena the one nearest the window and sat next to her. 'I'm whacked,' he said, yawning. 'The result of sleeping in a cabin with three snoring rhinoceroses last night. Wake me up when we reach the border.'

He settled back in his seat, rested his head on her shoulder and closed his eyes. Seconds later the weight of his head told Helena he slept, soon she sensed her own eyelids become heavier and heavier.

Chapter 7

HELENA WOKE with a start when the train jerked to a halt. Doors slammed open and footsteps resounded along the corridors. The engine stopped and uniformed officials strode past their carriage.

'We're at the border, miss. Next stop, West Germany,' said one of the soldiers.

'Thank you,' she replied.

Ned sat up and rubbed his neck. 'We should have brought pillows.'

The door slid open. An officer stood in the doorway. 'Passports, please,' he said in English. The soldiers handed theirs to him first and, after no more than a perfunctory glance at the photographs, he returned them, then held out his hand for Ned and Helena's. 'You're going to Germany?' he asked.

'Poland,' Ned answered for both of them.

The man whistled. 'Long journey. Good luck.'

'Thank you.' Ned took their passports from him and handed Helena hers. 'Do you think we'll need it?'

'Only if you eat there. The food wasn't good even before the shortages, now they deep-fry everything in old engine oil.' The officer tipped his cap and walked on.

Ten minutes later, after more door-slamming and whistle-blowing, the train moved slowly across the border.

'West Germany,' Ned said. 'The next customs check will be between West and East.'

'Hope you've packed several books to pass the time, mate,' said the soldier who'd spoken to Helena. He glanced at his companions, who nodded agreement. 'When we get leave, we go to West Berlin because it gives us an excuse to nose at East Germany. The way the papers carry on, anyone would think that all the people do there is build atomic bombs to lob at the West. The truth is, they're as scared of us as we are of them.' He lowered his voice. 'If you're carrying anything across for friends or relatives, put aside a few extras for the guards.' He winked at Helena, setting Ned's teeth on edge. 'If you haven't any goods to spare, marks will do – West not East German. If you don't slip the officials a bribe, they're likely to go through your luggage and take whatever they fancy.'

Helena didn't say anything but her thoughts turned to the airtight box in the duffle bag. She closed her eyes and formulated a silent prayer.

After a lunch of tepid pork cutlets, cabbage, mashed pototoes and apple cake in the dining-car, Ned and Helena returned to their carriage. Helena tried to concentrate on an article on Dali in *Studio* but woke disorientated hours later. The train had slowed, the sun was low in the sky, the servicemen had left and their carriage was full of elderly women. If the amount of luggage on the racks above their heads was any indication, they were all going on long holidays.

'Welcome back to the land of the living,' Ned said when he saw her blinking. 'You hungry or thirsty? They're still serving coffee and cake in the dining-car, or they were twenty minutes ago.'

She shook her head.

'I'll ask you again in ten minutes when you've woken up properly.'

'Have we reached the border?'

'We'll be stopping in a moment.'

'I didn't expect so many people to be travelling.'

The door to the carriage was suddenly thrust open. 'Tickets, papers, passports,' the uniformed officer barked in German.

Helena noted that there was no please, as there had been at the Dutch border.

One of the elderly women opened her handbag and handed over her passport first.

'Ilse Mohnke?' The official looked from her passport photograph to her.

'Yes.' The woman glared defiantly at him, but Helena noticed that her fingers were tightly knotted.

'Reason for journey?'

'Family visit.'

'Which is your suitcase?' He looked along the rack.

The woman pointed to a large trunk.

'Lift it down and open it.'

'I am seventy-five years old. I am recovering from an operation and have arthritis. I cannot lift that case,' she answered.

Helena and Ned who had studied German O-level were amazed at her temerity.

'If you can't lift it, who put it up there?' The official glanced at Ned, who pretended not to notice.

'A porter, when I got on the train.'

He muttered something under his breath and turned to the next woman. When she too refused to lift down her case, he made her open her large handbag. He rummaged through the contents and took out a bottle of brandy and a box of chocolates, passing them to his colleague at the door.

Ned and Helena watched as the officer moved on, searching the handbags of all six elderly women in their compartment, taking a tax from every one. Spirits, wine and chocolates were his favourites, but when he returned to Ilse, he relieved her of a bottle of perfume and a powder compact.

Ned handed him his own and Helena's passports. The officer opened them at the pages that held their photographs and stared at them for a long time.

'You are British?' he said in English.

'Yes.' Ned lifted his chin.

'Janek is a Polish name,' he observed, 'and according to this,' he tapped Helena's passport, 'you were born in Poland.'

'My mother emigrated to Britain shortly after the war,' Helena answered.

'You are visiting relatives?'

'No,' Ned asserted.

'You have presents?'

'Only things for our personal use.'

'Show me.'

Helena had pushed her duffle bag into the corner and was leaning on it. Ned lifted down the holdall he had bought on the boat to carry their duty free and London shopping. He opened it and the officer rummaged through it, removing a bottle of brandy and two of the four large slabs of chocolate Ned had bought on the ship. He passed them to his colleague, nodded to everyone in the carriage, walked back into the corridor, and slid the door shut behind him.

'So much for Communism and each according to his Marxist need.' Ned broke one of their remaining bars of chocolate into pieces and offered it around the carriage.

'Thank you,' said the woman called Ilse Mohnke. 'A word of warning: if you have any chocolate or brandy left, hide it as best you can. The shortages are worse in Poland and, from what I've heard, the customs' officers even greedier.'

It was dark when they reached the border between East Germany and Poland. Helena had hoped they'd reach Warsaw by midnight, but the customs' officials had delayed them for over an hour at the East German border, and the Polish officers were behaving as though they had all the time in the world.

They could hear people's voices raised in anger lower down the train, accompanied by thuds, which she presumed were suitcases being lifted down from the racks. She sought Ned's hand under cover of her cardigan and gripped it.

They now had the carriage to themselves, and Helena was surprised how much she missed the friendly elderly women who had disembarked, one by one, as they had crossed East Germany.

Their carriage door flew open, and two officers walked in, snapping at them in Polish. Helena took their passports and tickets from Ned and handed them over.

'You're English?'

'British,' Helena answered in Polish.

'You speak Polish?' One of the officials leaned against the door and eyed her in surprise.

'I learned it at shcool,' she lied.

'I didn't know that English schools teach Polish.'

'Some do.'

'Helena Weronika Janek is a Polish name.'

'Yes.'

Helena felt Ned's eyes burning into her. She knew he couldn't understand a word the man was saying apart from her name. But he had sensed her disquiet.

The official held up her passport. 'You were born in Poland?'

For the first time Helena understood her mother's fear of returning to her homeland.

'Yes.'

'Yet you live in the West?' He gave her a cold, thin-lipped smile.

'My mother took me there after the war when I was a baby.'

'Your mother isn't with you?'

Helena surreptitiously checked that her cardigan covered her duffle bag before leaning on it. 'She is dead.'

He thumbed through the pages of her passport. 'This is your first visit to Poland?'

'Yes.'

'Why have you come?'

'To see where my mother grew up.' She reached for Ned's hand again and squeezed it so hard he winced.

'You have relatives in Poland?'

'None that I know of.'

He looked at their passport photographs and back at them for the last time before returning the documents to Helena. 'You have currency?'

'Only British, and some Dutch and German. We were told that we couldn't buy Polish currency until we were in the country.'

'That is correct. Your money?'

Helena spoke to Ned in English. 'He wants to see our money, probably to make sure that we have enough to pay for our board and lodging in Poland.'

Ned pulled out his wallet. It contained some loose change, five pounds in English notes and about the same in guilders and West German marks, which he had bought on the boat. He handed it over.

The man opened the wallet and checked the notes. 'If this is all you have, you will have to return to West Germany,' he warned Helena in Polish.

'He wants to see the rest,' she said to Ned.

Recalling what the German woman had said, Ned reluctantly reached inside his shirt for the money belt he had tied around his waist. He unzipped it under cover of his clothes and took out fifty pounds in ten-pound notes and fifty in travellers' cheques, which he was hoping they wouldn't have to cash. He was careful to leave the American dollars, also bought on the boat, hidden in their separate pouch.

The man flicked through the travellers' cheques and returned them. Taking three ten-pound notes, he pocketed them and returned the rest.

'Ask him what that was for?' Ned said to Helena.

The man held up the notes. 'Tax,' he explained in perfect English. 'You object?'

'No,' Helena answered swiftly.

'I'd like a receipt,' Ned interjected.

'You can change money in Warsaw,' the man continued as if he hadn't heard Ned. 'There is an all-night bank in the railway station. These are your suitcases?'

As they were the only occupants left in the carriages, it was obvious the cases were theirs. 'Yes,' Ned answered, giving up on the receipt.

'You have gifts for the people in this lady's home village?'

Ned opened the holdall. The officer took a bottle of brandy, one of whisky and the remaining bar of chocolate.

'Enjoy Poland,' he said, then left their carriage and moved on.

At two o'clock in the morning, the taxi driver who had picked Ned and Helena up at Warsaw station deposited them outside an unprepossessing tower block hotel. Ned stepped on to the broken pavement and looked up at the concrete façade.

The driver lifted their cases from his cab and spoke to Helena. She paid him with the zlotys they had acquired at the bank in the station.

'Can't he find us anything better?' Ned asked.

'He said it's the only hotel that's open at this hour near the station. It's only for one night,' she reminded.

'From the outside I think I'd prefer the station waiting room.'

'For seven hours?' Helena led the way inside. The first thing that struck her was the overwhelming chemical smell. She walked over cracked vinyl tiles to a desk set against the far wall. A bored-looking young man was sitting behind it reading a newspaper. He didn't look up until she stood directly in front of him.

'Do you have a vacant room, a double, please?' she asked in Polish.

'For tonight,' he replied.

She almost answered, 'No, for next week,' but thought better of it. 'For tonight,' she confirmed.

He looked at a board behind him that held row upon row of keys. After staring at it for a few seconds he lifted one down. 'Passports?'

Helena handed them over.

'You'll have to sign the register. Both of you.'

'I hope you asked for a double room.' Ned dropped his case beside her.

'I did. But I'm not sure who will be protecting who.'

'You have the language; I have the muscle.'

Helena took the plastic biro the clerk handed her, filled in her own and Ned's details, signed her name and handed the pen to Ned.

'You are on the eighth floor. There is a problem. No hot water. The cold will be on from six until eight in the morning. The bathroom is next door to your room. Breakfast in the dining room is served from seven until nine.' The clerk pointed to a set of double doors that were glazed with hardboard.

Helena relayed the information to Ned. Resigned, he signed his name, dropped the pen on top of the book and picked up his own and Helena's suitcases, leaving her to carry the holdall and duffle bag.

'Another problem,' the desk clerk added. 'The lift is broken.' He pointed to a flight of stairs.

'The lift's broken,' Ned guessed.

'It is.'

He looked at the number on the key. 'I can't believe every room in this place is taken up to the eighth floor. Ask if he has a room free on one of the lower floors.'

'Do you have a room on a lower floor?' Helena stared pointedly at the rows of keys behind him.

'No.'

'Those keys indicate there are free rooms on the lower floors.' She pointed to the board.

'All of those rooms have problems.'

'All the other rooms have problems,' she relayed to Ned.

'What kind?'

'I didn't ask.'

Ned lifted the cases. 'I hope they aren't of the creepy-crawly kind. I don't fancy picking up fleas or body lice or bedbugs . . .'

'Shush, you're making me itch,' she panted as they began hauling the bags up the stairs.

The lights on the stairs were dim, but the corridor on the eighth floor was even gloomier. A single, bare, low-wattage light-bulb hung halfway down a passageway that stretched into black, impenetrable shadow.

Ned looked at the rows of closed doors and whispered, 'What number are we?'

'Eight-one-two.' Helena halted in front of the door to their room and slid the key into the lock. The door swung open before she turned it.

'So much for security.' Ned walked in ahead of her, flicking on the light switch. The floor was covered with the same brown plastic tiles as the reception area. The walls may once have been cream. The bed was covered with a garish, brown, red and purple nylon spread. Ned flung back the cover, single blanket and top sheet, and looked at the bottom sheet. He pressed his hand down on the mattress.

'What are you doing?'

'Checking for bed bugs; they gravitate towards heat. But bugs or not, we're sleeping on top of this bed, not in it.'

'Why?'

'It's damp. We'll spread our plastic macs out and lie on them.'

Helena opened the door to the corridor and Ned followed, he watched as she opened the door to the bathroom. She stepped smartly back into their room.

'Close the door – I can smell it from here. But, as you said, it's only for one night.'

'Rub it in, why don't you?' Exhaustion had made her irritable.

'Sunshine, we're in this together. And one night isn't so long. You washed your face and cleaned your teeth on the train, didn't you?'

'You know I did.'

'Then come here, lie down next to me and cuddle up. Given the state of this place I don't think we should undress. If the water comes on in the morning, we can wash and change then.'

'Change perhaps. I'm not washing in that bathroom. If it's like this in the capital, what is it going to be like in Mama's home village?'

'We'll find out tomorrow.' Ned yawned.

He shook their macs out on to the bed, and they lay down. He wrapped his arm around Helena's shoulders, pulled her head down on to his chest and, within minutes, his breathing slowed to the regular rhythm of sleep. But Helena was too tired to rest. Wide awake, staring into the gloom, she tried not to disturb Ned while stretching her cramped and aching muscles. The rank smell in the room seemed to have intensified with the darkness, and strange noises echoed from the corridor.

Ned had jammed both their cases against the door, but she tensed every time she heard a door slam, or footsteps echo in the distance. With that faulty lock, anything could happen. She imagined armed men breaking in and beating them up for their travellers' cheques and money. Given the thieving attitude of the customs' officials, any Westerner foolish enough to venture into the Eastern bloc was obviously regarded as fair game.

Long before light percolated through the thin nylon curtains, traffic noise started in the street below. She thought of Ned's father's reservations and her mother's fears about Poland. She reached down to the duffle bag she had placed beside the bed and felt the solid square shape of the airtight box Andrew John had given her. Only then did sleep finally overtake her.

Helena opened her eyes to see light straining through the nylon curtains and Ned watching her.

'It's six o'clock. Did you sleep well?' He wrapped his arm around her waist and pulled her even closer to him.

'No.'

'Neither did I after five o'clock.'

'What happened then?' She looked at the door. Their suitcases were still in front of it, exactly as Ned had left them.

'The local army decided to march up and down the corridor in hobnailed boots.'

'I didn't hear a thing.'

'You were out for the count. Cold bath here I come.' Ned rolled to the side of the bed and reached into his duffle for his toilet bag. 'Unless you want to use the bathroom first.'

She lay back and rested her head on her arm. 'No. you go.'

'You just want me to throw out the dead bodies and clean it before you use it?'

'Yes.'

Ned smiled. It was the sort of banter they'd exchanged before Magda had died. He went into the bathroom and flushed the toilet without lifting the lid in the hope that the smell would dissipate. It didn't. He turned on the tap in the sink. A trickle of cold water dripped into the basin. It was just as well he'd packed his electric razor. Ignoring the brown stains in the bath, he put in the plug and, despite the warning about hot water, turned on both taps. The hot tap coughed and wheezed but added no water to the thin, brownish stream that came from the cold. The only towel was thin, coarse and grey, and the soap was as hard as a rock. It refused to lather even when he left it lying in the water.

After washing as best he could and changing into fresh clothes, he returned to the bedroom to see Helena lying just as he'd left her.

'If we take the cases down to the dining room, we won't have to come back up again.'

'I wouldn't be happy leaving them here anyway.' She left the bed and scratched her arms. 'I wish you hadn't mentioned fleas last night. I've been itching ever since.'

Ned looked around. 'I wouldn't worry, sunshine. I've a feeling this is too downmarket for creepy-crawlies.'

The clerk at reception had been replaced by a thick-set, stocky man, who looked like a caricature of an Eastern European secret police-man.

Helena asked for their passports. The man moved his finger slowly down the list of half a dozen names on the register before opening a drawer and removing the forms they had filled out the night before. He took a sheet of paper and laboriously added up a list of figures, totalled the amount and handed it to her.

'Passports after you've paid,' he said in Polish.

Ned checked the amount. 'It's much more than the suggested amount for a night in a hotel room.'

'This is too high,' Helena complained.

'Not for a first-class hotel,' the man growled in English, parrying Ned's stare. 'Top class.'

'No lift, no hot water, damp sheets,' Ned countered.

'Top-class hotel,' the man repeated, holding out his hand for payment.

'Top-class hotels have working lifts and running hot and cold water twenty-four hours a day,' Ned insisted.

Anxious to put an end to the staring match, Helena spoke to the clerk in Polish. 'The lift isn't working. We had to carry our cases to the top floor and back down again. There was no hot water in the bathroom and the bed was damp.'

The man checked her passport. 'You are English?'

'I was born in Poland.'

'I'll take ten per cent from the bill,' he offered.

'Fifty,' Helena demanded, prepared to settle for twenty.

'You are a good Pole.' The man laughed. 'Half it is.' He took the bill, crossed out the amount and halved it.

'Thank you. We'll need a taxi to take us to the station after breakfast.'

'What time do you need to be there?'

'Nine o'clock.' Helena ventured a smile, and the man smiled back.

'It will be here at half past eight.'

Ned paid the bill. They retrieved the passports and headed for the dining room.

'Congratulations on saving us some money and me from getting punched by that heavy.'

'He wouldn't have hurt you.' Helena held the door open for Ned.

'I'm not so sure.'

'As for the bill,' she closed the door behind them, 'Mama brought me up to ask for a discount if I received bad service.'

'In that case, I suggest you go back to the desk and demand another twenty per cent. I hadn't expected much of breakfast, but this is worse than I imagined.' Ned surveyed the baskets of shrivelled bread rolls, oily blobs of margarine, dishes of dried-up jam, and plates of curled-up meat and cheese. 'Let's hope the coffee is drinkable.'

Ned shook Helena gently. 'The train is slowing from tortoise to snail pace. I think we're almost at Zamosc.'

Helena opened her eyes to find that she was lying on Ned's shoulder. She sat up and rubbed her eyes. 'I didn't mean to sleep. But it feels as though we've been travelling for months, not days.'

'Given the night's rest we had, you're forgiven. Besides, having the carriage to ourselves meant you didn't disturb anyone other than me with your snoring.'

'I don't snore.' Helena wrapped her arms around her duffle bag and rested her chin on it.

'How can you possibly know?' Ned eyed her in concern. 'You feeling OK?'

'I've felt better,' Helena conceded.

'It's probably that breakfast.' He glanced at his watch. 'Midday. I'm ravenous. How about we find somewhere to eat at the station and then go on to the village?'

'I'd rather eat in the village.' Helena left her seat and began to check her belongings.

'You can't wait to get there, can you?'

'No.' she replied honestly.

'Then we'll compromise. We'll look for food and eat it on the way.'

'What food?' she questioned. 'You saw the queues outside that shop in Warsaw. The taxi driver warned us that sometimes people wait all day just for a loaf of bread and a bag of potatoes. We'll be better off in the village.'

'What makes you think that?' Ned lifted down their suitcases from the rack.

'Food is produced in the country.'

'Nothing we had for breakfast ever saw anything as healthy as the country.'

'Then where did it come from?'

'I'd prefer not to think about it. But I'd stake my life on that butter never seeing a cow or a dairy. You have the name of the village?'

'As if I could forget it.' She opened the door to the corridor as the train juddered to a halt.

'I wish I spoke the language so I could help you, sunshine, but I can't, so it's over to you.' Ned picked up their cases and followed her.

'Is it our clothes, or have the locals a sixth sense when it comes to detecting Westerners?' Ned asked.

'Both.' Helena looked around the small station. There was a queue outside the ticket office. A bored-looking police officer was leaning against the wall next to it, watching everyone who walked in or out of the main entrance.

The noise was deafening. Porters in blue overalls rattled trolleys loaded with mail sacks, parcels and luggage over uneven stone flagstones. A woman with a high-pitched voice listed train arrivals and departures over a whistling tannoy system, which did nothing to help a young girl who was trying to soothe a fractious baby. Two drunks were singing a mournful duet in front of a one-legged man who was playing a piano accordion. And a pack of dogs was fighting in the street outside.

Helena hitched her own and Ned's duffle bags higher on her shoulder and gripped the holdall. 'We have to ask for directions to my mother's village, so we may as well go to the most obvious person.'

'PC Plod?' Ned picked up their cases and followed her.

'Ssh. More Polish people speak English than the other way around.'

'If you're trying to adopt a low profile, you're too late.' He returned the police officer's hostile glare.

Helena walked up to the officer and greeted him in Polish.

He straightened and moved away from the wall.

She explained that they wanted to travel on to her mother's home village and asked if it would be possible to continue their journey by train. He continued to look at her but said nothing. Assuming he'd had trouble understanding her Polish, she repeated her question slowly.

'Never heard of anywhere by that name,' he finally answered.

The clerk in the ticket office took a break between customers, slid back the glass panel that fronted his counter and leaned forward. 'No trains go there. There is a bus but it only runs once a week. On Thursday. It leaves here at seven in the morning and gets into the village at ten. It leaves the village at five in the afternoon and returns here at eight o'clock at night. Every Saturday the journey is reversed. The bus leaves the village at seven and gets in here at ten so the villagers can do their shopping. It leaves for the village at five.'

'You sure?' the officer questioned. 'I've never heard of the place.'

'It's the back end of a cabbage patch,' the clerk sneered. 'My mother-in-law's sister lives there.' He turned to Helena, and she sensed that he was eyeing her jeans and sweatshirt. She was beginning to wish she'd bought a pair of the polyester slacks the locals were wearing. 'It's small, a hundred people at most live there, and that's if you include those who live on the farms within a day's walk of the main square. There's nothing there for tourists.'

'We're not tourists,' Helena looked around for Ned. She was reassured to find him standing behind her.

'Why are you going there?' the officer asked.

'My mother was born there.'

The police officer looked from her to Ned. 'You're visiting relatives?'

It was the one question Helena was beginning to dread, simply because every official she met asked it. Her passport bore her surname. If she had relatives in the village, would they suffer if she acknowledged them? Would they suffer more if she didn't and it was subsequently discovered they were related?

'I have no relatives living there that I'm aware of.' She crossed her fingers under cover of her pocket. It was almost true. If she did have any relatives in the village, none of them had acknowledged her or replied to her letter. 'But my father is buried there. I would like to see his grave.' That at least was the truth.

'There's a hotel across the road.' The officer pointed towards the main entrance to the station. 'You can stay there until the bus leaves on Thursday morning.'

Now that Helena was within reach of her mother's home village, she had no intention of breaking her journey to accommodate the vagaries of the local bus timetable.

'There's a bus on Thursday,' she informed Ned.

Ned dropped the suitcases. 'Thursday! How far is the village?'

'It takes the bus three hours.'

'We'll have to hire a taxi.'

The officer heard 'taxi', a universal word. 'It will be very expensive to hire a taxi to take you that far,' he said to Helena.

'How expensive?' She asked.

'You'll have to negotiate with the drivers outside the station.' He nodded to them, then walked towards a telephone kiosk.

'Thank you,' Helena called after him. She waited until the queue in front of the booking office had dissipated. 'Do you know the village well?' she asked the clerk.

He carried on counting and stacking coins on the shelf below his counter, and spoke without looking at her. 'My mother-in-law's sister is poor. My wife and I visit there once a month to take her food and warm clothes. It's not easy for old people in Poland, especially in the country areas. I can give you her address. She has lived in the village all her life. If your mother was born there, she will have known her. She may be able to tell you things. She may even know if you have any relatives living nearby.'

Helena ignored the clumsy hint. 'Is there a hotel in the village?'

He laughed. 'A hotel? What for? Visiting stud boars and bulls?'

'Is there anyone who lets out rooms?' Helena persisted.

'There is a bar in a side street off the main square. You can't miss it. It's next door to the shop. They have a room they let out to visiting officials from the Ministry of Agriculture. But if it's occupied?' His grin widened. 'You'll have to return to the hotel here.'

'There isn't anywhere else?' Helena pressed.

'Between here and the village? A few barns and pigsties. Nothing a Westerner would want to stay in,' he mocked.

'You'd be surprised how tough we Westerners can be. Thank you for the information.' Helena turned to Ned. 'Let's go.'

'Where?'

'To find a taxi.'

Chapter 8

HELENA HAD EXPECTED to find a line of taxis waiting outside the station. There were none. She and Ned dropped their bags and looked up and down. Apart from a parked red Syrena, the car produced in Poland solely for domestic use, the street was remarkably empty, as devoid of people as it was of traffic.

'I feel as though I've stepped into one of those sci-fi films where we're the only people left on the planet.' Ned commented. 'But it's midday, so everyone must be taking a siesta.'

'This is Poland not Italy or Germany.'

'Then they're all queuing for food somewhere. If I knew where, I'd join them. I'm so hungry I could even eat that foul breakfast again.'

A man emerged from a building across the road and walked towards them. He looked at their suitcases.

'Taxi?' he unlocked the Syrena.

'That doesn't look like a taxi to me,' Ned said suspiciously.

'Taxi,' the man repeated.

Helena looked up and down the street again. Despite the police officer's suggestion that she barter with the 'drivers' outside the station there wasn't another car or person in sight.

The man opened the door, pushed the driver's seat forward and motioned them into the back of the car.

'That car hasn't any back doors. Once we're in there we'll be trapped. He could drive us into the woods, rob us blind and dump us miles from anywhere,' Ned whispered, mindful of his father's warnings. He picked up the suitcases. 'We'll look for a hotel and get reception to call us a taxi.'

'Norbert.' The police officer strolled out of the station and walked up to them. 'Don't tell me you're pretending to be a taxi driver again.'

'He's not a taxi driver?' Helena asked the officer.

'Not an official one who pays his licence fee.'

'When have I ever had an accident?' Norbert challenged the officer. 'I'm a good driver with a car. These people want to be taken somewhere. Where's the harm?'

'The harm is that you specialize in picking up gullible tourists and charging them ten times the going rate. And because they don't know any better, they pay you.'

'What's the difference, if they're happy and I'm happy? Everyone knows Westerners have money to burn.' Norbert winked at Helena, and Ned stepped closer to her.

'Not all of them are happy. A German couple came into the office to complain that you drove them into the woods, stopped the car and demanded twice what you'd originally asked for to return them to their hotel.'

'A misunderstanding,' Norbert dismissed.

Tired of standing in the broiling midday sun, Helena turned to the police officer. 'Where can we hire a real taxi?'

'That's a good question,' he pontificated. 'There aren't many in town and,' he gazed at the empty street, 'they all appear to be engaged.'

'You won't do better than me and my Syrena, miss,' Norbert coaxed. 'Together we'll fly you wherever you want to go. And so quickly you'll be amazed.'

'Even if you pay him upfront, he'll stop the car halfway and ask for more,' the police officer warned.

'Come on, sir,' Norbert whined, 'we all need to make a living.'

'A living not a fortune,' the officer emphasized.

'If we can't get another car then we'll have to take his,' Helena said decisively. 'How much would you charge?'

'To take you where?' Norbert asked.

Helena gave him the name of the village.

'It's three hours there and three hours back for me. There's no way I'll get a return fare.'

'How much?' Helena repeated.

119

Norbert glanced slyly at the officer. 'Dollars or zlotys?'

Helena hesitated. She knew it was illegal to give Poles foreign currency or trade in anything except zlotys.

Norbert broke the silence. 'I could do it for twelve dollars.'

'That's three days' pay,' the police officer told Helena.

Norbert scratched the side of his nose. 'Tomorrow and the day after I could make zilch.'

'Knowing you, that's not likely. What are you selling this week, Norbert? Stolen watches or fake Levi jeans?'

'The driver asked for twelve dollars.' Helena said to Ned in English.

'For five, I'll note the number of the Syrena and make Norbert promise to take you straight there and stick to the agreed fare,' the officer offered.

Helena recalled the policeman heading for the public telephone in the station after he left them. And Norbert's swift arrival after she and Ned walked out on to the street.

'Five dollars,' the officer repeated.

'You said he'd leave us in the woods,' Helena reminded.

'Not now I've helped you make the arrangements. He's not a bad sort and he's a good driver. He'll get you there in one piece.'

'Have you seventeen dollars?' Helena asked Ned. She had a hundred tucked into a money belt she'd tied around her waist but she didn't want to flaunt it publicly and she knew that Ned had broken his share of the dollars into small amounts and secreted them in various pockets in his shirt and jeans.

'Seventeen dollars is a lot,' Ned objected.

'Twelve for the driver, five for the officer. And please don't try to haggle. It'll draw attention to us and it's illegal to pay for anything in American dollars,' she murmured, when a man leaving the station stopped and stared at them.

'Even to a policeman.'

'A police officer's word will carry more weight than ours.'

Ned pulled a small leather bag from inside his shirt. He opened it and extracted three five dollar bills and two singles. Helena took them from him, slipped the officer five dollars and gave the rest to Norbert.

'Have a good journey.' The police officer turned on his heel and returned to the station.

Norbert walked to the back of his car and opened the boot. He lifted the suitcases from the pavement and piled them inside. 'Don't worry, you and your girlfriend will be fine with me,' he said to Ned in English. 'I know how to look after tourists from the West.'

'You certainly know how to charge them,' Ned complained.

Ned helped Helena into the back of the car and, conscious that there was no back door, sat behind the driver's seat. There was little he could do while Norbert was driving, but it comforted him to know that if they stopped, should it prove necessary, he could always throw the cord from his duffle bag around the man's neck and throttle him from behind. He reached for Helena's hand.

'All the Communists we've met so far seem to be on the make and take,' he observed quietly.

'Peter warned us what it would be like.'

'He was right. Anyway, as we've allowed ourselves to be picked up by what the people on Ponty market call a spiv, we may as well use him.' Ned leaned forward when Norbert sat in the driver's seat. 'I'm starving. Is there any chance of buying food on the way?'

'It will cost you.' Norbert turned and flashed a grin.

'I didn't expect you to conjure up a meal for nothing,' Ned answered.

'What do you want?'

'What can you get?' Ned tossed the question back at him.

'A large, well-cooked cold chicken, fresh bread rolls, butter, apples and plums.'

'Sounds good.' In spite of her determination to get to the village as quickly as possible, Helena's mouth was already watering.

'Five dollars.' Norbert held out his hand.

Ned reflected that their money wasn't going to last long at the rate they were spending it, but after only two days behind the Iron Curtain he wasn't anxious to make their stay a long one. 'Where do we get it?'

'I know a restaurant. You stay in the car. I'll go in the back door.'

'And pay a dollar for the chicken and a dollar for everything else,' Ned guessed.

Norbert laughed. 'A driver has to eat, too. But because I like you and your girlfriend, I'll throw in two bottles of beer at no extra cost. How's that for generosity?'

As Norbert had promised, the chicken was good, with plenty of meat, the bread rolls were so fresh they were still warm, and if the apples were wormy and the plums hard, Helena decided it would be mean-spirited to grumble. She and Ned gazed out of the car window at the passing scenery.

'The countryside's not as green as Germany,' Ned commented.

'The climate is drier,' Norbert informed him.

'Your English is very good,' Helena complimented between mouthfuls of chicken roll.

'It was the only subject worth studying at school. Poland's future lies in the West not the East. The Russians who live outside Moscow and Leningrad are even poorer than we are.'

'You've been to Russia?' Helena had been curious about the country ever since she'd read *Anna Karenina*, which Alma Raschenko had given her for her fourteenth birthday.

'My mother is Russian.'

'Do you speak the language?' Ned dropped a chicken bone back into the cardboard box in the basket and tore one of the wings from the carcass.

'Not as well as I speak English.' Norbert waved his hand in the air. 'What do you think of our Polish forest?'

'Very pretty.' Helena drank a mouthful of beer from the bottle.

'And haunted,' Norbert said. 'So many people were massacred there during the war that the peasants won't walk through it at night.'

'Polish people?' Helena moved to the edge of the seat.

'Poles, Jews, Russians and, when we Poles had the chance, Germans,' Norbert said with relish.

'Did you live here during the war?' Helena asked.

'I was born and grew up in the town, but I have no intention of dying there. When I save enough money I'm going to America. Have you been there?'

Ned had, but Helena kicked him to warn him to stay silent. 'What was it like here during the war?'

'Bloody and terrible for the survivors; even bloodier for those who were killed.'

'Did you fight?'

'I was only twelve when it finished. But my father joined the partisans and I ran errands for them. I remember the Russians marching in. I was six years old. They ordered everyone into the town square – men, women, children, old, young, sick, healthy. It made no difference. They separated out those they didn't like the look of, shot half and sent the other half to Siberia. When the Germans drove the Russians out in 1941, things became even worse. They killed people for amusement, cut food rations for Polish people to below starvation level, rounded up everyone who was young, fit and healthy, and sent them to work camps in Germany. But the Jews received the most savage treatment. My father's brother's wife was Jewish. She was murdered in Treblinka.'

'Did the rest of your family suffer?' Helena probed.

'I just told you, all the Poles suffered during the war. No one in the country escaped. Look over there.' He pointed to a roofless ruin, its crumbling stone walls barely visible beneath a tangle of ivy, brambles and weeds. 'That used to be a flourishing farm. My father knew the owner. He had over fifty cows.'

'What happened?' Even as Helena asked the question she dreaded hearing the answer.

'The Germans drove into the farmyard early one morning and accused the farmer and his two sons of helping the partisans. They shot the entire family, even the baby, stole all the animals and burned the buildings.'

'My mother told me a little of what is was like here during the war.'

'Your mother lived here?'

'In the village,' Helena confirmed.

'So that's why you want to go there. To see relatives?'

'No, but I want to see my father's grave. Is the village like this one?' Helena moved the conversation on.

About fifty houses were scattered either side of the sandy road. A few were brick but most were wood. All were in dire need of care, attention and a coat of stain or paint. Apart from a few vegetable plots, the gardens weren't tended, and the few flowers that bloomed were straggly and overblown, as if they hadn't been pruned in years.

'The village you're going to is smaller but not that different,' Norbert replied.

'Are all the people there farmers?' Ned asked.

'No. There are two factories close by. One makes jam, the other sausages. People either work in them or on the collective farm. A few of the older people still live on their own small plots of land.'

'This is just what I expected after talking to Peter,' Ned whispered under cover of the engine noise. 'In Communist countries everything belongs to everyone, but no one takes responsibility for or cares for anything, including the houses they live in, which are left to rot. After last night's fiasco I dread to think where we'll be sleeping tonight. A village is bound to have less to offer than Warsaw.'

'That doesn't necessarily mean the accommodation will be as bad.' Helena leaned close to Norbert. 'The clerk in the railway station said something about a bar in the village. Do you know where it is?'

'Yes.' Norbert nodded.

'He said there is a room there that they rent out.'

'I didn't know.'

'Do you know of anyone else that rents rooms there?' Helena hoped there'd be a small hotel or boarding house the clerk hadn't heard of.

'No, but I'll take you to the bar. If they haven't a room to spare they might know of someone who does. So,' he leaned back in his seat, 'are you planning to do much sightseeing while you're here? Because if you are, there are castles and churches that I could show you.'

'No, thanks. We just want to go to the village,' Ned interrupted.

'But if you give us your telephone number, we'll let you know when we're coming back. Provided, of course, we don't spend all our money in the village and have none left to pay you the return fare.'

'There's nothing to spend your money on in the village,' Norbert said authoritatively. 'I'll give you the number of the bar nearest my apartment. I call in there once a day to pick up my messages. So telephone at least a day before you want to come back. Two days would be better.'

'How much longer before we get there?' Helena wrapped the food they hadn't eaten, and settled back in her seat.

'An hour.' Norbert glanced back at her over his shoulder.

'I have no idea why but the closer we get to the village the more nervous I feel,' she said to Ned.

Ned looked out of the window. 'We've come a long way from Pontypridd. It's strange to think that your mother grew up here.'

'She told me that she and all the other people from her village who were sent to Germany were marched out along the main road to the town. It took them two days to get there and when they reached the railway station they had to sleep on the platform because there wasn't anywhere else. The next morning they were loaded on to goods wagons.'

'I suppose this must be the road.'

Helena looked through the window and tried to imagine her mother and all the other young people being forced to march along it at gunpoint by armed guards. She recalled one of the few conversations she'd had with her mother about the day her father had been murdered and Magda had been taken from her home.

'*They rounded us up and marched us out as we stood. None of us was allowed to say goodbye to our families or go into our homes to fetch so much as a comb or toothbrush or coat. And the sun hadn't risen. It was cold that morning . . . so cold . . .*'

'How long ago did your mother go to the West?' Norbert broke into her thoughts.

'She went to Britain from Germany in 1947.'

'She never returned to Poland after the war?' he guessed.

'She didn't, but she told me about the village and her life there. She never mentioned a bar.'

'That's because she wouldn't have been allowed in there. In Poland women stay home at night.' Norbert slowed the car and turned right at a crossroads.

'You mean before the war,' Helena said.

'And now. No self-respecting woman will go near a bar in any village or small town in Poland, although widows and respectable married women can go to the side doors to buy beer.'

'Is there a priest in the village?' Ned asked quickly, afraid that Helena might start a lecture on women's liberation.

'Priests are outlawed,' Norbert informed him curtly.

'We know.' Knowing that Ned had only asked about priests to avoid an argument, Helena made a face at him. 'But my priest at home said that many priests have stayed on in Poland and operate secretly.'

'Ask questions about them and, English or not, people will think that you are working for the secret police. What was your mother's name?'

Helena hesitated, before deciding that as she had come to bury her mother's ashes and find out what she could about her mother's life here before the war, it was ridiculous to keep her name secret. 'Magdalena Janek. Have you heard of her?'

'No. But hundreds if not thousands of people left here during the war and never returned. Who could blame them? Not me. So many people were killed, entire families wiped out. There was nothing for some people to come back to. And I've heard that life is soft and easy in the West.' He slowed the car as they approached another crossroads. 'All milk and honey with machines that do the work for you. Unlike that poor man over there.' He pointed to a field where an old man was ploughing a field with an ox.

'I am a teacher and I have worked hard to get where I am,' Helena informed him, irritated by his assumption.

'And you?' Norbert eyed Ned in the mirror. 'Are you a teacher, too?'

Not wanting to broadcast the fact that he was a doctor, lest people begin regaling him with lists of their ailments, Ned said, 'Yes, I teach science.'

'Clever you. I have no time for science. It has no relationship to

126

money, and that's the only thing I am interested in. But here we are. This is the village.'

Although Magda had been reluctant to talk about her husband's death, she had loved talking about her home village. Helena knew there was a large square in front of the church where people congregated on summer evenings. And when the musicians in the village brought out their piano accordions and violins, there had often been impromptu concerts and dances.

She'd imagined it as large, shaded by oaks and sycamores, and ringed by benches. The reality was very different.

The square was larger even than she had expected, or perhaps it seemed larger because it was barren. There were no trees, no lawns, no flowers and no benches. It was ringed by stone buildings, which were the same pale, sand-washed colour as the compacted dirt on the ground. There were no pavements.

Norbert drove straight across it and she caught a glimpse of the church, which was fronted by high gates. He then left the square and drove down a narrow lane scarcely wider than the car, stopping outside a square wooden building that sported a pair of half-doors. They reminded Helena of the saloon doors in Hollywood Westerns.

'This is the bar.' Norbert switched off the engine and climbed out of the car.

Helena wrapped her arms around her duffle bag. 'I'll go in and ask if the room is free.'

Norbert moved the front seat forward and helped them out of the car. Ned glanced into the bar. The walls might once have been whitewashed, the floor was compacted dirt, covered with cigarette butts and spittle. Half a dozen unshaven, unsavoury characters were sitting around on cracked Formica stools.

The men – they were all men, just as Norbert had said they would be – were nursing glasses filled with beer, and small clay cups that might have contained coffee or tea, although, given the bleariness of their eyes, Ned doubted it.

'We can't stay in this place,' he protested to Helena.

She pushed open the half-doors. 'This is the bar, not the room for rent. Now we're here we may as well look at it.'

A young man sat next to a middle-aged man behind the counter. They both rose to their feet when Helena entered. The older man's body shook as he moved, and he gave Helena the vacant, childlike smile peculiar to the slow-witted. The younger man, who was tall and well-built, with black curly hair and deep blue eyes stared at her. It was a full minute before he shook the hand she offered him. 'Josef Dobrow. Welcome to our village, but not, I'm afraid, to our bar. Young ladies are not allowed in here.'

'I know, and I won't stay after we have discussed our business. Thank you for the welcome.' There was a clean-cut, open directness about Josef Dobrow that suggested friendly honesty. Helena liked him on sight.

'You are English?'

'Welsh.'

'Welsh?' He looked at her quizzically. 'What is Welsh?'

'Wales is a part of Britain, like Ireland and Scotland,' Helena explained.

'I'm sorry. I have never heard of it.' He switched to English. 'I hope you won't mind me practising my English. I have so few opportunities to speak it in the village.' He shook hands with Ned. 'How can I help you?'

'A man in town told us that you have a room we might be able to rent,' Helena said.

'Women can't come in here,' one of the customers barked.

'I'm not here for the bar,' Helena explained in Polish.

'There is only one room,' Josef warned.

'My husband and I only want one.' Aside from the fact that there was only one room on offer, she had found Ned's presence in her bed comforting in this alien country. 'Is it vacant?'

'We should discuss this outside.' He led the way out on to the street. 'I only work here in the summer. Anna, who owns the bar, rents the room. It is a simple attic, accessed by an outside staircase.'

'Does it have a bathroom?' Helena was longing to soak in a full-length tub of hot water.

'Lavatory in the back yard. Running cold water in the washhouse. You won't find any better in the village.'

Helena remembered the only alternative was three hours' drive away. 'We'll take it.'

'You haven't seen the room or asked how much it is.'

'We were told how much our accommodation would cost when we applied for our visas.'

'Anna usually throws in breakfast and supper for the fixed rate, although she's never rented to Westerners before. But if you're determined to take it, you'd better bring your things in.'

'Thank you.' Helena walked over to Norbert, who was leaning against his car smoking a cigarette. 'We can take our suitcases in.'

Ned followed her. 'Is it wise to take it before we see it?' He had been uncharacteristically silent during the exchange.

'I told you what the railway clerk said: it's here or nowhere.' Helena lifted the holdall from the seat of the car.

'And if the bed's full of bugs and lice?'

'We'll itch. Norbert,' Helena shook the driver's hand after he'd unloaded their cases, 'thank you for the sumptuous picnic and the ride.'

'Good to do business with you.' Norbert produced a notepad, scribbed down a number, tore off a sheet and handed it to Ned. 'For the return journey.'

'Thank you.' Ned tucked the slip of paper into his top pocket.

'If anyone here says they can take you cheaper,' Norbert waved the flat of his hand from side to side, 'we can — how do you say? — negotiate.'

Ned drew him aside, as Helena followed Josef around the side of the building. 'First negotiation begins right now. I'll buy you a beer, if you hang around until after we've checked out the room. I've a feeling that we may be going back sooner than Helena thinks.'

Norbert slapped Ned on the back. 'A beer and sausage it is.'

'I didn't say anything about sausage,' Ned remonstrated.

'You ate all the chicken. A Polish family of four could have lived off that for a month.' He walked through the half-doors and shouted for service.

While Norbert tried to explain his order to the old man behind the bar, Ned went outside to stand guard over their suitcases, which they'd left on the pavement. Norbert joined him a few minutes later. 'Do you want me to help you take these up to the room while the old man finds someone who will take my order?'

'As Helena hasn't returned, it appears we're staying.'

Ned studied the stone house that adjoined the wooden bar. It was large enough to be called a mansion. Ornate, decorative stonework around the windows and doors suggested that no expense had been spared in its construction. But time and lack of maintenance had taken their toll, as they had on all the buildings in the street. Its stonework was in desperate need of cleaning and its window frames of painting. It looked cold, austere and unwelcoming.

Norbert picked up the lighter suitcase and walked around the side of the building, entering a narrow archway cut into the wall of the house. Ned followed and found himself in an enclosed yard the size of a tennis court. It was walled in on their left by the back of the bar. Ahead was a barn, built from the same stone as the house, that loomed two and a half storeys high. On their right was what appeared to be a stable block, although there was no sign of horses.

The roof of the barn had been built out to cover a wooden veranda. Crates of empty bottles were stacked ten high alongside rows of wine kegs and barrels. A wire chicken run, which contained about two dozen white-feathered hens, filled the far corner between the barn and the stable block. Adjoining it was a pig pen housing a sow and a litter of piglets. Everything looked clean and orderly, but the smell from the pig pen and chicken run hung heavy and acrid in the still, warm air, and Ned blanched.

'Not used to farm smells?' He turned. Helena was sitting on a roughly made bench beneath an outside staircase, which led up to a wooden annex bolted on to the second floor of the house itself. The bench faced an even more primitive table.

'Neither are you,' Ned retorted.

'But I'm coping better than you. It must be something in the blood. My mother was a farmer's daughter, after all.'

Ned heard raised voices coming from within the house. He looked quizzically at Helena.

'The landlady doesn't appear to be too keen to rent the room to foreigners,' she whispered.

'It'll take me half an hour to eat. I'll be in the bar if you want to go back to town.' Norbert dropped the suitcase he'd carried into the yard, and returned to the street through the archway.

Joseph appeared a few minutes later. 'Anna doesn't think the room is suitable for Westerners.'

'As it's the only one for miles around, can't we at least see it?' Helena pleaded.

'She wants to know why you've come to this village.'

'I was born here. My mother's family lived here for generations.'

'Your mother didn't travel with you?'

Helena glanced self-consciously at her duffle bag. 'She died last month.'

'I am sorry,' Josef said sympathetically. 'Do you have relatives in the village?'

'I hope so, but I'm not sure. That's one of the reasons I'm here. To find out if any of them still live nearby. My mother's name was Magdalena Janek; she left here during the war—'

'Left?' Josef interrupted.

'She was taken by the Germans, who used her as a slave labourer. Perhaps if I talked to the landlady . . .' Helena rose to her feet.

'Leave it to me,' Josef cut in. He went back into the house. A few seconds later they heard a woman's voice raised in anger. A very long ten minutes after that Josef re-appeared. He held up a six-inch iron key. 'Anna says you may look at the room, and if you think it's suitable you may stay for a day or two – but no longer. She doesn't want the authorities asking questions about her guests, which they will do once they find out she has rented to people from Britain.'

Ned picked up the suitcases.

'Wait until you've seen the room. I'll help you to carry those up, if you decide to take it.' Joseph walked to the foot of the staircase and opened a door in the back wall of the house. He showed them a concrete-floored cubicle that held a bench toilet seat. 'Lavatory.'

Ned looked in. The stench of raw sewage was overpowering.

'The village has no mains drainage. There's a cess pit under the barn. It's emptied twice a year in spring and autumn, but this facility is just for the house. The bar has its own lavatory on the other side of the building. The customers don't come into the yard.'

'That's comforting to know,' Ned commented.

131

Helena hoped Joseph hadn't picked up on the sarcasm in Ned's voice.

'The wash-house.' Joseph opened a door next to the lavatory. The cubicle was slightly larger, and a brass tap was set high on the wall above a drain in the floor. There wasn't a sink, but a wooden barrel stood on a three-legged stool. 'The water from here also goes into the cess pit.'

'Only one tap? There's no hot water?' Ned guessed.

'You need hot water in summer?' Joseph said in surprise.

Ned recalled Norbert's comments about Westerners being soft. 'I can manage without.'

'There is a boiler in the kitchen. Anna uses it to heat water to wash clothes. If you want hot water, she will probably heat it up for you – at a price.' Joseph closed the door. 'The room is up here.' He walked up the staircase that led on to an outside landing.

'Looks like they're offering us the old hay loft. I only hope that there aren't any rats up here.' Ned followed Helena up the rickety, weathered staircase.

'No room could be as bad as the one we had last night,' Helena declared.

'I wouldn't be too sure of that if I were you.' Ned's optimism was rapidly dissipating at the thought of living without a flushing toilet and hot water for as long as it took Helena to arrange the interment of her mother's ashes.

Josef unlocked the door of the room and moved aside. Helena went in and looked around. It was the first rustic Polish room she had ever seen. It could have served as an illustration for the grand-mother's cottage in *Red Riding Hood*.

The walls and floor were pine, as was the furniture. Some pieces were more basic than others, but none was as coarse as the table and benches in the yard. There were two beds, both large, and separated from one another by a curtain that had been pulled back against the wall. Both appeared to be sturdy, or in Pontypridd terms 'rough and ready'. If it hadn't been for their size Helena would have assumed they were products of a junior woodworking class. Plumped high with feather eiderdowns, they were covered by ornately worked blue, red and green embroidered and tasselled spreads. The tiled washstand held a plain, white utility jug and pitcher. The washstand itself was an elegant piece from a bygone age, as were the carved dressing table and mirror.

A clean but empty wood-burning iron stove stood in the corner. A table and two chairs, of the same ilk as the beds, were set in front of the gable window. The table was covered with a cloth that matched the bedspread, and a glass vase of dried flowers was set in the centre along with an ashtray. The chair cushions were decorated with the same design as the tablecloth, as was the cushioned cover of the built-in window seat.

A red and dark-blue hand-woven, Bokhara carpet hung on the wall behind one of the beds. Helena touched it.

'That's Anna's prized possession and a family heirloom,' Josef informed her. 'Her grandfather brought it back from Russia. He used to trade horses there before the war.'

'It's lovely,' Helena said sincerely.

'That's why Anna keeps it here. It's too good for the public rooms and it could get damaged in the house. Anna's brother – you saw him behind the bar – can be clumsy and careless. The wardrobe is in here.' He opened a door set into the eaves.

'The room is lovely. We'll be very comfortable here. Thank you for talking the landlady into renting it to us.' Helena held out her hand. 'I didn't introduce myself properly earlier. Helena Janek – John,' she blurted, remembering that she had told him that she and Ned were married, forestalling any objections the landlady might have in renting the room to two single people. It might be the 1960s in Western Europe but she wasn't sure that the sexual revolution had spread behind the Iron Curtain.

'Pleased to meet both of you.' Josef shook hands again.

'Would you like us to pay in advance?' Ned unzipped the in-side pocket of his jacket and lifted out one of the many wallets he carried.

'You can sort that out with Anna after I've told her that you're taking it.'

'It might help if I see her,' Helena suggested.

'You will see her soon enough,' Josef said casually. 'Will you be staying two days?'

'Possibly longer. I hope that will be possible.' Helena looked through the window down into the yard. The old man was pouring a bucket of water into the trough in the pig sty and she wondered if the mysterious Anna was running the bar.

'It could be,' Josef replied honestly.

'As I said, I'm here to look up my mother's family, if there are any left. My mother was a Niklas before she married.' She hoped that Josef would be able to tell her if any of her relatives still lived in the area. 'Do you know anyone by the name of Janek or Niklas who lives near here?'

'Some people with the surname Niklas live near the village,' Josef said shortly.

'My mother's brother Wiktor Niklas survived the war, as did her sister Julianna. Of course, Julianna might not be a Niklas now. She is probably married. But my grandmother's name was Maria ...' Helena's voice trailed away as Josef went to the door. He'd obviously stopped listening to her.

'I'll bring up your cases and tell Anna that you're staying.'

'Thank you. When can I meet her?'

'When Anna decides.' Josef ran down into the yard.

Chapter 9

NED FOLLOWED JOSEF down into the yard. 'Here, let me take one at least,' he protested, taken aback by the nonchalant way Josef picked up both the heavy cases.

Josef handed Ned the lighter of the two, and ran up the staircase with the other. He left it just inside the door. 'I hope you will be all right here,' he said. 'If you need anything I'll be in the bar or the yard. If you can't see me, shout.'

'We'll be fine. I didn't expect to find anything this comfortable in a small village.' Helena struggled to conceal her disappointment at the way he'd brushed off her enquiries.

'Anna furnished this room with all the personal pieces that belonged to her and her two sisters. I know it's not what landladies usually do, but she likes people to feel at home here.'

'Are her sisters still living here?' Helena asked, anxious to turn the conversation back to the village and its occupants.

'One was shot and killed by the Germans; the other disappeared.'

'Disappeared?'

'The Germans took her. It happened a lot in wartime. To the people she left behind it would have seemed as though your mother had disappeared.'

'No, it wouldn't have, because my mother wrote to them as soon as she could after the war.' Helena dragged the suitcase to the wardrobe.

'Are you hungry?' Josef changed the subject.

'No, thank you. We ate on the way here, but we would like to eat later if that is all right,' Ned answered.

'Anna serves supper at seven.'

'That's fine.' Ned put the second suitcase on one of the beds.

Josef gave Ned the enormous key. 'It would be wise to lock the door, even if you only go down to the lavatory or wash-house. We can't watch this room all the time, and some people are stupid enough to think that all Westerners carry sacks of gold. Most of the villagers are honest, but not all.'

'Thank you.' Helena took the key from Ned and laid it on the table.

'Oh.' Josef turned back just as he was about to leave. 'I almost forgot. We will need your passports to register your stay here with the authorities.'

'Of course.' Helena fished hers out of her duffle bag and Ned handed his over.

'If you need anything in the next half hour, I will be in the bar.' Josef walked out on to the landing and closed the door behind him.

'And there's me thinking what a nice trusting soul he was – right up until the moment he took our passports. That makes us virtual prisoners here.' Ned stretched out on one of the beds and closed his eyes.

'We'll be free again after we pay our bill.' Helena lay beside him. 'Soft enough for you?'

'Too soft.' He opened one eye and looked at her. 'Josef kept staring at you.'

'I'm a westerner.'

'Was I reading too much into Josef's conversation, or didn't he want to talk about any family you might have in the village?'

'He didn't seem to want to discuss them,' she admitted. 'Although he said there are people by the name Niklas living close by.'

'Which means you want to go looking for them?'

'I'd like to find my father's grave first.'

'Exhausted as we both are, you'd rather be up and out of here, wouldn't you?'

'I'd like to walk to the churchyard, yes,' she admitted. 'But you don't have to come with me.'

'As if I'd allow you to wander around by yourself. Let's go.' Ned groaned before rolling off the bed.

Helena picked up her duffle bag.

'You could leave that here,' he suggested. 'We have a key.'

'It might not be the only one to this room.' Helena knew she was being irrational, but she wasn't prepared to allow her mother's ashes out of her sight until she could bury them in her father's grave.

'No one would bother to make two keys that size,' he insisted.

'Probably not,' she agreed in a tone that said she wasn't convinced but wasn't prepared to argue the point.

Knowing she had no intention of leaving the duffle bag, he held out his hand. 'At least let me carry that for you.'

'It's not heavy.'

'It would be even lighter if you took the magazines and your toilet bag out of it.'

Helena set it on the bed and took everything from it except her purse, which contained some of the zlotys, and the casket in its airtight box.

'Do you want to wash your hands and face before we go?' Ned asked.

'No, I'll wash before supper. You?'

'I've a feeling that I'm as clean as I'm going to be while we remain here.'

'Do you mean the village or Poland?'

'Both.'

'Admit it, you don't like washing in cold water.' She picked up the duffle bag.

'Only a masochist would. As for washing before supper, I just hope it's worth washing for.'

They left the room, and Ned locked the door behind them.

'I'm sure it will be as good a meal as the mysterious and strangely hostile Anna can provide,' Helena replied.

Ned eyed the slops in the trough in the pig pen. 'That's what bothers me.'

Helena and Ned left the yard and walked under the archway into the street. Neither of them had noticed the village shop when they'd arrived because its shutters had been drawn. But it was now open. There was no door or window, simply an outside counter that faced the street. Two men stood behind it. Piled high in front of them was a hillock of enormous river carp. A line of women and children snaked down the street to the front of the counter, where one of the men was chopping the fish into chunks.

Ned felt the eyes of every woman and child burning into him as they passed. Helena clutched her duffle bag closer to her chest.

'So everyone in the village will be dining on fish tonight,' Ned commented.

'Including us.' Helena noticed a woman handing over a card to one of the men. He glanced at it before cutting her a piece of fish that he wrapped in newspaper. 'Rationing must still be in force here.'

'Peter said something about food distribution committees controlling the supply to the grocery shops. You'd think they could run to greaseproof paper for hygiene's sake. I dread to think what bacteria are on that newspaper.'

'Not so loud,' Helena cautioned. 'You can't assume that no one speaks English here. Josef's is perfect. And besides, I thought newsprint didn't harbour germs.'

'That's all you know. Wouldn't you say that Josef's English is too perfect for a barman?'

'How do you know Josef's a barman?'

'He was serving behind the bar when we walked in,' Ned reminded her.

'He could be Anna's son.'

'Wouldn't he call her mother, not Anna, if he was?'

'Possibly.' She avoided a cat that was gorging on a piece of carp skin. 'But some people call their parents by their Christian names.'

'I'd liked to have seen you try it with Magda,' he smiled.

'She would have soon put me to rights.' Helena returned his smile at the thought.

'Wouldn't she just.' Ned knew that Helena was remembering Magda's insistence on everything being done properly, according to the Polish code of conduct she had been brought up to respect. But his spirits soared at the brief return to their former good humour.

'Josef's obviously well educated. I suppose he could be living here because he's related to Anna; not necessarily her son, but a nephew or cousin perhaps.' Helena was glad when they turned the corner and left the shop, its smell and its queue behind them.

'He could be a Party spy, billeted with her in order to keep his eye on any Westerners crazy enough to venture this deep into wild, unchartered, untamed Poland.'

'You are paranoid.'

'Ssh . . . don't look to your right. He's about to join us.'

'Possibly because he's friendly and he'd like to help us?' Helena suggested.

'I don't think so. He's still staring at you as though he knows you but can't quite place you.'

'You don't like him, do you?'

'No more than I'd like anyone who looks at you the way he does,' Ned muttered.

'That's ridiculous . . .' Helena muttered. 'Hello, Josef.'

'I talked to Anna,' Josef announced. 'She agreed that you can stay until you have finished your business here.'

'Thank you,' Helena said sincerely.

'And I thought you might like someone to show you around the village, as you haven't been here before.'

Although Helena was still smarting at Josef's refusal to give her any information about the Janek and Niklas families, she decided it was worth trying him again. He didn't look much older than her, so it was unlikely he knew much about what had happened in the village during the war, but he was clearly at home in the place and seemed to know it well.

'My mother often talked about the good times she and her brothers and sister enjoyed before the war,' she began. 'Apparently there were dances and parties in the square in the summer. Is the square this way?' She'd made a note of the direction when Norbert had driven them in, but she wondered if she'd lost her bearings since they'd left the house.

'It is.' Josef fell into step beside them.

'Do you have time to spare?' Ned enquired pointedly.

'Yes.' Josef smiled. 'You are suspicious of me?'

'Not particularly,' Ned lied.

'Yes you are. I know how the Western press portray Communist countries.'

'You do?' Ned met Josef's steady gaze.

'They regard the Communist Party as evil, war-mongering and controlling, and its officials as busybodies who are paid to pry into the population's private lives to make sure that everyone toes the Party line. As for the people, you think we are all cold-hearted automatons.'

'And how do you regard Westerners?' Ned turned the tables.

'People who live in countries full of decadent millionaires who know the price of everything and the value of nothing. Your rich step over your starving homeless as they frequent expensive restaurants to buy a meal for a price that would keep a person for a month. But I am astute enough to know that neither image is true. You and Helena are no more decadent than I am a cold-hearted automaton. I work here, in this village. I am the schoolmaster.'

'So that's why you are free now,' Helena said.

'It's the summer holidays. They are longer in the villages than they are in the towns so the children can help bring in the harvest. We work harder during the autumn term and have a shorter winter holiday to make up for lost time.'

'And are you helping with the harvest?' Ned asked.

'No. I am helping Anna in the bar. I live with her and her brother, and try to make all the necessary repairs to the house and outbuildings at this time of year. It's a battle to keep a place that age watertight.'

'How old is it?' Helena asked.

'The barn and house are over five hundred years old; the stables and bar only two hundred.'

'You mentioned winter holidays. I thought Communists didn't celebrate Christmas.' Ned wrapped his arm around Helena's waist, as though he were staking a claim to her.

'Poland may have a Communist government, but people still put up Christmas trees and decorate them with home-made sweets and biscuits. They even sing carols in the village square – and live until Twelfth Night to tell the tale,' Josef added in amusement. 'Old customs die hard, and the Party recognizes that religion is important to some people, especially the old. The hardliners may not be happy about it, but they know better than to try to outlaw it entirely.'

Helena threw caution to the wind. 'Is there a priest in the village?'

'Two. One who has taken orders and an apprentice who hasn't, but does the job as best he can.'

'Two?' she echoed in amazement.

'Officially there are none, but Anna's brother is the first.'

'The old man?' Ned asked.

'Stefan wasn't always as you see him now. The Germans tortured him for carrying food and information to the partisans. He hasn't been the same since. Anna nursed his body back to health, but his mind remains beyond the doctors' healing.'

'That's horrible,' Helena said.

'Some people say he is lucky to have survived. Anna disagrees. She said he was a strong, proud man who would have hated living as he is now.'

'You said there were two priests,' Helena reminded him.

'You're looking at the other.'

'You? But—'

'I told you, things are different here in the country. My father was taken by the Germans during the war; my mother was shot here, in the village, by the SS when I was three years old. I didn't have any other family to take me in, so the village priest sort of adopted me. Stefan was his curate. And, as Anna had just lost her younger sisters and parents, the priest asked her to care for me as a favour to him – and, I think, for her own sake. She fed my body; he my soul. When the Communists took control after the war, they locked up the church and the priest's house. He and Anna moved into the house next to the bar, which was empty because the owner had been killed. After working six twelve-hour shifts a week in the meat factory, the priest carried on baptising babies, burying the dead and marrying people. He wasn't allowed to use the church, so he conducted the ceremonies in people's homes. He brought me up and supervised my education. When I returned to the village after university to run the local school, I helped him. He died two years ago. I haven't taken Holy Orders but, as there was no one else to do his work – you've seen what Stefan is like – I simply carried on where he left off.'

'The Catholic priest in Pontypridd told us that some priests were still working undercover in Poland, but we didn't expect to find one as young as you,' Ned commented.

Josef shrugged. 'It may not suit the Pope or the Vatican to have an unqualified lay man giving the Holy Sacrament, but it suits us Poles. And it doesn't mean that we, as a nation, are any less devout than those who have the services of fully ordained priests.'

'Then you are a Catholic?' Desperate to find someone who would understand her mission to bury her mother's ashes in her father's grave, Helena opted for a direct approach.

'The villagers trust me to conduct the ceremonies that mark the important days of their lives. It is a sacred trust and I treat it as such. I conduct them the old way, but I am also careful to fill in the Party paperwork. That way, no one in authority can complain.'

'Isn't that a little cynical, not to mention hypocritical?' Ned asked.

'If you don't mind me saying so, Ned, it is obvious that you haven't been in Poland long.' Josef paused, as the street ended and the square opened out in front of them. 'It won't take you long to see all that this village has to offer. Is there anywhere you would like to go first?'

'The church,' Helena said decisively.

'As I told you, it is closed and has been since 1945. Anyone caught tampering with the locks would be taken away.' He lowered his voice to a theatrical whisper and leaned close to Ned. 'Locked in dark dungeons, tortured and never seen again.'

'I don't mean inside the church.' Helena's mouth twitched at Ned's annoyed expression. 'My mother corresponded with her family after the war. She told me that they had put up a headstone in the churchyard to mark my father's grave. I would like to see it. That's if we are allowed to go into the churchyard?'

'We still use it to bury people because we have no other cemetery. Your father's name was Janek?'

'Yes, Adam Janek. Have you heard of him?'

Josef glanced at her quickly, then turned aside. 'Yes.'

'What have you heard?' she asked, but Josef was already striding ahead into the dusty square. A dozen children were playing a game of catch there. They saw Josef and rushed over.

'My pupils,' he explained. 'Do you mind if I tell them that you are from Britain?'

Helena was irritated by Josef's refusal to answer her question, but it didn't stop her from smiling at the children. 'Of course not,' she said.

After prompting from Josef, the children lined up in front of Helena and Ned, and said, 'Welcome to Poland' in English.

Helena thanked them in Polish, and they ran off.

'That makes me wish that I'd taken the trouble to learn a few words of the language before we came here.' Ned watched the children return to their game.

'It's not too late. You're in the right place to learn.'

They walked to the church. The wrought-iron gate was thick with rust, and creaked loudly when Josef lifted the chain that held it in place and pushed it open.

Planks of pine had been nailed over the church windows, and metres of metal chains, held in place by enormous padlocks, stretched across the doors.

'Are they expecting it to be stormed by troops?' Ned asked.

'It's no more than they've done to other churches in the area. As you see, the local people have pasted posters on the door to commemorate their dead. It's customary to do so every year for the first three years and every seven after that. In the old days they would have been put up inside, with masses said and candles lit for the souls of the departed.'

The weather-stained posters bore the photographs, names and dates of the deceased. Some were so faded they were almost indecipherable. Others looked as though they had just left the printing press. But although the church was boarded up, the graveyard was immaculate. The grass verges neatly cut, the trees trimmed and fresh flowers on most of the graves.

'This is a wonderful surprise.' Helena dropped her voice to a whisper without knowing why. 'I expected to find the cemetery overgrown and the graves derelict and neglected.'

'The people in this village honour their dead,' Josef said, 'especially the martyrs who died during the war. That is Anna's sister's grave.' He pointed to a granite tombstone, decorated with a sculpted angel. A white rambling rose obscured the name and dates.

'Beautiful flowers,' Helena commented.

'Anna planted the rose. She says the blooms remind her of Matylda, and if she can't see the name and the dates she can pretend that she is still alive.'

They walked around the corner of the church. There were fewer flowers in front of the older graves, but the stones were still clean and the area around them tended.

'Everyone in the village does what they can to keep this churchyard neat and tidy,' Josef said proudly. 'After all, unless we leave the village to make a life elsewhere in the world – and not many of us are able to, or even want to – we will end up here.'

'You have a rota?' Ned asked.

'We don't need one. If someone visits a family grave and sees that someone else's headstone needs cleaning or that a plot needs weeding, they do it.'

'But the grass is freshly cut.' Helena stared at a photograph of two young children set behind a glass plate sunk into one of the headstones. The grave was tiny, the image heartbreaking.

'The retired farmers see that as their responsibility.'

'Do you know where my father's grave is?' Helena asked, suddenly impatient.

'Yes. The Janek tomb is one of the largest.'

'Are other members of my father's family buried there?'

'Adam Janek's grandparents, great-grandparents and generations before records began. Also his parents, brother and two sisters. They died during a diptheria epidemic in 1934.'

'You're very well informed.' Ned kept his arm around Helena as they followed Josef around the back of the church.

'This graveyard was my playground when I was a child. The old priest who brought me up used to spend what little free time he had keeping it tidy. I liked to think that I was helping him. Although I suspect now that I must have been more of a hindrance. Also the Janek family were important – in their day.' He frowned at Helena, as if something was bothering him, then pointed to a large area separated from the rest of the graveyard by a high stone kerb. 'That is the Janek family plot.'

'It's vast! There must be two dozen graves there.'

'According to the records, sixty-nine Janeks are buried in the ground. The old priest took the registers from the church before the Communists sealed it up. I have kept them safe. They are in Anna's house if you want to look at them. The earliest recorded Janek burial was in 1598. The last in 1943.'

'My father's,' Helena guessed.

'Adam Janek's,' Josef confirmed.

'I've seen a picture of the memorial. It's a stone cross.'

'There it is.' Josef pointed to a grave on the edge of the plot. The inscription was simple. Helena translated it for Ned.

'*Adam Janek, born 21 January 1919, martyred for Poland 26 June 1943. A loving husband and father.*'

Suddenly she gripped Ned's arm so hard he winced.

'What is it?' he asked, alarmed by the wild look in her eyes.

It was Josef who translated the rest. '*Also his daughter, Helena Weronika Janek. Born 5 June 1943, martyred 26 June 1943.*'

Ned stared at the dates. 'Magda never told you that you had a sister?'

'It's not my sister.' Helena's voice was husky with shock. 'That birth date. Don't you see?'

Ned stared at it, not wanting to believe what was etched into the stone. 'It's the same as yours,' he said when he could bear the silence no longer.

Chapter 10

NAUSEOUS AND LIGHT-HEADED, Helena sank to the ground. She could barely comprehend what she was seeing.

Also his daughter, Helena Weronika Janek. Born 5 June 1943, martyred 26 June 1943.

Ned crouched beside her and reached for her hand. It was icy. He looked up at Josef, who was watching both of them with concern. 'Could there be some mistake?'

'What kind of mistake?' Josef asked.

'I don't know,' Ned snapped. 'Adam Janek was killed in a massacre. People died alongside him. Perhaps there was a mix-up with the bodies and the wrong baby was buried in this grave.'

'A mix-up in this village?' Josef said sceptically. 'Everyone knew everyone in 1943, just as they do now. And every one of the nineteen people who were murdered by the Nazis that day is listed on the memorial in the square. Adam Janek's daughter's name is chiselled below that of her father's.'

'Helena told you that she was looking for her father's grave. She said his name was Adam Janek. You brought us here, yet you gave her no warning that he was buried with his daughter, who has the same name and birth date as Helena.' Ned knew he was being illogical. But he wanted to blame someone for Helena's pain. And, as he had taken an instant dislike to Josef, he was the obvious target.

Josef hesitated. 'I knew Adam Janek was buried here with his daughter, yes. But I'm not an expert on the Janek family. I assumed Helena was another daughter.'

'You said you knew this graveyard—'

'But not the name of every single person buried here,' Josef interrupted. 'Look around you.'

Ned did. They were marooned in a vast sea of hundreds of memorial stones, crosses and iron grave-markers.

'Did Magda ever mention that she'd had another child, Helena?' Ned drew closer to her.

'Not one with the same name and birth date as me,' she answered in a hollow voice.

'Is it possible that your mother gave birth to you after she left here, and named you for the child she had lost?' Josef asked.

'How?' Helena raised her eyes. 'My father was killed in 1943 . . .' She faltered as she realised that Adam Janek couldn't possibly have been her father.

'Your mother could have been raped,' Josef said gently. 'It happened to many women during and after the war. Or she could have met another man who was also killed during the war. Did she marry again?'

'Not to my knowledge. There was a man, a British soldier, but she already had me when she met him, and he married someone else shortly afterwards. I only found out about him after Mama died.' Helena wondered just how many secrets Magdalena Janek had carried to her grave. For the first time her mother's last words to Father O'Brien made sense: '*Tell Helena I'm sorry . . .*'

'As she'd lost one child and her husband, you would have been the only person left in her life,' Josef extrapolated. 'If she hadn't married again, and wanted to keep you, it would have made perfect sense for her to give you her husband's name and the name of the daughter she had lost. It would have meant that she could remain respectable. It might also explain why your mother didn't return to this village after the war. Catholic or Communist, rightly or wrongly, women who bear illegitimate children are still regarded as a disgrace by some people in these rural areas. And, unfortunately, so are their children.'

'You must have been born after Magda left the village, Helena.' Ned was clutching at straws but he desperately wanted to ease the pain etched on Helena's face.

'Auntie Alma said I was four years old when she first met my mother.'

'But you might have been younger. Magda could have told a white lie to cover up what she would have considered shameful.'

'There is a world of difference between a one- and a two-year-old child, and Bob Parsons said I was two when he first met my mother in 1945,' she reminded him.

'There must be someone in this village who knew Magdalena Janek,' Ned said to Josef.

'Plenty, I should think,' he replied. 'But who knows what happened to Magdalena after the Germans took her? Very few people who were marched away by the Nazis returned. And of those who did, none wanted to talk about what the Germans had done to them.'

'But some did come back,' Ned persisted.

'A few.' Josef said. 'But if you want to find out what life was like for your mother before the war, Helena, you should talk to the people who lived here then. They often talk about the Janeks, especially when they reminisce about the good old days.'

'Why the Janeks more than anyone else?' Helena asked.

'Because, before the war, the Janeks were the richest and most influential landowners in the area. Adam Janek was the last of them. After the massacre the only people who lived on Janek land were tenants, who would have paid rent if there had been anyone left to pay it to.'

'Will the older people talk to me about my mother and my . . . Adam Janek?' Helena had a suspicion that Josef wasn't telling her everything he knew.

'Possibly. But no one who survived the massacre talks about it willingly, even now,' Josef cautioned.

'Can you remember it?' Helena asked.

'I'm not sure.'

'Were you there?'

'I was three years old. I think I remember a little, but it's likely that I imagined it, to fit in with what the priest and Anna told me when I asked them about it years later.'

'Knowing something about what happened to my mother that day, even a second-hand account, would be better than nothing,' Helena pleaded.

Josef frowned. 'All I can recall is a series of images almost like ... how do you say it? ... like snapshots. I have a vision of standing in the square with everyone else from the village. I looked up at the adults, saw fear in their eyes and felt afraid because people I had always regarded as strong were terrified. I think I pulled on my mother's skirt because I remember blue cloth, and I raised my arms, but I can't remember if that was because everyone had their arms up or I was hoping that my mother would pick me up. I can't picture her face. The only likeness I carry of her now is the one I have seen in old photographs. A young man — I am sure that I remember him only because there were so few young men left in the village during the war — was arguing with a Nazi officer. The priest told me later he was Adam Janek. I will never forget the sound of the gunshots that ended the argument — and I am sure that *is* a real memory, because for years afterwards I couldn't stand any kind of loud noise. Even now, I only have to hear a bang to feel sick. The last image I have in my mind is one of bloody corpses piled in the square. Someone — not the priest because he was kneeling and giving the Last Rites — carried me away while I was crying for my mother. That is it.'

'No one told you anything more about the massacre?' Josef's pain had been palpable when he had been talking about it, but all Ned could think of was Helena's burning need to know the truth.

'The priest did, when he thought I was old enough to understand. He said that my mother had deliberately shielded my body with hers when she fell. He persuaded me that I owed it to her to work hard and live my life as honestly as I could to honour her memory. Her name is also on the monument. Anna's sister Matylda is there, too.'

'I'd like to see the monument.' Helena rose to her knees.

Ned helped her to her feet.

They retraced their steps back to the gate. The air in the church-yard was redolent with the scent of roses, and buzzing with the hum of bees and whirring of insect wings. Dandelion seeds floated among the stones, and gathered in diaphanous clouds on the paths. It was a quiet, peaceful place, and Helena realized she still wanted to leave her mother here. Despite the lies Magda had told her. She believed, really believed, that Adam Janek had been the one great love of her mother's life, and the village Magda's first and only true home.

'I'm sorry.' Josef fastened the chain back on to the churchyard gate. 'It must be a dreadful shock after travelling all the way from Britain to find out that the man you thought was your father couldn't have been.'

'I came here to bury my mother's ashes in his grave. Nothing has changed my mind about that,' Helena said determinedly. 'She loved Adam Janek to her dying day. Their wedding photograph hung in pride of place in our living room.'

'Her ashes?' Josef looked surprised. 'She has been cremated?'

Helena nodded. 'The priest gave me a dispensation because he thought it would have been too difficult for me to arrange to ship her body here. Who do we have to ask for permission to open Adam Janek's grave?'

'The people in the village look after the churchyard. The Niklas family put up the memorial to Adam Janek.'

'With money my mother sent them,' Helena clarified.

'Will there be a problem?' Ned asked, as they stopped in front of a square stone monument near the gate.

'I can't answer that. The village and the family would have to decide. As you see,' Josef indicated the monument, 'a list of everyone who died in the square that day.'

Posies of wild flowers lay on the plinth beneath the stone. They were limp, shrivelled by the summer sun. Helena moved one into the shade.

'The children in the village put those there. Most have a relative on the list,' Josef explained.

Helena read the inscription above the list of names: '*Martyred for Poland and freedom.*' As they were in alphabetical order Adam and Helena Janek's were halfway down. Just their names and ages: Adam Janek aged twenty-four; Helena Janek three weeks. Of the nineteen who had been shot, fourteen were women, the youngest eleven, the oldest eighty. There had been two babies. She looked for and found a Dobrow: Ludwika aged twenty.

'Ludwika was your mother?' she asked Josef.

150

'Yes.'

Helena gazed at the monument. Heat rose from the sandy earth. The children had gone but she could hear their voices, faint and shrill, in the distance. Cooking smells emanated from the houses, carrying with them pungent traces of the peppery spices her mother had used: paprika, oregano, ginger, marjoram, cinnamon, mint ...

'We should be getting back if we are going to clean ourselves up before supper,' Ned said.

Helena realized that she had been standing in front of the monument for some time. She turned to the square and visualized the scenes her mother had painted so vividly on dark winter evenings in Pontypridd: the doors of the houses wide open; people wandering in and out with trays of glasses and plates of food; musicians playing ... The road that led out of the square was little more than a lane, and barely the width of two cars, but just as Magda had said, fruit trees had been planted either side of it, stretching as far as she could see.

'We used to walk and eat ourselves to school when the fruit ripened. And such fruit, Helena. Like you've never tasted. Apples, pears, plums ...'

'That road leads to the farmhouse where my mother's family lived. She said it was a mile or so outside the village. Does the Niklas family still live in that house?' Helena asked Josef.

'A family by the name of Niklas lives in a house along that road, yes,' Josef answered cautiously.

'I must see them.'

'Not now, Helena,' Ned pleaded. 'You're upset. Leave it until the morning.'

'But—'

'Your arrival will be a shock. Have you written to tell the family that your mother is dead?' Josef asked.

'I couldn't find an address among my mother's things, so I wrote to them care of the post office or shop.'

'A letter like that wouldn't have been forwarded by the authorities,' Josef said flatly.

'Has anyone in the village mentioned the letter, Josef?' Ned asked.

'I haven't heard anyone talk about it.'

151

'Then my mother's family doesn't know that she is dead, or that I was coming here.' Helena clutched her duffle bag.

'You said that your mother told you that she was marched out of here by the Germans the same day that your father was killed.'

'Yes?' Helena picked up on the suspicious tone in Josef's voice.

'She never returned?'

'No.'

'And she sent her family money to pay for the memorial stone on Adam Janek's grave?'

'I told you she did,' Helena said impatiently, not understanding Josef's train of thought. 'My mother wrote to her family at least once a week. She often read me extracts from the letters she received from my aunt, uncle and her mother in return.'

'Did your mother tell the Niklas family about you?'

'Of course,' Helena retorted indignantly. 'When my mother read the letters she always gave me the good wishes they sent to both of us.'

'In that case, they must have known that you weren't Adam Janek's child,' Josef pointed out.

Ned couldn't bear the thought of Helena turning up on her grandmother's doorstep only to be hurt once more. 'Did you ever read the letters yourself?' he asked her.

'No,' Helena admitted. 'My mother always said there were things in them about what had happened to her family during the war – horrible things that she didn't want me to know.'

'So you never actually saw these letters?' Josef pressed.

'I saw them in my mother's hand. I saw the Polish stamps and postmarks. And I saw the parcels my mother packed for her relatives and gave to Auntie Alma to pass on to the Polish sailors who docked in Cardiff. My mother paid them to post the parcels in this country for her, so they wouldn't have to go through customs' checks. And, after seeing your thieving officers, I can understand why. My mother also used to send photographs of me. She ordered extra copies of every school photograph I had taken . . .' Helena saw Josef and Ned looking oddly at her, and realized she was being too emphatic. As though she were trying to conceal her own doubts about the veracity of the letters.

'Ned's right. You will have plenty of time to contact the Niklas family tomorrow.'

'You do know them, then?'

'I keep telling you, everyone knows everyone here. But I have been away from the bar long enough. Anna will need help to restock the shelves for the evening trade.'

'Anna's sister was killed in that massacre. Was she there?'

'I told you, the Germans assembled everyone in the village in the square.'

'Do you think she will talk to me about it?' Helena asked.

'I don't know,' Josef replied honestly. 'But she grew up here, so she would have known your mother and Adam Janek.'

Helena took a last look up the lane. 'We'll go there tomorrow,' she said to Ned.

'I think you should write to them first, and ask if you can call,' Ned suggested.

'All these food smells are making me hungry.' Josef began to walk back towards the bar. 'Anna always serves *flaki* and baked river carp with horseradish on a Monday. Both are excellent. You are in for a treat.'

'What's *flaki*?' Ned asked Josef, anxious to talk about something – anything – other than Adam Janek and Helena's family.

'Tripe soup.' Josef smiled. 'It's very good. Hot and spicy.'

'I'll take your word for it.' Ned had never eaten tripe, and had no intention of doing so.

'You don't have to. You can soon eat it and judge for yourself.'

Ned saw the preoccupied expression on Helena's face. 'Try not to think about your mother for a few hours, sunshine. I promise I'll help you to find out the truth about your father.'

'There really isn't any chance that he was Adam Janek, is there?' The enormity of her discovery was only just beginning to sink in.

'No, sunshine, there isn't,' Ned said finally.

Helena, Ned and Josef walked back in silence. The shop was now closed and the street deserted, yet it still stank of fish. When they reached the bar, Ned and Helena looked over the half-doors. It too was deserted, apart from a blousy, middle-aged woman with

153

dyed blonde hair, who was sitting behind the counter reading a newspaper. They both presumed that she was the mysterious Anna. There was no sign of her brother. Josef pushed open the doors.

'Would you like to meet your guests, Anna?'

'Not in the bar, no,' she admonished in Polish. 'You know women aren't allowed in here.' She eyed Ned and Helena. 'I'll talk to you in the yard.'

'Our landlady would like us to walk around into the yard. She will meet us there,' Helena translated for Ned.

Josef went behind the bar and tied on a canvas apron. 'See you later.'

'Thank you for taking us to the churchyard and the monument.' Helena said.

He smiled. 'My pleasure.'

Helena and Ned walked around the corner, through the archway and into the yard. Their landlady was already sitting on the bench beneath the outside staircase, smoking a cigarette. A tray of small glasses and a glass bottle of clear liquid stood in front of her.

'Hello, Mrs . . .' Helena held out her hand, but their landlady ignored it.

'Anna will do. It's what everyone in the village calls me. And you are Helena and Ned John?' Her voice was harsh, curt and abrupt, but Helena could detect a slight slurring in her speech. She wondered if Anna had been drinking.

'Yes.' Helena sat at the opposite end of the bench and Ned perched on the edge of the table.

'It says Janek in your passport.'

'We have only just married.' Helena hated lying, but now she'd started she felt she couldn't stop.

Anna ground her cigarette to dust in a tin ashtray. 'Josef told me that your mother was Magdalena Janek and that she has died.'

'Two weeks ago.'

'Did you marry before or after she died?'

'Before,' Helena answered reluctantly. It wasn't just the lies she was telling. She wasn't accustomed to being on the receiving end of so many direct questions.

Anna looked pointedly at the engagement ring that Helena was wearing. 'You decorate your wedding bands with diamonds in the West?'

'I liked the ring,' Helena murmured truthfully. 'Did you know my mother?'

'If she was the Magdalena Janek who lived in this village, yes, I did.'

'She was Magdalena Niklas before she married my father.'

'Then she is the woman I knew.'

'We've been to the churchyard. Josef showed us Adam Janek's grave.'

'He has a fine memorial cross.' Anna opened the bottle and poured out three measures. She pushed one towards Helena and another towards Ned.

'He does. And no, thank you.'

'Drink it,' Ned ordered. 'You've had a shock.'

'Getting drunk won't help,' Helena bit back.

Ned picked up his glass and sniffed it. 'You'll hardly get drunk on a thimbleful of local vodka.'

'So you used the name Janek before you were married.' Anna drank her measure of vodka down in one.

'Yes.'

'Did your mother tell you that Adam Janek was your father?'

'Yes.'

Anna replenished her glass. 'Poor Adam; he was very young when he died. And he only had time to father one child – a girl with the same name as you.' She looked at Helena appraisingly.

'So we found out in the churchyard.' Helena lifted her glass and sniffed the contents, but didn't drink it.

'Adam Janek was very good-looking.'

'So my mother always told me.'

'His family were the most important landowners for miles around. He was the last of them.'

'I've already told Helena and Ned that.' Josef brought two stools out of the bar and set them on the opposite side of the table to the bench. He took one and pushed the other towards Ned. 'Stefan is watching the bar, Anna. I told him to fetch me if anyone comes in.'

'The Janeks were exceptional. Wealthy and kind,' Anna continued, as if Josef hadn't spoken. 'If someone on one of their farms was
too sick to work and couldn't pay the rent, they would waive it.
Not many landlords before the war were that concerned about their
tenants, I can tell you.' She stared down into her glass of vodka.

Helena opened her duffle bag and brought out her purse. She
opened it and showed Anna a photograph of her mother, which she
had cut to fill a clear plastic slot. It was in colour, the last one taken
of Magda, at Alma's staff Christmas party.

Anna looked at it for a few seconds. 'Yes, that is the Magdalena
Niklas that I knew. Older, careworn, not as pretty as I remember,
but still her.'

'Please,' Helena begged, 'can you tell me anything about my
mother and Adam Janek?'

Anna poured herself another measure of vodka. 'What do you
want to know?'

'My mother told me many stories about what it was like to grow
up in this village, but she only talked once about her last day here.'

'The day of the massacre?' Again Anna drank the vodka in one.
'Yes.'

Josef spoke to Ned in a low voice, and Helena realized with
gratitude that he was translating her conversation with Anna.

Recalling what Josef had said about the villagers' reluctance to
talk about the killings, Helena searched for a less horrific memory
that her mother had entrusted to her. 'Mamma told me about her
wedding to Adam Janek. She said the whole village came, and there
was dancing, feasting and music in the square for three days and
nights.'

'Theirs was the last big wedding here before the war. Magdalena
was the prettiest girl in the village, so it seemed only right that
she caught the richest man. The whole countryside came together
in those days to celebrate a wedding. And a Janek wedding was a
once-in-a-lifetime occasion. Everyone wanted to pay their respects
to the bride and groom.'

'My mother said that she travelled miles to get the material for
her dress. And it was real silk.' Although Helena hated herself for
thinking of her mother as a liar, after discovering that Adam Janek

couldn't possibly be her father, she felt the need to check every single thing Magda had told her.

'Adam arranged for Magda and her mother to pick it up from someone he knew in Cracow, and the Niklas family made it up beautifully. That dress was the envy of every girl in the village. My sister Matylda was fifteen years old when your mother married Adam Janek, and Magda promised Matylda that when it was her turn to marry she would lend her the dress. When Matylda turned sixteen there was no stopping her nagging to be allowed to marry. She used to say, "There won't be any expense, Magda will loan me her dress . . ."' Anna pulled a pack of cigarettes from her pocket. 'But by then it was wartime and Matylda's boyfriend was no Adam Janek. He wasn't just poor. He was fighting and living with the partisans in the forest. My parents were afraid that his life would be a short one. With good reason, as it turned out. It's just that they never thought that Matylda's life would be short as well.'

'Adam Janek didn't fight?'

'Not with the partisans. He thought it his duty to be the spokesman for the village. The Germans controlled everything, and made more and more demands on us every day, for food, farm produce, workers to send into the Reich. My parents were over forty, so we thought they'd be safe. But they weren't. They were taken in 1942 and never came back. I tried to find out what had happened to them. But it was as though they had vanished from the face of the earth.' Anna's hand shook as she struck a match and lit another cigarette.

'I'm sorry.'

The silence grew in intensity unil it was almost palpable. When Josef moved closer to Ned, the thud of the stool legs landing on the dirt floor of the yard startled Helena, making her jump.

Anna broke the silence. 'It all happened a long time ago,' she said harshly, adding, 'You're here to ask about your mother, not my sister and parents. The old wives in the village had almost given up hope of Magdalena and Adam having a child when their daughter was born. They had been married some years, and tongues had begun to wag – that one or the other was barren. But then Helena arrived and proved the gossips wrong. You always expect men to want boys

157

but Adam doted on that baby. For three weeks he was the happiest man on earth then . . .' She drew heavily on her cigarette.

'My mother told me that the German soldiers came into the village without warning and rounded everyone up.'

'I knew they were coming, and so did my brother and the priest, because the partisans called here in the early hours of that morning. About one or two o'clock. This bar was a meeting place. Partisans came late at night to barter with the farmers, who sold them black market food. Messages were passed on, and guns, ammunition and petrol stolen from the Germans were delivered to and distributed through our back door. The Germans were suspicious. They raided us many times but never found anything. The partisans told us there were rumours in the town that the Germans were planning some kind of action. They'd had a tip-off from one of the clerks who worked for the Nazis, and were going into the woods to warn the other partisan groups to move further away from the roads. But we knew what "action" meant. The Germans had cleared the Poles out of many villages to make room for the ethnic German settlers they had brought in from the Baltic States like Latvia and Lithuania.'

'Why?' Helena asked.

'To Germanize Poland. That was the German plan. To re-settle Poland with Germans, who could control the country. We Poles would only be allowed to stay in our homeland as labourers and servants. We learned that early on in the invasion when the Germans closed all the high schools and made it illegal to educate any Polish child beyond the age of twelve.'

'My mother told me about that and the effect it had on her younger brother and sister,' Helena said.

'Lack of secondary education was the least of our problems at the time,' Anna continued. 'Children can always be educated at home. After the partisans left, my brother went to Adam Janek to ask his advice. Afraid that the Germans were going to conscript more people to work in the Reich, Adam suggested that my brother take all the young people into the woods and hide them. Adam, Stefan and the priest were still going from house to house at four o'clock in the morning, telling people to pack a few necessities and run to

158

the woods when the German convoy drove in.' Anna waited until Josef had finished translating what she'd said.

'The Germans parked a tank in front of the church. We all knew that they could – and would, if the mood took them – blow up the village, because other villages had been razed to the ground. Soldiers jumped out of the lorries they'd parked behind the tank, and went round the houses, rousing everyone from their beds and demanding they go into the square. Because of Adam, my brother and the priest, most people were dressed. When we assembled, the Germans started separating the young people from the old. There weren't many young men; most were with the partisans. Adam had his arm around Magdalena and he was holding Helena. He tried talking to the commanding officer. He spoke good German and Russian as well as Polish. The priest told me later than Adam was asking why they wanted to take the young people. The commanding officer ignored him. One of the soldiers tried to snatch Helena from Adam's arms. He refused to let go of the baby or Magdalena. The soldier knocked Magdalena back, pulled out his gun and shot baby Helena. The bullet passed through her body, killing both her and Adam. That started a panic. Everyone ran, and the Germans opened fire. When they stopped shooting there were nineteen bodies in the square. The soldiers went into houses to look for more people. A few young girls had hidden in an old wooden house in the lane leading out of the square. The Germans saw them, set fire to the house, and shot them when they tried to leave. It wasn't the only house they burned to the ground that day.'

'And my mother?'

'Magdalena was pushed into line along with fifteen other young women, two young men and about a dozen young children and babies.' Anna closed her eyes for a moment as though trying to shut out the memory.

'Why did the Germans take babies and children?' Helena asked.

Anna ignored the question. When she spoke again her voice was clotted with tears. 'The ones the Germans had picked were marched out. My brother and the priest read the Last Rites over the corpses. We women who were left fetched sheets to cover the dead. We buried them. Later those strong enough went into the woods to join the partisans. I stayed to run the bar because everyone insisted that it was a necessary meeting place and post office for messages between the partisan groups. That's all I can tell you about the massacre.' Emotionally drained, Anna stared down into her empty glass.

'The people who were marched away with my mother — Josef said some of them returned.'

'Not many.' Anna stood.

'Are they still in the village?' Helena persisted.

'One or two of the men.' Anna placed her glass on the tray.

'Are my mother's brother, sister and mother still here?'

'Yes.'

'They live in the house my mother grew up in?'

'Yes.' Anna looked at Helena. 'Think about what I have just told you before you rush to see them. Some things are best left.'

'But they are my family—'

'Like Adam Janek was your family?' Anna said cruelly. 'I have to make supper now. You and your ... husband will eat out here. I don't want you in the bar or in my house. Understand?'

Helena was too stunned to answer, but she knew from the way that Anna had said the word husband she didn't believe she and Ned were married.

'Look after the bar for me, Josef,' Anna turned and walked into the house.

Chapter 11

NED SAT ON the edge of the bed and watched Helena sit in front of the dressing table. 'Helena, I know you feel—'

'You can have absolutely no idea how I feel.' Helena tugged her hairbrush through her hair. It was tangled after the walk but she made no allowances for the knots. The brush dragged painfully against her scalp, and still she kept tugging and tearing.

'I know you're angry with Magda—'

'How would you feel if *your* mother suddenly told you that your father wasn't your father?'

'Grateful because we have so little in common,' Ned shot back without thinking. 'Sorry, that was an appalling thing to say. I have no idea how I'd react. But it's not as if you knew Adam Janek.'

'Of course I knew him! Mama told me all about him. How wonderful he was, how handsome, how strong, how brave, how rich. How he stood up to the Germans when no one else would. How he did everything he could to stop them from taking people from the village, and how he was gunned down in cold blood for trying. But now I know he couldn't possibly have been my father. Do you realize what that makes Mama?'

'Calling your mother names isn't going to help, Helena.' Ned spoke softly in an attempt to calm her.

'My mother was a liar. There, I've said it. And it makes me feel as though I can never, ever trust a single thing she told me. My entire life is based on a lie. I'm not even Helena Janek. She is dead, buried in the village churchyard with her father. Somewhere out there is my real father. I don't know who he is, and I may never know. He could be a thief, a murderer, a rapist or worse. I'm not Helena

161

Weronika Janek. I never was. I'm just another bastard without even a name to call my own.'

'Steady on, Helena.' Ned left the bed, crouched beside her chair and took her hand. 'You're still the girl I love. Soon you'll be Helena John. Nothing and no one can ever change that.'

'You fell in love with Helena Janek.'

'I fell in love with *you*. Not your name.'

Unable to meet his gaze, she looked at the floor. 'I'm sorry. I know I'm shouting at you. You didn't have to come to Poland with me—'

'Yes, I did.'

'Because you loved me?'

Ned's blood ran cold to hear her use the past tense.

'I know no one will love me more, but I now realize that you can never understand me. I am only just beginning to understand myself. Did I allow Mama to push me so hard to succeed because somehow I knew she wasn't telling me the truth about my father?'

'There's no way you could have possibly known Adam Janek wasn't your father. Parents don't bring up their children to question what they tell them, and Magda was more autocratic than most.'

'But that's the whole point. I allowed her to make all my decisions for me when I was growing up because it was easier than confronting her and risking an argument. I shouldn't have taken everything she told me at face value. I could have, *should* have, asked more questions about her family, and written to them myself. After all, they're my relatives as well as hers. And I should have made her talk about what happened to her during the war to make her so ambitious for me.'

'She just wanted you to have what the war had denied her.'

'The war!' she mocked. 'Don't you see, that's not true? It was never true. Mama wanted me to be successful because I am a nameless bastard. Have you any idea what that means to a Catholic?'

'Set aside your religion, Helena, please,' he begged. 'And think about your mother. We don't know everything that happened to her – not yet. But what we do know is that she was marched out of here in 1943 and two years later she ended up in Germany. Somewhere along the line she had you. Whoever your father was, he wasn't

162

able or willing to help Magda, so she took sole responsibility for you. And she loved you. Enough to give you the name and identity of her dead daughter – her much-loved daughter. And through it all she cared for you and protected you. That couldn't have been easy when she was at the mercy of the Germans.'

When Helena didn't answer him, he continued.

'Think back to what Bob Parsons told you. He said that his mother objected to you, not Magda. If Magda had agreed to give you up, he would have married her and she could have lived with him and his mother in Pontypridd.'

'Remember what Josef said,' she said coldly. 'If Mama had returned here after the war with a bastard we would both have been ostracized. Have you considered the possibility that she never had any intention of marrying Bob Parsons? She told Bob that she didn't receive his letter telling her not to come to Wales. But what if she had received his letter, and made the journey to Pontypridd anyway?'

'I don't understand why you think she would do that,' Ned said.

'Because it was the only way she could get us out of Germany and the Displaced Persons' camp. She didn't have any money, so she couldn't buy her own ticket to Britain or anywhere else. If she'd remained in the camp, the chances were, sooner or later, we'd both be repatriated to Poland. Then along came Bob Parsons. Given the conditions in the camp, she probably thought Pontypridd was as good a place as anywhere in the world. It was certainly far enough away from Poland. She probably paid Bob back the money he gave her out of guilt. She *used* him.'

'You can't be sure, Helena. Don't keep thinking the worst of her, because if you do you'll drive yourself mad.'

Helena's only reply was to tug the brush through her hair again.

Disheartened by the argument, and bitterly upset by Helena's assertion that he could never understand her, the last thing Ned felt like doing was eating. But when he followed her down into the yard and smelled the food, he discovered he was hungry. However, even the tripe soup proved more enjoyable than the company.

After her outburst, Helena withdrew into silence. Anna set the soup tureen and bread board in front of them on the table, ladled the soup into two bowls, and disappeared without a word. Josef joined them a few minutes later. He helped himself to soup, tore a hunk of bread into pieces, which he sprinkled on top of his soup, sat on one of the stools he'd carried out earlier, and started eating.

'I have to relieve Anna in the bar in a few minutes so she can eat while the food's hot,' he explained in reply to Ned's quizzical look.

Ned nodded and glanced at Helena. She was stirring her soup, occasionally lifting a spoonful out of the bowl, only to pour it back in untasted.

'Anna asked me to remind you that she doesn't allow young girls in the bar, but if you would like a drink after supper you could stay here, or take drinks up to your room. It's quite pleasant sitting there with the door open. I know because I lived there for a month last spring when I repaired the roof on the main part of the house.'

'We'll do that. Thank you for the suggestion.' Ned found himself talking to the air, as Josef took his empty bowl and disappeared.

Anna walked through the yard shortly afterwards, went into the house and re-emerged with plates of carp, potatoes and spinach, which she set in front of them.

Ned heard her talking in the house a few minutes later, and realized that she and her brother were eating inside. He wondered if their landlady was hostile towards everyone who rented the room, or if she reserved her antagonism for Westerners.

He cleared his plate while Helena ate a morsel of fish, but any thoughts he'd had about scolding her faded when he saw the grief in her eyes. After the meal he went into the bar, asked for two bottles of beer and glasses, then carried them up to their room. Helena was already there, curled in one of the chairs, a magazine on her lap. But from the way she was flicking restlessly through the pages he knew she wasn't reading.

'I brought you a beer.' He set the glasses and bottles on the table next to her.

'Thank you.'

'Helena . . .'

'Please, Ned,' she said, looking up at him, 'I don't want to talk, not now.'

'I wasn't suggesting we discuss what happened today.'

'Then what?' she challenged.

'You can't go on like this.'

'Like what?' she demanded.

'You've just made a devastating discovery. Perhaps it would be better if we did talk about it.' He sat in the chair opposite hers and poured his beer.

'There's nothing to say,' she said tonelessly.

'After travelling the best part of three days and two nights to get here, we should at least make plans for tomorrow.'

'No.' She dropped her magazine, left her chair and walked out on to the landing.

'Helena—'

'I don't want to talk. I don't want a beer. I just want to be left alone.' She returned to her chair and lifted her sweater from the back of it. 'I'm going for a walk.'

'I'll come with you.'

'I'd rather go alone.'

'Helena!' Ned leaned over the rail at the top of the staircase and shouted after her. But she didn't turn around, and disappeared through the archway. Ned ran down the stairs but when he reached the street there was no sign of her and, without knowing whether she had turned right or left, he decided there was little point in following her.

Instead he went into the bar. Anna was sitting on a stool behind the counter talking to two old men. Josef was crouched in front of the shelves behind Anna, stacking bottles into crates. He looked up when Ned entered.

'You'd like more beers?'

'No, thank you.' Ned hesitated for a moment before blurting. 'Helena's gone for a walk.'

'Alone?' Josef asked.

'She wouldn't allow me to go with her.'

'She'll be safe enough. There aren't many wild boars or wolves

165

left in the woods.' Josef handed a full crate to Ned. 'Could you put that by the door, please?'

'It's not wild boars or wolves I'm thinking of. What if she gets lost?' Ned took the crate and dropped it by the door that led into the yard.

'She seems a sensible girl to me. I think she'll look around and note the landmarks so she can find her way back.'

'That's all you know,' Ned muttered.

'You quarrelled?' Josef guessed.

'Not really,' Ned said defensively. 'But she's been strange ever since we returned from the churchyard this afternoon.'

'What do you expect?' Josef asked. 'Her whole world has changed.'

'I wanted to talk to her about it, but she wouldn't even discuss it.' Ned leaned on the counter. 'I'd go after her if I knew where to look.'

Josef straightened up. 'The village isn't that big.'

'I suppose I could start with the churchyard.'

'In the dark?' Josef raised an eyebrow. 'I wouldn't advise it. It's been used as a burial ground for hundreds of years. The older coffins have collapsed and the ground above them is pockmarked with holes. Some of the paths have sunk and are uneven. If you fall, you could hurt yourself, and crying out wouldn't help. It's rumoured the place is haunted – people would assume you were a ghost.'

'It would be just as dark for Helena.'

'I think she has more sense than to return there at this time of night.' Josef wiped his hands on a bar rag. 'Anna's expecting a delivery tomorrow. They only give her full bottles to the number of empty she can supply, and even want to see evidence of any broken bottles. I promised I'd crate all the empty bottles, carry them through to the yard, and set aside the broken ones. But if you'll take over, I will look for Helena.'

'Would you?' Ned asked in relief. 'She wouldn't listen to me, but she's likely to be more polite to a stranger.'

Josef rolled down his sleeves, and spoke rapidly to Anna in Polish.

She nodded and carried on talking to her customers.

'I told Anna you're taking over. I hope you finish the crating and stacking before I get back.' He smiled. 'And thank you. A walk in the fresh air is a much better prospect than shifting heavy loads around the yard.'

Ned watched Josef leave. Although the bar was unpleasantly warm, he shivered. He couldn't help feeling that his initial impression of Josef had been right. The man couldn't be trusted, especially around Helena.

Helena walked quickly along the street. She neither knew nor cared where she was heading, although she had instinctively chosen the route that led to the square. Night had fallen, warm and close, cloaking the village in grey and purple shadows that softened the harsh lines of the houses, obscuring the signs of neglect that were so glaring in the daylight: peeling paint, weather-worn and splintering window frames and fascias, and patched roofs. Welcoming lights shone out from behind curtained windows, and she caught tantalizing scents of spicy cooking, accompanied by the soft hum of voices and tinny musical tones of radios.

She tried to visualize the lives being played out within the houses, lives ruled by a rigid Communist regime that, by dint of rationing, even dictated what food people would eat on any particular day. But was the life of this generation so very different from that of her mother's family before the war.

Magda had always stressed how happy she and everyone in her village had been before the Russian and Nazi invasions. But she had also talked at length about the hard work that was involved in running the farm, how she and her brothers and sister had been given chores from an early age. If there hadn't been a war, her mother's life would undoubtedly have been a continuation of that lived by farming families in this corner of Poland for centuries: living off the land; rare trips to cities; ambitions curtailed by the needs of the family farm; adherence to social boundaries set in medieval times, when children had been expected to follow in their parents' footsteps, and replace them when age and infirmity took their inevitable toll.

If the tides of war hadn't carried Magda away, her life would have been quiet, uneventful, its highlights family weddings and baptisms. Her mother would have no more thought of travelling to Wales than going to the moon. Yet, almost half of her life had been lived in industrialized Pontypridd with its factories and coal mines, which must have seemed like another world after this rural backwater.

The square opened out in front of Helena and she stopped, amazed by how much larger it appeared in moonlight. Was it her imagination, or were the lights that shone from the houses here much stronger than those in the street? She moved closer to the churchyard wall and gazed at the scene, imprinting it on her mind.

She had the oddest feeling that only a thin curtain separated the present from her mother's world; that if she tore it down she would be able to step into the past and see the scenes Magda had described so vividly. The sounds from the houses around her faded, and the strong, sweet tones of violin and accordion, playing the country dance and gypsy tunes her mother had hummed, filled the air.

She saw Adam Janek – tall, upright, handsome, with piercing blue eyes and a confident air of authority, just as her mother had described him – a sepia photograph come to life, as he crossed the square to where her young mother was standing with her sister, Julianna. She watched him bow over Magda's hand, before leading her into the centre of a group of dancers.

She saw her great-grandmother, sitting in a huddle with the other elderly widows, all dressed head to toe in black, even stockings and shoes, in full mourning for husbands who had died in the previous century. Her farmer grandfather lifted his fifth glass of local beer high and smiled benignly across the square at her mother, Adam, uncles, aunts, the world in general and her grandmother in particular, who was sipping home-made wine and gossiping with the other village matrons. Her mother's voice echoed through her mind: *'I never saw my father and mother dance. Not once. But my mother loved gossiping with the neighbours, and my father loved drinking and talking to the other farmers when work was done for the day. And they both liked seeing us children dancing and enjoying ourselves.'*

A breeze blew across the square, rattling loose casements, picking up and scattering the fine dust that coated the ground. It stung her eyes and face. She wiped it away with her handkerchief, and the ghosts she had conjured dissolved into the darkness. The only dancer left in the square was the moonlight.

A stray cat darted before her so quickly she barely had time to see it before it was gone. A dog barked in a side street, and a door slammed somewhere.

She glanced behind her at the dark, forbidding churchyard, full of whispering trees. Then she looked towards the lane that led to the house her mother had always referred to as home. She could wait no longer.

When Ned had offered to take over Josef's task he was unaware that there was a lean-to shed next to the bar that was full of bottles of varying shapes and sizes. Anna took him by the elbow and showed him the shed, bottles and crates. Although she couldn't speak a word of English, she managed to make him understand that he could not place bottles of differing sizes or types in one crate, and that each type of bottle had its own specific crate.

Leaving the bar in the hands of a trusted customer for a few minutes, she beckoned him into the courtyard, switched the light on in the barn and showed him exactly how she wanted the crates stacked.

What Ned had assumed would be half an hour's work stretched into two hours and, as the minutes ticked by, he began to wonder if Josef had found Helena and, if so, where they both were. And what exactly they were doing that was delaying their return.

For as far back as Helena could remember, she had lived an urban life. First in the flat above the shop in Taff Street and later the room she had shared with Ned in Bristol. The nearest she had come to the countryside was the year she had spent in a university student hall, when she had occasionally seen squirrels scampering across the lawns.

The lane that led to the Niklas house was narrow, and after she passed the last of the houses on the outskirts of the village there were no more lights, only unfenced fields, trees and moonlight. In the places where the branches overhung the road she couldn't even

169

see her hand when she held it up in front of her face. But worse than the intermittent pools of pitch darkness were the noises.

Strange scurrying in the bushes conjured images of giant rats. The hoot of an owl froze her blood. Distant howling – could it be wolves? – sent terror crawling over her skin. And a snuffling in a ditch reminded her of an article she had read about a wild boar killing a hunter.

Magda had only described happy daytime rambles, not fearful night walks. Whenever her mother had travelled by night it had always been as a passenger on a farm cart. And on Sundays, when the family had attended the church, or made formal visits, the farm pony and trap had been used.

Magda had described her daily trips to and from school with her brothers, sister and the children of the farm labourers who lived outside the village. In winter there had been sledging and skiing, snowball fights and skating on nearby lakes and ponds. In spring they had enjoyed the fragrance of cherry, apple, plum and pear blossom on the trees that bordered the road. In summer they had watched the fruit grow and slowly ripen until they judged it just short of ready when they had picked and ate it slightly green, because if they'd waited the fruit-pickers would have left none for them. But the blossom had long gone and it was too dark for Helena to make out any fruit.

Helena stopped several times, searching across the fields for lights, but she saw only darkness. After she had walked for half an hour, the woods closed in again and she could see nothing beyond the trees. More peculiar scratching and scrapings gave her a reason to quicken her step. She turned a corner and there, on her left, set back from the road behind an orchard illuminated by a perfectly round, low-slung moon, was the Niklas family farmhouse, exactly as Magda had described it.

After her mother's lies about Adam Janek being her father, Helena hadn't known what to expect. But the house *was* large, three storeys high. Lights were on in two rooms on the ground floor and one on the second floor. She walked up to the orchard gate so she could take a closer look, and spotted a light burning in one of the outbuildings. She could hear a man talking softly.

She stood there, allowing her imagination free rein just as she had done in the square, immersing herself in the past that Magda had painted so vividly. Lost in thought, she only noticed that a cloud had scuttered across the moon when the world was plunged into darkness. Startled back to the present, she heard the unmistakeable sound of footsteps.

Heart thundering, she stood stock still, hoping that whoever it was would pass by without seeing her, but just as suddenly as it had covered the moon the cloud moved on.

'Helena?'

'Josef,' she whispered, recognizing his voice.

'I thought I'd find you here.'

'You've been looking for me?' She was angry at the inference that she couldn't take care of herself.

'Ned asked me to find you. He was worried.'

'If he was that worried, why didn't he come himself?'

'Because he said you wouldn't talk to him, and thought a stranger would be better. Although I don't feel like a stranger.' He leaned on the gate beside her. 'Farmers don't appreciate visitors at this time of night. They go to bed early.'

'They're still awake. The lights are on and I heard someone talking.'

'That doesn't mean whoever it is wants to talk to you,' he warned.

She tried to decipher his features but it was difficult in the darkness. 'Do the Niklas family still live on this farm?'

'People by the name of Niklas live here, yes,' he answered guardedly.

'My mother told me that her father and older brother were killed in the war, but her younger brother Wiktor, sister Julianna and mother survived. Do Wiktor and Julianna live here?' she persisted.

Josef sighed. 'The farmer's name is Wiktor. He lives with his mother, sister, wife and children.'

'Is his sister married?'

'No.'

'How many children——'

'Don't you think that you should leave the questions for your uncle, Helena?'

'If he is my uncle.'

'Anna recognized your mother from the photograph you showed her, didn't she?'

'Yes.'

'Then you've no reason to think that he isn't your mother's brother.' He left the gate and turned back towards the road.

'I can't help feeling that Anna didn't tell me everything she knew about my mother and Adam Janek,' Helena said quietly.

'People around here would rather forget the war than talk about it. Being a war orphan, I can understand why.' He held out his hand. 'Come on, I'll walk you back.'

She fell into step beside him but didn't take his hand. 'I know your mother died in the massacre and your father was taken by the Germans, like my mother. Did you have any relatives who survived the war?'

'I didn't say that my father was killed.'

'He survived?'

'He was marched away by the Germans and didn't come back. But the priest told me that someone from the town had met him in a Displaced Persons' camp after the war. He probably decided to make a life for himself in the West.'

'He never tried to contact you?' she asked in surprise.

'He may have thought I was dead. Either way, it hardly matters now. The priest, Anna and Stefan became my family.'

'You never looked for your father?' she persisted.

'Why should I? If he'd heard I'd survived he would have known where to find me. He was the grown-up, I was the child. If any searching had to be done, it should have been done by him.'

'And you never think of him?'

'Never,' he insisted resolutely.

'Family is everything.'

'You learned that from your mother?'

She knew he was mocking her but said, 'I won't rest until I find out who my father was.'

'You may never rest again.'

'There has to be a record of my birth.'

Josef threw back his head and laughed. The sound echoed eerily around the quiet road.

'What's so funny?'

'You were born during the war.'

'So?' she countered irritably.

'Records were kept in villages like this one that had a church open at the time but if you were born in Germany to a Polish slave labourer, the chances are your birth was never registered. And even if it was, Germany was flattened after the war. Buildings were bombed, whole towns burned, including records offices.'

'But I have my birth certificate. I needed it for my passport.'

'Your birth certificate or Helena Janek's?' Josef interrupted.

Helena faltered. Even her birth certificate must belong to the girl buried in the churchyard. 'A copy of Helena Janek's.'

'Not the original?'

'It bears the stamp of the Displaced Persons' camp. My mother applied to have it issued there.'

'She would have found it comparatively easy to give you the identity of a child whose birth was registered in a Polish parish church.'

'As opposed to that of an unregistered bastard born in Germany?'

'You can't be sure of that,' Josef said sympathetically. 'But what does amaze me is that your mother was allowed to keep you. Most Polish women taken by the Reich were sterilized. If they weren't and became pregnant, they were either sent back to their families or to a concentration camp.'

'That still leaves me without a name or birthday to call my own.' Helena burned with anger. 'I wish my mother were here, in front of me right now ... I'd ...'

'Shout at her?' he suggested.

'Demand to know the truth.'

'The truth?' he repeated. 'The truth is that you, like me, are alive to enjoy this beautiful world when so many other children who were born the same time as us are not.'

'Alive without a history.'

'You know who your mother is,' he reminded her.

'But I can't even be sure that I was born in 1943.'

'You know that you certainly couldn't have been born any earlier. The question is, how much later?'

'There are photographs of me that were taken when I was a year old, and some of me and my mother at the Displaced Persons' camp in July 1945.'

'And you look how old?'

'My mother told everyone I was two. No one questioned it.'

'The chances are that, after being in a labour camp, both you and your mother were malnourished, so no one would have questioned you being small for your age.'

Helena did some rapid calculations. Her mother had given birth three weeks before being taken by the Germans in June 1943. She couldn't possibly have had another child much before April 1944, which would have made her only fifteen months old in July 1945. She hadn't had a great deal of experience of small children, but she did know the difference between a one-year-old and a two-year-old. And Bob Parsons had seemed sure of her age.

'Have you noticed how beautiful the sky is in the country?' Josef said. 'I hated having to study in Warsaw because of the lights. The sky looked different there. It wasn't so clear, and the stars weren't so bright.'

'I can't think about the sky.'

'You should. Just look at it and you'll see why. It's beautiful. It's also late, you must be tired, and tomorrow is another day. You'll drive yourself mad if you keep asking yourself questions that have no answer, Helena.'

'I will go back to the farm tomorrow.'

'It would be better to send the Niklas family a note first.'

'Why?'

'Because your grandmother is a frail old lady who has been through a great deal,' he warned. 'The sudden arrival of a grand-daughter she might not know she had, to announce the death of a daughter, could make her ill.'

'Of course my grandmother knows about me,' she snapped.

'You are sure of that?'

'As sure as I can be.'

'Because of the messages she sent to you in letters your mother read to you?'

She bit her lip. 'Yes.'

'If you like, I will take a note to them tomorrow and explain why you are here. The Niklas family put the cross on Adam Janek's grave. They have more right than anyone to decide whether or not your mother's ashes should be buried with him.'

'I think I should have a say in the matter too, as it was my mother who paid for the memorial.'

'Don't you think it might be better to try the tactful approach first?' he suggested mildly.

'I suppose so,' she conceded ungraciously. 'And if they say yes?'

'I'll check to make sure no one in the village has any objection. If they don't, I'll open the grave and arrange a ceremony.'

'Thank you.'

'Don't thank me yet. I haven't done anything and, as the decision isn't mine to make, I may not have a say either way. It might be as well if you consider an alternative resting place for your mother's ashes in case the family or the villagers refuse to allow you to bury them in the churchyard.'

'They may refuse me permission to bury them in Adam Janek's grave but they can hardly refuse to allow me to bury them in the churchyard. Not if I bought another plot.'

'Have you looked around the churchyard? There isn't an inch to spare.'

'There must be room somewhere. My mother's casket isn't very large.'

'All the plots belong to local families.'

Tired of trying to find answers to problems that seemed insurmountable, Helena said, 'I suppose I could scatter them somewhere, but I don't want to think about that unless I have to.' She sighed. 'What should I say in my note?'

'That is entirely up to you. But I advise you to keep it short and simple. And don't sign yourself Helena Janek. That alone would be enough to give any Niklas a heart attack.'

*

Careful to observe every rule of Polish grammar that Magda had taught her, Helena eventually wrote:

Dear Uncle Wiktor,

I am Magdalena Janek's daughter, and I have brought my mother's ashes back to the village so she can be buried in the grave of her beloved husband Adam Janek. She talked constantly about him and their wedding, and she loved him until the day she died.

I would very much like to meet you, my aunt and my grandmother. My mother told me so many stories about you and what it was like to grow up in the village. I hope you will allow me to call and see you. I have given this note to Josef Dobrow to deliver because he thought it might be too much of a shock for you to see me unannounced. Looking forward very much to receiving your reply.

Helena bit the end of the biro and stared down at the coarse-grained paper in the exercise book Josef had given her to write the note. How could she sign herself? *'Love Helena'* would be too much, and it wasn't just the Janek part of her name she couldn't use. Helena Janek was buried in the churchyard.

In the end she settled for, *'With all good wishes, your niece.'*

Chapter 12

'WHY DIDN'T YOU come and tell me you'd returned from your walk?'

Ned walked out of the back door of the bar and confronted Helena, who was sitting on the bench beneath the staircase. Josef had switched on an outside lamp, and she looked pale and tired beneath the glare of the single, naked bulb.

'Because I've only just got back. What on earth have you been doing? Your face and clothes are filthy.'

'Didn't Josef tell you? I took over his chores here so he could go and find you. And don't try to tell me you weren't with him.'

'Why should I deny it?' She stared at him in amazement. 'You're jealous!'

'Do I have reason to be?'

'I can't cope with this on top of everything else.' She looked down at the note she'd written to her uncle. Unable to think of anything else to say, she tore the sheet from the exercise book and folded it.

'Cope with what? My concern?' he challenged. 'You storm off—'

'I told you I was going for a walk.'

'You wouldn't allow me to go with you.'

'So you sent Josef to get me.' She didn't know why they'd started shouting at one another, but now she couldn't stop.

'I was afraid you'd get lost.'

'I'm a grown woman, Ned, not a child. And you're being ridiculous.'

'Am I?' he demanded testily. 'We're in a strange village in a foreign country—'

'It might be foreign to you. But my mother lived half her life here and I speak the language.'

'And everyone in the village goes out for a walk at this time of night just in case a foreign tourist decides to ask directions?'

'Sarcasm as well as jealousy, Ned? What's got into you?'

He placed his hand on the table to steady himself. 'Josef told me that you walked to the Niklas house.'

She looked up at him defiantly. 'I did.'

'We could have gone there together.'

'When, Ned? You didn't want to go earlier.'

They both fell silent when Josef walked into the yard with two bottles of beer and two glasses. He set them on the table. 'These are on me. You did a good job of stacking the bottle and crates, Ned.'

'Thank you.' Ned picked up a glass and a bottle. 'But I didn't have much choice.'

'Anna can be a slave-driver.' Josef turned to Helena. 'Have you written your note?'

'Yes, in my best Polish.' She unfolded it so he could read it.

'I'll take it to the Niklas house first thing in the morning.' He slipped it into his pocket.

'Thank you.'

'I have to help Anna but I'll see you at breakfast. And thank you again for stacking those crates, Ned.'

Helena left the table as soon as Josef returned to the bar. 'I'm going to bed.'

'If you hang on I'll come with you.' Ned held up the second bottle of beer. 'Aren't you going to drink this?'

'I don't want it.'

Ned watched her go. Picking up both bottles and the glasses, he went into the bar. Josef was serving behind the counter. Ned sat at a corner table watching the locals play chess, wondering what he was doing in a dirt-floored bar in a remote area of Poland. Not helping Helena, that was certain. But since Magda had died he hadn't even been able to talk to her.

He finished both beers, took the bottles and glasses to the counter, said goodnight to Josef, and went upstairs. Helena was in the bed nearest the door, her face turned to the wall.

He sensed she wasn't asleep but he undressed, slipped on his pyjama trousers, took his toilet bag and went down to the wash-house in the yard. She was in the same position when he returned. He crept in beside her. She kept her back resolutely towards him. When he drew close to her she moved away. He risked resting his hand lightly around her waist but she shrugged it off.

Exhausted by their argument and her rejection, he left the bed, climbed into the second one, and closed his eyes.

Ned woke with a start. The room was in darkness but he knew Helena wasn't in bed. He switched on the lamp at the side of his bed and saw her sitting, wrapped in a blanket, on one of the chairs. He went to her.

'Can I do anything?'

She shook her head, but tears glistened on her lashes.

'Come back to bed?'

'I will in a little while. Please leave me alone.'

Ned lifted his hand, intending to stroke her hair from her eyes. But something held him back. He turned back to the bed and climbed into it, wishing he could think of some way – any way – to help her.

When Ned next woke, the attic room was warm, bright – and empty. He took his wristwatch from the bedside table and looked at it. Seven-thirty. Helena was nowhere to be seen. Her bed was made and her duffle bag gone. Grabbing his clothes and toilet bag, he ran halfway down the outside staircase before remembering Josef's advice about keeping the door locked when they weren't in the room. He returned, locked the door, went down into the yard, washed and dressed. There was still no sign of Helena, or anyone else, when he left the wash-house.

He returned to their room, made his bed and checked around. As well as the duffle bag, Helena's cardigan had gone. Hoping she was having an early breakfast and not another walk with Josef, he headed back down into the yard.

Helena was sitting at the outside table with Stefan. Anna was clearing her cup and plate. As the cup was half full of coffee and there was untouched food on the plate, Ned suspected she had left the table the moment Helena had sat down. Breakfast was certainly plentiful. There were fresh bread rolls, Polish sausage, cheese, jam, butter, a pot of coffee and a jug of water on the table. Helena was drinking coffee, but there were no crumbs on her plate.

Determined to forget the disagreements of the day before, Ned smiled and said, 'Good morning,' to Anna and her brother. Anna nodded, and Stefan gazed at him silently. He turned to Helena. 'You were up early.'

'I couldn't sleep, so I walked up to the churchyard again.' Helena moved her duffle bag beneath the bench so he could sit next to her.

'Coffee?' Anna asked Ned in Polish, holding up the pot.

Ned nodded and smiled, making a mental note to learn the Polish for please and thank you, if nothing else.

'Josef took my message to the Niklas farm early this morning,' Helena informed him.

Ned glanced at his watch. 'It's only just eight o'clock now.'

'They're early risers in the country. He went at six.' Helena poured herself a glass of water.

Ned helped himself to a bread roll and reached for the butter dish. 'He hasn't returned?'

'No.'

Anna and Helena held a brief conversation in Polish. Stefan smiled vacantly before filling a tray with the dirty breakfast dishes. Anna went into the house, and he followed her like a dog trained to walk to heel.

'Anna told me to tell you to take as long as you like over breakfast,' Helena translated.

'I hope you thanked her for me.' Ned forked a slice of cheese on to his plate.

'I did.'

'Aren't you eating?' He ventured, risking another outburst at the implied criticism.

'I'm not hungry.'

'You didn't eat anything at supper last night and hardly any of the chicken in the car yesterday. Carry on like this and you're going to make yourself ill,' he warned.

'I'm too nervous to eat.'

'Nervous about what?'

'I'm not sure what I'll do if my uncle refuses to allow me to bury my mother's ashes in Adam Janek's grave.'

'Wouldn't it be better to wait and see what he decides, before worrying about what to do should he refuse?'

'Probably.' She started at the sound of conversation behind them.

Josef entered the yard accompanied by a middle-aged man, whose hair and eyes were so dark he could have been a gypsy. Helena rose to her feet and looked anxiously at the man.

'Helena, this is Wiktor Niklas. Wiktor, this is Helena John and her husband Ned.' The fact that Josef introduced them without mentioning the name Janek wasn't lost on Helena – or Ned, despite his lack of Polish. Helena also noticed that Josef had made no reference to her relationship to Wiktor.

'Is the coffee hot?' Josef asked.

'Yes,' Helena stammered, trying not to stare at Wiktor.

'Please, Wiktor, sit down.' Ned pulled out a stool for their visitor in front of the place setting Anna had laid for him. 'I'll get myself another cup and plate.'

Remembering her manners, Helena spoke to her uncle in Polish. 'I am pleased to meet you, Mr Niklas.'

He nodded to her, without meeting her eyes. Then he took the coffee pot and poured himself a cup.

Josef returned. 'Mr Niklas would like to see the photographs you have of your mother, Helena.'

'Of course.' She left the table.

'Where are you going?' Ned asked.

'To our room to fetch the box of photographs.'

'Stay there.' He rose to his feet and went to the stairs. 'I'll get them for you.'

'Bring down the bottle of brandy and the chocolates as well, please,' Helena called after him. 'The large box from my suitcase.'

'That won't leave us with much to give anyone by the way of presents,' Ned cautioned.

'I know.'

After Ned left, Helena lifted her duffle bag on to her lap, removed her purse, opened it and showed Wiktor the same photograph she had shown Anna. 'This is the last photograph that was taken of my mother.'

Wiktor looked at it for a moment. 'She's not quite as I remember her, but there is enough of a similarity for me to recognize my sister Magdalena. How did she die?'

'A brain haemorrhage. The doctors found old, healed fractures in her skull. It's possible they contributed to her death.'

'Was she ill for a long time?'

'No, she was never ill – well, hardly ever,' Helena continued, conscious that she was talking too quickly to cover her unease. 'Only a few headaches, and coughs and colds in winter.'

'You were with her when she died?'

'No.' Helena felt the colour flooding into her cheeks when she recalled what she'd been doing while her mother lay dying in Father O'Brien's car.

'She was alone?'

'She was with a priest. He was driving her to a church Sunday school party; she was very active in our local Catholic church.' Helena wished she could stop the words from tumbling out.

'A priest. He gave Magdalena the Last Rites?'

'Yes.'

'Then she was a good Catholic to the end.'

'The Church was very important to my mother. She brought me up in the faith.' Helena expected Wiktor to make a comment on his own religious beliefs, but he didn't.

'Josef tells me that you want to bury Magdalena's ashes in Adam Janek's grave?'

'Yes.' Helena crossed her fingers beneath the table.

'You had her body burned.'

'I asked the priest to arrange a dispensation so my mother could be cremated. Everyone told me that it would have been very difficult, if not impossible, to transport her body here from Britain.'

'Magdalena told you that she wanted to be cremated and her ashes buried in Adam Janek's grave?' he questioned.

'No, my mother never talked to me about her death, or where she wanted to be buried.' Helena couldn't lie, not with those dark, probing eyes, so similar to Magda's, watching her. 'But she often spoke about Adam Janek and her childhood here. She used to say that it was the happiest time of her life.'

'Yet she never returned.'

'In her heart she never left.'

'Did she ever tell you why she didn't come back here?' His face was stern, intractable, his features so fixed she found it impossible to read them.

'No. But it is difficult to travel from Britain to Eastern Europe. You need visas—'

'I meant after the war, when other people who had been taken by the Germans to work in the Reich returned to Poland.'

'Not really, other than to say that she thought there would be better opportunities for my education and future in Britain.' Magda's explanation sounded lame, and Helena wondered why she had never thought to question it before.

'My sister paid to have you educated?'

'I gained a scholarship and went to university on a grant from the British government.'

'And how did my sister keep herself and you?'

'She managed a cooked meat and pie shop in a market town in Britain, Wales, called Pontypridd. But she wrote to you—'

'We received a few letters,' he interrupted.

'She sent you parcels, food, clothes—'

'Occasionally.'

Helena hadn't known what to expect from her mother's brother, but she certainly hadn't anticipated such cold, suspicious reserve.

'My grandmother and my aunt—'

Again, he cut her short. 'Here's your husband with the photographs.'

Ned walked down the stairs carrying the box of photographs in one hand, a bottle of brandy in the other, and the enormous box of chocolates tucked under his arm.

Helena took the brandy and chocolates from Ned and handed

them to Wiktor. 'These are for you, my grandmother and my aunt.' She set the photographs on the table.

'I will give them to the family.' Wiktor set the gifts aside.

Helena tried to forget 'the family' instead of the 'your family', opened the box and spread the photographs on the table. Wiktor stared at them for a long time before pointing to one that had been taken in Ned's house at Easter. 'My sister looks happy.'

'She did her best to accept and adapt to her life in Britain after the war,' Helena said guardedly.

'And she went to mass every week.' He thrust his thumb down on a photograph of Magda with Father O'Brien.

'Yes.' As it was obvious that the photographs had been taken in the company of the priest, Helena could hardly refute it, but she remained acutely conscious that she was in a Communist country.

'Is this the priest who was with her when she died?'

'Yes. He is Irish. His name is Father O'Brien.'

'He looks a good man.'

'He is.'

'And this photograph?' He picked up the only one in a frame: Magda and Adam on their wedding day.

'Hung in our living room.'

Wiktor stared at it for so long, Helena wondered if he had fallen into a trance.

'You're right. My sister did love Adam Janek,' he declared. 'If the heads of the families in the village agree, you can bury my sister's ashes in his grave. Although I would have preferred to bury her body.'

'So would I,' Helena agreed. 'But it would have been difficult, if not impossible to arrange—'

'So you said.' Wiktor waved his arms and her explanations aside. He looked to Josef. 'You will find out if there are any objections in the village?'

'You know the people here, Wiktor.' Josef set down the salami roll he was eating. 'If you agree to the interment of your sister's ashes in Adam Janek's grave, so will everyone else.'

'You will arrange to open the grave and conduct the ceremony, Josef?'

'When?' Josef asked.

'Tomorrow morning, nine o'clock.' Wiktor pushed his chair back from the table, picking up the brandy and chocolates.

'May I call on my grandmother and aunt to show them these photographs of my mother?' For all her efforts to remain calm, Helena's voice wavered with emotion.

'No, but I will come here tomorrow after I have buried my sister's ashes. We will talk then.'

Helena was devastated by her uncle's attitude, but tried to remember Magda's insistence on politeness at all times. 'Thank you. Just one more thing: I would like to put my mother's name and dates on Adam Janek's gravestone . . .'

'I will arrange it.' Wiktor pulled his cap from his pocket and flung it on his head.

'But the wording—'

'Josef will take you to see the stonemason. You will give him the date of Magdalena's death, but I will pay the bill.'

Wiktor walked swiftly through the archway as though he couldn't bear to be in Helena's company a moment longer.

Helena waited until her uncle had left before blotting her tears in her handkerchief. Then she gathered the photographs from the table and returned them to the box. 'Thank you for persuading my uncle to allow me to bury my mother in the churchyard, Josef.'

'All I did was hand him your note. What hymns would you like sung at the burial service? I take it you want a Catholic mass?'

'Please, but it might be more fitting if my mother's family choose the hymns and how my mother should be buried.' Helena couldn't help wishing that they could have made the decisions together.

'I'll call on Wiktor again this afternoon.'

'Is there anywhere around here that I can buy flowers?' Helena asked.

'Flowers?' Josef smiled. 'If the women want them for the house, they go out and pick them.'

'For a funeral wreath?'

'What could be better than wild flowers, especially for your mother who grew up here?'

'You're probably right,' she conceded.

'But there will be a market tomorrow morning, at six in the square. Someone may bring roses to sell.'

'I'll look there, thank you.'

Josef buttered another roll and pushed slices of sausage into it. 'I have work to do. I'll see you later.' Taking the roll, he walked through the back door into the bar.

'Well?' Ned asked impatiently, when Helena didn't volunteer any information.

'My uncle has agreed that my mother can be buried in Adam Janek's grave tomorrow morning at nine o'clock. Josef is arranging it.'

'And the conversation you had with Josef after your uncle left?'

'Was about flowers. Sorry, I didn't mean to exclude you. I didn't even realize that we were speaking in Polish.'

'I know you didn't.'

'What's that supposed to mean?' Upset by Wiktor's frosty reception, she turned her anger on Ned.

'Nothing.'

'You've been—'

'Please, Helena, let's not quarrel,' he pleaded. 'We've both been under a lot of pressure. It's time to finish what we came here to do and move on. As Magda will be buried tomorrow morning, we should look for a telephone, get in touch with Norbert, and make arrangements for him to drive us back to town the day after. There we can try to make reservations for our return journey. But even if we don't succeed, we can jump on a train. We may not have a reserved seat but—'

'I can't leave here the day after tomorrow.'

He struggled to hold his exasperation in check. 'Why not?'

'My uncle said he'd visit me here after the funeral tomorrow. I have to talk to him. I have so many questions, and I want to meet my grandmother, my aunt, and my uncle's children.'

'If he'd wanted you to meet them he would have taken you back to the farm with him this morning.'

'They're busy. It takes a lot of hard work to run a farm. My mother always said that no one in the family ever had a minute to themselves.'

'Sunshine, don't take this the wrong way—'

'I won't take it any way because you're about to say something horrid. Frankly, I'd rather you didn't say anything at all.' She pushed the box of photographs into her duffle bag.

'All I was going to say is, I don't understand Polish but your uncle didn't exactly seem over-friendly towards you.'

'It's as Josef said – my coming here is a shock. One moment Mama was writing letters to her family and sending them parcels of luxuries. The next, I turn up in the village and announce that she has died. It's bound to take time for them to adjust, just as it has for me.'

'Of course,' Ned agreed. But he couldn't help thinking that Helena hadn't begun to accept Magda's death herself. And probably wouldn't until her mother's ashes were buried.

'Then there's my grandmother. She's elderly and in ill-health. She's already had to bury her husband, one of her sons, her son-in-law and baby granddaughter. My mother's death will be a heavy blow at her time of life.'

'All the more reason for your uncle to introduce her to the granddaughter she has never seen.'

'He *will* introduce me,' she countered.

'When?'

'Soon.'

'He told you that?'

'Not in so many words,' she conceded impatiently. 'But that's why he's coming here tomorrow after the funeral. To talk to me and make arrangements for me to meet the rest of the family.'

'I hope you're right, for your sake.' Ned refilled his cup of coffee.

'Of course he wants me to meet them. They're my family!' Her voice rose precariously.

'Yes, they are, Helena,' Ned agreed. 'I would just hate to see you disappointed, that's all.'

'I can't sit around here all morning. I have to see Josef. My uncle said he would take me to see the stonemason who is adding my mother's name and dates to Adam Janek's memorial.' Helena picked up her duffle bag, went to the back door of the bar and knocked on it.

Ned watched Josef open the door and smile at Helena. He pushed his plate aside, left the table and went up the stairs. The thought of Helena turning to Josef for help had taken away his appetite.

'Your uncle meant old Henryk. He's the only stonemason we have left in the village.' Josef carried a bucket of pigswill across the yard, emptied it into the trough in the sty, stood back and watched the sow push her piglets aside so she could dip her snout into the mess. 'I don't know why Wiktor didn't make a note of your mother's date of death.'

'I don't either.' Helena hadn't considered it at the time, but now she thought it odd.

'But you heard Wiktor; he wants to pay the bill and so he'll decide the wording. I wouldn't argue the point if I were you,' he warned. 'He is a proud man and probably sees it as his responsibility to arrange his sister's memorial.'

'The last thing I want to do is argue with my uncle. Josef, can I ask you something?'

'There's an old Polish saying: "You can ask what you like, but you may not always receive an answer."'

'We have a similar saying in Britain. I can't help feeling that all of you are keeping something from me . . .'

'I told you, people in the village hate talking about the war, and, given the way your mother left here, they're not going to be anxious to tell you anything about her.'

'That's all?'

'What else could there be?'

'I don't know.'

'I've finished doing what I have to around here for an hour or so. We could visit the stonemason now, if you like?'

'That would be wonderful. Thank you.'

'I could take a message . . .'

'I'd rather go myself. That way I know there'll be no mistake.'

'I am a school teacher. You can trust me with a simple message.' When she didn't answer him, he said, 'But as you're intent on going, we'll walk the long way round past the small lake. You may even find some flowers for tomorrow.'

'I'd like that. Let's go.'

'Don't you have to get your coat?'

'My cardigan is warm enough.' She was suddenly loath to face Ned, and wanted to leave before he returned downstairs, saw her with Josef and became even more jealous than he already was.

Ned emerged in time to catch a snatch of Josef and Helena's Polish conversation, as they walked through the archway that cut through the house. He ran after them and glimpsed Helena's long blonde hair as they rounded the corner of the street. Furious with her for shutting him out, he returned to their room. Anna was there, tidying up. He grabbed his jacket, muttered sorry, and ran back into the yard.

If Helena could go for a walk, so could he.

'Is this the nearest lake to the village?' Helena asked.

Josef was leading her down a path that cut through a thickly wooded area.

'Yes. It's a fifteen-minute walk from the square – or a ten-minute run – and has been a favourite playground for the village children for generations. You'll soon see why.'

They walked into a clearing. A gleaming expanse of sun-dappled water, fringed by dark conifers, lay in front of them. Josef stepped on to a wooden pier that jutted into the lake, walked to the end, sat down and dangled his legs above a bank of reeds.

Helena sat next to him, and noticed a small rowing boat tied to a mooring ring. 'Does that belong to anyone?'

'Possibly, but whoever owns it doesn't mind everyone in the village using it. I'll take you out in it some time. There's a small island around that curve. You can't see it from here. Every stray duck and swan in this part of Poland has made it their home.' He leaned back on his hands and looked across at a family of wild ducks swimming beneath the overhanging trees on the opposite bank. 'This is my favourite place on earth. The one place I have almost always enjoyed peace and quiet. I say almost,' he added wryly, 'because occasionally there were other children around when I was growing up. But more often than not, I had the place to myself. There were only two other children my age in the village, and, as their fathers were farmers, they had more chores to do around their houses and yards than I did.'

'So you spent most of your time alone?'

'The Communist government wasn't kind to priests after the war. After the authorities locked the churches and outlawed religion, many monks, nuns and priests fled to the West. My foster-father was one of the few who didn't. He insisted that the villagers needed him more than ever, which was true. But he was given a job in the meat factory and forced to work six twelve-hour shifts a week. Anna was busy looking after the bar and her brother, as well as running the house, so, apart from homework checks and meals, I was more or less left to my own devices.'

'Was your foster-father forced to work in the factory because he was a priest?'

'Because there was a shortage of manpower after the war. Everyone around here worked long hours – factory-workers, farmers – and my foster-father chose to carry on working after his factory shifts, conducting mass, christenings, weddings and funerals, which meant that I saw far more of Anna than I did of him.'

'Did he conduct the ceremonies in secret?'

'Not so secret. Everyone knew it was going on in people's houses. As I said to you, the authorities turn a blind eye most of the time.'

Helena breathed in deeply. 'It's certainly beautiful here.'

'You'd never think that two miles down the road there are two large factories that employ over two hundred people.'

'You wouldn't,' she agreed. 'My mother told me that the country-side around the village was beautiful, but I didn't expect to find it unchanged. I thought, like Britain, there'd be more building – new houses, shops and factories to replace those that were destroyed during the war.'

'Our country is poor and although a great deal was destroyed during the war a fifth of our population was killed, so there was no need to do much more than re-build the parts of our cities and towns that were destroyed. Our government didn't have to cater for an increase in population like yours.' He glanced across at her and smiled. 'You look quite at home here.'

'I feel it,' she concurred.

'In the land of your ancestors. Wiktor Niklas was right; it is odd that your mother never returned, not even to see her own mother.'

'She was terrified of the Communists.'

'Why? She became a naturalized British citizen, didn't she?'

'We both did.'

'So why didn't she come here with her British passport? No one could have done anything to her, and she would have been able to see her mother. I think that would have meant a great deal to the old lady.'

'You know my grandmother?' Helena asked eagerly.

'I keep telling you, everyone here knows everyone else.'

'What is she like?'

'Ever since I can remember, she has seemed the oldest of the old women, probably because, like every widow here, she always wears black. But she and the other women who lost children during the war were always kind to me. Every time Anna sent me to the Niklas farm on an errand, Granny Niklas gave me something: a cake, a slice of pie, a piece of cheese.'

'Did she ever talk about my mother?'

'Not to me. She only ever mentioned her son Wiktor, daughter Julianna and her grandchildren, but that's hardly surprising, as they are the only ones I knew. But, enough about the village. Tell me about yourself. What do you intend to do after you have buried your mother here?'

Helena thought for a moment before answering. 'I'd like to get to know my mother's family, especially my uncle, aunt and grand-mother, and find out if my mother's childhood was as idyllic as she told me. But most of all, I'd like to know why she lied to me about being Adam Janek's daughter.'

'The Niklas family won't be able to answer that last question.'

'But they must know someone who was taken to Germany at the same time as my mother.'

'That's something you can ask your uncle tomorrow.' He rose to his feet. 'Much as I hate to leave this place, Anna will be looking for me to help her before too long. We should go and find old Henryk and talk to him about the gravestone.'

'I suppose so.'

'Why so reluctant, all of a sudden?'

'Because I could sit here all day.'

'Now you know the way, you can come back later.' When she didn't move he said, 'Ah, the Polish part of you wants you to stay in this country.'

'Possibly.'

'But you have to go back to Britain to work?'

'Not until September when I start a new teaching post.' She climbed to her feet, and took a last look at the lake.

'You can't deny your blood heritage.'

Josef's words made Helena think of Alma. What had she said? *'It's something in the blood. A bond between a person and their birth country that transcends logic. I can't explain it better than that. But what I do know is that no matter how hard an exile works to build a new life, how good that life is, or how cruel or hateful the government in their native country, people born behind the Iron Curtain will always feel as though they belong there and nowhere else.'*

'My father might not have been Polish,' she said.

'But your mother was, and many people believe religious and mystical heritage is passed on through the maternal line. You should think about staying here, Helena. This country needs all the intelligent women and teachers it can get.'

'But I'm married to Ned.'

'Are you?'

She looked into Josef's deep blue eyes, and saw that he knew she wasn't.

Chapter 13

'SO YOU ARE taking a new teaching post in September?' Josef said, breaking the silence, as he and Helena walked away from the lake.

'Yes, in my old school.'

'And you are happy about it?'

'I was. But when I heard that I'd been given the job, I was living at home with my mother. She was pleased because teaching positions in Wales are scarce, and it meant that I could stay in my home town close to her.'

'Does Ned teach in that school, too?'

Helena paused. 'Ned is a doctor, not a teacher. He never tells people what he does when he first meets them.'

'In case they bore him with details of their illnesses?'

'You understand.' She followed him through the woods. 'How old are the children you teach?'

'From six to twelve years old, then they go to the secondary school in the town.'

'A three-hour drive away?' she said in surprise.

'They have a bus, and you can do your homework while you travel. I know because it's a journey I made for many years myself.'

'How many teachers are in your school?'

'You're looking at the entire staff.'

'How many children are there?'

'Only fourteen. Even now, nearly twenty years after the war, the population hasn't recovered from the German massacres and deportations.'

'But fourteen children all of different ages and abilities, working on different things at different paces. It can't be easy to teach them.'

'It's easier than working in the meat factory like my foster-father,' he said philosophically. 'And we have interesting class discussions. The big ones help the little ones.'

'What do you teach them?'

'I imagine the same things that are taught in British primary schools: mathematics, spelling, grammar, literature, history, geography and languages. Russian first, then English and French. No one wants to teach or learn German. The war is too raw a memory.'

'You're right – apart from the languages, the Communist syllabus isn't so different from ours,' she agreed.

'You don't teach your young children languages?' He was amazed.

'We British are very insular. Our borders are the sea.'

'Unlike the French, who teach their primary school children English and German.'

'How do you know?'

'Because I spent a year studying French literature in Paris.'

'The Communists allowed you to do that?' It was her turn to be amazed.

'The government paid for me to study there.'

'So you could become a village schoolmaster?'

'I will only be teaching in the village school for one more year, then I go the secondary school for two years, and then back to the university to teach education students. It's the Socialist way. Work upwards from the bottom.'

Helena thought of her college tutors. Most had been theorists with no practical experience of teaching. 'That's a good system.'

'We think so. Here's old Henryk's house.'

'Did he know my mother?' She saw the exasperated expression on Josef's face. 'Sorry. I should know by now that everyone knows everyone in the village.'

'Come on, I'll introduce you.' Josef opened a small wicket gate and they went into a garden. A wire chicken run was set back, well away from beautifully tended beds filled with cabbages, leeks, tomatoes, lettuce, peas and beans.

The door to the house was open and an old woman was sitting on the step shelling peas. She smiled, showing twin rows of toothless gums.

'Wiktor said you'd be around, Josef. Is this the young English lady the whole village is talking about?'

'Her name is Helena and she speaks excellent Polish, Olgan,' Josef warned.

Helena debated whether or not to call the elderly woman by her Christian name. She felt it would sound disrespectful if she did, but Josef hadn't mentioned her surname. In the end she settled for a simple, 'Hello.'

Olgan took Helena's hand and shook it enthusiastically. 'Welcome. Henryk will be pleased to see you. You will have a cup of tea with us?'

'We've only just had breakfast, thank you, Olgan,' Josef smiled, shaking his head.

'Please, come in, make yourself at home. I will get Henryk.'

Helena entered the wooden house. The front door opened directly into a large room that served as kitchen, living and dining room in one. Just like the attic she and Ned had rented there was a plethora of embroidered cushions and cloths – on the large table, the backs of two easy and four upright chairs – as well as tapestries on the walls. Olgan indicated the two easy chairs on either side of the hearth, and Helena and Josef sat down. The heat was oppressive, which wasn't surprising as the fire was blazing. There was an appetizing smell of baking bread in the air.

'It's my cooking day,' Olgan explained. 'I will get Henryk. He is milking the cow.'

'They run a farm at their age?' Helena asked when Olgan disappeared.

'Smallholding,' Josef explained.

A few minutes later Olgan returned with her husband. Helena had never seen a man so bent and gnarled. He looked as though a summer breeze would flatten him, yet he was carrying a log almost as large as himself. He dropped it outside the door. Josef and Helena rose to meet him.

'Helena, this is Henryk.'

The old man brushed his hand on the back of his trousers before taking hold of Helena's hand, lifting it to his lips and kissing it, cavalier fashion.

'You know Wiktor Niklas has given Helena permission to bury Magdalena Janek's ashes in Adam Janek's grave, Henryk?' Josef checked.

'Yes. It's a pity there are no Janeks left, but I suppose a Niklas is the nearest Adam Janek has left to a relative.' Henryk smiled at Helena, and his eyes disappeared, swallowed by wrinkles. 'Wiktor called in earlier. He said you would give me the date of Magdalena Janek's death.'

Helena took the stub of pencil and scrap of paper he gave her, and wrote it down. 'Would it be possible to put "beloved mother of Helena" below my mother's name and dates?'

Henryk shook his head. 'There's only room for Magdalena's name and dates. And that's all Wiktor wants,' he added.

Helena bit her lip to stem the tears that started in her eyes. She was beginning to feel that by bringing her mother's remains to Poland, she was losing her a second time. This time to their Polish family, who, for whatever reason, were intent on excluding her.

'I promised Wiktor that I would add Magdalena Janek's name today before the service tomorrow,' the old man added.

'Thank you.' Helena didn't know why she was thanking Henryk. Again she had the feeling that people couldn't wait to be rid of her.

'We must be going, Henryk. We'll see you tomorrow.' Josef rose and made his way to the door, Helena trailing behind him.

'You can go on to Anna's. I want to visit the churchyard again,' Helena said when they reached the square. 'There's something I want to check.'

'I'll come with you.'

'There's no need.'

But Josef followed her anyway, as she headed towards the church. She slipped the chain from the gate, and walked to the Janek plot. Then she stood and stared at Adam Janek's gravestone.

'*Adam Janek, born 21 January 1919, martyred for Poland 26 June 1943. A loving husband and father. Also his daughter, Helena Weronika Janek. Born 5 June 1943, martyred 26 June 1943.*'

She knelt before the cross and, using the nail of her little finger as a measure, traced out the amount of space that would be needed to put Magdalena Janek and her dates. There was definitely room for another line which could have read 'beloved mother of Helena'.

'There *is* room,' she murmured.

'For another Helena?'

It was only then she realized that her mother's brother would never countenance the ambiguity of two Helena Janeks on a gravestone. Not after her visit here. Everyone would know what it meant.

'I'm sorry, but it's what your mother's family want, Helena.' Josef wrapped his arm around her. Instinctively, without thinking what she was doing, she rested her head on his shoulder.

Ned walked through the open church gate, turned the corner and saw Helena and Josef standing, wrapped in one another's arms, in front of Adam Janek's grave. His first instinct was to run up to them, tear Helena away from Josef, and demand to know what they were doing.

Then he recalled how her love for him had seeped away since Magda's death. And how powerless he had been to prevent it.

He walked away before either of them could see him.

Ned was sitting at a table in the bar that gave him a prime view of the street when Josef and Helena returned. Helena glanced above the half-doors and saw him looking straight at her. Mindful of Anna's frequently repeated edict that women were not allowed in the bar, she pointed around the corner to the passage that cut through the house. Ned ignored her.

Josef touched her arm. 'I have to work, but if you need me I will be in the yard or bar.'

'Thank you for taking me to see old Henryk, and coming with me to the churchyard.'

'It was my pleasure.' Josef entered the bar, nodded to Ned, and tied on his canvas apron before going into the yard.

By the time Helena had walked through the archway, Josef was hard at work, shifting crates of beer that had been delivered and stacking them in the barn. Helena climbed the outside staircase to the attic room. It was only when she stood in front of the door that she realized she didn't have the key.

She sank down on the wooden landing and leaned against the warm, stone wall. It was an hour short of midday, but the sun was relentless, and the yard stifling. Helena sat and watched Josef move crates. He was engrossed in his task, and she knew he wasn't aware of her presence.

She closed her eyes, turned her face to the sun and mulled over the events of the morning. For all her insistence that her aunt and grandmother must be too busy with farm work to see her, she knew Ned was right. Either they didn't *want* to see her or they didn't know she existed. And if it was the latter, her Uncle Wiktor wanted to keep it that way. But why?

She set her duffle bag down carefully, so as not to jar the box inside. Opening the roped top, she removed the box of photographs Ned had brought to the breakfast table. She gazed at the framed photograph of Magda and Adam Janek on their wedding day. After seeing the churchyard she could pinpoint exactly where they had been standing; to the right of the gate and the left of the church door. They looked so young, so happy, so hopeful ... Who could have predicted their lives would be wrecked by war and tragedy so soon afterwards?

She returned the frame to her bag and flicked through the snapshots. She almost didn't need to look at them. She had studied them so often she only had to close her eyes to conjure the images.

She gazed at the earliest photograph of her that her mother had possessed. It was a close shot, so close that, if it hadn't been for the trees and imposing building in the background, it could have been taken in a studio. She was staring wide-eyed at the camera, her mother's distinctive embossed wedding ring clearly visible as she held her. But Magda's hands were the only part of her that could be seen. Helena had always thought it odd that her mother wasn't in the picture. When she had asked her why, Magda told her that the photographer had only wanted to take her.

But now she knew that Adam Janek couldn't possibly be her father, another reason came to mind. Her staunchly Catholic mother hadn't wanted to compound her 'sin' by appearing with her illegitimate child in a photograph that might have made its way back to her family, friends and priest. Was she the product of an illicit love affair or rape? Love or lust? The only fact she could be certain of was that Magda had never married again, because she had kept the name Janek until the day she died – an outwardly respectable widow.

Her mother had set great store by respectability. Whenever Helena had wanted to do something Magda disapproved of – like wear mini-skirts, go for a drink in a pub with Ned, or stay late at a party – her mother had always begun her lectures by saying, 'What will people think? No decent girl would behave that way' and invariably finish with 'in my day . . .'

She and Ned had constantly reminded her mother that it was the 1960s. Old morality was being thrown out of the window, and it was good riddance to a hidebound society that labelled an illegitimate child as a 'product of sin', and unmarried mothers as 'fallen women'. But could it be true? Were there sound reasons behind the Church's attitude towards children born outside marriage? Would she have to pay for the sin her mother and father – whoever he was – had committed? Did her illegitimacy lessen her worth as a person?

She recalled the strict moral principles inculcated in her during her education in the Girls' Grammar School, and imagined the gossip would arise if it became known that she had no claim to the name Janek, or even the Christian name Helena. That her entire life was based on a lie, her identity stolen from a dead baby. The headmistress and governors of the school would never have given her a position on the staff. They might have interviewed her politely enough, but would have looked down on her. Just like the children who had been born to unmarried mothers during the war, the ones who had been taunted and called GI bastards in the playground.

'Enjoy yourself with Josef?' Ned was standing on the steps. The expression on his face chilled her despite the baking heat.

'He introduced me to the stonemason,' she answered, aware that Josef was probably within earshot.

'Really?' he queried sceptically.

'We also walked to the lake. It's only a quarter of an hour from the square. It's beautiful. Quiet and still . . .'

'And afterwards you went to the churchyard?'

'Yes.' She realized that he had either followed her and Josef, or seen them there. 'I asked the mason if he'd put "beloved mother of Helena", but he said there wasn't space. I wanted to check for myself.'

'And was there space?'

'Yes.'

'So you went back and argued with him?'

'As Josef reminded me, I'm in no position to argue. My uncle is paying to have my mother's name added, not me, so I have no right to dictate the inscription. And, now people know there are two Helena Janeks, it might look odd . . .'

Ned leaned on the rail. Helena looked so forlorn sitting on the landing surrounded by photographs that his anger faded, but not the jealousy that had given rise to it. 'It might,' he agreed.

'I feel that in bringing my mother's ashes here to be buried, I have returned her to her Polish family.'

'I thought that was the point of the trip.'

'I didn't realize that I would lose her all over again,' she murmured.

'Was it that realization that made you turn to Josef?'

'Pardon?'

'I saw you in his arms.'

'In his arms? I don't understand . . . I was upset. He . . .'

'I saw what he was doing.' Ned pulled the heavy key from his pocket, reached over her and unlocked the door to their room.

'Ned, you're being ridiculous.'

'Am I?' he asked coldly.

'Of course you are. There's nothing between Josef and me.'

'I'm glad to hear it.'

'Sarcasm—'

'I'm not being sarcastic.' Suddenly weary of arguing with her, he changed the subject. 'It's lunch-time. Anna has made an enormous pot of what looks like spinach soup. It's on the outside table.'

Helena gathered the photographs together and returned them to the box. 'I'm not hungry.'

'You look as though you should be in bed.'

'I'm going for another walk. This is my mother's home village. Who knows when, if ever, I'll return? I'd like to explore. I haven't even taken any photographs yet. I'd like some reminders of the square, the church and the Niklas farmhouse.'

'I'd wait until you've spoken to your uncle before taking any there, if I were you.' Ned stepped past her, went into the room and opened the window. 'It's stuffy in here.'

She rose to her feet and joined him, dropping her cardigan on the chair.

'Can I come with you?' he said eventually, trying to make amends.

'If you want to.' She shrugged.

'Helena, are you all right?'

She wanted to scream that she wasn't all right. Would never be right again. That she couldn't bear being cold-shouldered by her mother's brother, or thinking such dreadful things about her mother, but most of all she couldn't bear that he was talking to her as if she were one of his patients.

'Helena—'

'I'm fine.' She straightened her T-shirt and hitched her duffle bag higher on her shoulder. 'If you want to come, let's go.'

Yet again, Ned felt that Helena was shutting him out. When she bothered to reply to his attempts at conversation she did so in monosyllables. She ignored all his suggestions about composition when she took photographs of the square and churchyard. Afterwards, and only at his prompting, they walked out to the lake where she finished one film and put another in her camera.

They returned to the bar, ate dinner at the table in the courtyard with Josef, and then went to their room. She unpacked the black suit and blouse she had brought with her, hung them up and checked that her low-heeled court shoes – the only shoes she had brought with her aside from her canvas running shoes – were clean. Then, just as she'd done the night before, she went to bed before Ned and turned her face to the wall.

Knowing he wouldn't get any more conversation out of her that night, Ned checked his own clothes, then sat in one of the chairs and read his James Bond. But when he climbed into the second bed an hour later, he knew she was as wide awake as he was.

Recalling what Josef had said about the market in the square opening at six o'clock, Helena set her travelling alarm clock for five, but she was awake at half past four. Light was already shining through the thin cotton curtains when she slipped out of bed, switched off the alarm, and picked up clean underclothes and the jeans and T-shirt she had worn the day before. She wrapped her robe around her nightdress and went down to the wash-house.

The local farmers were laying their wares out on trestles when she wandered into the square half an hour later. There were only a dozen traders, and their efforts were amateurish compared to the stall-holders of the colourful twice-weekly markets in Pontypridd. The only produce on offer was home-made or grown: cheese, butter, eggs, sweet and sour cream, and yoghurt on the two dairy stalls; cured sausages and salamis on the meat stall, but no fresh meat; and mounds of potatoes, carrots, cabbages, turnips, swedes, spinach, kohlrabi, tomatoes and lettuces on the eight vegetable stalls. Another stall offered cloudy bottles of homeopathic remedies labelled as cure-alls for animals and humans, neatly arranged in rows next to a mess of fuses, electrical wires, sockets, rusting tools and bits of metal she couldn't identify. Nothing looked as though it had travelled more than a kilometre or two from beyond the village.

She found what she wanted on the last stall she looked at. Next to a few dozen bunches of radishes, mint and strings of garlic lay ten short-stemmed cream roses. As they were the only flowers she had seen, she paid the old woman manning the stall her asking price, and watched while she wrapped them in a sheet of damp newspaper.

'You will make it difficult for the rest of us, buying without bartering. You could have got those for half the price.'

Taken aback by the venom in the reprimand, Helena glanced over her shoulder to see Anna staring at her. 'As they were the only flowers here I thought I'd better grab them before someone else snapped them up,' she retorted.

'Only rich Westerners have money to spare for flowers.' Anna examined the potatoes on the next stall. After checking them for firmness, she ignored Helena and barked her order to the man behind the counter.

'Is this the foreigner everyone is talking about, Anna?' the stall-holder asked as he weighed out the potatoes.

The landlady shrugged dismissively. 'People round here have nothing to talk about except the price of carrots – and you're asking too much for these.'

'Everyone?' Helena echoed in surprise.

'You don't know you're famous?' It was Josef. He pushed his way between her and Anna. 'Westerners are rarer than hens that lay golden eggs in this part of Poland.'

'Her Polish is good,' the stall-holder commented.

'My mother taught me.' Helena answered him directly.

'And your mother was Magdalena Janek?'

'She was.' Helena began to realize just how much gossip her appearance in the village had given rise to. 'Did you know her?'

'I remember her, but not well. I was a child when she left, but not as young as Josef here.' He slapped him on the back. 'But my mother knew her. We will all be at the church at nine o'clock to see her laid to rest.'

'All?' Helena looked at Josef.

'Everyone who knew your mother will be there, and probably everyone who has been born since. It's the Polish way. We laugh, cry, celebrate and mourn together.' He picked up the sacks of potatoes and carrots that Anna had bought. 'I'll take these back for you, Anna, and return for whatever else you buy.'

'I won't be buying much more, certainly not more than I can carry.' Anna counted her change and put it into her purse. 'When you've carried those sacks down to the cellar you can lay breakfast for Helena and Ned in the courtyard.'

'What it is to be worked like a slave,' Josef joked before falling into step alongside Helena. 'Are you going back to the house?'

'Yes.'

He looked over his shoulder. 'It's not much of a market to a Pole; it must seem even less to a Westerner.'

She searched for something to say that wouldn't sound patronizing. 'It's a typical local farmers' market.'

'You have one like it in your home town?'

'No, because the town I grew up in is much larger than this village and well known for its market, which sells everything people want, as well as things that they don't.' A woman bumped into her, jarring her duffle bag. She lifted it from her shoulder, set the flowers on top, wrapped her arms protectively around it and carried it in front of her.

'I visited Wiktor yesterday evening. He chose a well-known Polish hymn for the service, "Święta Miłość Kochanej Ojczyzny". Which roughly translates as—'

'"Sacred Love of the Beloved Homeland,"' Helena interrupted. 'It was one of my mother's favourites. It is also very fitting.'

'I'm glad you consider it appropriate. He asked me to keep the service short. I hope you approve.'

'Given the way that my uncle has taken over the organization of my mother's funeral service, I'm not in a position to approve or disapprove.'

'This can't be easy for you,' Josef observed.

'I will be glad when it is over.'

'And then you and Ned will return to Britain?' he probed.

'Soon,' she replied vaguely.

'If you don't have to return until you start teaching in September you should stay a while, explore the countryside and see some of our beautiful cities. Warsaw is grand again now that it is being rebuilt. And the medieval quarter of Gdansk is very atmospheric.'

'Anything to get me out of the village?' she challenged.

'This village is small and boring.' He shifted the sack of potatoes on to his shoulder and tightened his grip on the smaller sack of carrots.

'Only to people who live here. After living in a Welsh town and an English city I find it fascinating. And I have relatives here, which gives me a good reason for wanting to stay.'

'Another week and you'll be bored witless.' He stopped, an

enthusiastic expression on his face. 'Anna could spare me for a few days; I could apply for a permit, take you around the country and show you the sights.'

'And Ned?'

'He could come if you want him to. Although he isn't your husband.'

They both knew it wasn't a question.

'No,' she confirmed, then changed the subject. 'Why is my uncle so cold towards me?'

'You will have to ask him that when you talk to him after the ceremony,' he answered evasively.

They began walking again.

'But you know why?' she pressed.

'Try to put yourself in his position. He has lost his sister twice. Once when she was marched away by the Germans, and now when you have returned her ashes to her birthplace.'

'Why should I put myself in his position?' she demanded. 'And why should I consider his feelings when he doesn't care about mine? My mother was the only relative I have ever known. I have just discovered that the man I always thought was my father isn't. And although this is the third day I have spent in the village, I still haven't met my grandmother or my aunt.'

'They'll be at the graveside.' He spoke softly, in sharp contrast to her heightened tones.

'Will they?'

They reached the bar, and he dropped both sacks outside the half doors. 'I spoke to them when I visited the Niklas farm yesterday. They are coming to the ceremony.'

She gripped the corner of the building to steady herself. 'Has Wiktor told them about me?'

Josef unlocked the shutters that fastened over the saloon half door and hauled the sacks inside the building. He hesitated before replying. 'You will have to ask him that, Helena.'

She looked at him for a moment before turning on her heel and walking through the archway.

*

Ned and Helena were leaving the breakfast table when Josef entered the yard and drew Helena aside.

'How big is the box containing your mother's ashes?'

'Why do you want to know?' she asked suspiciously.

Ned wrapped his arm around her waist. The warmth of his hand permeated through Helena's T-shirt, and her first instinct was to shake him off. Then she remembered that in an hour they would be in the churchyard, in full view of everyone in the village, and the last thing she wanted was to cause yet another argument between them before the ceremony.

'I have to open the grave,' Josef answered.

Helena lifted her duffle bag from her shoulder, opened it, took out her purse, hairbrush and make-up bag, and carefully removed the airtight box.

Josef held out his hands. She hesitated for a second before handing it over.

'The casket is inside.'

'A casket not an urn.' Josef lifted the lid on the plastic box and peered inside.

'The undertaker in Pontypridd assured me that the wood is the best quality oak. It should last for years.'

'You would like it to be buried without the outer box?'

'Please.'

'Thank you. Now I know what size hole to dig. Do you want me to take it to the churchyard?'

Helena clenched her lips together and fought back the tears pricking at the corner of her eyes. 'No, I will carry it.'

'The ceremony is due to begin in an hour. Can you bring it to the churchyard in half an hour?'

'I'll bring it to you as soon as I have changed.'

'Here.' Josef handed her a length of cream ribbon. 'I thought you might like this to tie your roses together.'

'Thank you.' She took it gratefully. 'Where did you find it?'

'Anna's old sewing box. I told her it was for you.'

Helena ran her fingers over the smooth satin and thought of Anna's sister, Matylda, the young girl who had been shot almost before she had begun to live her life. 'I must thank her.'

'I already have. I'll see you in the churchyard.'

Helena returned her personal items to the duffle bag, clutched the casket to her chest, and ran up the outside staircase.

Josef looked thoughtfully after her. 'Helena has been carrying the burden of her mother's ashes for so long, it is going to be hard for her to let them go.'

'But when she does, she will be able to move on.' Ned looked Josef in the eye. 'We both will.'

Helena changed into the black suit, black silk blouse, stockings and shoes she had bought for Magda's funeral in Pontypridd. She applied a discreet layer of foundation, lipstick and mascara, tied her blonde hair into a knot at the nape of her neck and draped her mother's black lace shawl over her hair. When she finished dressing she took the roses from the newspaper and tied them together with the ribbon Josef had given her, teasing the ends into a decorative bow. Only then did she remove the casket that contained Magda's ashes from the airtight box.

She laid the posy of roses on top and looked back at her duffle bag. It seemed strange to leave it, but her money and valuables were in the belt around her waist and she no longer had any reason to carry it with her.

'Would you like me to carry the casket to the churchyard for you?'

She looked at Ned as though she were seeing him for the first time. He looked tall and handsome in his dark suit, white shirt and black tie, with his auburn hair brushed back from his forehead.

'No, thank you. I've carried my mother this far. I can take her to Adam Janek's grave.'

'Are you ready?' The question hung, unspoken, between them. 'Are you ready to let Magda go?'

'Just one moment. I have something else to do. I was going to do it at the graveside but on reflection it will be best done in private.' She set the box on the table, lifted the flowers from the lid and opened it.

Trying not to look at the contents, she unclipped Magda's locket from around her neck. She opened it and studied the photograph it contained of Adam Janek.

'Are you sure you want to bury that with your mother, Helena?' Ned asked, concerned.

'Adam Janek wasn't my father. I have no right to wear it.'

'You told me that Magda always wore it, in which case it must have meant a great deal to her. It won't do any good in the earth. And neither will her wedding ring,' he added when he saw Helena take it from her pocket. He moved closer to her. 'You will value them. Not because they are gold, but because they were your mother's treasured possessions. If you can't bear to wear them any longer, put them away and think of them as your mother's gifts to the grandchildren she will never know.'

She looked up at him through dark, bruised eyes. 'You really think I should keep them?'

'I do,' he said decisively. 'You may not be Adam Janek's daughter, but you are the child of Magdalena Janek. You should cherish her possessions.'

She stood silently for a moment before closing the casket. Her fingers trembled as she lifted the locket.

'Here, let me.' He took the chain from her and re-fastened it around her neck, then watched her replace the flowers. 'Ready?'

'Yes.'

'Then let's go.' He opened the door.

Chapter 14

JOSEF WAS STANDING behind the stone cross that marked Adam Janek's grave. His white shirt, collar and black tie were neatly pressed, his dark suit shiny, the sleeves and trouser legs too long, the shoulders too wide as if it had been tailored for a taller, broader man, and Helena wondered if he had inherited his foster-father's suit along with his ecclesiastical duties. He was holding a worn, leather-bound prayer book. A carved wooden crucifix bookmark hung from its pages and she watched it sway in the slight breeze that was ruffling the leaves of the trees and bushes.

Wiktor and an old woman, who looked so like Magda Helena knew she could only be her grandmother, stood on Josef's right. Beside them was another younger woman, whose eyes and hair were as dark as Magda's had been. A mousy-haired woman and four children, all of whom appeared to be of secondary school age, hung behind them. Helena presumed they were Wiktor's wife and children.

Wiktor deliberately turned away from her and Ned when they walked to the grave. Not wanting to cause a scene, Helena didn't acknowledge the Niklas family but went to Josef.

She looked down at the casket. Now that the moment had finally arrived for her to relinquish it, she couldn't bring herself to hand it over. She gripped it tightly and dropped a kiss on the smooth planed surface of the oak before re-arranging the roses so they lay in the centre. A shadow blocked out the sun. She looked up. Josef was in front of her. He held out his hands.

'It is time, Helena.'

She was aware of Ned moving closer to her. She allowed Josef to take the casket. Wiktor stepped forward. Josef held out the casket, and, like Helena, Wiktor kissed it. Josef crouched down next to the hole he'd dug, and Helena knelt beside the grave, neither seeing nor heeding the dirt that clung to her stockings and skirt.

The hole Josef had dug was three feet deep, and a foot wider and longer than the casket. He laid the box with its covering of cream roses in it, and a whisper rippled through the churchyard. Helena glanced over her shoulder. For the first time she realized that the churchyard was full of people. She recognized Anna, old Henryk and Olgan, the stall-holder who had sold her the roses, and the men she had seen drinking in the bar. They had entered so quietly she hadn't even been aware of their presence until now. And every one, even the small children, was standing so still and so silent, that she found it unsettling.

Her uncle lifted an immense wreath woven from green fir branches and dozens of artificial red roses. Josef took it from Wiktor and laid it on the mound of earth he had taken from the grave.

'Please, will you leave my roses on the casket?' Helena asked Josef.

'If that is what you would like.' He opened the prayer book.

'The family flowers go on the grave,' Wiktor barked.

Ned helped Helena to her feet, and she was more grateful for his presence than she had been since they'd reached Poland. A lone violinist struck up a tune and a hundred voices rose in unison singing the old, nationalistic hymn that her mother had often hummed while she'd worked in their flat or the shop. *'Sacred love of the beloved homeland, you are felt only by worthy minds . . .'*

Helena mouthed the words Magda had taught her, but she couldn't bring herself to make a sound. Instead, she lifted her head and looked up at the sun-washed, cloudless blue sky. Crows flew overhead, their cawing blending with the music. The peppery, pungent scent of lilies, left as offerings on the surrounding graves, mingled with the sickly sweet perfume of full-blown roses that had been planted around the churchyard. She was suddenly certain that, despite Magda's fear of the Communists, she would have loved to have visited this village one last time.

The hymn ended. Josef gave a brief eulogy. Helena suspected that Wiktor Janek had told him what to say, because Josef made no mention of her being Magda's daughter. Instead, he recounted how happy Magda had been growing up with her brothers and sister on the family farm, and how she had been driven from her home by the Nazis during the war and forced to make a life for herself elsewhere. A life he didn't elaborate on.

Then Josef began the mass. As the people made the age-old responses to the ceremony, Helena reflected that, although Poland might be outwardly Communist, no government could ever hope to gain complete control over people's minds and souls. Far from dead, the old beliefs were obviously very much alive and being passed on to new generations. The service drew to a close, and the task she had set herself, which had seemed so impossible in Pontypridd, was complete.

She had brought her mother back to the churchyard where she had been christened, confirmed and married. Magdalena Janek undoubtedly belonged here. But two questions remained, burning into her consciousness. If she wasn't Helena Janek, then who was she? And just where did *she* belong?

People moved away as silently as they had appeared. Josef took the spade from the mound of displaced earth that he had piled behind Adam Janek's memorial cross. He offered it to Helena, but before she could take it, Wiktor snatched it. Helena could smell alcohol on his breath as he sank the spade into the earth. He lifted a chunk of crumbling sandy soil and dropped it on to the box. Although Helena had been expecting a noise, the sound of the dry dirt rattling on the polished oak startled her, sending her taut nerves jangling.

Josef held out his hand, ready to take the spade from Wiktor and hand it to Helena. According to Polish custom, each member of the immediate family should be invited to fill in a grave, but Wiktor lifted his rose wreath from the mound and continued dog-gedly to wield the spade. When it became obvious that he wouldn't relinquish it, Helena looked at her grandmother.

The old woman was staring intently at her. Helena braved a smile and stepped forward, but the younger woman, whom she had presumed was her aunt, moved between them. Deliberately turning her back on Helena, she led the old woman away. Helena blanched.

She had never experienced such naked hostility before.

Wiktor Niklas continued to fill in the grave. His face turned crimson, but he only paused to wipe away the beads of perspiration that collected at his temples and on his neck above his tight white collar. Every time he broke his rhythm, Josef held out his hand to take the spade, but Wiktor pretended he hadn't seen him.

When Wiktor had returned all the dirt to the hole, he battered it down with the flat of the spade before treading around the edges. Only then did he place the wreath on top of the grave. He propped the spade against the church wall, thanked Josef for conducting the ceremony and walked away.

'I'm sorry.' Josef looked at Helena and Ned with sympathy.

'It's not your fault that my uncle is determined to ignore me.' Helena looked at the new inscription on the cross. Old Henryk had been as good as his word. Her mother's name and dates had been inscribed below that of her husband's and daughter's. She traced the letters with her finger. 'I had my mother all my life until a few weeks ago. Her mother, brother and sister hadn't seen her in over twenty years. I knew when I made the decision to return her remains to Poland that I would lose her to the rest of the family. I just didn't expect them to shut me out.'

'Come on, I'll buy you both a drink,' Ned offered.

'All the men in the village will be there,' Josef warned.

'That won't affect us in the courtyard.'

They followed the masculine crowd heading towards the bar. When they reached the yard, Ned turned to Josef and Helena.

'Beer?'

'As it's too early for vodka.' Josef pulled out a stool from under the table for Helena. 'But it will have to be a quick drink. Anna will need me to help her serve that lot.'

'Helena?'

'Small beer, please.'

Ned opened the back door into the bar. Loud voices raised in anger resounded into the yard, and Helena looked inside. Wiktor was sitting at a table, shouting at Henryk and two other men. He slammed his fist on the table, sending the glasses rattling. She stood.

'You can't go in there,' Josef reminded her.

'My uncle promised that he'd talk to me after the funeral.'

'He started drinking early this morning, before the mass.'

'I know.' She looked Josef in the eye. 'Will you get him or shall I?'

Slowly, reluctantly, Josef left his chair and went into the bar, just as Ned walked out with three glasses of beer.

'Your uncle hasn't your mother's temperament, that's for sure. Magda could be cantankerous but I never saw her aggressive,' Ned commented.

'Josef is asking him to come here. Be polite if he does,' she pleaded.

'He can't speak English.' Ned set the beer on the table.

'Voice tone and body language are universal,' she muttered when Wiktor raised his head and looked at her through the open door. His eyes were cold and unforgiving.

Josef returned to the yard, and picked up the beer Ned had bought for him. He raised the glass. 'Cheers. Your uncle will join us in a few minutes but be careful. He's in a very bad mood.'

'I could see that in the churchyard.' Helena toyed with her glass.

'He was bad then, but he's worse now. Watch out.'

'You wanted to see me; I'm here.' Wiktor swayed in front of their table.

'Please, sit down,' Ned said in English, rising and pulling out a stool for Wiktor. Wiktor might not have understood Ned's words, but the gesture was obvious. However, he made no attempt to sit.

'I wanted to ask your permission to visit the farm and see my grandmother and aunt ...' Helena began hesitantly.

'Your what?' Wiktor was perspiring heavily but he made no attempt to wipe the sweat from his face.

'My grandmother and aunt. My mother's mother and sister ...'

'You really believe that my sister, Magdalena, was your mother?' He threw back his head and roared.

Chilled by the sound, it took all of Helena's courage to reply. 'Of course she was.'

'Look in the mirror and tell me what you see,' he sneered. 'A

213

tall, slim, healthy blonde girl with blue eyes. You're no Pole.' He spat out the words. 'God only knows where my whore of a sister found you but there's only one thing you could be – an Aryan Nazi. And a whore. Just like the bitch that brought you up.'

The silence that blanketed the courtyard and bar was so absolute, so total, that Helena heard a cockroach scratching as it crossed the dirt floor. Shattered by her uncle's contempt, she slumped, jarring her spine against the wall of the house.

Ned realized Wiktor Niklas was furious, but he didn't understand why. He looked to Josef in the hope of receiving a translation but Josef appeared to be as paralysed by shock as Helena.

It was left to Anna to break the spell. She charged out of the bar, bottle in one hand, glass in the other, and brandished both in Wiktor's face. 'No one calls any woman such names, or uses language like that in my place and gets away with it. No one! Do you understand me, Wiktor Niklas? No one. Get out! Now!'

'You'd rather serve a Nazi bitch than an honest Pole,' Wiktor taunted. 'But then, you always did.'

'You're drunk, but not so drunk you don't know what you're saying. I just told you to get out!' Anna shouted.

'I've buried my sister—'

'And I'm sorry that she's not here to see what you are doing to her daughter,' Anna interrupted.

'She's no more Magda's daughter than you are, Anna.' Wiktor narrowed his Slavic eyes. 'She's a—'

'Young girl. Now get out, before I have you thrown out.'

Wiktor squared up to Anna. 'Just try—'

'She doesn't have to; I'll do it for her.' Josef stepped between Anna and Wiktor. He glanced at the men in the bar who had gathered around the back door. 'Do I have to send someone to telephone the police, or will one of you take Wiktor home?'

Two men left the bar and stood either side of Wiktor.

'I'm not going anywhere.' Wiktor lashed out wildly at Anna, who side-stepped. His intended blow fell wide of the mark, but the back of his hand connected with Helena's cheek. There was a loud crack as she jerked sideways and hit her head on the stone wall of the house. Both Josef and Ned leapt forward, but Josef was quicker. He caught Wiktor's arm and twisted it high behind his back, before pushing him towards the men.

'Get him out of here.'

Wiktor was unceremoniously frog-marched through the archway.

Blood poured from Helena's head. She closed her eyes and swayed. Ned caught her before she fell from the bench. He crouched next to her and examined the wound.

'Does she need a doctor?' Anna said, looking worried.

'Ned's a doctor.' Josef gazed anxiously at Helena.

'A doctor!' Anna repeated sceptically.

Ned didn't understand what Josef or Anna had said, but he recognized the scepticism in Anna's voice. 'If you have a first aid kit, get it,' he shouted.

Josef translated the order, and Anna ran into the house.

Dazed, Helena struggled to focus. 'I'm all right, there's no need to fuss.'

'Sit still,' Ned commanded, concern making him brusque.

Anna returned, holding a wooden box decorated with a hand-painted red cross. Ned was squeezing together the jagged edges of the wound that had opened above Helena's ear with both his hands, so Josef took it from her.

Anna looked around for some way in which she could reassert her authority. 'The entertainment is over,' she shouted at the men still crowding in the doorway. 'Go back into the bar, all of you. If you want a drink, ask Stefan to serve you. And make sure you pay him. If my takings are down, the price of beer will double until I make up the loss.'

The men retreated, the last one in closing the door behind him.

Ned gave Josef a hostile look. 'I need antiseptic, cotton wool and a plaster.'

Josef took out a small brown bottle. He unscrewed the cap, upended it on a pad of clean cotton wool, which he handed to Ned. The antiseptic smelled like nothing Ned had encountered before, but he cleaned the wound with it.

'Who told you I was a doctor?' Ned asked him.

'I did.' Helena shuddered when Ned applied a second coating of the cold antiseptic.

'Why? We agreed—'

'Josef is hardly going to ask you to practise brain surgery. And this really is nothing,' Helena snapped irritably as the wound stung painfully to life.

'It's bruised, but it's a scrape more than a cut. It's not deep enough to need stitching,' Ned announced authoritatively.

'It's bleeding a lot for a scrape,' Josef observed.

'Any injury to the head will bleed profusely,' Ned lectured. 'Pass me another pad of cotton wool and two plasters.'

Josef did as he asked. 'Helena should sleep. I'll help you to get her upstairs.'

'We can manage without your help, thank you.' Ned said managing to make it sound like an insult. 'And Helena needs to rest, not sleep. She could have a mild concussion.'

'I'm fine, really.' Helena looked at Anna, switching to Polish. 'Thank you for saying what you did to my uncle.'

Anna sniffed. 'If I were in your shoes I'd be only too happy to disown him.'

'I rather think he has disowned me. But all the same, thank you.'

'I would have said it to any man who was abusing a young girl in my house. I'll make you some mint tea. It's good for shock.' Anna went into the house.

Josef re-packed the first aid kit. 'I have to go to the bar. Anna's brother can't be trusted to manage things there for long.'

'Josef, about my mother . . .' Helena began.

'We'll talk later.' He said firmly, then disappeared into the bar.

'The slightest dizziness, you tell me at once,' Ned instructed Helena.

'How many times do I have to tell you that I really am fine?'

'Two dozen more before I'll believe you. Come on, I'll help you up to our room. We'll take the chairs out on the landing. You can sit in the fresh air and drink the tea Anna is making.'

She remained where she was. 'You didn't understand what my uncle said.'

'No, I didn't,' Ned conceded, 'but I know a drunk when I see one. He wasn't aware of his own name, let alone what he was shouting.'

'He called Mama a whore.'

'You and I both know that's ridiculous,' Ned countered. 'Magdalena Janek was the most respectable, religious woman I've ever met.'

'He also said I wasn't my mother's daughter.'

'What?' Ned stood stock-still.

'He told me to go and look in the mirror. It could be true, Ned. Mama and I were nothing alike . . .'

'To say that you're not Magda's daughter is as ludicrous as calling your mother a whore,' Ned dismissed. 'Why would a woman, a slave labourer, struggle to keep a child that wasn't hers in wartime? And afterwards in the Displaced Persons' camp, where conditions were appalling. We both heard Magda talk about what it was like there. How hard it was to survive between food shortages, bomb-ings—'

'Perhaps she found me and couldn't bring herself to abandon me. Perhaps there weren't any orphanages . . .'

'Remember what Bob Parsons told us? He said that his mother wouldn't have had any objections to him marrying Magda if she hadn't already had a child. Think about it, Helena. I can't come up with one good reason why Magda would have brought you up if you were someone else's.'

'My mother had lost everyone she loved and everything she owned – husband, daughter, home, friends, country. She had nothing. Perhaps she just saw me lying on a bombsite, picked me up . . .'

'People don't pick up children and adopt them the way they do stray dogs. Not in wartime,' Ned argued.

'Yes they do.' A slim, silver-haired woman walked through the arch and joined them in the yard. 'And if you'd lived through a war as I had, young man, you would know that some people do exactly that. Anna, for example.'

A loud crash from the doorway of the house made them all jump. Anna had dropped the tray carrying the mint tea. Teapot, cups, saucers and sugar bowl lay smashed on the ground in a welter of broken china, hot water and scattered leaves.

Ned rushed over and helped her pile the broken crockery back on to the tray.

'I forbid you to talk to this woman,' Anna said sharply to Helena.

'What did I ever do to you, Anna, to make you so angry with me, even after all these years?' the woman said.

'You know what people around here think of you,' Anna replied.

'Considering what happened to me after the war, how could I forget?' The woman calmly pulled out a stool and sat down.

'I couldn't believe it when I saw you standing in the churchyard. I never thought you'd find the courage to come here again, not after all the trouble after the war.' Anna snatched the tray from Ned.

'The trouble after the war was none of my making, Anna.'

'What do you want here?'

'To talk to Magda's daughter.' She smiled at Helena. 'I knew you when you were a toddler. But I doubt you remember me, child.'

'I don't,' Helena said in bewilderment.

'You can have nothing to say to Helena or Ned John,' Anna declared.

'Oh, but I do, Anna. Private things that were known only to Magda and me.'

'Made-up things,' Anna taunted.

'Not lies, Anna.' The woman kept her voice low and even. 'Some people like to keep all the doings in this village secret, but I hear things, even in town. And when someone told me that Magdalena Janek had died and her daughter had brought her ashes back to the village to be buried with Adam, I wanted to pay my respects. Magda was a good friend to me. At one time, my only friend. I knew some people in the village wouldn't want me here, but I have as much right as anyone to mourn her, if not more.'

'That doesn't mean that you are welcome in my house.' Anna gripped the tray so hard her knuckles turned white.

'This is a public bar.'

'Not this courtyard. It is part of my house. And the bar is men only.'

'I don't need to be reminded that this house is now yours or that the bar is men only.' The woman opened her handbag and took out a pack of cigarettes.

'What's going on?' Ned asked, regretting his lack of Polish more than ever.

Helena ignored him. 'If you knew my mother, I would like to talk to you,' she said, taking advantage of the silence that had fallen between the two women.

'I knew your mother, child. And if you want to talk to me, then we'll talk.' She glanced at Anna as though daring her to object. 'But perhaps not here.'

'*I* will talk to you first. Privately.' Anna carried the tray back into the house, and the woman followed her.

'Helena—'

'Quiet, Ned. They could return at any moment.'

They waited in silence for the women to re-emerge. It was the longest ten minutes of Helena's life. She hadn't known what to expect, but Anna was tight-lipped when she returned to the yard.

'You can talk to this woman, but not in the courtyard,' Anna announced. 'Take her up to your room. No one can see her there. And you?' she glared at the visitor. 'You will remember what I said.'

'I will Anna.'

Ned carried the two comfortable chairs in their room out on to the landing. He gave one to the woman, the other to Helena, and sat on the doorstep between them.

'Your English is very good,' he complimented the visitor, who had still made no attempt to introduce herself.

'Like Magda, I was a slave labourer in Germany during the war. Afterwards I worked as a Russian-Polish-German interpreter. I couldn't speak English when the war ended but I soon learned. The Americans and the British had more black market goods to offer than any of the other Allied soldiers.'

Anna walked up the stairs with another tray of tea. She set it on the floor next to Helena's chair.

'That is for Helena,' she said. 'She needs a hot drink.'

'I can see that she has hurt herself,' the visitor replied in Polish.

'She didn't hurt herself; Wiktor Niklas hit her.'

'Then he hasn't changed.'

'If by that you mean he still drinks, he does.'

'Won't you sit with us, Anna?' the woman asked.

'I have a bar to run.' But Anna hesitated.

'As I said, I can only talk about how Magda and I were sent into Germany to work.'

'You call what you did work?' Anna sneered.

'What Anna doesn't want me to tell you,' the visitor said to Helena, 'is the *kind* of work the Germans made me do during the war.' She watched Anna intently. 'Magda and I were marched out of this village together and shipped out of Poland to Germany on the same train, but we ended up in different places. I was sent to an army brothel—'

'And my mother?' Helena began to tremble. Whatever her mother had done during the war she'd had no choice. She was certain of that much.

'Was sent to work in a children's home.'

'You're sure?' Helena weakened in relief.

'Absolutely certain. I was in the Displaced Persons' camp at the end of the war when the Americans brought in your mother, together with half a dozen other women and eighty children they'd found in the home.'

'I'm sorry, I interrupted you,' Helena apologized.

'It's understandable if Magda didn't tell you much about what had happened to her during the war.' The woman continued to watch Anna, who was lingering at the top of the stairs.

'She told me hardly anything. Whenever she talked about the past it was usually about the good times here, in this village.'

'The good times.' The woman shook her head sadly.

'I'm sorry, you must have suffered dreadfully during the war,' Helena said sympathetically.

'And not just during the war,' the woman answered. 'When I saw what kind of place the Germans had put me in I tried to fight. For that, I was beaten and starved. After a month of fighting – and starving – I learned to do as I was told because I wanted to survive.

After the war I lived in a Displaced Persons' camp for six months because I had no papers and no relatives left in Poland who would vouch for my identity. My *friends* didn't even answer the letters I sent them. I wouldn't be here now if one of my High School teachers who'd fought with the Free Polish Army hadn't recognized me. He organized papers, so I could return here, to my home village. I had hoped to be welcomed. But someone knew where I had been and how I had been used. My friends and such family as I had left – not blood relations – thought that I would have been better dead than disgraced.' She paused. 'So-called friends slammed their doors in my face. I left and went into town. People there were kinder. I was able to find a job and a room.'

'I didn't refuse to allow you into this house,' Anna protested.

'Then we have different memories, Anna. You told me there was no room here for me.'

'There wasn't.'

'Not even a space on the floor where I could have slept on a blanket?' The landlady didn't answer. 'When I was driven out of this village, you didn't lift a finger to help me, Anna.'

'Weronika—'

'Now that you have told these two young people my Christian name, would you like to tell them my surname?' She looked at Helena. 'I am Weronika Janek. Adam Janek was my brother. Magda, Anna and I were close friends – once.' Then she repeated it in English, for Ned's benefit.

Anna looked at Weronika for a moment before turning and walking down the stairs. Weronika's use of the past tense wasn't lost on anyone.

221

Chapter 15

THE METAL 'SAVERS' on Anna's shoes rang on the wooden treads of the staircase. Helena followed the sound of her footfalls as she crossed to the back door of the bar, and started when she slammed it shut behind her.

Weronika sat back in her chair, tapped a cigarette from the pack she was holding, then held it up. 'Do you mind?' she said in English.

'No, please go ahead.' Helena took the tea Ned had poured for her, grateful that he hadn't pressed her for a translation of the conversation.

He handed a cup to Weronika, but she waved it aside. 'No, thank you. Anna would choke if she knew that I was drinking her tea.'

'I didn't know Adam Janek had a sister. My mother never mentioned you,' Helena said.

'She made a new life for herself, so she had no reason to tell you about me. We can't always be looking to the past. And I came here to talk about Magda, not myself.' She took a lighter from her handbag and lit her cigarette. 'As you are here, Magda obviously told you about this village. Did she also tell you about the massacre?'

'Yes. And I have seen the memorial to the people who were killed. Mama told me that I was Adam Janek's daughter. But after seeing the inscription to Helena Janek on his grave I now know that he couldn't have been my father. What I don't know is who my father was, or why my mother gave me the identity of her dead daughter.'

Weronika gave her a sad smile. 'I wish you were the first Helena Janek. It would be wonderful to have one relative alive in the world, especially a niece. Adam and I were very close. There was only fifteen months between us.'

'Were you younger or older than him?'

'Younger. He was the best big brother anyone could have had.' Weronika smiled at a happy memory, which she didn't share. 'I wrote to Magda after I left the Displaced Persons' camp and returned here. She replied to my letters until she left for Britain to marry Bobby Parsons. I only received one letter from her afterwards. It was about three years later. She said that you were both doing well. She told me that she was managing a shop and had been able to rent a fine apartment from her employer. She also said that the schooling and opportunities for you were good. I hoped that she'd continued to do well for herself. I was fond of my sister-in-law and would have liked to have kept in touch with her. But she simply stopped answering my letters.' She flicked the ash from her cigarette into the ashtray Ned had fetched from the room. 'I think there were too many unhappy memories between us for her to want to keep in contact.'

'You're not the only one who hasn't any relatives. And it's hard to accept that I'm not Adam Janek's daughter after believing it for so long.' Helena's hand shook as she lifted the teacup to her lips, and Ned knew that cold logic and hard fact hadn't entirely persuaded her to relinquish the father her mother had given her.

'I thought Magda would go crazy with grief after seeing Adam and Helena killed. But instead of being moved by your mother's tears, the soldiers beat her and me, forced us into the line of people they had chosen, then marched us out. On the road we met people who had been taken from other villages. There were a lot of young men and women our age. I suppose I might have been thought pretty at the time.' There wasn't a hint of boastfulness in the remark, only an underlying sadness.

'Mama told me that it took two days for you to walk to the railway station in the town.'

'It did, and your mother was in agony. We all thought that she was dying. She couldn't move her arm, she was dizzy, sick, and her head was bleeding. When she complained of headaches to the doctor in the Displaced Persons' camp, he told her that it was because her skull had been fractured. I think it probably happened when the soldiers beat her at the time they took us, although Magda told me that she was often whipped after we were separated.'

223

Helena dug her nails into the palm of her hand to stop herself from crying. She simply couldn't bear the thought of her mother defenceless and mistreated.

'We slept in ditches at the side of the road the first night, and the station platform the second, before being loaded on to cattle wagons. We weren't given any food or water. All we'd had to drink was what we'd been able to scavenge from puddles. The children were screaming—'

'Children?' Ned interrupted. 'You had children with you?'

Weronika looked at Ned in surprise. 'Didn't you know? That's why they took Magda. The Nazis saw the damp patches on her blouse, realized she'd been breast-feeding Helena, and made her feed the younger babies on the journey. Not that she refused. It was hard enough to march without suffering from engorged breasts and milk fever. She told me after the war that they sent her on to a children's home and used her as a wet-nurse.'

'A wet-nurse?' Helena repeated in bewilderment. 'I can understand the Germans taking people for slave labour, but why would they take children?'

'We didn't know, not then. But no blonde, blue-eyed child was safe from the Nazis. Women in brown uniforms used to travel around the towns and villages. The Germans called them the Brown Sisters, but there was nothing sisterly about them. Sometimes, when soldiers came into a village, like they did here on the day of the massacre, the Brown Sisters would come with them. They would wait while the soldiers assembled the people, then they would examine the children and take the fair-haired ones.'

'And the parents?' Ned asked, horrified by the thought of such wholesale kidnapping.

'If they objected, they were shot, as Adam was when he refused to hand over Helena. His daughter followed him in looks. He was fair-haired and fair-skinned, unlike Magda.'

'So you were the second fair-haired child your mother gave birth to,' Ned commented, in an effort to reassure Helena that Magda had been her mother.

'But why did the Nazis take Polish children?' Helena persisted.

'For Himmler's Lebensborn project.' Josef climbed the stairs and joined them. 'Anna sent me to ask if you want anything.'

'You mean she sent you here to spy on us and listen to what I'm telling Helena.' Weronika corrected. 'You are Josef Dobrow?'

'Yes.'

'I knew your mother.'

'You also know Anna and her penchant for wanting to know everyone's business.' Not in the least embarrassed at being found out, Josef sat on the top step.

'Anna told you about me?' Weronika asked Josef.

'Yes. I am pleased to meet you and sorry for the reception you received here at the end of the war.'

'And you were how old?'

'Six.'

'I forgive you for not championing me.'

'Lebensborn?' Ned said thoughtfully. 'Life fountain – spring of life?'

'You haven't heard of it?' Josef looked incredulous.

'No,' Ned replied frankly.

'As your country won the war, I thought you would have. There were many articles printed about it in the newspapers here after the war. But Poland was badly affected by what happened. And not just Poland. Norway, France, the Ukraine – all the countries the Germans occupied. Himmler established the Lebensborn Foundation to safeguard, promote and protect what he called pure German blood.'

'The mythical blond, blue-eyed Aryan, the master race,' Ned mused.

'I researched the project,' Josef explained. 'Initially, all Himmler did was set up luxury maternity hospitals for SS officers' wives. Later, he opened children's homes for the illegitimate offspring of the SS. If the mother or father didn't want them after they were born, they were put up for adoption by Party members, or brought up in one of the Lebensborn boarding schools or orphanages.

'But the project didn't result in as many children as Himmler wanted, so he ordered the kidnap of "Aryan" children from countries occupied by the Nazis. He decreed that fair-haired children were

225

throwbacks to their German ancestors who had been driven from their lands. The children were examined by Lebensborn doctors. If their Aryan credentials were medically established, they were given to Nazi Party members to bring up, or sent to Lebensborn institutions where they were trained to become active and useful Party members.

'I discovered the kidnapped children were first taken to holding centres where they were examined by Nazi doctors. Their skulls, noses and bones were measured, to ensure they complied with the Aryan ideal. Their eyes were tested for colour – blue and green being the two most acceptable. Then, if they passed all the tests, they were sent to the Lebensborn homes. There, the older ones were taught German and Nazi doctrine before being placed in boarding schools or offered for adoption. The babies who were too young to know what was going on were passed on right away. The original identities of all the kidnapped children in the project were erased before they were given to their new families, so they became German in every way.'

'Were there any children who didn't pass the racial tests?' Ned asked.

'Our government believes thousands, but as there are so few records, and the ones that do exist have been doctored, it's impossible to verify the actual number,' Josef divulged.

'They were returned to their parents?' Helena said hopefully.

'They were sent to concentration camps. There are eye-witness accounts of hundreds of them being gassed on arrival.' Josef spoke as though he were quoting from a textbook, but his eyes betrayed his pain.

'And after the war?' Ned asked. 'Were the ones who had been adopted returned?'

'A few,' Josef answered. 'Perhaps twenty thousand out of those who were taken. No one is really sure of the numbers. The government estimates that three hundred thousand children were taken. But as so many came from villages where all the adults were killed and the buildings burned to the ground, it's impossible to tell.'

'That doesn't make it any less of a tragedy for every family who lost a child.' Weronika stubbed out her cigarette in the ashtray. 'The ones that found their way back to Poland after the war were mainly the older children. There were a few in the Displaced Persons' camp with Magda and me. The Nazis stole children up to fifteen years of age if they thought they possessed the right mix of Aryan blood.'

'But there must be records . . .' Helena began.

'I told you, the children's original identities were erased.' Josef was uncharacteristically abrupt. 'If they were babies when they were taken, they would look on their adoptive parents as their own. If they were old enough to have memories of their real families, they were told that their parents had died or abandoned them.'

Weronika took another cigarette from the pack. 'One of the boys in the camp was twelve when he was taken from his mother. When he refused to memorize his new name or speak German, he was beaten and sent to a labour camp. I am surprised Magda didn't tell you any of this.'

'She never mentioned it.' Helena returned her cup to the tray.

'She didn't tell you the Germans had made her work in a Lebensborn home?'

'No.' Helena shook her head.

'It *was* a Lebensborn home?' Josef checked.

'A big one outside Munich,' Weronika said. 'Most of the staff fled when the Americans drew close. Magda and some of the other women who worked there didn't fear the Allies, and they absolutely refused to leave the children, so they stayed. When the Americans liberated the home, there were about 300 children there, aged from six months to six years old. But that was just one home. The babies were sent to orphanages, the older ones to the camp with Magda and the other women.'

'The British and the Russians found others.' Josef leaned back against the outside wall of the house. 'But before they reached them, the Germans burned what few records of the children's origins they'd made.'

'You seem to know a lot about these homes,' Ned commented.

'I've made it my business to study them,' Josef said.

'I can guess why. You never found him?' Weronika lit her cigarette.

Josef shook his head. 'No, I didn't. Did you or Magdalena Janek see him on the journey?'

'He was still on the train when I was taken off it with most of the other girls.'

'And Magda?'

'Was ordered to stay on the train with the children.'

Helena and Ned listened intently, trying to follow the conversation.

'Did Magda ever mention him when you met up with her at the end of the war?'

'She talked about three of the children who had been taken from this village.'

'They stayed with Magda.'

'Yes,' Weronika confirmed. 'Magda said she saw them in the home she worked in, but only for the first few months. Then they were taken away for adoption. They never returned.'

'You have been looking for someone who was taken that day?' Helena asked Josef.

'My brother, Leon. He was six months old.' Josef turned to Weronika. 'Was he one of the babies Magda saw in the home?'

Weronika shook her head. 'If he was, Josef, she never mentioned his name, but then she wouldn't have called him by his Polish name if he had been in the home for any length of time. She, like the children, would have been punished for clinging to the past and her language.'

'So much tragedy,' Ned murmured when Josef left them to return to the bar.

'Sad times, sad country,' Weronika agreed. She glanced at her watch. 'A friend had business this way. He brought me here and arranged to pick me up in the square. I mustn't keep him waiting.'

'Do you have to go right away?' Helena looked at Ned. 'The photographs . . .'

'I'll get them.' He disappeared into the room and returned with Helena's box.

'You brought photographs of your mother?'

'And one that was taken on her wedding day to your brother.'

'I remember seeing it.' Weronika took the frame Ned handed her and gently stroked her brother's outline. 'Adam looks so young, so handsome ...'

'Is there a shop here that will make a copy, so you can have one?' Helena asked.

'Here?' Weronika laughed too loudly as she wiped a tear from her eyes. 'No. Perhaps in Warsaw or Cracow.'

'If we can't have a copy made here, I will get someone to do it in Pontypridd and send one to you,' Helena promised.

'Thank you. I will pay for it.'

'No, please. It would be my pleasure. You were kind enough to come here and see me.' Helena paused. 'You said that you met my mother again after the war in the camp?'

'Yes.'

'And I was with her.'

'Obviously. You were a sweet little thing.'

'Did she tell you that I was her child?'

'No, because I knew that you couldn't be. Helena's birth was a difficult one, and the doctor warned Adam that Helena would be Magdalena's first and last child.'

'Did you just tell her, Weronika?' Anna was on the stairs, a bundle of clean towels in her arms, her eyes flickering between them.

'She has a right to know the truth, Anna,' Weronika said, switching to Polish.

'I hoped you'd see sense.'

A peculiar buzzing filled Helena's head. She saw Anna and Weronika's lips move, sensed Ned crouching beside her, his face full of concern and love.

But who was the girl he loved?

'Since we arrived here a couple of days ago, Helena has discovered the man she always thought was her father wasn't. This morning the man she assumed was her uncle physically attacked her, and now you tell her that the woman who brought her up wasn't her mother. I wish we had never come to Poland!' Driven by the devastating effect of Weronika's revelation on Helena, Ned lost his temper.

'Stop it, Ned,' Helena pleaded. 'Now I know this much, I have to find out the truth.'

Weronika poured another cup of tea for Helena, and handed it to Ned to give to her. 'I am sorry I upset you, Helena. But I believe that everyone has the right to know who their parents were and where they came from.'

'What right have you to tell Helena things Magda chose to keep from her,' Anna demanded bitterly, reverting to Polish. 'Magda must have loved Helena to keep her through the war and afterwards. To take her to Britain—'

'Magda couldn't have loved Helena more if she had been her natural daughter, Anna,' Weronika interrupted. 'I saw just how much Magda loved Helena in the camp. Enough to die for her if need be. Although I did wonder why Magda had given you the name Helena Weronika Janek,' she said to Helena in English. 'That poor mite had so little in life. I thought the least Magda could have done was allow her to keep her own name. But then, if Magda hadn't used Helena's name she would have had trouble getting you papers.'

Anna sat heavily on the top stair, and gazed down into the courtyard.

'Did everyone in the camp know I wasn't Magda's daughter? The other women from the orphanage? Bob Parsons?'

'I think everyone else assumed that you were Magda's child. The women and children who had been in the children's home with Magda might have known differently, but if they did, no one mentioned it.' Weronika frowned with the effort of remembering. 'You were so small, so tiny and so close to Magda. In the camp it was as though the two of you were one. You slept in the same bunk, and I swear I saw Magda soothing you in the night before you even cried out. She would have done anything for you, anything at all. Everyone there had lost everything they owned, but Magda would work day and night, doing all sorts of menial work in exchange for a few balls of wool or a piece of cloth to make you a dress. And you were so bright, so cheerful, so chatty. You gave every one of us hope for the future.'

'Did she tell you where she found me?' It had taken all the

courage Helena possessed to ask that question, and she was terrified of hearing what the answer might be.

'I never asked. I simply assumed that you had been given into her care in the home.'

'You never once talked about it?'

'There were many things that we avoided talking about. Things we were ashamed of, although none were our fault. The camp seems a long time and another world away. I think that if I considered you at all, I probably thought Magda had lost a child in her beloved Helena and found another. Not to replace her daughter, because, from what I have seen of mothers, I don't think it's possible to replace a lost or dead child with another. But you gave Magda a reason to go on living.'

'You never considered the feelings of my real mother and father?'

'Germany in the spring of 1945 was awash with orphans. You were lucky to have Magda.'

'How many children did they take from this village?' Ned asked.

'A dozen. All under two years old. One died in the cattle truck that took us to Germany.'

'How many returned?' Helena didn't know why she was asking.

Weronika said, 'That is easy to answer. None. And I was the only woman.'

'Is there anything else that you can tell me about Mama ... Magda?'

Weronika turned to Anna, who was backing down the stairs. 'Unfortunately not. But Anna was Magda's friend, too. She may be able to tell you more.' She glanced at her watch again and picked up her handbag. 'I will give you my address.' She took a cheap biro and small notebook from her bag, and wrote on a page before tearing it out. 'That is the address of my flat and also the shop where I work. The telephone number is the shop's. But there are no telephones in this village. If you want to phone me you will have to go to the post office in the next village, which is seven kilometres away.'

'So we have discovered.' Ned had already tried, and failed, to book a call to his father.

231

Weronika left the chair. She went to hand the photograph back to Ned, then looked at it again, holding on to it for a moment.

'I will send you a copy,' Helena promised.

'I know you will. And it was good to see you again, Helena, although I would never have recognized you if I hadn't been told who you were.'

Helena rose to her feet and embraced her.

'We'll walk you to the square,' Ned offered.

'There is no need.'

'Please. I would like some fresh air and the walk will do me good.' Helena touched the cotton wool Ned had taped over the cut above her ear. It still stung but it wasn't as painful as it had been. 'You said that you lived in a house here in the village, Weronika. Did my . . . Magda ever live there?'

They began to descend the staircase.

'Yes, with Adam and me. Our parents and brothers and sisters died in a diphtheria epidemic before the war.'

'Is the house still standing?'

'Oh, yes.'

'Could you take us to it?' Ned asked when they reached the courtyard.

'You're standing in it. When the Communists closed the church and the priest's house at the end of the war, the priest moved in here.'

Helena recalled Josef telling her that his foster-father had moved into an empty house at the end of the war. 'This was the Janek house?'

'One of them. Anna's father, mother and sisters used to live in a room above the bar,' Weronika said loudly in Polish, so Anna who was feeding the chickens could hear her. 'But it's more comfortable in the house, wouldn't you say, Anna?'

The landlady chose to ignore her.

'So, you owned it?' Helena asked.

'Communists don't recognize personal property. Besides, when you get to my age, you realize that all you'll ever own is the pit you are buried in. And most people even have to share that.'

'You sound like an old woman, yet you can't be much older than my mother was.' Helena took Weronika's arm.

'If you measure my years, I'm not much over forty, but in terms of what I have seen and done, I am centuries old, child.' She looked at Helena and laughed. 'Don't look so tragic. Life is a joke. And if you're coming with me, come. I don't want to keep my friend waiting.'

Helena was aware of the villagers, particularly the older ones, watching from their windows, as she, Ned and Weronika strolled up the lane towards the square. One man opened his front door and stood on the step, glaring at Weronika, which made Helena think that he had been waiting for her to pass. Weronika calmly nodded to him. He spat after her, missing her shoes by barely an inch. Ned turned around, but Weronika touched his arm.

'Don't, he's not worth it.' She spoke first in English, then more loudly in Polish so the man would hear.

Helena looked at her in admiration. 'I'm not sure I could be so forgiving after what they did to you after the war.'

Weronika shrugged. 'I knew what I was letting myself in for when I came to pay my respects to Magda.'

'But you have done nothing wrong!' Helena exclaimed.

'During the German Occupation there were mothers who poisoned their daughters rather than allow the Nazis to take them. Some people believe that the girls who were sent into forced labour and survived, like me, should have killed ourselves or been killed on our return. The people who suffered the least were always the first to tell us we had no right to live. But there were times when I wondered if they were right. I have been tempted to take my own life many times, especially when I remembered what the Nazis did to Adam and little Helena. And how I stood by and watched.'

'The only time Mama . . . Magda talked to me about the massacre, she said that she'd thought about killing herself, too. But if she had, it would have been allowing the Nazis to win.' What Helena hadn't said was that Magda had insisted that she had to live to look after her daughter. And it hurt now, knowing that couldn't possibly be true.

233

'It must be agonizing for you to know that neither Magda nor my brother was your parent, Helena,' Weronika said. 'I can't even begin to imagine the pain you are suffering. But console yourself with the thought that Magda loved you very much. And if she didn't tell you anything about your real parents it was either because she didn't know who they were, or she wanted to spare you. Given the way that the Lebensborn homes were run and the children's original records destroyed, I think it far more likely that she didn't know.'

'You believe that?'

'Yes.' Weronika looked at her challengingly. 'Did she make a good life for herself and for you?'

'I think she was as happy as she could be,' Helena replied. 'Although, looking back, I can see now that she suffered from homesickness.'

'I was afraid of that. I feel responsible for Magda going to Britain. As soon as I received my papers I returned here. After the villagers drove me out I wrote to Magda at the camp to warn her what she could expect if she came back with you.'

'I wouldn't have been accepted?' Helena stopped walking.

'A blonde, blue-eyed Lebensborn child? No, you wouldn't have been accepted. It was hard here after the war. People like Wiktor Niklas would have resented every mouthful of food Magda gave you, for all that she was his sister. I rather suspect the villagers would have made both your lives even more unbearable than they made mine.'

'When Magda wrote to tell you that she was going to Britain, did she say she loved Bobby Parsons?' Helena asked.

'No. I knew that she didn't. Although he was besotted with her.'

'How do you know she didn't love him?' Even now, Helena couldn't blame her mother for re-writing her early years as a fairy tale, or retreating into fiction; it was kinder than the unbearable truth of the years she had spent as a prisoner of the Germans.

'Because I had seen your mother in love. She and my brother lived for one another. Even as children it was obvious they were meant to be together. They never so much as looked at anyone else.'

'Mama always said that their wedding day was the happiest of her life.'

'Adam's too.' Weronika's face lit up, making Helena think of sunshine illuminating a frost-covered landscape. But her smile faded when she looked around the deserted square. Weronika glanced at her watch again. 'I have time to take a last look at my brother's grave. And it will be a last look. I won't come here again.'

'Do you mind if I . . .' Helena glanced at Ned. '*We* come with you?'

'Not at all. After all, it is also the last resting place of the woman who was your mother in every way that mattered.'

Ned opened the gate to the churchyard and replaced the chain after Helena and Weronika had walked through it. A shrivelled old woman, draped in voluminous black, was crouched over a grave, scrubbing a memorial stone with a brush. As she worked she talked, judging by the conversational tone, to the person in the grave. Helena made a detour to give her privacy.

'I wonder if our dead can hear us.' Weronika said as they headed for the back of the church and the Janek plot.

'Everyone would like to know the answer to that question, but I've always thought that even if they can't, the living wouldn't want to believe it.' Ned stopped when they reached Adam Janek's memorial stone.

Weronika looked at her brother's grave. It had been tidied up after Wiktor had filled it in. The loose dirt had been swept up and the ostentatious wreath of artificial roses moved to the side of the stone cross.

'My mother . . . Magda hated artificial flowers. She thought they were in bad taste,' Helena commented. 'She liked single rosebuds. She used to say, "One is—"'

'"Perfection. Take time to study it, because to cut any more than one from the bush would be greedy and deprive other people of the pleasure of seeing its beauty."' Weronika finished for her.

'It's strange to think that you knew her as well as me.'

'The Magda I like to remember was not the woman I met in the camp at the end of the war, but a happy young girl, who loved music, dancing, cooking and single rosebuds.'

235

'We had a vase at home that she kept on the sideboard below her wedding photograph. She used to buy a rose from the flower-seller at the local market every week when they were in season.'

'You didn't have a garden?' Weronika asked.

'No.'

'We used to grow roses in pots on the veranda in front of the barn. Magda always kept one in a silver vase next to a photograph of my parents.'

'The first piece of silver I remember my mother buying was a rose vase.' Helena watched Weronika lift Wiktor's wreath from the earth.

'Allow me.' Ned took the wreath from her and moved it out of sight behind the headstone.

'Magda had exquisite taste, unlike her thieving brother.' Weronika opened her handbag and took out a roll of cardboard. She upended it and shook out a single red rose. 'If Wiktor knew we'd moved that monstrosity, Ned, he'd punch me first, then you. But he'll never find out. He wouldn't dream of coming here to pay his respects now the public show is over.' Weronika laid the rose in front of the memorial, stood in front of it for a few minutes then crossed herself. 'Goodbye, Adam. Goodbye, Magda. Be at peace together.'

'I hope they are,' Helena whispered.

'Adam was a good brother to me and Magda a good sister.' Weronika ran her fingers over the letters carved into the stone. 'It's heart-breaking to see their names here when I remember them in childish writing on their drawings and school exercise books. When they married, they were so in love and wrapped up in one another I thought I'd feel awkward living with them. But they never made me feel in the way. But it couldn't have lasted, even without the war.'

'Why not?' Helena ventured.

'Because I would have married, and moved out of the family house.'

'You were planning to marry?'

'To a doctor. But the leaders of our communities – the doctors, lawyers and teachers – were the first people the Gestapo rounded up and shot. They were buried in mass graves. I never found out where they took him. Only that he didn't return. I don't even have a place to pray for him.'

Weronika took one last look at the memorial with its single rosebud. 'I am tempted to place that wreath in the bin. But then, trust Wiktor. After robbing Adam and Magda blind, he has the gall to spend their money upon a wreath both of them would have hated.' She led the way back around the side of the church.

'My uncle robbed Magda and Adam?' Helena asked in amazement.

'When I returned, I asked Anna for my clothes, personal things, and the photographs and mementoes that had belonged to my family. She told me that Wiktor ransacked the house the day after the massacre and moved all the valuables and furniture to the Niklas farm. He led the campaign to keep me out of the village. Perhaps he was afraid that if I stayed I would want the Janek family possessions. But we weren't the only people he stole from. There were many empty houses here after the war.'

'That's what Josef told me.' Helena opened the gate.

'You said there were other women who worked with Magda in the children's home. Were they also sent to the Displaced Persons' camp at the end of the war?' Always analytical, Ned had been mulling over everything that Weronika had told them.

'Yes. The Americans brought them in by truck.'

'Did you keep in touch with any of them?' Ned fastened the gate.

'No.'

'Why not?' Ned walked Weronika and Helena to the war memorial.

'We got on well enough together, but we had seen so many horrible things that all we wanted to do was return to our homes, forget the horrors of war and pick up the threads of our lives. Or in my case, start living a new one.'

'Is there anyone we can talk to who was in the home with Magda? Who might have known anything about Helena or her real parents?'

'So that is why you're asking,' Weronika said slowly. 'About six or seven women came into the camp from the children's home with Magda but only two were Polish. I think the others were Latvians.'

'Can you remember the names of the Polish girls?' Ned pressed.

'One was called Irena, another Marta, but if I ever knew their surnames I have forgotten them.'

'Did they say what part of Poland they were from?' Ned urged.

'Cracow and Lublin. Adam and I had often visited our cousin who lived in Cracow, it was where your mother bought the silk for her wedding gown,' Weronika informed Helena.

'She told me.'

'Irena – who was from Cracow, Magda and I used to reminisce about the city. We talked for hours about the shops and planned expeditions to buy clothes, useless clothes like silk, satin and organza evening gowns, gold jewellery, high-heeled slippers and furs – and food. Such wonderful food!' She laughed. 'You can have all the caviar, champagne, fried chicken, asparagus and rich cream cakes you want when you're shopping with your imagination.'

'Was a register made of Polish people who were sent into the Reich as slave labourers?' Ned asked.

'I don't know. Girls who were taken and used like me would want as few people as possible to know what had happened to them so they would never sign any official papers. As I told you, all most of us wanted to do at the end of the war was forget about it – not that we could.'

'What about the children?' Helena asked hopefully. 'Perhaps one of the older ones would remember me? They might have seen Magda with me . . .'

'If they did they would hardly have thought it surprising. Magda worked there, she would have always had children with her. I doubt anyone would have noticed that she had one with her any more often than another. And all the children in the home would have been blond and blue-eyed.'

Weronika looked up as a car drove into the square. 'And here is my friend.'

Norbert's red Syrena drew up in front of them. A well-dressed elderly man was sitting in the back of the car. Norbert opened the door, climbed out and held out his hand to Weronika to help her into the back.

Weronika didn't introduce her friend. Turning back to Helena, she held out her hand, then dropped it and embraced her. 'It was good to meet you, my almost-niece and the nearest person I have left to a relative. You have my address safe.'

'I do.' Helena returned Weronika's hug and kissed her cheek.

Ned shook her hand. 'Perhaps you will come and visit us some-day, Weronika.'

'In England?'

'Wales. It's part of Britain – like Ireland and Scotland.'

'Thank you. I will,' Weronika answered. 'When I am old and drawing my pension. The government won't allow me to leave before. But I don't have so long to wait. Another twenty years or so.'

Norbert settled Weronika in the back of the car before replacing the seat. 'I heard that you managed to bury your mother's ashes,' he said to Helena.

'Yes,' Helena said briefly, not wanting to elaborate.

'You still have the telephone number I gave you?'

'I do.' Ned patted his pocket.

Norbert glanced at his passengers. 'I must go. But I'll see you soon?'

'When we leave,' Helena assured him.

'But only if your price is right,' Ned called after him.

Chapter 16

HELENA AND NED watched Norbert drive off. When the car rounded the corner of the square, Helena waved goodbye and Weronika blew back a kiss. Ned rested his hand around Helena's waist. For once she didn't shrug it off.

'I'll talk to Josef again about the Polish children who were kidnapped by the Germans,' Helena turned towards the narrow street that led to the bar. 'From what he said, he seems to have done a great deal of research while he's been looking for his brother.'

Ned watched as the dust stirred by the car began to settle. 'By all means talk to him, but given the number of children who were kidnapped and the various countries they were taken from, I doubt you will find any answers as to who your birth parents were.'

'I have to start looking for them. They could be looking for me.'

'And they could be anywhere.'

'I have to try and find them.'

'You were taken in wartime. They could have been killed. In fact, that might be why Magda looked after you. Because she knew that your parents were dead. The more I consider it, the more I think that's the most likely scenario.' He pulled her even closer to him. 'If they had lived, she would have told you about them.'

'Unless I was just one more child who came into the Lebensborn home with her birth identity erased. Magda may well have known nothing about my life before I was given into her care, in which case I'll never know who I am.'

'But I know *exactly* who you are: Helena soon-to-be-John, the girl I love and want to marry. Can't you be content with knowing that much about yourself?'

'It isn't enough.'

Much as Ned was reluctant, he felt he had to put the question to her. 'And if you discover something you can't live with?'

'It's not a question of not being able to live with whatever I find out about myself, because there's simply no alternative. I *have* to try to find out who I am. The truth can't possibly be any worse than what I'm imagining right now.'

'Which is?'

'That I'm the result of some bizarre breeding programme. Or that my mother was an innocent young Pole who was raped by an SS officer.'

'Helena, you can't spend the rest of your life roaming around Europe searching for people who lost a child during the war. There are hundreds of thousands of families who lost children in one way or another.'

'I can try,' she countered stubbornly.

'Sunshine, please—'

'I'm trying to look at this sensibly and logically.'

'Then allow me to say something sensible and logical. For whatever reason, Magda decided to tell you that you were her and Adam Janek's daughter.'

'Her motive was obvious,' Helena snapped. 'She wanted to give me a respectable background.'

'And also because she also wanted you to be happy and feel secure. We might never find out where she picked you up, or who your parents were, but you could waste a lifetime on a futile search.'

'It's my lifetime to waste.'

'It's my lifetime, too.'

Her face was serious when she looked up at him. 'I'd rather know something dreadful about myself than not know anything at all.'

Anna was sitting at the table in the courtyard, a glass and a pitcher of home-made lemonade in front of her when Ned and Helena returned.

'We went to the churchyard so Weronika could pay her final respects to her brother and Magda,' Helena explained.

'Did she tell you any more lies after you left here?'

Helena struggled to keep her voice even. 'None.'

'You can't trust that one. Everyone knows what she is.'

'A woman who was enslaved by the Germans, as was my mother.' Helena spoke quietly but firmly.

'You've done what you came to do. You've buried Magdalena's ashes with Adam Janek. You can sleep here tonight, but tomorrow you go.'

'And if we can't get to the town?' Helena asked.

'That's your problem.' Anna staggered as she made her way into the house, and Helena realized she was drunk. She returned with two clean glasses, left them next to the pitcher, and stumbled into the bar without saying another word.

Josef emerged a few minutes later with a crate of empty bottles, and overheard Helena translating what Anna had said to Ned.

'Anna is not very good with strangers,' he said awkwardly. He dumped the crate on the veranda in front of the barn, and glanced at the table. 'That lemonade looks good. I'll get a glass and join you. I'm due a break.' He went into the house and returned with a glass.

Helena and Ned sat opposite him at the table.

'We'd like to talk to you——' Helena began.

'I'll have a word with Anna about letting you stay longer, but I can't promise anything.' Josef filled his glass and passed the jug to Helena.

'Thank you.' Helena poured lemonade for herself and Ned. 'But I didn't want to talk to you about Anna. Do you know if there is a register of children who were kidnapped by the Nazis for the Lebensborn project?'

'Register sounds very grand. There are lists of parents who are looking for their children. They have given their sons' and daughters' original names — which isn't much good when the children were taught to forget them; that's if they were old enough to remember who they were in the first place — their ages when they were taken, the places they were taken from, their ages now, and their dates of birth, which the Nazis frequently changed. There are photographs and descriptions of the children as they were when kidnapped. But I doubt anyone will recognize young men and women from their baby pictures. There is also a very much shorter list made by children who can remember being taken. They have given what information they can recall of their original family and left current photographs. But for every Lebensborn child who knows they are adopted, there are hundreds if not thousands who don't. And some that do are still in Germany with their adoptive parents simply because they had nowhere else to go after the war.'

'East Germany?' Ned asked.

'East and West. The register covers all the children that the Nazis kidnapped in the Reich and occupied territories.'

'Would it be possible to track down the children who went with Magda to the Displaced Persons' camp from the children's home?' Ned persisted. 'Weronika said there were eighty of them.'

'Some as young as six months old,' Josef reminded.

'And some as old as six. A six-year-child might remember seeing my mother with a baby.'

'As a wet nurse it was Magda's job to look after the babies, Helena,' Josef interrupted. 'They probably wouldn't have noticed which baby she was looking after at any one time. And the children weren't kept in the homes for long. The purpose of Lebensborn was to Germanize them so they could be brought up by Nazi families. The older ones, who were more difficult to place, were sent to special boarding schools, but most of the babies and toddlers selected for Lebensborn were passed on after a few weeks in the homes, sometimes only days. Once given a new identity they disappeared into their new families. And most of those families weren't prepared to relinquish their adoptive children after the war. They simply kept quiet about their origins.'

'But it's worth trying to find out if there is a child who can remember my mother and me,' she pleaded.

To Ned's extreme annoyance, Josef covered Helena's hand with his own. But the thoughts he voiced were the same as Ned's. 'What if you find out something you don't want to know, Helena?'

'Everyone has the right to know who they are,' she insisted.

'Start down this road and you will probably end up as just one more bitter Lebensborn child who will never know her origins.'

'I know what I'm letting myself in for. Ned and I talked about it.'

'Talk in the early days is easy. But years and years of disappointment are very difficult. I know what that can do to a person.'

'But my case is different from yours. You're looking for a baby who was taken.'

'And you are probably one of the babies. Our cases are not so dissimilar.'

'I could have been taken from a family here, in Poland—'

'Or France, or Norway, or Holland, or even Germany – the illegitimate child of a married SS officer and some girl he picked up in a bar one night.'

'And raped?' She raised her eyes and looked at him.

'If that is the case, better you never find out. And you won't,' Josef predicted. 'The people who ran the homes took care to burn the records of the illegitimate children before the Allies reached them.'

'Have any records survived?' Ned moved along the bench until his thigh pressed against Helena's.

Josef removed his hand from Helena's. 'A few. Mainly details of the new identities the children were given after they went into Lebensborn. That's what makes the kidnapped children—'

'Like your brother?' Ned interrupted.

'Like Leon,' Josef agreed, 'so difficult to trace. It is almost impossible to match new identities to old when you have little knowledge of the old. All I have of Leon is a photograph taken shortly after he was born. But I have put it in the register together with my own photograph in the hope that if he is alive, one day he will find out about his origins, start looking for his real family, discover the entry I made and see a similarity between us.'

'You looked alike?' Ned asked.

'I don't know. All I remember of him is a bundle in a shawl.'

'That is your only hope of finding him?' Helena's disappointment was evident in her voice.

'Perhaps now you realize just how difficult it is to identify your roots when you have been separated from your family and your papers have been destroyed.'

'It seems impossible.'

'I am afraid it is, Helena.'

Anna opened the door to the bar and shouted to Josef. He left the stool. 'I will ask her if you can stay until the weekly bus leaves.'

'Thank you.' Ned slipped his arm around Helena's shoulders. 'You need to rest. Let's go up to our room while Anna is still prepared to rent it to us.'

At Ned's insistence, Helena sat in a chair on the landing, a cushion behind her head and one of the suitcases beneath her feet. But she couldn't rest or settle; her mind remained fixed on the ceremony and her conversation with Weronika. She watched Ned as he sat reading his James Bond novel in the chair opposite her. Gradually his head sank lower, and when the book fell from his hands she knew he was asleep.

She went into their room and picked up her duffle bag. It felt odd without the weight of the casket that had contained Magda's ashes. The plastic box Ned's father had given her was on her bed. She set it beside the wickerwork waste paper basket, never wanting to see it again.

She felt restless and confused. She had been given irrefutable evidence that she wasn't Magda and Adam Janek's daughter, but memory – and her heart – dictated otherwise.

She recalled her childhood, all the dark winter nights she had woken with minor ailments – a sore throat, a cough, a rare nightmare. How Magda had always been there within seconds, smelling of toothpaste and lavender water. How she had wrapped her strong, comforting arms around her, cuddling and comforting her before fetching her a soothing drink. And her last assurance before returning to her own bed: *'Don't worry, Helena sweetheart. Everything will be fine in the morning.'*

Only things would never be fine again. She felt crushed, alone and unequal to facing the world – and that was without taking Magda's legacy of lies into account. She sank down on the bed, opened her duffle bag and did what she had always done when faced with seemingly insurmountable problems. She reached for a notepad and pencil, opened the book, drew a line down the centre of a clean page and stared at it.

Would making a plan of action help her find out who she really was? What could she write that would help her trace her origins, when almost everything Magda had told her had been untrue? She was an adult. She had been about to marry. She had a degree and a teaching certificate. She had been given a responsible job by influential, well-educated people who had faith in her ability to teach literature at Pontypridd Girls' Grammar School. So why did she feel like throwing herself to the floor and screaming at her mother – who hadn't been her mother at all – for putting her in this awful situation when Magda couldn't even hear, let alone answer her?

Ned woke with a start. Looking in from the landing, he saw her sitting on the bed next to her open duffle bag. 'Are you searching for painkillers? I have a couple of aspirins in my suitcase.'

'I don't need them.'

'Are you sure your head isn't hurting? That you don't feel nauseous or dizzy?'

'Just for once, stop being a doctor.'

'I tried, but my fiancée gave my secret away to the locals,' he sniped back.

'And you'll never let me forget it, will you?'

'I don't understand why you had to tell Josef what I do for a living.'

'We were talking about teaching – the difference between the Polish and British curriculum. He asked what your subject was, and the truth slipped out. Anyway, what difference does it make? After the way you started barking orders when Wiktor Niklas pushed me into that wall, everyone realized that you were a doctor anyway.'

Ned knew Helena was upset and angry, but the last thing he wanted was for her to continue taking her anger out on him. 'Please, let's not quarrel.'

'You're only saying that because you're losing.' She thought about what she'd said then, and murmured, 'I'm sorry, that was childish of me.'

'What are you doing anyway?'

She lifted up the notepad. 'Trying to think things through. Making a list of what little I do know about myself.'

'You are blonde, blue-eyed and beautiful. Kind, generous and loving – very, very loving,' he added softly, exercising every ounce of willpower he possessed to remain where he was. 'You hate arguments, cruelty of any kind to humans and animals. You love children, liquorice, good literature, the theatre, and drinking pints of beer in the pub with your friends. And you're sentimental. Remember the blow-up chair?'

'None of which is the slightest bit helpful.' She made an effort to subdue her irritation. 'Ned, don't you see? I can't possibly consider marrying you when I don't even know who I am, or what secrets Magda might have hidden about my family. My real parents could have done horrible things. And if it became public, that knowledge could destroy your life and that of your parents. I could be the child of Nazis, murderers . . .'

'I'm not interested in your parents, just you. And the only thing that would destroy my life is if you left me.'

'Ned—'

'You're under enormous stress,' he interrupted, not wanting to give her any more time to voice worse scenarios. 'You have to come to terms with the fact that you're not your mother's biological daughter. That everything Magda told you about your family is a tissue of lies. You have to accept that much before you can go forward. Come back out here and sit in the fresh air,' he coaxed. 'I'll get us a couple of drinks and we'll brainstorm together. One small beer isn't going to make any difference, even if you do have concussion. This local stuff is incredibly weak.'

'It will still make me sleepy.'

'Then I'll find Josef and ask him if there's any of Anna's lemonade left. But I warn you, if I see Anna I'll retreat back up here empty-handed.'

'Coward.' Her face ached when she tried to smile, and she realized how long it had been since she had tried.

'I'm happy to admit it.'

When Ned returned ten minutes later with two glasses of lemonade, Helena was sitting on the landing. 'I talked to Josef. He offered to lend me his push-bike so I can ride to the post office in the next village. I'll book a telephone call and leave a message at the number Norbert gave us. He can pick us up. That way we won't have to wait for the bus.'

'Will Anna allow us to stay until Norbert comes?'

'She's asleep – or,' he lowered his voice, 'more likely lying in a drunken stupor. Josef did say he won't ask her until she wakes. But he also said that although she's often threatened her paying guests in the past, she's never actually thrown anyone out of this room.'

'There's always a first time.'

Ned handed her one of the glasses and set the second on the floor next to his chair. 'Then let's hope she doesn't rouse herself from her torpor until the morning.' He looked around. 'I need paper and pen. Like you I can't think without making notes.' He went into their room and emerged a few minutes later with a blank exercise book and biro. 'Let's start with what we do know. Magda had you with her when the children's home was liberated in May 1945, and Weronika and Bobby Parsons said you were about two years old.'

'Did Magda pick me up by chance, or did she deliberately choose a child the same age as the one the Nazis had murdered so she could use the baptism record of my namesake?'

'That's the first question.' Ned made a note. 'Weronika also said that the Americans brought you and Magda into the Displaced Persons' camp from a Lebensborn home near Munich.'

'The first Lebensborn home was opened east of Munich.' Josef was struggling up the stairs with four enormous box files. 'I've left Stefan in charge of the bar; he'll fetch me if someone comes in, but after the way our customers drank this morning it will take them hours to sleep off the after-effects. I predict the bar will remain deserted until this evening. So I thought I'd show you these so you could see what an impossible task you are facing.' He dropped the files next to Helena's chair.

'These are the records of your search for your brother?' she asked.

'And all the notes I made about the Lebensborn project.' He sat on the top stair, lifted a file on his lap and opened it.

'If you and Magda were in a children's home in Munich in 1945 the chances are it was this one.' He removed a large envelope and extracted a photograph. 'Steinhöring, the first Lebensborn home opened by Himmler in 1936. It offered Aryan women a place where they could deliver their illegitimate babies and keep the births secret from their families and the outside world to avoid social disgrace. It closed early in May 1945 when American troops moved in. According to eyewitnesses, the SS burned all the home's records before they fled. But others who were there insist that the Americans fought the Nazis, and tried to stop them escaping into the mountains. During the fighting, the files were dumped into the Isar river and washed away. Whichever story is right, you can be sure that the identities of the children who were left in the home, and some of those who had already been placed with German families, were permanently lost.'

'Possibly including mine.' Helena took the photograph from him. She studied the image of the magnificent four-storey house with its typical Bavarian balconies decorated by window boxes. Leaving her chair, she went into their room and brought out the box of photographs she had brought from Pontypridd. Opening it, she removed her earliest baby picture. There was no mistake. The house in the background was the same. She passed both photographs to Josef.

'This proves it,' he said. 'You were definitely in Steinhöring.'

'With Magda. You see the wedding ring on her hand. It is quite distinctive. I have it with me.'

Ned took the photographs. 'Do you know of any other children in the home who had come from Poland?'

'Two boys,' Josef divulged.

'Do you know where they are now?'

'Yes.' Josef opened another file and flicked through the envelopes. 'Neither has found their parents, and both live in Warsaw.'

'You have their addresses?'

'Yes. I interviewed both of them a few years ago.'

'So we could visit them?' Ned smile encouragingly at Helena.

'There's no point. When I spoke to them they could recall very little about their time in the home.'

'But they might remember something about Magda or Helena. Something that didn't seem important when you spoke to them.'

Ned knew the chance was slim, but it was the only lead they had.

'Before going to the expense of travelling to Warsaw you could write to them and ask if they remember Helena's mother,' Josef replied. 'But it's not likely. One was three years old at liberation, the other two.'

'But it gives us somewhere to start and something to do,' Ned persisted.

Despite Ned's apparent enthusiasm, Helena suspected that he saw the quest as a way of keeping her occupied until lack of progress forced her to face the fact that she probably would never discover her origins. And then what? No doubt he hoped that she would forget all about it, return to Pontypridd, calmly marry him and carry on living the life they had planned. Only she knew that she never would be able to forget the mystery that surrounded her birth.

'Your lemonade is getting warm.' Josef returned his photograph of Steinhöring to the envelope.

Helena looked at the mass of newspaper cuttings and envelopes in the file he had opened. 'Can I borrow these files, please, Josef?'

'Be my guest.' Josef set the one he was holding on top of the others. 'As I said, they're mainly lists of names and addresses, and although it looks like a great deal of information, none of it is useful to anyone who isn't looking for a specific person. And even then the accounts are fragmentary. Take me, for example. After five years of continual searching I still don't have any idea where my brother is, or even if he's alive.'

'What gives you the strength to keep looking for him?' Helena lifted one of the files on to her lap.

'The knowledge that, if he is alive, I have one relative left in this world. A part of my parents and a part of me that makes him family. And that Leon might be as lonely without me as I am without him. If that sounds stupid—'

'No, it doesn't,' Helena said eagerly. 'Because that is exactly how I feel.'

'Then you too—'

'Feel incomplete, yes.'

Ned watched and listened to Helena and Josef with increasing despondency. Their respective searches were drawing them together.

Already they understood one another well enough to finish the other's half-spoken sentences. And, in some ways, for all the deprivation and poverty here, Helena was more at home in this backward Polish village than he had ever seen her in Pontypridd. Or could it be that her fluency in the language and familiarity with the culture had highlighted another side of her that he had never seen before.

The thought made him even more jealous of Josef than he already was. He only wished he could talk to Helena as easily and understand exactly why she was so intent on embarking on a search that, in the unlikely event it might prove successful, could well destroy what little peace of mind she had left.

For the next hour Ned pretended to study the photographs in the files, looking for a similarity between a baby girl and Helena. In reality, the faces of the children he scanned barely registered. Engrossed in listening to Helena and Josef's conversation, he started guiltily when Helena turned to him.

'Sorry, were you talking to me?' he asked.

'Who did you think I was talking to?' She thrust a photograph at him. 'Do you think that looks like me?'

He took the photograph and studied it. 'The mouth is similar to yours but the ears don't match.' He looked up at hers to check. 'The shape of the ears are one feature that never changes from birth unless they are doctored by plastic surgery, and yours, my love,' he inserted the two last words for Josef's benefit, 'show no sign of being surgically altered.'

'What about this one?' Josef handed him another baby photograph.

'The eyes slant down, not up as Helena's do.'

'And this?' Helena handed him a photocopy of a passport-sized shot of a blonde baby.

'Straight hair. Yours is naturally wavy, so it would have been curly when you were a child.' Eaten up by jealousy, unable to sit idly by and watch Josef and Helena a moment longer, he left his chair. 'I think I'll cycle to the post office.'

'When are you going to tell Norbert to pick us up?' Helena asked.

'As soon as he can.'

'But—'

'I don't fancy trying to sleep rough in the square or the church-yard.' Ned checked his pockets for change.

'Anna won't throw you out,' Josef said authoritatively.

'How can you be so sure?' Ned asked.

'I've been thinking about it. You're Westerners, and the government is anxious to bring foreign currency into the country. Anna won't risk you complaining to the authorities. If you do, they could take away her licence for this room, and she makes quite a few extra zlotys from Ministry of Agriculture officials.'

'We can't think of leaving here yet, Ned,' Helena pleaded. 'I want to talk to more people.'

'You've done what you came here to do. It's time for us to go home.' Ned unconsciously reiterated what Anna had said to her earlier.

'When I came here I thought Magda and Adam Janek were my parents. Now I know differently. Please, Ned. Stay and help me look through the photographs in these files. We might be lucky and find a match that's worth further investigation.'

Ned gazed into Helena's eyes. He couldn't refuse her anything, especially when she was wearing a half-pleading, half-anguished expression. He sat down again. 'All right, sunshine, hand me one of the files.'

There was still no sign of Anna that evening. Josef served Helena and Ned Krupnik, a thick barley soup with a lot of vegetables, a little smoked venison and a loaf of heavy, close-baked rye bread. They ate, as usual, at the table in the yard. Afterwards Helena returned to their room, piled the box files on to the table, pulled one of the chairs from the landing inside, switched on the lamp and continued to wade through the papers.

'Would you like me to carry on looking at the photographs?' Ned said unenthusiastically when he walked into their room half an hour later with a couple of bottles of beer and two glasses.

'You don't have to if you don't want to.'

He set the beers on the table and brought in the second chair, leaving the door open. It was a beautiful evening. The air was still, the sun had tinged the grey roof of the barn opposite with red and gold. If it hadn't been for the smell of the chickens and pigs below, he might have felt the scene was perfect. He poured his beer. 'As I've looked through all of them once without coming up with anything, is there something else that I can do?'

'Given that you can't read Polish, nothing I can think of,' Helena replied absently, engrossed in the report she was reading.

'Any other suggestions?'

'Read your James Bond.'

'Helena—'

'Sorry, I didn't mean that the way it sounded.' She shuffled a sheaf of papers. 'It's just that these make depressing reading. Endless accounts of how children were taken, together with lists of their likes and dislikes, and anecdotes related by their relatives to illustrate behaviour in the hope that will enable a lost child to be returned to his or her birth family.'

'Doesn't it make you feel very grateful that you had a mother who loved and cared for you?' Ned asked.

'I can't think about Magda or who I might or might not be any more.' Helena gathered all the papers together and returned them to the files.

'Beer?' He held up the bottle he'd bought for her and a glass.

'No, you drink them. I'm going for a walk.'

'To the churchyard?' he guessed.

'Yes, to take photographs of the grave before the sun sets. I meant to do it earlier but I was so busy talking to Weronika I forgot.'

'You'd be better off waiting for the morning.'

But Ned found himself talking to an empty chair. Helena had gone without inviting him to accompany her.

Chapter 17

EVER SINCE HELENA had arrived in the village, she had constantly thought, 'My mother walked here', or 'My mother looked at this church, this house, this street . . .'

Now, as she walked towards the church, she no longer wondered what Magda had done or seen when she had lived in the village. The ties to the place were Magda's. She had none. But was there another village, town or city in Poland that she could claim as her birthplace? Or had she been taken from another occupied country? That would mean that she had no right to the Polish heritage Magda had passed on to her.

She walked across the square, swinging the duffle bag that held her camera. Ned was right. It was too dark to take photographs. She would have to come back in the morning. She knew she had hurt Ned by not asking him to accompany her, but all she wanted was to be left alone with her thoughts.

It was strange, a complete reversal of their relationship in Bristol. There, she had been the insecure one, never quite believing that handsome, smart, intelligent Ned was hers. Now she resented his attempts to protect her. It was as if by trying to keep her safe, he was suffocating her, giving her no space to think or breathe, let alone be herself – whoever that might be.

She debated whether or not to ask Ned to walk with her as far as the Niklas farm in the morning so she could take a photograph of it. Then she realized there was no point. She had no more claim to a history that connected her to the Niklas farmhouse or the Niklas family. Wiktor Niklas couldn't have made it plainer that he wanted nothing to do with her, and was intent on keeping her away from his mother and sister.

Twilight thickened around her, casting deep blue and purple shadows over the tombstones as she walked through the gate into the churchyard and around to the Janek plot. She stopped suddenly.

A woman was hunched on the ground in front of Adam Janek's stone cross. A black crocheted shawl covered her head and shoulders. She was holding out her hands and her fingers moved swiftly, clicking the beads of a rosary, as she muttered the age-old, Catholic prayer: 'Hail Mary, full of grace. Our Lord is with thee. Blessed art thou among women, and blessed is the fruit of thy womb, Jesus. Holy Mary, Mother of God, pray for us sinners now and at the hour of our death. Amen.'

No sooner did the woman reach the end of the prayer than she began at the beginning again, chanting as if she were hypnotized, her lips moving in synchrony with her fingers. Feeling like an interloper, yet loath to move, lest she make a noise that would disturb the woman, Helena froze.

After a few minutes the woman turned and looked at Helena. It was only then that Helena recognized Magda's younger sister, Julianna.

'I am sorry,' Helena apologized. 'I didn't mean to disturb you.'

Flustered, Julianna grabbed hold of the cross to steady herself, and rose stiffly from her knees. She turned back to the grave, hurriedly crossed herself and thrust the rosary into the pocket of her voluminous dark skirt.

Helena held out her hand. 'I am Helena, your sister Magda's adopted daughter.'

Julianna put her head down and refused to look Helena in the eye. 'I know who you are. I saw you at the service today. Wiktor said we mustn't talk to you.'

'Why doesn't Wiktor want me to talk to you, Julianna? The last thing I want to do is hurt you or your mother. Magda told me stories about you and her two brothers, what it was like for the four of you growing up on the farm. How you played together as children. She also told me about the cooking lessons your mother gave you girls, how she taught both of you to make cheese and butter and run a dairy, and look after the livestock.'

'My sister wasn't your mother.'

255

'So I discovered today, but Magdalena always told me that I was her and Adam Janek's daughter. And it is difficult for me now to think of her as anything other than my Mama.'

Julianna hesitated, then, still looking down at the ground, asked, 'Was Magda happy in the West?'

'She had a good job. She managed a cooked meat and pie shop. We lived in a busy market town, but Magda missed Poland, you and all her family. We had lots of friends, but I don't think they compensated for the people she had left behind here.'

'You never went hungry?'

Helena knew that she shouldn't have been surprised by the question, but it illustrated the privations the Polish people had suffered during the war. 'No, Mama – Magda – earned a good wage, and a nice apartment came with her job.'

'And clothes? Before the war, when she lived here, Magda used to love pretty clothes.'

'She liked to dress well, and she could afford to. We weren't rich, but there was always enough to buy a few luxuries.'

'I must go. I shouldn't be talking to you.'

'Why, Julianna?'

'You know my name.'

'I know a lot about you. As I said, Magda used to talk about you and Wiktor and her mother all the time. And she used to pray for your father and your brother, Augustyn. I have photographs that will tell you more about Magda's life in the West than I can. Please, can I visit you at the farm and show them to you and your mother?'

'Wiktor wouldn't allow it.'

'Then visit me in the village. My husband Ned and I,' Helena swallowed hard as she repeated the lie, 'are staying in Anna's house.'

'Wiktor says Anna is a bad woman. And he doesn't like me to leave the farm. I was only able to come here now because he is sleeping. He got drunk this morning and has been asleep since.'

'I know. I saw him.'

'The men who brought him home said he hit you.'

Helena instinctively fingered her cut, which was still covered by the cotton wool Ned had plastered over it. 'It was an accident.'

'Wiktor doesn't mean to hurt people but he gets angry when he drinks. It isn't easy for him to run the farm by himself. The collective wants too much from us, and there is only his wife, me and Mama to help him. And Mama can't do much these days. She is old and tires easily.'

'I know Magda wrote to you. Did she ever mention me?' Helena asked.

Julianna shook her head. 'Never.'

'Are you sure?'

Julianna glanced nervously over her shoulder. 'I have to go. Someone could see us and tell Wiktor, and then, drunk or sober, he would be very angry with me – and you. There's no saying what he would do to both of us for disobeying him.'

'Who is going to see us here?' Helena looked around the deserted churchyard. When Julianna followed suit and didn't draw away, she was encouraged. 'If we move back here behind the gravestones and close to the wall of the church, no one will be able to see us from the path.' Helena shrank back behind Adam Janek's cross and moved into the shadows. 'Come on, we'll whisper, so no one can hear us.' She held out her hand. Julianna didn't take it, but she did move alongside her.

'Just for a few minutes,' she conceded.

'Magda sent you parcels every month—'

'No, she didn't,' Julianna whispered.

'She didn't send you parcels?' Had Wiktor kept them and the contents for himself? Helena wondered.

'At Christmas, and for Mama's and my birthdays, but not every month. Magda sent good warm clothes for Mama and me, and tins of food. Ham and salmon and chocolates. Wiktor's boys loved the chocolate.'

'But the letters . . .'

'There was always a letter in the parcels. A short note, wishing us good health, luck and happiness. They always finished with her love and a sentence or two about how well she was doing. But there were never more than three a year. Except early on, just after she went to the West, when she sent a special letter with a money order to pay for Adam Janek's memorial cross.'

'But I watched her write the letters and pack the parcels – one, sometimes two a month – with clothes, food and photographs of me. Magda used to give them to a friend who passed them to Polish sailors on Cardiff docks so they could be posted here in Poland to avoid being opened by customs.'

'I told you, we only ever had three parcels a year.' Julianna's voice sounded harsh in the darkness.

'But you wrote back—'

'Wiktor would never let Mama or me reply to Magda's letters. He said if Magda had still been decent and cared anything for us, she would have returned at the end of the war to help us run the farm. But he says . . . says . . .'

'What, Julianna?' Helena saw she was trembling, and her heart went out to her. She longed to embrace her, but she was afraid to try.

'That Magda, like Weronika, had been . . . used by the German soldiers. Mama says he is wrong, but he always argues that if Magda had been pure she would have come back after the war. Then, when you came to the village with Magda's ashes, he said it was proof that Magda was no better than Weronika and he'd been right all along. That Magda . . . my sister . . . was a . . .'

'But Wiktor knew that I couldn't be Magda's child. Weronika said that after Magda gave birth to Helena she couldn't have any more children. And Helena, like Adam Janek, was murdered by the Germans. You all saw it happen.'

'Wiktor says you are some whore's German bastard.'

Helena didn't attempt to deny it. She couldn't disprove it any more than Wiktor could prove it. 'I think it's likely that Magda picked me up in the children's home where she worked as a nurse.'

'We heard that Magda had worked in a children's home, but Wiktor said the Germans used the Polish girls they took for only one thing, and he wanted none of the Germans' dirty leavings in his house. He can't help being the way he is. It was horrible here during the war. Things happened . . . dreadful things. He changed.' Julianna sat down suddenly on the Janek kerbstone as if her legs would no longer support her. 'Wiktor was very different before the Germans came.'

Now that Julianna had begun to talk – really talk – she couldn't stop. Once again Helena heard the stories of Magda's childhood, told in a different voice but with the same accent, stories that confirmed everything Magda had told her about her pre-war life. And, as Julianna painted the same idyllic childhood, village and rural life that Magda had, Helena sat next to her and listened.

Time and distance had probably gilded the memories of both women, but their essence was undoubtedly true. The past remained treasured and untarnished by the horrors of the war that was yet to come, the untimely and premature deaths of so many friends and relations, and even Wiktor's cruelty, as he had been transformed by bitter experience into a vicious bully.

These were recollections that had not only warmed Magda's life but also her family's. For the first time Helena realized that Julianna and Maria Niklas had needed them even more than Magda because their drab, regimented Communist lives were so much bleaker than Magda's had been in Pontypridd. She recalled what Peter Raschenko had said in Ronconi's café the evening before they had left for Poland: '*I guarantee that after Poland, you'll look at this place in a new light. It may not be Paradise, but compared to Russia and Poland, it's almost Utopia.*'

Ned was still looking at the photographs in Josef's folders when he heard a crash and an agonizing scream. He ran on to the landing in time to see Josef rush from the bar. Stefan was in the yard wailing and rubbing his eyes. Josef grabbed him and spoke rapidly in Polish before charging into the house. Ned raced headlong down the stairs and followed.

He found himself in a large kitchen. Footsteps echoed in a stone passage and he hurried after Josef, who was sprinting up a magnificent wooden staircase. At the top was a galleried landing studded with half a dozen doors. One was open. Josef disappeared through it. Ned rushed after him.

Anna was lying on her side on the wooden floor. She was groaning, her eyes were rolling and her legs and arms were covered with blood. A splintered chair lay beside her.

But all Ned could look at were the photographs on her night-stand.

Framed snapshots of Helena at various stages of her childhood had been neatly arranged around a large studio portrait of her in graduation cap and gown. Below it was a silver rose vase that held a single red rose.

'Anna needs help,' Josef shouted.

Ned tore his attention away from the photographs and looked down at Josef, who was cradling Anna's head.

'Leave her,' he commanded, the trained doctor taking control. 'She needs to be in the recovery position.' He moved two empty vodka bottles that were lying on the floor, and rolled Anna on to her left side. After checking her airways were clear, he picked up a glass from the nightstand. He sniffed it. 'Neat vodka?'

'She drinks it that way,' Josef informed him bleakly.

'She drank all this today?'

'There were no bottles here when I helped Anna change the beds and take down the laundry this morning.'

'Not even in the wastepaper basket?'

'No.'

Ned set the glass back on the nightstand before kneeling next to Anna. Her skin was pale and clammy, with an unmistakeable bluish tinge. He pinched the skin on the back on her hand but she didn't react. He forced open her mouth. She retched, and a stream of clear liquid flowed from her lips. Her tongue lolled.

'I'll fetch the first aid box.' Josef went to the door.

'There's a small black bag in the bottom of my suitcase. Can you get that instead? And a bucket, lukewarm drinking water – if it's been boiled so much the better – salt, a large beaker, cup, spoon, and a funnel if you have one. And towels. Lots of towels and wash-able blankets. You have all that?'

Josef nodded and ran out. Stefan, who was still wailing and grind-ing his knuckles into his eye sockets, entered a few seconds later. Anna groaned when Ned checked her airways again, and Stefan's wails heightened to a scream.

'Anna will be all right.' Ned hoped the tone of his voice would reassure Stefan, but he regretted that he hadn't learned rudimentary Polish as he'd intended. Stefan's cries became louder and more irritating, and Ned suppressed the uncharitable wish that Josef would return and shut the man up.

After checking Anna's airways once more, he examined her. Her arms and legs were covered in bloody cuts. None was deep, although several were pierced by large splinters from the shattered chair legs. And, although her skin was spattered with angry red blotches, her bones were intact beneath the bruises. He ran his fingers lightly over her spine and torso.

'Will she be all right?' Breathless, Josef returned with Ned's bag, a bucket and a bundle of towels.

'There doesn't appear to be any serious damage to her arms, legs or spine, but I think she may have cracked her ribs.' Ned inspected her skull for swellings or dents, but he found nothing. 'Does the local hospital have an X-ray machine?' He took the towels from Josef and heaped them over Anna, in an attempt to raise her body temperature.

'Yes, but our nearest hospital is in Zamosc and it's always busy. Even if we got Anna there, she could wait for days to be X-rayed.'

'There'd be a problem getting her there?'

'Some of the farmers have horses, carts and tractors, but it would take hours to reach the hospital in one of those, and it wouldn't be a very comfortable journey for Anna.'

'No one has a car here?' Ned didn't know why he was asking. The only car he had seen in the village was Norbert's.

'No.'

'She should be in hospital.'

'There's no way you can get her there before morning. And by then she will have sobered up.'

'If she's alive.' Ned looked at the empty bottles again.

'It's that serious?' The colour drained from Josef's face.

Ned didn't hold any false hope. 'Yes.'

'I know Anna. If she is going to die, she'd want to die here, in this house. But if she woke up in hospital she wouldn't thank you for taking her there. And not just because she hates leaving Stefan.' He gestured towards Anna's brother, who was sobbing quietly now.

261

'She doesn't like hospitals?'

'The local one, no.'

'Why?'

'Because she's been there a few times,' Josef admitted.

'For alcohol-related injuries?'

'She's been better lately — at least, she was before you and Helena arrived. You've seen her at her worst. And Weronika Janek upset her this morning. She's always felt guilty about taking over this house.'

'She could have allowed Weronika to stay here after the war.'

'Wiktor and some of the villagers threatened to burn the place down if she so much as allowed Weronika to step over the doorstep. I was a child and unable to help her. Stefan — well, you can see how he is. She made a choice to reject Weronika and protect us, but it wasn't an easy one for her. I know she feels terrible about it.'

'And the priest?'

'Was away in Warsaw at the time, giving evidence at a war crimes trial. By the time he returned, Weronika was long gone. I know he spoke to Wiktor and the other men about their attitude, but it didn't do much good. Everyone in the village promised to treat the women who had been enslaved by the Nazis respectfully, but they didn't. After Weronika, they weren't put to the test again. Word got out, and most of the women avoided returning to their homes in rural areas, settling instead in the cities where they weren't known.'

Ned glanced at the wreckage strewn around the floor. 'It looks like Anna sat on the chair, overbalanced and toppled backwards.'

'Two years ago she fell into the mirror, smashed it and cut her wrists.' Josef pointed to an empty frame above the nightstand.

'That gives her another five years of bad luck according to the saying. Pity the chair broke and the floor was wood. If it had been carpeted she would have had a softer landing. She hasn't hit her head as far as I can tell, but it's difficult to diagnose concussion in a patient who is this drunk. I can't see any damage to her skull, but she has severe bruising on her abdomen and, from the way she winces when I touch her, I'm certain she has cracked her ribs.'

'That also wouldn't be the first time.' Josef crouched beside Ned. 'Should we get her up on the bed?'

'Yes. The first thing we need to do is empty her stomach, before the alcohol is absorbed into her system. For pity's sake, tell Stefan she'll live. Perhaps then he'll quieten down enough for me to think.'

Josef spoke to Stefan and guided him out of the door. Ned removed his stethoscope from the bag that Josef had brought him; he almost hadn't packed it. As he drew closer to Anna, the smell of alcohol was overwhelming.

'Two bottles of that rot gut would be enough to kill any normal person,' he muttered.

'It's the cheap local brew.' Josef picked up the pieces of chair scattered around Anna and cleared them into the corner to give Ned more space.

'Bring that bucket and bowl over here.' Ned pointed to a large bowl under a water jug on the old-fashioned washstand. Josef brought it, together with the bucket he'd carried upstairs.

'Help me lift her on the bed.' The room was furnished in similar style to the one he and Helena were sharing, with rustic pine furniture and elaborate embroideries. 'Better fold back that tapestry bedspread, and lay her on something that can be easily washed. I'll see to the cuts after I've pumped her stomach.'

Josef rolled down the bedspread, eiderdown and top sheet.

'You take her shoulders; I'll take her legs. Try not to move the towels,' Ned ordered. 'On three. One, two, three ...'

As soon as Anna was lying on her side on the bed, Ned removed a length of rubber tubing from his bag. 'Did you find a funnel?'

Josef took one out of the bucket together with a beaker, packet of salt and jug of warm water. He watched Ned heap large spoonfuls of salt into the beaker, pour water on top and mix it with a spoon.

'You're going to force her to drink that.'

'It should make her sick. As I said, the vodka in her stomach is better out than in. Hold her head firmly while I slide the tube in place.'

Half an hour later it was difficult to see who was more damp – Ned or Anna. Despite Josef's efforts to keep her still, Anna hadn't taken kindly to having her stomach washed out, and as much of the salt water had gone over Ned's jeans as inside Anna. But once he'd managed to get what he considered enough of the fluid into her, he'd withdrawn the tube and she brought up a quantity of alcohol tinged with traces of blood.

'Now we need to get some real fluid into her.' Ned took the glass he'd left on the nightstand and emptied the remaining vodka into the bucket. 'If we were in a hospital I'd just set up a drip, but as we're not, it will have to be the old-fashioned way.'

'Which is?' Josef asked.

'Cup and spoon. And water is all she should drink for a while. Her liver is grossly enlarged.'

'I'm surprised she still has one,' Josef said.

'How long has she been drinking this heavily?'

'She doesn't all the time, just binges now and again. It started after the priest died three years ago.'

'He kept her drinking in check?' Ned took surgical tweezers from his bag and set to work removing the wooden splinters from Anna's arms and legs. As he removed each one, he swabbed the area with antiseptic and covered it with a square of gauze that he took from a pack in his bag.

'He didn't have to.' Josef moved the bucket away from the bed. 'She would have been too ashamed to allow him to see her drink more than an occasional glass of home-made cherry wine. I wish you could have known the priest. He was a remarkable man. I have never witnessed such faith in humanity in any other person, Catholic, Atheist, Marxist or Capitalist. He took life, death, tragedy and joy in his stride, rejoicing with people during the good times and helping them to pray through the bad. Anna and Stefan were shattered by his loss, and I couldn't be here immediately afterwards because I was completing my last year in university. When I came back here to teach I caught Anna drinking vodka one morning when she was making breakfast. I tried talking to her but nothing I said made the slightest difference. Running the bar didn't help, either. For every drink she poured a customer she poured herself one "to keep them company".'

'Alcoholism is a common disease among publicans in Britain.'

Josef looked surprised. 'When I was in France they told me alcohol was expensive in your country.'

'It is, but it doesn't stop people from drinking.'

'Like Russian soldiers. I've heard that if they can't get the real thing they'll drink anti-freeze.'

'They must lead short lives.'

'But, they'd argue, happy ones. I went to see the local doctor when I moved back here. I tried talking to him about Anna but he refused to believe her drinking was a problem. Probably because excessive drinking is a fact of life in all the Soviet states. People see it as a solution to their difficulties. The bottle offers instant oblivion and an escape from miserable reality. In Anna's case, the loss of the priest, as well as her family during the war.'

'Not all her family.' Ned nodded to the display of photographs.

Josef took a deep breath. 'No.'

'I can't understand why I didn't notice the resemblance when I first saw her. Is she Helena's mother?'

'I don't honestly know. Anna had two sisters ...'

'Her aunt, then?'

'I've no idea. I don't remember Anna's sisters, although I've seen photographs of them.'

'With a baby?'

'No.'

'But you knew that Helena was related to Anna when we walked into the bar,' Ned persisted.

'I recognized Helena as the girl in these photographs.'

'Did you ever ask Anna who she was?'

'Anna told me that she was the daughter of a dear friend of hers who lived in the West. I knew she had a friend in the West because of the letters and parcels we received every month.'

Ned remembered seeing Magda pack the parcels. 'Clothes, food, tights, make-up, chocolate?'

'Soap powder, shaving cream, jeans and cologne for me. Magda Janek was a good friend to Anna and to me. I always had more to eat and more toys than any other kid in the village.'

'And all the time Magda told Helena that she was sending them to her family.' Ned returned the pack of gauze to his bag.

Josef glanced at the photographs once more. 'Anna will kill me when she wakes up and finds out that I allowed you into this room.'

'You didn't. I came in here to see why she screamed,' Ned reminded him.

'Anna never remembers much about what happened when she wakes after one of these bouts. I could tell her she fell in the kitchen, and that I carried her up here.'

'And treated her?'

'I've looked after her before when she's hurt herself.'

'As badly as this?'

Josef sighed. 'I could say that I sent for the doctor. I don't suppose you would consider not telling her you were here?' He looked at Ned hopefully.

'Not a chance.'

'I was afraid you'd say that.'

'Are you surprised? Helena's going out of her mind thinking she's the result of some Nazi breeding experiment! You can't expect me to keep quiet about this.' He nodded towards the photographs.

'Anna's put up with so much in her life—'

'So has Helena since we arrived here,' Ned said shortly. He paused, thinking. 'Anna didn't want us to stay here because she was afraid that Helena would find out that either she or one of her sisters was her birth mother.' He took a breath. 'Is Helena illegitimate?'

'I don't know, and that's the truth. I told you that the priest brought me to Anna the night of the massacre. I don't remember much before that night – and I certainly don't remember ever seeing Anna with a baby since.'

'I hope you're around to do some translating tomorrow,' Ned said harshly.

'Don't think badly of Anna. You know, she told me to do all I could to ensure that Magda's ashes were buried with Adam Janek. It wasn't easy to persuade Wiktor Niklas to allow us to open the grave. But Anna gave me money, and Wiktor has never been able to resist the lure of cash he hasn't had to work for.'

'How much did you pay Wiktor?' Ned wondered why he hadn't realized that Josef had bribed Wiktor. Josef had spent at least two hours on the morning before the ceremony at the Niklas farm. It wouldn't have taken him that long simply to make arrangements.

'Two hundred dollars.'

'*Two hundred* . . . Where did you get that kind of money?'

'Anna had a hundred. Government officials occasionally pay her in dollars. It's illegal but they're fond of Anna. And I had dollars from my year in Paris. I had a part-time bar job and I changed my wages into dollars. It is, or rather was, my fall-back money.'

'Two hundred dollars was all of your and Anna's savings?'

'Most of our foreign savings. There's no point in hoarding zlotys. There's not much that you can buy with them other than food if you can find it, and a man can only eat so much.' Josef picked up the last pieces of chair and heaped them on to the pile in the corner. 'All that is fit for now is the stove.'

Ned removed the last splinter from Anna's arm. 'I've finished but we still need to get her temperature up. Do you have any washable blankets that we can put on top of these towels and the sheet?'

'I'll go and look. Don't you want to strap up her ribs first?'

'The modern thinking is to leave the ribs to heal naturally without strapping them.' Ned ran his fingers over the bruised area on Anna's torso to make sure the bones hadn't splintered.

'In Poland we strap them up,' Josef said firmly.

'It's more important we get her temperature up at the moment. If we don't, you'll have to call an ambulance.'

'What ambulance?'

'You don't have ambulances here?'

'One to cover a hundred square miles,' Josef informed him. 'That's why we use carts and tractors to take people to the hospital.'

'What happens is someone has a heart attack in one of these small scattered villages?'

'They die.'

Josef left the room again and returned after a moment with four blankets, which Ned heaped over Anna. Then he opened a drawer in the dresser and took out a linen sheet. 'Anna will expect you to strap up her ribs; it's what they did the last time she cracked them.'

'When she's warmer, I suppose I could bandage her.' Too concerned about Anna to argue, Ned checked her pulse again.

'She'll kill me for doing this. It's one of her last pre-war ones.' Josef took a pair of nail scissors from a manicure set on the nightstand, and made a series of small cuts in the sheet a couple of inches apart. After replacing the scissors in the leather folder, he proceeded to tear the sheet into strips.

Ned took them from him and rolled them into bandages.

When Josef had torn the last strip he said, 'I must go down and close the bar. I told Stefan to throw everyone out, but no one listens to him.'

Ned pulled the blankets to Anna's chin. 'Go. I can manage here.'

Josef opened the door, then hesitated, looking back at the photographs. 'Where's Helena?'

'She went to the churchyard for a walk.'

'You won't tell her, will you?'

'About the photographs or Anna's drinking?'

'Either,' Josef pleaded.

'I will tell her about both, but not until I have spoken to Anna – if she comes round.'

'I thought she'd be fine now?'

'That depends entirely on how much alcohol is left in her system, and without a blood test it's impossible to gauge. She could still choke, stop breathing, or die of heart failure. But I promise you, I'll do all I can to keep her alive. I'd like to hear her explanation about these photographs.'

'That will be difficult when she only speaks Polish and you don't. I doubt she'll let me translate.'

'Then she can tell Helena to her face, and I want to be there so I can read Anna's expression.'

'Anna's never been good at lying or keeping her emotions hidden. You can see that from the way she treated you and Helena when you arrived here.' Josef paused. 'If I see Helena, I'll tell her that Anna has had an accident and you're examining her.'

'You'll be back?'

'After I've locked the bar. If you want me before, just open the window and shout down.' Josef turned and left the room.

Ned gazed at the human wreckage sprawled on the bed. 'God only knows what has driven you to try to kill yourself with drink, Anna. I only hope it's not something that's going to affect Helena too badly.' He checked her temperature again before picking up the first bandage he had rolled.

Chapter 18

WHEN HELENA LEFT the churchyard she had to push past a tide of disgruntled men heading up the narrow street towards her. To her surprise, when she reached the bar it was in darkness. The shutters had been pulled down and locked over the half-doors. She walked around to the archway that cut through the house and found Stefan sitting by the table in the yard, his head buried in his hands, sobbing.

She sat beside him and put her arm around his shoulders. 'Whatever's wrong, Stefan?'

He lifted his tear-stained face. 'Anna . . .'

'What's happened to Anna?'

'She fell. She's covered in blood . . . she . . .' Too upset to continue, he buried his head in her shoulder.

'Anna had an accident.' Josef appeared at the back door of the bar. He locked it behind him.

'What kind of an accident? Is she badly hurt?' Helena asked in alarm.

'She fell over on a chair in her bedroom. According to Ned, she's cracked a few ribs. He's with her now. Given the primitive state of our local hospital we decided it wasn't worth the three-hour journey to take her there.'

'Is there anything I can do?'

'I don't mean to be unkind, but I don't think so.'

'You said Ned's with her.'

'He is.'

'Then she's unconscious or . . .' Helena debated whether or not to say it, but honesty won. 'Drunk?'

'As I told Ned, you haven't seen her at her best. She hasn't always been the way she is now.' He went to the barn and checked the padlock.

'She must be very unhappy.'

'No more so than any other woman her age in Poland.' Anxious to change the subject, he said, 'Can I get you something? Coffee, beer, vodka?'

'Nothing, thank you.'

'Did you enjoy your walk?'

'Yes, I met Julianna Niklas in the churchyard.'

'She spoke to you?'

'We had quite a conversation. I invited her and her mother to visit me here, but I doubt they'll come.'

'So do I. Her brother would never allow it.' Josef's features were thrown into sharp relief by the light of the unshaded bulb that hung from the rafters of the veranda, and Helena was shocked by how drawn and exhausted he appeared.

'You look dreadful. Anna will be all right, won't she?'

'I hope so. Ned's doing all he can.'

'Ned is a good doctor.'

'He seems to know what he is doing.' Josef sat at the table and patted Stefan's shoulder. 'Go to bed, Stefan. You can't do anything right now.'

Anna's brother lifted his tear-stained face. 'Can I take her breakfast in the morning? I'll make the coffee and butter the rolls.'

'You can take Anna breakfast tomorrow. You can even look in on her now. But don't make a noise or disturb Doctor John while he's treating her.'

'Goodnight, Helena.' Stefan touched her hand. 'It's good that you have come here at last.'

'Thank you, Stefan.' Helena watched him amble away like an obedient dog. She frowned. 'That was an odd thing to say.'

'He means well but he doesn't know what he is doing or saying half the time. He is a heavy burden on Anna. I've just checked the bar and he's washed the glasses in drain cleaner instead of liquid soap. I've left them soaking in cold water but I have a feeling Anna will have to find the money to replace her stock.'

'I'm sorry. I could help out while I'm here . . .'

'You're forgetting that ladies, especially young, pretty ones, are not allowed into the bar.' He went to the door of the house and listened for a moment, but all was quiet. 'I think I'll make coffee anyway. I could do with a cup. Can I tempt you to change your mind, Helena, if I add the promise of a cinnamon biscuit?'

'If you're making coffee, then yes please. But don't bring out the biscuits on my account.'

'Who said anything about you? I could eat a plateful myself.'

After Josef had disappeared, Helena sat back on the bench, leaned against the wall and stared at the yard. She tried to envisage it as Weronika had described, with rose bushes planted in tubs on the veranda, and perhaps a wooden table and chairs. Had the Janeks also kept pigs and chickens in the yard? Josef and Anna had told them they were the biggest landowners for miles. So they wouldn't have had to do it from necessity. They could have easily afforded to keep this area as a private walled garden.

She imagined a round table covered by an embroidered cloth and set with the fine porcelain and silverware her mother had loved, including a silver rose bowl. In summer Magda, Weronika and Adam would have sat there, drinking coffee and eating their breakfast rolls.

What had they talked about? Improvements to the farms they owned and rented out? Possibly. The people they knew in the village, the births, deaths, marriages, all the minutiae of village life? Probably. Planned meals for the visits from Magda's family and friends? The coming baby that had meant so much to all of them. And, later, the German invasion and war. Definitely. Had they realized how catastrophic the war would be for them?

Josef returned, set a tray of coffee on the table, and sat on a stool. 'Thank God the temperature's cooled. It was roasting in the bar at six o'clock.'

Helena took the cup he handed her. 'What happened to Wiktor Niklas to make him the way he is?'

'Life.'

'Julianna said he was a different man before the war. That it changed him.'

'The war changed everyone in the village and the country, but I suppose there's no harm in you knowing. He was engaged to a girl. The partisans caught her with a German soldier.'

'The soldier raped her?'

'Wiktor didn't believe it was rape.'

'Why not?'

'Not all Polish girls hated the Germans.' Josef took his cigarette from his shirt pocket and offered Helena the packet. She rarely smoked but took one. He pushed another between his lips, struck a match and lit them both.

'Did the girl say she'd been raped?' Helena ventured.

'She insisted that the man had attacked her.'

'What happened?'

'The partisans killed both of them, slowly and horribly.'

'Poor girl if it was rape. And poor girl and soldier if it wasn't.'

'Poor Poland. It was a war. The Germans imposed severe reprisals on the civilian population whenever one of their own was killed. The day before the girl was caught with the soldier, the Germans shot the entire family of the partisan leader, including his elderly parents and two-month-old nephew for aiding what they called "fugitives". The partisan leader passed the death sentence on the soldier and the girl because he thought it fitting: the German to pay for what his comrades were doing to Poland; the girl for betraying her country.'

'Did Wiktor see her die?'

'The partisans gave him the knife to do it.'

Helena drew on her cigarette. 'I don't want to hear any more.'

'That was the incident that led to the massacre in the village. The partisans didn't bother to hide the soldier's body. The next morning the tank rolled into the square.'

'So Wiktor was to blame for the massacre.'

'Blame?' Josef blew a smoke-ring at the sky. 'How can you blame young men who were whipped into an orgy of killing? As I've said, it was war. And those who haven't lived through it have very little idea what it was like. For every German soldier who was killed by the partisans, the Germans shot a hundred innocent civilians and turned a hundred more peace-loving Polish farmers into vicious partisans. And you have to ask yourself what the Nazis were doing in Poland in the first place. The Teutons and their *Lebensraum*.'

'Living space. Mama ... Magda told me the Nazis believed that they were entitled to all the land in Poland.'

'Because it had been colonized by German tribes before records were made – or so they said. It's easy for us to sit here and blame the partisans for their excesses, but we never had to live through the war as adults. Who knows what we would have done in similar circumstances? Let's change the subject.'

'Not before I thank you for explaining why Wiktor hates women.'

'The problem is he thinks all women are loose by inclination. Except possibly his mother. His wife and Julianna have a dog's life, literally. They are allowed as far as the farmyard gate, and no further without him. If he ever finds out that Julianna went to the churchyard alone this evening, he'll whip her. The villagers pray he never has a daughter. If he did, he'd probably lock her in the attic and feed her through the keyhole lest she dare look at a man. Anna told me that was why he was so hard on Weronika when she returned. If it had been his decision he would have hung every girl who came back from Germany after the war simply because he was convinced that they had worked willingly in the brothels.'

'If Magda knew her brother's views on women who had been forced to work for the Reich, it would have given her another reason not to return here. I hadn't realized how much the war still affects everyone's lives in Poland.'

'It didn't happen that long ago. Only the children can't remember it. Unlike Britain, we were invaded and occupied. It shatters a people's pride when foreign soldiers tell them what they can and can't do in their own country. And the Russians and the Germans didn't just order us about; they were cruel bastards, if you'll pardon the expression. And here we are talking about the war again.'

'It's hardly surprising. Since I discovered I'm a product of it, that's all I can think about.'

'Poland may still be affected by the last war but we have a new one to fight. France, Britain and even West Germany have gained their freedom from the Fascists. We Poles fought and died in our millions only to be enslaved by the Soviets.'

'I thought you were a free Communist state.'

'If you think Poland is free, you are blind.'

'But you are a Communist.'

He lowered his voice. 'Am I?'

She looked at him, and he laid his hand over hers.

Stefan knelt beside Anna's bed, holding her hand and stroking it. She hadn't moved in over half an hour. To Ned's relief, her temperature was almost normal, her breathing steady and her pulse strong, if too fast for his liking. He gathered the rubber tube he had used to pump her stomach, the beaker, tweezers and soiled towels, threw them all into the bucket, closed his medical bag and glanced around the room to check he hadn't forgotten anything.

Stefan gazed at him beseechingly.

'I'm still worried about her, but not as worried as I have been.' Ned knew Stefan couldn't understand a word he was saying but he had spoken simply to reassure himself. He pointed to Anna, Stefan and the door, moving his fingers to indicate that Stefan should come and get him if there was any change. The old man nodded, and Ned hoped that he'd understood.

He picked up his bag and the bucket, and went to the door. There was a robe hanging on a hook on the back of it, and he caught sight of the label: Marks and Spencer. Yet another example of Magda's generosity.

He went down the stairs and through the passage to the kitchen. When he stood in the doorway he realized why Anna had refused to allow him and Helena inside the house. The room was large, furnished with enormous old-fashioned pieces. And stacked on the open shelves were British tins of food. Biscuit tins, toffee tins, even toothpowder and polish tins. The door to the walk-in pantry was open and he saw a neat stack of John West tins of ham and salmon.

He dropped the rubber tube and tweezers into the massive stone sink. There was a kettle on the range. He filled it from the cold water tap set above the sink, opened the ring, and put it on to boil before standing in the doorway that led into the dark yard.

'Ned, is that you?' Helena called to him.

'Yes.' He stepped out, and saw Helena and Josef holding hands at the table.

'How long have you been there?' she asked.

'Not long. You have a good conversation with Josef?'

Helena pulled her hand away from Josef's. 'Do you remember what Magda used to say whenever you caught us speaking Polish? One of the problems of being bilingual is having to think about which language you are using.'

'We were talking about what it was like here during the war.' Josef rose to his feet.

'Really?' Ned raised an eyebrow.

'I met Julianna Niklas in the churchyard,' Helena explained defensively. 'She told me that Wiktor was aggressive because of what had happened to him during the war. I asked Josef if he knew anything about it.'

'How is Anna?' Josef asked anxiously.

'Out for the count. But I'll stay with her tonight in case she starts retching again and chokes.'

'I'm a light sleeper. I could make myself a bed on her floor,' Josef volunteered.

'And what would you do if she stopped breathing? You didn't even have the sense to put her in the recovery position.'

Josef knew how to lose an argument graciously. 'You want me to make a bed up on the floor for you?'

'I think it's best, don't you?'

'I'll go and do it. Goodnight, Helena.'

'Goodnight, Josef.'

Josef piled their coffee things back on to the tray and went into the house.

'You look tired,' Ned said to Helena.

'I am.'

'Then go to bed.' He handed her the key to their room and their fingers touched. Hers were cold.

'Ned?'

'Yes?' His eyes gazed searchingly into hers.

'Nothing.' She rose and went to the foot of the stairs. 'Good-night.'

He watched her climb up to their room, unlock the door and close it behind her. He saw her switch on the light and draw the curtains. Only then did he walk back into the house.

Ned found Josef carrying an armchair into Anna's room. He'd also taken up a kitchen chair and laid out a makeshift bed on the floor with sheets, pillows and blankets.

'There's not much point in both of us sitting up with Anna.' The last thing Ned felt like doing was spending the night with Josef.

'I won't sleep until I know she is going to be all right. But as you pointed out earlier, I wouldn't know what to do if she did start choking, so I guess that makes us companions until morning.' Josef dropped the armchair in front of the kitchen chair and tossed a blanket and pillow on it. 'If you find the floor too hard you can sit in the armchair and put your feet on the wooden chair. I'll take the floor.'

Irritated by the inference that Josef was more used to the hardship of sleeping on a floor, Ned snapped, 'I slept on the floor more often than not when I was a student.' He instantly regretted his outburst, knowing it made him sound petulant.

'As you wish.' Josef shrugged. He sat sideways on the window seat, lifted up his feet, leaned back against the wall, and gazed across at Anna.

Despite what he'd said about the floor, Ned pulled the easy chair close to Anna's bed, sat on it and checked her pulse and breathing again.

'How is she?' Josef asked.

'Her pulse is slower than it was.'

'Is that good or bad?'

'Good. She's lucky she fell when she did. It was worth a few cracked ribs. If she'd lapsed into an alcohol-induced stupor, it's possible you wouldn't have found her in time for me to empty her stomach. Two bottles of spirits drunk in quick succession can be lethal. The vodka I washed out of her could have caused heart failure.'

'Is there a chance that this will stop her from drinking herself into this state again?' Josef asked.

'You said you've often seen her drunk.'

'But never as bad as this.'

'When she wakes, I suggest you tell her what happened, because she won't remember a thing. The realization that she almost died might make her think twice before she reaches for another bottle.'

'I suspect all the lecture will do is slow down her drinking.' Josef continued to stare at her, lying white and still in the bed. 'She was . . . is . . . a wonderful woman. Warm, loving, kind and funny. She gave me all the emotional support I needed when I was a child.'

'Isn't there anywhere she can get help?' Ned tucked Anna's hand back beneath the covering blankets and towels.

'What kind of help?'

'In the West we have centres and organizations that help people to stop drinking. They hold meetings—'

'In this village?' Josef interrupted. 'You saw the number of men here this morning. The only place big enough to hold a meeting, apart from the barns, which are full of hay and chickens, is the bar. If the villagers have business to discuss that affects everyone, like the introduction of a new agricultural quota, they allow women in.'

'You could keep the bar closed during the actual meetings,' Ned suggested.

'I could try but I wouldn't succeed,' Josef predicted. 'All it would take is someone to demand a beer and vodka, and if I wouldn't serve them they'd bring their own home-made liquor. Before you know it, everyone would be drunk, and instead of a temperance meeting there'd be a party.'

'There's an organization which you can telephone if you are trying to stop drinking . . .' Ned faltered.

Josef laughed. 'If it's a choice between drinking with your friends or walking seven kilometres to the nearest post office to book a telephone call that could take a week or more to place, most people would walk only as far as the bar.'

'You're right,' Ned conceded. 'Our Western ways wouldn't work here. Have you asked Anna why she drinks?'

'Her reply is always the same – "to be sociable".'

'That's the reason we all give. I used to drink too much when I was a student. But that was before I worked in a hospital's casualty department. A teenager who'd downed two bottles of whisky to celebrate his eighteenth birthday was brought in one night. Despite everyone's best efforts, the boy died.'

'It happens all over the world. You can understand young people going wild once in while, but people of Anna's age?' Josef shook his head. 'I wish she would hand the bar over to someone else. She has enough to occupy herself with running the house and looking after Stefan.'

'If she gave it up what would she do for money?'

'That's the problem,' Josef said. 'She's too young to retire, and working in one of the local factories, which is the only other job she could get around here, would mean leaving Stefan on his own for most of the day. You've seen what he's like; he can't be trusted to look after himself. It's easier for her when I'm around, but the school will be opening for the autumn term next month. And I won't be in the village for ever. Next year I'll be teaching in the town.'

'Will you still live here?'

'Yes, I can travel on the school bus, although it will be a long day.' Anna moved restlessly, and Josef lowered his voice. 'But I can't leave Anna, not when she's like this. If it weren't for her and the priest I would have been put in an orphanage. It's doubtful I would have survived. I certainly wouldn't have been educated. Government institutes after the war had nothing, and a lot of the kids died of malnutrition.'

'So you feel obligated to Anna?'

'No more than any child does to their parents. Since the priest died, she and Stefan are all the family I have left. Until I find Leon. Do you have a family?'

'Father, mother, six sisters and a brother.'

'Big family,' Josef commented.

'Four of my sisters are war orphans that my mother adopted.'

'So many children were brought up after the war by people who weren't their parents. The priest told me that most people in this

279

world are kind. On balance I think he was right, although I have met plenty who are anything but.'

Ned picked up the photograph of Helena in her graduation cap and gown. It had been taken less than two months before, but it felt like years. His parents had driven down to Bristol for the ceremony, bringing Magda in their car. He recalled how emphatic Magda had been in ordering two large copies of Helena's photograph. One for her and one for her 'family' in Poland. She must have sent it almost the day she received the prints. Josef's voice broke in on his thoughts.

'You know, Helena is completely at home here. She almost seems more Polish than British.'

Ned replaced the photograph on the nightstand. 'Magda brought Helena up to speak, read and write the language. It was only natural. A link to the *old* country for both of them.'

'She wanted Helena to be Polish,' Josef contradicted.

'Let's wait for Anna to tell us where Helena came from, shall we? As for Helena, I assure you, she might speak Polish but she's all Welsh.' Forgetting his earlier resolve to sleep on the floor, Ned moved the second chair and swung his feet on to it.

'Would you try to prevent Helena from leaving Britain and moving to Poland if she wanted to?'

'That is the last thing Helena would want to do.' Ned was astounded by the question.

'But if she did, would you try to stop her?' Josef repeated.

'You make it sound as though I order Helena about.'

'Don't you?' Josef's blue eyes probed into Ned's.

'Helena and I don't have a master-slave relationship. I love her and she loves me. Enough to wear the ring I bought her.' Ned struggled to keep his voice even. He wondered if Josef was deliberately trying to goad him into losing his temper. If so, he was going about it the right way.

'But you aren't married.'

'Who told you?'

'Helena. But I had guessed from the way you behave towards one another.'

'We would have been married if Magda hadn't died. We had

the church booked, the ceremony planned. We'd bought a house together—'

'Is that what marriage means in the West. Buying a house together?'

The sneering tone in Josef's voice set Ned's teeth on edge. 'We have to live somewhere. I thought it would be better if it was in a place of Helena's choosing. And she chose Pontypridd.'

'Didn't Helena decide to live in the town because it was where Magda lived, and she wanted to be close to the woman she thought was her mother?'

'It was where Helena grew up. She has many friends there. As for the house, she picked it, not me,' he added vehemently.

'Why so angry, Ned? If she's prepared to marry you, then she obviously wouldn't consider returning to Poland.'

'It wouldn't be returning. Even if she ever lived here, she can't remember it.' Ned glared at Josef, then checked Anna's pulse and breathing again. Not because he needed to, but because it gave him something to do other than argue with Josef.

'Any change?' Josef asked.

'She's still the same.'

'Thank you for looking after her.'

'As a doctor I couldn't have done otherwise,' Ned said ungraciously. He closed his eyes and tried to relax. But it was difficult when he was so conscious of Josef's presence in the room.

He tried to block him out by concentrating on the steady rhythm of Anna's breathing and listening to the small noises of the house as it settled for the night: the creak of the floorboards, contracting after the heat of the day; the irritating buzz of a solitary fly as it circled the lightbulb above them; the ringing of footsteps on the cobblestoned street outside . . .

Ned knew he'd slept, because when he next opened his eyes, the main light in the bedroom had been switched off and the door was open. The lamp on the landing was bright enough for him to read the clock face on the nightstand. The hands pointed to a little after four. He glanced across at the window seat. Josef was sitting there, watching him.

He left the chair and checked Anna's pulse and breathing again.

'How is she?' Josef asked.

'I think she'll be all right now.'

'You may as well go up to your room and sleep in a comfortable bed for what's left of the night.'

'I don't want to disturb Helena. She hasn't slept well since Magda died.'

'In that case, I'll go downstairs and make some coffee – or tea. Which would you prefer?'

'Tea would be good, thank you.' Ned returned to the easy chair. 'Have you slept?'

'No. But as Anna seems to be making a recovery, I can catch up tomorrow afternoon.'

'What about the bar?' Ned asked.

'It won't hurt to shut it for a few hours. After what has happened to Anna, I think it might do the regulars good to stay sober for once.'

Ned didn't drink the tea Josef made. He woke with a start two hours later to see Josef kneeling on the window seat, opening the curtains. The sun had risen and the haze in the east promised another hot and sunny day. He swung his legs to the floor and stretched his arms. He felt stiff and grubby, as he always did whenever he slept in his clothes.

In contrast, Josef had already shaved and washed. He wore a clean white cotton shirt, black polyester trousers, and smelled of Old Spice, which Ned assumed Magda had sent to Anna in one of her parcels.

Ned left his chair and leaned over Anna. Her breathing was steady, her skin had lost its blue tinge, and her hand was warm when he lifted it from beneath the covers to take her pulse.

'She's out of danger?' Josef asked.

'Yes. But she needs to drink plenty of water today, at least three litres. And she should eat light food. Scrambled eggs, toast and fruit would be good,' Ned advised.

'She usually eats bread rolls for breakfast with cheese and ham.' Josef straightened the blankets on Anna's bed.

'Eggs would be better.' Ned went to the door. 'I need to wash and change.'

'Breakfast in the yard in an hour?'

'Please. And as soon as Anna wakes, tell her she has to talk to Helena.'

'She won't want to.'

'If she refuses, I'll tell Helena about the photographs and the contents of Magda's parcels which are in the kitchen. And that is not a threat. I don't want Helena tormenting herself with thoughts about her origins for a minute longer than it takes Anna to wake and prepare to meet her.'

'You really would tell Helena?'

'Absolutely. Better she have a drunk for a mother – if Anna is her mother – than no knowledge of her real family. You have half an hour after Anna wakes to persuade her I am serious, Josef.'

Breakfast was a silent affair. Josef laid the table for Helena and Ned in the yard, but neither he nor Stefan joined them. Ned presumed they were eating in the house. As he was drinking his last cup of coffee, Helena stood to leave the table.

Ned hadn't slept well, but the dark half-moons beneath Helena's eyes suggested she had slept as badly. 'You going somewhere, sunshine?'

'To the lake to take some photographs.'

'I'd leave it until this afternoon, if I were you.'

'Why?'

'The weather and the light will be better,' he suggested lamely.

'It couldn't be more perfect now.' She sat down again, and he could see from the way she tensed her fingers that she was preparing for another argument.

'I'd like to go with you this afternoon – that's if you want company. As for this morning, as soon as Anna wakes, she will want to see you.'

'Why?' she demanded suspiciously.

Josef carried an empty tray out of the house before Ned could answer. He set it on the table and proceeded to clear the dishes.

'I was just telling Helena that Anna will want to see her this morning,' Ned prompted.

'She woke half an hour ago. Stefan has taken up her breakfast.' Josef lifted Helena's empty coffee cup on to the tray.

'And you told Anna—'

'About last night, yes.' Josef interrupted. 'She is ashamed of herself. She said she didn't mean to get into that state. But one drink led to another until she didn't know what she was doing. She promised me it won't happen again.'

Having had some professional experience of alcoholics, Ned knew just how little Anna's promise was worth, but he refrained from making a comment. 'Did you also tell Anna that I had treated her?'

'Yes.'

'And that we want to see her?'

'We?' Josef dropped the plate he was holding on to the tray. 'I told Anna you wanted her to talk to Helena—'

'I want to be there, too.'

Helena watched the argument bounce between Josef and Ned with increasing bewilderment. 'What is going on between you two? I thought Anna was drunk and had an accident?'

'She did and she has. She's cracked her ribs.' Josef slammed the sugar bowl on to the tray so hard that granules scattered.

'Then why does she want to see me?'

'Ask Ned.'

Helena turned to Ned. 'Why should I see Anna?'

'Anna will tell you.' Ned left the table. 'Is she getting up?'

Josef picked up the tray. 'I thought she should stay in bed today and rest.'

'She can stay in bed if she insists, but not for more than one day. Sitting up in a chair in her room would be better, and sitting outside so she can breathe fresh air better still. I'll go up and check on her. Perhaps Helena can come up afterwards.'

'You want me to sit here and wait until you call me?' Helena asked caustically.

Ned ignored her tone. 'I won't be a moment.'

'Does Anna want to throw us out?'

'You know she does,' Ned answered.

'And you want me to try and talk Anna into letting us stay until you can arrange for Norbert to pick us up?'

'I'll be back in a moment.' Ned walked into the house.

Josef picked up the tray and followed him.

Chapter 19

NED KNOCKED ON the door of Anna's room. She called out something he didn't understand, and he entered tentatively to see her propped up on pillows in bed, an untouched tray of scrambled eggs and breakfast rolls alongside her on the mattress.

Ned waited for Josef to appear so he could translate for them. In the meantime, Anna looked anywhere but at him. He tried to smile to put her at her ease, but the smile died on his lips as he caught sight of Helena's photographs again. When he recalled how distraught Helena had been when she had discovered that Adam and Magda Janek weren't her parents, and that she had grown up believing lies, he couldn't forgive Anna for causing her such pain. It was a relief when Josef finally joined them.

'Ask Anna how she is feeling?' Ned snapped without any preliminaries.

Josef spoke to Anna and translated her reply. 'Very sorry for the trouble she has caused you, and embarrassed by her behaviour. She assures you that she will never drink again.'

'I meant in a medical sense,' Ned explained. 'Has she any pain from her ribs, or are any of the cuts on her arms and legs stinging more than the others?'

Josef spoke to her again, and Anna replied, looking at him, not Ned.

'Anna says the pains are not so bad and she will be fine. She is grateful to you for looking after her and pumping her stomach. I told her about sitting up, and she said she'll probably get up later today.'

'Ask her when Helena can come to talk to her.'

'I spoke to her about that earlier. She said that no young girl, let alone one as intelligent and beautiful as Helena, would want a drunk as her mother. It would shatter her.'

'Then Anna is her mother?'

'She doesn't want Helena to know,' Josef answered.

Ned saw that he was torn between his feelings for the woman who had been as much of a mother to him as Magda had been to Helena, and Helena's right to know the truth about her birth. 'Please, ask Anna if she thinks it better that Helena believes she was snatched from a loving home by the Nazis after they murdered her parents? Or that Helena goes through life, constantly searching for her real parents and suffering the torment of a fruitless quest? You've spent years searching for your brother without success so you know what it's like to look for someone you may never find. If Anna doesn't tell Helena who she is, she has no hope of discovering the truth.'

Josef translated, and Anna glared at Ned. He parried her look. After what felt like the longest two minutes of Ned's life, Anna finally dropped her gaze. She turned to Josef and spoke sharply to him.

Josef replied, and Ned could tell from his tone that he was pleading with Anna. Unable to understand what they were saying, or to stand the suspense, he went to the window seat. Someone — either Josef or Stefan — had cleared the make-shift bed and extra chairs, and tidied and swept the room. The corner where Josef had heaped the broken chair was clear, and the embroidered coverlet had been draped back on the bed.

'Anna thinks it's best that Helena doesn't know the truth. She says it's her secret, and no one else's now that Magdalena Janek is dead,' Josef translated, clearly trying hard to keep his own emotions in check.

Ned looked at Anna. When she refused to meet his steady gaze, he moved closer, forcing her to look at him. She screwed her eyes shut, as though she were in pain.

'It's not just your secret, Anna. It affects Helena, so it is her secret, too.'

Josef translated, and Anna replied rapidly, stumbling over her words.

'She is afraid Helena will ask her questions about her father, and she doesn't want to tell Helena that she is illegitimate.' Josef met Ned's gaze.

'Helena wouldn't care whether she was illegitimate or not. And any truth has to be better than the belief that she is the result of an SS breeding experiment.'

Josef spoke to Anna once more, but she continued to shake her head.

Ned played his last card. 'If she continues to refuse to talk to Helena, I will go downstairs and tell Helena that Anna is her mother.' He moved towards the door.

Anna hadn't understood what Ned had said, but his sense of purpose was unmistakable. She grabbed Josef's arm and cried out hysterically.

Ned waited, his hand on the door.

Anna spoke urgently to Josef.

'Well?' Ned asked when she fell silent.

Josef closed his hand reassuringly over Anna's. 'You can bring Helena up, but Anna insists on seeing her alone.'

Ned hesitated.

'It wouldn't make any difference if you were here, Ned. You wouldn't be able to understand what Anna was saying and Helena can tell you about it afterwards.'

Ned nodded and left the room.

Helena was still in the yard. She and Stefan were leaning over the wall of the pig-sty. Stefan had lifted out one of the tiny piglets, and Helena was scratching it behind the ears.

Ned joined them. 'I can see you wanting to exchange the bungalow for a farm when we return to Pontypridd.'

'Much as I like animals, I think it would be too much hard work. Besides, I'd never be able to part with a single creature, especially if I knew they were going to be slaughtered.' She paused. 'I've been talking to Stefan. He said something odd to me yesterday evening – "It's good that you have come here at last." Anna is my mother, isn't she?'

Ned took a deep breath and steeled himself for an outburst. 'Yes.'

'You knew all along and you didn't tell me?' Her eyes darkened in contempt. 'How could you?'

'I only began to suspect it last night when I went to Anna's bedroom after she fell. When you go up you'll see why. I didn't know for certain until a few minutes ago. Josef confirmed it.'

'I thought we could tell one another everything.'

Emotions Ned had fought to keep in check since the day Magda had died finally erupted. 'Like you tell me everything? I know something is dreadfully wrong between us, Helena, but I haven't a clue what it is, or what I can do about it. You stopped talking to me properly weeks ago. I've never felt so hopeless and useless. Sometimes, I can't help feeling that you don't even want me here ...' He looked up, saw Josef watching them, and made an effort to control his temper. 'As I said, I didn't find out until a few minutes ago, and now isn't the time or place to argue. Go and talk to Anna. We can sort out our problems later.'

'I'm not so optimistic,' she snapped bitterly.

A lump rose in Ned's throat. Suddenly he felt certain that he was about to lose Helena, and was powerless to stop it. There was no way he could force her to stay with him. And even if he could, he wouldn't want to. Their relationship had been built on love, trust and respect. He had never loved her more, and loving her meant wanting what she wanted for herself. If her happiness depended on sacrificing all that they had been to one another and never seeing her again, that was his price to pay. He felt something move on his cheek, and realized that tears were falling from his eyes.

Josef pulled a bunch of keys from his pocket and unlocked the door to the bar. Stefan returned the piglet to the sty and went to help him.

'I'll wait for you here.' Ned leaned on the wall and looked down at the pigs.

Helena didn't move and Ned didn't turn towards her. Still staring into the sty, he said, 'Go through the kitchen into the inner hall and up the stairs. Anna's bedroom door is the second on the right. It will probably be open. And remember, Helena, I love you very much. That's why I insisted that Anna talk to you.'

*

289

Unlike Ned the night before, Helena had time to look around when she walked through the house. She saw the tins with English labels in the kitchen – and noted they were the brands Magda had favoured. A cardigan that was draped on the back of one of the kitchen chairs was identical in colour and style to one of Magda's. She even recalled her buying two a few Christmases ago, saying, 'This shade of blue will suit my sister.'

She went to the foot of the stairs. The inside of the house was far grander than it appeared from the outside. The oak newel post and banisters were beautifully carved in a fruit and flower design, and the treads were highly polished, with a sheen that bore testimony to centuries of loving care. As Ned had said, one of the doors on the galleried landing was open. She walked up to it and knocked.

Anna called out, 'Come in, Helena,' in a weak and tremulous voice.

Helena went into Anna's bedroom and stared just as Ned had done, mesmerized by the display of photographs.

'Please, won't you sit down?'

Helena walked across the room to the window seat, although she could have sat on a chair that was closer to the bed.

Anna plumped up a pillow, moved it behind her head and sat up.

'All those parcels – Magda sent them to you?' Helena felt it was a stupid way to begin a conversation, but she couldn't wait to have her suspicions confirmed.

'Yes,' Anna admitted.

'And that's why you didn't want Ned and I to stay here, because you were afraid that I would find out that you knew Magda and me ...'

'Ned and Josef want me to tell you about the past. I think some things are best left unsaid. It's better you believe the stories Magda told you.'

'But they weren't the truth,' Helena protested.

'Magda wrote to me every month. Her letters were all about you and your life together. She tried to be your mama in every way that she could, Helena, just as I tried to be Josef's.'

'I knew that you were my real mother before Ned told me because of something Stefan said.'

'Since the Germans beat him, my brother can't be trusted. God help him.' Anna crossed herself. 'He has the mind of a child.'

'You gave birth to me. You are my mother,' Helena pressed, needing to hear it from Anna.

'I am a drunk, middle-aged woman with a dubious reputation, who runs a seedy village bar. You are an elegant young lady, a person of some importance, a teacher whose young man is a doctor. You wouldn't want to own me as your mother.'

'I can't disown you when I don't know you, Anna. Please, I'd like to hear how I came to be with Magda.' Helena said angrily. 'What happened to separate us? Did you give me up willingly? Do I have any brothers or sisters? Did you abandon me or give me to Magda? Who was my father? Did you love him? Did he love you?'

'Too many questions.' Anna waved her hand as though she were physically pushing Helena's words aside.

'The last thing I want to do is upset you by bringing up the past, but I have a right to know who I am,' Helena pleaded.

'I will try, if you sit and listen quietly. When I have finished I will do my best to answer any questions you may have. But remember, this is your doing, not mine.'

'May I ask just one question before you start? Do I have a name of my own?'

'When you were two weeks old you were baptised Lena Matylda Leman, after my mother and my sister.' Anna sank back on to the pillows.

'Lena . . . I like it and it's not so very different from Helena.'

'That is what Magda said.'

'Thank you for telling me, Anna. I won't ask any more questions until you have finished.'

'And afterwards you will hate me.'

Helena didn't answer. Anna had stated a fact, not asked her a question. And she wasn't prepared to lie. Not before she heard Anna's story.

Helena leaned back against the wall. She drew up her knees,

wrapped her arms around her legs and looked at Anna. The ivory cotton on the pillow behind the landlady's head was the same shade as her parchment-dry skin. Her bleached hair, which Helena had only seen swept up and caught in a French pleat, hung limp and unkempt below her shoulders, and her blue eyes were bloodshot and watery.

'People say everyone believes their childhood days were golden,' Anna began hesitantly. 'It's a lie. Josef was three years old when his mother was killed, and the bullet that ended her life ended his childhood. Before, I used to see him laughing as he ran and played around the village. When the old priest brought him to me the night of the massacre I knew that his laughter had died along with his mother. He woke screaming night after night for years afterwards, as he waited for the Nazis to return and murder me, the priest and him.'

Anna reached for the jug of water next to her bed and poured herself a glass. 'But my childhood . . .' She smiled, and for the first time Helena caught a glimpse of the vibrant happy woman she could have been. 'I don't just remember golden days; I lived them. I have no need of an imagination because nothing could better my memories. I could never make up my mind which season I loved the most. In the summer, as soon as school closed for the holidays, Magda, Weronika and I used to spend our days in the woods around the lake. We'd roam until it grew too hot to walk, then swim, pick berries and mushrooms, light fires and bake potatoes in the embers. We spent hours reading books aloud to one another, wrote stories and poems . . . Weronika and I were luckier than Magda. She never had as much free time as we did. She had to work on the farm, helping her mother in the dairy, or her brothers to clean out the pigs or the chickens. We were known as the three witches – in a good way – because we were always together.

'Every autumn we helped bring in the harvest on every farm for miles around, because in return we'd be invited to the harvest suppers in the barns, and there was music, dancing and young men.

'Winter meant skating parties on the lakes, snowball fights and sleigh rides. My sisters and Stefan would always come with us. This was before Stefan went to the seminary. Wiktor, Adam and

Magda's oldest brother Augustyn used to take us to town whenever they went to pick up stores for the farms.

'Wiktor was the joker in those days. You could rely on him to make everyone laugh; sometimes at his expense, mostly at ours. He would tie our plaits to the back of the carts whenever he gave us a ride, just to hear us scream when we tried to climb off. He'd pull knotted string and bits of leather and fur from his pocket, tell us it was a dead rat, and chase us round the village. He was never nasty, not like he is now. He'd spend hours nursing an animal rather than kill it. Once he hid a runt in his bedroom and fed it from a baby's bottle when his father threatened to let it starve to death. His mother was furious when she saw the mess the piglet had made in his bed. And whenever we went anywhere he would take as many girls and boys from the village as wanted to go. Ten or twelve of us would cram into a cart or sleigh meant for four.'

Anna closed her eyes. 'But then we grew up.'

Helena had heard all this from Magda a hundred times and more, but she sat quietly as she had promised and waited. Anna sensed her thoughts.

'I'm boring you. Magda must have told you all these stories. We wrote more about the old days than our new lives in our letters. Perhaps Magda, like me, clung to her past because she preferred it to her present. I know I did. From an early age we knew our destinies would be different, but we thought we would carry on living here together, if not in the village then the town, close enough to visit and keep our friendship.

'Weronika was the sophisticated one. Money meant little to us as children; there has only ever been one shop in this village and all you could buy in it before the war were things that weren't produced on the farms or sold in the weekly market, like paraffin oil, candles, sewing thread, needles and, occasionally, magazines and comics. Occasionally, because the grown-ups told us that magazines and comics were a waste of money. But our mothers bought them when they thought no one was watching. How else would they have known what was fashionable and what was not? And if our fathers complained, they used to say, "What else can we use to line the kitchen drawers?"

'The Janeks were the richest family in the area. If any farmer was in trouble because his animals were ill or his crops had failed, he went to Weronika's father to borrow money. Mr Janek never refused. And twice a year, in spring and autumn, Weronika and her brothers and sisters would visit Cracow with their mother to stay with their cousins and shop.

'They had furniture, clothes, jewellery and household goods like no one else. Some – the few things Wiktor left when he ransacked this house – are still here. But they never boasted about their money or possessions. And every time Weronika returned from the city she brought Magda and I dress-lengths of beautiful material, the same quality as the ones she bought for herself. Magda's were always red, and mine were blue – our favourite colours.

'The greatest tragedy of our childhood was the diphtheria epidemic that swept through the country in the winter of 1934. Weronika's parents and all her brothers and sisters except Adam died, as did many of the young and old people in the village.

'Adam was only nineteen, but he took over his father's business and looked after Weronika. On her seventeenth birthday Weronika became engaged to the son of the doctor who lived in town. Some said it was a match arranged by their fathers when they were children. Maybe it was, but Weronika had stars in her eyes whenever she looked at the doctor's son. Just like Magda with Adam.

'So Magda married her Adam,' she continued. 'Weronika lived with them while her doctor's son went to Warsaw to study at the university. She kept the business books for Adam, as well as embroidering her future married monogram on table and bed linen. With Magda married and Weronika dreaming about her wedding, which was planned for the spring of 1940, I felt out of step with my friends for the first time in my life. Then my father invited the eldest son of one of the farmers to our house. I didn't discover until much later that he had asked my father if he could call on me. We were far more formal in our courting in those days.

'I knew what my parents hoped would happen. The bar didn't bring in much money. My mother tried to help by cooking and selling food, but few people bought her meals because everyone ate at home except the village's two widowers, one bachelor and the travellers who went from village to village selling animal feeds and cures.

'We girls were a burden. There was nowhere for us to work where we could earn money while we continued to live at home, and my father wouldn't hear of any of us going to the town, let alone the cities. The farms were run by families, and no farmer would pay wages when he could make his son or daughter work for bed and board. My mother wanted the three of us to marry well so we would never have to worry about money as she'd had to do all of her married life.

'My parents had a sitting room behind the bar. We use it to store the empty bottles now. There was a couch there where my brother slept before he went to the seminary. Upstairs were two bedrooms; my sisters and I shared one, and my parents slept in the other. It was crowded, and the bar downstairs was always noisy. But Adam and Weronika allowed us to play in their yard and use the library in their house whenever we wanted to study.'

Anna's bloodshot watery eyes grew misty. 'I was telling you about my young man. I had known him all my life, but only really noticed him when he asked me to dance at a harvest supper in 1938. His family's farm was large and they owned it outright. The house was beautiful and in time it would be his, as would all the land, because his family followed the tradition of handing their wealth down to the eldest son. He was a fine catch for the daughter of a poor bar-keeper.

'As well as the farmhouse, the family had a little house not far from the farm. His widowed grandmother lived in it. She was frail and the time was coming for her to move in with his parents. It was the way then. The little house would have been free for the farmer's oldest son to set up home there with his bride. Then, in time, when the young couple had a family, the son's parents grew old, and the rest of their children had left the farm, the cycle would begin all over again.

'My parents were happy for me when he asked my father for my hand. They thought my life was mapped out, and so did I. I wasn't a farmer's daughter but I wasn't afraid of hard work. My fiancé's mother offered to train me. I used to walk to the farm early every morning to help with the milking. Afterwards I would work in the dairy or the fields, and my young man would drive me home in the cart in the evening.

'When Germany declared war and the Russians and Germans invaded Poland, the Polish army called on all men to fight for their country. Every man in the village went. Some didn't return. Weronika lost her fiancé, but Adam, Magda's brothers and my young man returned when it was clear that we had lost the war, days after the first German troops crossed the border.

'Adam called a meeting in the bar. It was decided that he should stay in the village to protect it as best he could. He was a gentleman farmer. The invaders needed food; he could oversee production. My fiancé ...' Anna clamped her hand over her mouth for a moment. 'He took his father's old hunting rifle, went into the forest and joined the partisans along with Wiktor. Brave but foolish young men. As if it were possible to fight tanks and machine guns with old hunting rifles.

'We tried to carry on as before. My eldest sister helped my father in the bar, and Matylda ...' Anna's voice broke. 'Matylda was very beautiful. She could have had any man in the village, but she fell in love with a poor boy, a farm labourer. His family could offer her nothing and my father was furious. For a year she and my father didn't speak a word to one another. It broke my mother's heart.'

Helena saw Anna's love for her sister etched into every line on her face.

'Our lives changed. The Nazis gave every Pole a ration card, which entitled us to nine hundred and thirty calories a day, half of what we needed to stay healthy. They were like locusts. They would turn up in the village without warning, at any time of the day or night, order us into the square, and search our houses for partisans, weapons and hoarded food. They took whatever they wanted – silver, jewellery, paintings, linen. If we objected they would set fire to the house. Anyone – man, woman, or child – suspected of helping the partisans or hoarding food would be hanged and we would be forced to watch.

'The first time it happened, the priest and my brother, who had returned here as a curate, appealed to the officers. They were both taken away. When they returned a year later we didn't recognize them. They were so changed, thin and broken. It was the beginning of the end for Stefan. His spirit had been crushed. The beatings the Germans gave him later only finished what they had begun when they took him in 1941.'

Anna tensed. 'We fought back every way we could. My father would harness the cart with our one remaining old horse and pick up barrels of beer from the farmers – in those days we had no large breweries. He would hide guns smuggled in from Russia amongst the kegs, and move hunted men from one village to another. He took Jews who'd been in hiding as close to the Russian border as he dared, and distributed food, which the farmers had risked their lives to hoard, among the partisans.

'Someone informed on him. I never found out who. The Germans offered food, money and favours as rewards to anyone who betrayed a Pole working for the underground. I don't even blame the traitor, unless he or she sold my father for money. Perhaps they hoped to buy the life of a son or a husband. When the soldiers came for him they took my mother and older sister as well. I was left to look after the bar and Matylda.

'I did what I knew my father would have wanted me to: fight the Nazis every way I could. The next day I harnessed the horse and cart and carried on smuggling for the partisans. I went to my fiancé's camp as often as I could, using the excuse that I was taking him news of his family, but we both knew I went only to see him.

'In the summer of 1942, I was driving the cart through the forest with my sister Matylda when a group of German soldiers stopped us. They were drunk . . .'

Helena gripped the edge of the window seat.

'I was terrified. I had heard stories about what the Germans did to young girls, and not just stories. I had seen their corpses abandoned at the side of the road.'

She raised her bloodshot eyes. 'It was different between young men and women in those days. Matylda and I were virgins. All of us faced death every day under the Germans, but our young men wouldn't make love to us, no matter how much they wanted to, because they thought it would demean us in the eyes of the Church and decent society.'

'You wanted to?' Helena asked when she could bear Anna's silence no longer.

'I was frightened. I didn't know what to expect. I had been brought up a strict Catholic and knew nothing. No one talked about what love between a man and woman could be like in those days, not even mothers and daughters. Sex was something that went on in the fields between animals. We had seen the results when cows calved and horses foaled. But every Sunday in church we were told that men and women were different from beasts. The church preached that sex before marriage was a mortal sin, and we were terrified of going to hell. So, my fiancé never did more than kiss me.

'But when Matylda and I were trapped on that cart by those foul, drunken pigs – which is too good a word for them; no pig would have done to another pig what they did to us – I wished that he and I had never listened to the priest. I wished that we had made love every time we had been alone together. But it was too late. I looked at Matylda, and the expression on her face will haunt me until the day I die.

'They pulled us down from the cart, tore our clothes off, stripped us naked – hit us when we screamed and . . .'

Helena felt sick to the pit of her stomach. She had never seen such self-loathing and disgust on anyone's face. 'You don't have to tell me any more.'

'Yes, I do. I have lived a lie for so long I was in danger of believing it. It is time for the truth. And I am telling you this for my sake not yours. What I am about to say, I have never said outside of the confessional. The old priest who gave me absolution is dead. Now I need absolution again – from the one person who had the right to expect me to protect her, the one person I have failed most in my life.'

'My father was a drunken German rapist.'

Silence closed in, thick, suffocating. Anna whispered, 'They took Matylda first. They did unspeakable things to her, and all the time she screamed, pleading with them to kill her, they laughed. I begged them to take me instead, but they laughed. She was prettier. That was why they took her first. She was prettier.'

Chapter 20

HELENA FELT AS though time and everything else in the room, including Anna, had been frozen, as though she were in a painting, brushed into a corner, fixed and immobile. The staccato tick of the alarm clock on the table next to the bed seemed to shatter the silence. The room whirled around her. Anna was dry-eyed. Beyond tears.

'When they finished with Matylda they threw her to the side of the road. She was covered in blood. I didn't know whether she was alive or dead. One of them grabbed my arm. I could smell the sour herrings and beer on his breath ...'

Helena braced herself. A part of her wanted to tell Anna to stop. Yet she couldn't. She needed to hear the truth about her parents. Wasn't that what she had told Ned? No matter how terrible, she would learn to live with the knowledge of who she was, if she could be certain that it was the truth. She looked up and saw Anna watching her intently, an odd expression on her face. Then she continued.

'A car drove up and stopped. Two German officers climbed out and walked over to us. The soldiers stopped beating me and jumped to attention. I fell to my knees and asked the officers to kill Matylda and me quickly, to put us out of our misery.

'They were kind, gentle. They picked up our clothes and took two coats from the soldiers. They covered Matylda with one and gave me the other. They asked me where we lived.

'I was terrified that they would go to the village and kill everyone there, so I wouldn't tell them. They sent the soldiers away, put us in their car and took us to a doctor, who stitched Matylda's wounds and warned me that the worst injuries were the ones that couldn't be seen: the ones in her mind. He was right. When he had finished treating Matylda, the officers drove us back to the cart. I asked them to go away. They did. Fortunately the horse knew the way home. We returned here and I put Matylda to bed. She didn't say a word that night, or for almost a year afterwards.

'Somehow, one of the officers found out who we were and where we lived. The next morning he came to the bar. He brought food, medicine and apologized for what the soldiers had done to Matylda. He wanted me to go to the authorities to complain. That is how naive he was. I thanked him but told him not to come near us again, because if the people in the village saw a German officer visiting me they would think that I had become a collaborator. He asked if he could meet me again – and I looked into his eyes and knew. I thought he did, too.

'I told him that I couldn't risk being seen with him but I would try to go to the lake on Sunday. I went. He was there. He told me that he wasn't really a soldier but a scientist, an archaeologist. He had been drafted into an SS unit that excavated ancient burial grounds and villages in Poland and Russia to look for signs of early Germanic settlements. It was part of the Nazis' plan to claim that the whole of Eastern Europe had been settled by German tribes.

'He was a German, one of the enemy, yet I *knew* that he was the one for me, just as Adam had been the one for Magda. I thought about my fiancé and realized my feelings for him were childish infatuation. This was love – the real thing. We arranged to meet at the lake twice a week. We met ten times in all. And the first time we met we made love. Not because he forced me, but because I knew it was the right thing for us to do, that the Church was wrong. There was no sin in what we did.

'My time had come. I finally understood what Magda and Weronika had been trying to tell me when we had talked about love. The officer wanted to make plans for us for after the war. He told me how delighted his mother would be when he introduced us. But all I wanted to talk about was what was happening to us now. We never had much time. Matylda was ill and I couldn't leave her for long.

'One night, as I was walking back to the village from the lake, I heard gunfire and men shouting in German and Polish. I hid until it

300

was quiet then crept back here. The next morning I heard that the partisans had attacked a convoy of SS as they left the archaeological dig.

'He did not meet me the next Sunday. I was devastated because I thought he'd been hurt, or worse. What I didn't know for a week was that my fiancé had been killed that night. A month later I discovered that I was pregnant. I confessed to the priest and told him who the father of my child was, but no one else knew or suspected the truth. My fiancé's mother and father, like everyone in the village, assumed the child I was carrying was his.'

'Your fiancé never knew about you and the German officer?'

'No, Jerzy never knew about us.'

'His name was Jerzy.' Because Anna hadn't mentioned his name until now, Helena had been wondering if he was related to someone she'd met in the village.

'Jerzy Leman. His parents insisted that you be given his name when you were christened. One more lie that I went along with. Before you were born I was terrified that people would find out that the child I was carrying wasn't Jerzy's, although, logically, there was no reason for anyone to do so. I knew the priest would keep my secret because the confessional is sacred. Like my German lover, I had blonde hair and blue eyes, so the chances were that my child would be blonde and blue-eyed, too. Jerzy's hair had been light brown, his eyes grey, so no one's suspicions would be aroused if the child was fair.

'I had been careful, so had my German. We had never written a letter to one another. We met on Sunday and Wednesday evenings at the lake at seven o'clock in the evening. If one of us didn't turn up it would be seven o'clock the next Sunday or Wednesday. I never told anyone about him, not even Matylda, and he swore that he never told anyone about me. I believed him.

'It was almost as dangerous for my German as it was for me. The Nazis regarded us Poles as sub-humans. It was a crime for an Aryan to degrade his blood by having relations with a Pole. Rape was accepted. Polish women could be used and abused, but not loved. And marriage between a Polish woman and a German man was out of the question. That would have been a race crime.

'I was sick the whole time I carried you. I couldn't keep food down. Magda and Weronika cared for me, and Matylda tried to help. I had to close the bar. There was no more beer to be had, or spare food, so I had no excuse to take out the horse and cart even if I had been well. And all the time I carried you, I loved you and looked forward to your birth, because I believed that you would be born out of love and a living reminder of all that my German lover had been.

'One evening, two weeks before you were born, I saw my German. He came into the village with a convoy that was looking for partisans. He wasn't dead at all. As usual, we were ordered into the square. He saw me, looked at my stomach and winked at me – then he winked at another girl. A girl who was rumoured to have taken to walking in the woods in the evening.

'I understood. The Germans who had raped Matylda and almost raped me were more honest. They took what they wanted by force. My German lover – the man I believed had been destined for me – had only been pretending. There had been no great tragic love affair. He had fooled me and I had fooled myself. I had been used, just as Matylda had, only more gently.

'You were born at two o'clock in the morning on 7 April 1943. Magda helped the midwife, and when Matylda heard you cry she came into my room and spoke for the first time in nearly a year.

'I couldn't bear to look at you. You were a reminder not of my love but my stupidity. I was too sick to feed you or look after you. Now I think I made myself ill so I wouldn't have to look after you. I can't remember a single thing that happened during the month after you were born. And all that time, my sister Matylda nursed you, fed you, bathed you and took care of you.

'It was Matylda who carried you to the church for your baptism and named you Lena after my mother and Matylda at my insistence. As she had taken it upon herself to look after you, I think in some twisted way I wanted to believe you were hers. She was a better mother to you than I could ever have been.

'Jerzy's mother and father went to your baptism. They assumed you were their grandchild, but their kindness was more than I could bear. The villagers were kind also, especially considering that you had been born a bastard. Because Jerzy had been killed fighting the Germans I was almost accorded the status of a widow.

'Two nights before the massacre, German soldiers burned down Jerzy's farm and killed all his family. I don't have to tell you what happened on the twenty-sixth of June.'

'The day of the massacre,' Helena murmured.

'The soldiers assembled us in the square. As usual, Matylda was carrying you. The Brown Sisters took all the blonde blue-eyed babies, including you. Like Adam Janek, Matylda fought to keep you. And the soldiers shot Matylda, just as they shot Adam Janek. I wished then, as I wish now, that they had shot me.'

Anna took a deep breath and began to speak more quickly. It was as though she couldn't wait to tell the rest of her story.

'The Brown Sisters passed the children and babies they had taken to the people they had picked out. The way I describe it you might think it was orderly. It wasn't. It was all noise and confusion. The German officers were barking orders, the soldiers were firing guns, people were shouting, babies were screaming. It was chaos. And I stood calmly in the middle of it, with Matylda lying dead at my feet, watching as you, Magda and Weronika were marched out of the village at gunpoint.

'It was the last time I saw you before you walked into the yard with Ned. One of the young girls was carrying you, a tiny baby wrapped in a shawl. Magda tried to take you, but her left arm was hanging limp at her side. I think the Germans had broken it when she tried to stop them from killing Adam and Helena. I was crying, but my tears were for Matylda, Magda and Weronika. All I felt as I watched you go was relief. Relief that I wouldn't have to look on the living face of my stupidity and foolishness again.

'If the priest hadn't brought me Josef that night I would have killed myself. I had already laid out the kitchen knives and was choosing one to cut my wrists. The old priest couldn't be with everyone, so he tried to give each one of us a reason to live. Every single house had lost someone, either killed or taken. And we all knew that being taken was practically a death sentence.

'Josef needed me, and to be needed by someone meant every-thing to me at that time. I couldn't do anything for Matylda, Magda,

303

Weronika, my parents, my oldest sister or you, but I could look after Josef, poor Stefan and the priest. And the priest kept reminding me that nothing is for ever. That one day the war would end and you would find your way back to me. Little did he know that was the last thing I wanted.'

'But I have found my way back to you,' Helena said softly.

'Not as my child. As Magda's. I didn't hear from her until after the war ended. A month after Wiktor hounded Weronika out of the village, I received a letter from Magda. Weronika had written to tell her that everyone in Poland believed that the girls who had been taken by the Nazis had been used only for one purpose, and that they were all regarded as whores.

'Magda told me that a miracle had happened. She had managed to keep you safe and with her. It hadn't been easy. But by changing your records for newcomers into the home, and pretending that you had a temperature or diarrhoea whenever it was your turn to be adopted, she kept you so she could return you to me at the end of the war.

'I wrote back to her but I didn't tell her the truth. I made excuses. I said that I didn't have enough food to feed Josef and myself. I was ill. It was as much as I could do to look after Josef. It would be best if she didn't return to the village for her own sake because she would be treated the same way that Weronika had been.

'Magda replied and said she couldn't understand any mother not wanting their own daughter, which was understandable given what had happened to her Helena. She enclosed a photograph of you, the first of many. You looked just like your father and, so help me God, I still didn't want to see you. I never answered the letter. How could I even begin to tell Magda the truth without admitting that I'd had an affair with one of the enemy?

'The next time I heard from Magda she said that she'd had an offer of marriage and was going to make a new life for herself and you in Great Britain. From the little Weronika had said when she'd returned, I knew she hadn't recognized you in the Displaced Persons' camp. There was no reason for Weronika to suspect that you were anything other than a Lebensborn child Magda had picked up to replace the child that had been killed. And Magda hadn't enlightened her.'

'Why not?' Helena asked, momentarily forgetting her promise not to ask questions.

'Because Magda wanted to write to me and break what she thought was marvellous news herself. I didn't hear from Magda for over two years. When she was settled in Britain she started sending me parcels and photographs of you. I was pleased. I had proof that she was giving you a better life than I could have given you in Poland. It seemed right and made me feel less guilty. I had Josef; Magda had you. Neither Magda nor I were truly happy because we couldn't forget those we had loved and lost during the war, but we got on with our lives.

'The Cold War began, you and I were the wrong sides of it, and I thought that I would never see Magda or you again.' Anna fell back on the pillows. 'Now you know everything. You were born to a mother who was not only a traitor to her country but too much of a coward to love you. You had a father who was a good-looking, charming philanderer and a Nazi. A young aunt who loved you enough to sacrifice her life trying to protect you. And a foster-mother who loved you enough to risk her life in the Lebensborn home to keep you with her. A foster mother who would have given you up to a mother who didn't want you at the end of the war, simply because she thought it was the right thing to do, even though it would have hurt her unbearably. I know from her letters just how much Magda loved you. She never understood why I didn't want you back.'

'Do you know why Magda didn't tell me the truth?'

'We never wrote about it. But I think we both knew that the truth would upset you, and we wanted to protect you. It's easy to delay making difficult decisions. To say, "I'll think about this or that tomorrow."'

'And my father?'

'I never saw or heard from him again.'

'His name?'

'Johann Schmidt, he said.'

'John Smith,' Helena translated.

Anna smiled grimly. 'I was very young and naive.'

'You loved him?'

'I believed that I loved him. With all my heart and soul, I thought I did.'

'And that is the truth?'

'Yes.'

Helena rose from the window seat and went to the door. 'Thank you. I know this hasn't been easy for you.'

'I'm sorry.'

'You have nothing to be sorry for. You were used and hurt. What happened wasn't your fault.'

'Such forgiveness.' Anna reached out and Helena took the hand offered to her. 'I only wish you could have been mine. For a while you were Matylda's, but you were, and still are, Magda's daughter.'

Chapter 21

JOSEF WAS SITTING in the kitchen when Helena walked down the stairs into the hall. He lifted the coffee pot when she appeared in the doorway.

'I've made fresh. Would you like a cup?'

'Please. I think Anna could do with one as well.' Helena pulled out a chair from the huge scrub-down pine table and sat down.

'Did Anna tell you everything you wanted to know?'

'And more.' Helena rested her elbows on the table, propping her chin on the palms of her hands. She felt drained, emotionally, mentally and physically. She couldn't even begin to think through everything Anna had told her. But there was one thing that she wanted to do as soon as possible before she changed her mind. And she needed Josef's help to carry it out.

Josef filled a cup with coffee, and put the sugar bowl and the milk jug in front of Helena. Then he made another cup, poured in a splash of milk, and carried it up the stairs. When he returned, he sat opposite Helena. 'So what happens now?'

'In what way?' She picked up the milk jug.

'The future way. Are you going to stay here and look after your mother? As you see, she needs help. And now that Magda is dead, you have no reason to return to Britain.'

'Except Ned,' she said quietly.

'He doesn't understand the Polish side of you.'

'Helena?'

She looked up and started guiltily. Ned was leaning in the open doorway that led into the yard. Her cheeks burned before she remembered, with relief, that she and Josef had been speaking in Polish.

'Sorry, Ned, my mind was elsewhere.'

'That's understandable.'

She had to fight the urge to shout, 'Stop being so bloody sympathetic!'

'You've talked to Anna?' he asked.

'Do you mind if we discuss what she said later?'

'Not at all.' Ned gave her a reassuring smile.

Josef pushed the coffee pot and a clean cup towards the edge of the table. 'Coffee, Ned?'

'No, thank you. But may I borrow your bicycle?' Josef nodded. 'I thought I'd go to the post office and put in a call to the number Norbert gave us. Even if he gets the message today, he may not be able to pick us up until the day after tomorrow. Is that all right with you?' When she didn't answer immediately he added, 'We could wait for the bus, but Norbert's car will be quicker and more comfortable.'

'Fine,' she murmured absently.

Ned wanted to ask her if she intended travelling with him or not, but it was a question that might lead to an argument. And for that they didn't need a witness. Least of all Josef.

'If anyone else has a bicycle we could borrow, you could come with me,' Ned suggested. 'You look as though you could do with some fresh air.'

'I have things to do.'

Ned waited for a few minutes. When Helena didn't elaborate, he stepped out into the yard. 'I'll be going, then. See you later?'

'Yes.'

'Bye.'

Helena waited until she heard Ned wheel the bicycle through the archway before finishing her coffee. She left her chair and carried the cup to the stone sink. 'Can you spare me an hour, Josef?'

'If Anna is all right and doesn't want anything.'

'Will you visit the Niklas farm with me?'

He came towards her and slipped his arm around her shoulders. 'Is that wise? Wiktor hates you.'

'That's why I'd like you to come with me.' She moved away from him.

'I make a lousy bodyguard,' he warned. 'I lack the killer instinct required to punch people on the nose.'

'I don't want anyone to fight on my account. But I saw the way the men deferred to you when you ordered Wiktor to leave here.'

'Wiktor didn't defer to me,' he said dryly.

'Only because he was drunk. The others did. And I don't want to confront Wiktor. He, his mother and Julianna were Magda's real family. I have some personal things that I intended to bury in her casket. Ned persuaded me to keep them for my children, if I have any. But after speaking to Julianna, I think she and Maria would treasure them simply because they were Magda's.'

'Or because you believe that Magda's most treasured possessions belong in the country she never left in her heart?'

'That, too,' she agreed.

'Give me ten minutes. If Anna is all right, I'll go to the milkman at the end of the street. He has a spare horse and a trap he uses to take his family out on Sundays. If I can borrow them, we'll drive to the farm. It will save time.'

Josef knocked on Anna's bedroom door quietly lest she had already fallen asleep again. When there was no answer he opened it. Anna had left her bed and was kneeling, dressed in her robe, in front of her nightstand with her back to the door. She was facing two photographs: Helena at her graduation; and the old village priest.

'Forgive me, Father, for I have sinned . . .' She turned around, still clutching her rosary beads.

Josef saw tears staining her cheeks and had to fight to keep his own emotions under control. 'You didn't tell Helena the truth?'

'What do you mean?' She refused to meet his eyes.

'I have just seen her. She is sad, upset, but not devastated. The truth would have broken a sensitive girl like her.'

'What do you know about the truth?' Anna asked in alarm.

'I know that her father was one of a gang of German soldiers that raped you and your sister Matylda.'

'The priest told you?' Anna's face suddenly drained of colour.

Josef shook his head. 'I overheard the two of you talking one night shortly before he died. I couldn't help it. I had made him tea.

I was bringing it to him in the yard but you were sitting with him, crying. I crept away before either of you saw me.'

'If I'd told Helena about her real father, I'd burden her with all the misery, guilt and anger that has blighted my own life.' Anna's lips were as white as her cheeks. 'I intended to tell her everything, but the look on her face when she heard how the beasts had treated Matylda was enough. I knew then that the truth would destroy her, just as surely as those soldiers destroyed Matylda's life and mine.'

'So you told her she was Jerzy Leman's illegitimate daughter?'

Anna shook her head. 'No. If I'd done that she would have gone looking for Jerzy's relatives, and old Henryk was his uncle. I wanted to spare Helena pain, but not at the expense of giving Henryk false hope that a member of his family had survived.'

'So what did you tell her?'

'A lie.' She leaned against the bed. 'It's easy for me to lie and act the coward. I have done it all my life.'

'Anna . . .'

'You are like the priest. Always looking for good in every situation. But there is no good to be found in some things, only evil. When I discovered I was pregnant I went to the priest. He told me that my child was a gift from God, an innocent baby who deserved life. And God had given me a way to respectability of sorts for me and my child. Jerzy was dead, but he had loved me. And everyone would assume the child was his. I even remember his exact words: "A child can only bring comfort." And the thought of their family living on through Jerzy's child did comfort his parents before they were killed. So I did not suffer as Matylda did. When her young man was told what had happened to her he wrote her a letter. She opened it, hoping for sympathy. But he told her that he never wanted to see or touch her again. I will never forget the look on Matylda's face when she read that letter, and I saw that same look again on Helena's face today when I told her about the rape. I couldn't tell her the truth, so I invented a German. A philanderer who fooled me into making me love him and deserted me when I was pregnant. I didn't give him a real name, a death or a grave because I didn't want her to go looking for him, too. You are a priest, Josef . . .'

'Only what passes for one in this backwater. And you are my foster-mother.'

'I have to do penance for my sins.'

'You don't remember what the old priest told you that night in the yard, the night I listened in?'

Anna stared at him with anguished eyes.

'It is time to stop doing penance, Anna. The sin wasn't yours, yet you have punished yourself for it all your life.'

'But my child—'

'*I* am your child, Anna. You gave the child you bore the best gift you could have at the time: a new life in a country of opportunity with a mother who loved her.'

'Sometimes I have trouble believing that you are not the old priest's son. You are so like him.'

Josef gently took the beads from Anna's hand and helped her to her feet. 'Enough punishment, Anna. It is time to start living the rest of your life in peace.'

'What's left of it.'

'You have years in front of you.' He guided her back into bed.

'I wish I could believe it.' She grasped his hand. 'You love her.'

'I do.' He kissed her cheek.

'What are you going to do about it?'

'I don't know – yet.'

If Helena hadn't been so preoccupied with thoughts of Anna, she would have enjoyed the novelty of driving out in a horse and trap. The sun beat down relentlessly, and the countryside basked in the midday heat. The air was still, heavy, the only movement the bees and butterflies as they hovered around the immature fruits that hung from the trees lining the road.

The fields stretched on either side, their crops creating a patchwork of light and dark greens interspersed with gold as far as the eye could see. Helena gazed over them as she sat bolt upright on the bench seat next to Josef. She gripped the side of the trap to steady herself, as he tried to rein in the horse and urge it on at the same time.

'I never was as good a horseman as the farmers' sons because I wasn't able to practise,' he apologized. 'When I was twelve I asked

311

Anna to buy me a pony; instead she managed to get me a bicycle. Our milkman has a young and an old horse. I would have preferred the old, she's slower but steadier, but he alternates them on his round. This one is only half-trained, and too frisky for me. Horses always sense an amateur driver.'

'It's quicker than walking,' Helena commented for the sake of conversation.

'Don't you think the road looks different from the way it appears at night?'

'Not particularly.'

'There are no frightening shadows or noises to scare you.'

'I wasn't frightened the last time I walked here,' she lied.

'No?'

'No,' she repeated, glancing at him.

'Helena . . .' His tone was serious.

'That's the farm ahead, isn't it?' she interrupted.

'Yes.'

She picked up her duffle bag. 'If Wiktor won't let me near the house, will you talk to him for me?'

'As we agreed.' Josef heaved on the reins, halted the trap, jumped down and tied the horse to the gate. 'As long as Wiktor remains polite.' He held out his hand to help her down. She took it.

'Thank you. Josef.'

'But if he has been drinking, we leave. No arguments; we go immediately,' he emphasized. 'Understood?'

'Understood,' she echoed.

Julianna was cleaning out the hen house when Josef and Helena walked into the yard. Alerted by their footsteps, she turned, saw them, and rushed out of the chicken run, only remembering to fasten the gate as an afterthought.

Josef said, 'We're looking for Wiktor, Julianna.'

She pointed to the cowshed before darting into the house.

'So much for Julianna,' Josef muttered under his breath.

'She's shy, and having a brother like Wiktor doesn't help.' Hoping to keep her canvas shoes clean, Helena picked her way carefully across the yard.

It was odorous but cool in the stone-built cowshed. The only light came from two narrow iron gratings, one above the door and another opposite the stalls. Helena and Josef heard Wiktor's voice interspersed with lowing as they entered. When their eyes became accustomed to the gloom, they saw him standing beside a cow in a stall at the far end. They walked towards him, their footsteps resounding over the stone floor, but Wiktor didn't look up or away from the cow.

'Hello, Wiktor.' Josef stopped in front of the stall. 'Fine-looking heifer you have there.'

'She's about to calve, that's why I brought her in here,' Wiktor said gruffly. 'What do you want? And why have you brought the—'

'Helena.'

Wiktor sneered. 'Don't you mean the piece of rubbish that Magda picked up in Nazi Germany?'

'No . . .'

Helena gave Joseph a warning prod, and tried to visualize Wiktor as the amusing young man Anna had described: the tease who had fastened girls' braids to the back of a cart, the boy who couldn't watch a runt die of starvation, so hid it in his room. But it was no use. She couldn't equate the bitter, red-faced, hard-featured, middle-aged drunk with the young boy Anna had spoken of.

She glanced sideways at Joseph. He nodded briefly. From somewhere she summoned the courage to speak. 'I'm here, Mr Niklas, because I'd like to give your mother and sister keepsakes.'

'What kind of keepsakes?' Wiktor peered at her, greed in his eyes. She recalled both Weronika and Anna saying that he had ransacked the Janek house after the massacre.

'Magda always wore a locket—'

'A *solid gold* locket that Adam Janek gave her when Helena was born. There was a picture of him inside it.'

Helena opened her duffle bag and drew out the box of photographs. She opened it and lifted out the locket and Magda's wedding ring.

Wiktor moved away from the cow and took the locket from her.

She pointed to the side. 'You press the button there to open it.'

'I remember.' He touched the catch and it flew open. 'You want to give this to my mother?'

'No, to Julianna.'

'The gold will be wasted on her. She never goes anywhere.'

'It's not an ornament, it's something to remember her sister by,' Helena said. 'I would like to give your mother Magda's wedding ring.' She held it out.

'I remember this also. It's old. You can't get heavy embossed rings like this any more.' His eyes narrowed as he looked suspiciously at her. 'Why don't you want to keep them?'

'They were Magda's. They should go to her blood relatives.'

His voice was hoarse, cracked. 'If you are giving these things away, what are you keeping?'

'My memories of the woman I called Mama, and the photographs I have of her.'

'And that is enough for you?'

'She was my mother in every way that mattered. It's enough.' She held out the box of photographs. 'I thought I'd ask Julianna and your mother if they'd like to choose a photograph each as well.'

'You can go into the house and see them,' he conceded gruffly.

'Thank you.' She followed Joseph to the door.

'Don't stay long,' Wiktor called after them.

'We won't,' Joseph replied.

'Did she ever talk about me?' Wiktor shouted as they reached the door.

Helena turned back. Wiktor was standing at the entrance to the stall, watching her.

'Magda,' Wiktor barked. 'You said she talked to you about the farm and her family in Poland.'

'She did.'

'Did she mention my name?'

'All the time,' Helena answered.

He nodded and disappeared back into the stall.

Julianna, Maria and Wiktor's wife were sitting at the table in the farmhouse topping, tailing and slicing green beans as if their lives depended on the level of production. An enormous pot containing glass jars and rubber seals was boiling on the range. Around it were rows of gently steaming preserving jars that had already been sterilized. Those waiting to be boiled were stacked on a side table. All the windows and the door were open, but the atmosphere in the kitchen was steamy and sweltering, more Chinese laundry than Polish farmhouse.

Helena recalled Magda telling her about the mammoth baking and preserving sessions, presided over by her mother, and how all the women in the household had taken part.

The three women looked at her and Joseph, but none spoke.

Helena risked a tentative smile. 'Good morning. I see that harvest still starts early on the Niklas farm, just as Magda told me it did.'

The women continued to stare at her through round, frightened eyes.

'It's all right,' Joseph reassured them. 'We have spoken to Wiktor. He gave us permission to come in here. Helena wants to give you something of Magda's to remember her by.'

A voice boomed out behind them. 'Put that box you showed me on the table and let them see the photographs.' It was Wiktor.

There was a clear space at the end of the table. Helena set the box down, took out half a dozen of the most recent pictures of Magda, and laid them out. Then she removed Magda's locket and wedding ring. Julianna gasped when she saw them.

Helena reached for Julianna's free hand, opened it and pressed the locket into it, before taking Maria's hand and giving her Magda's wedding ring. She pointed to the snaps. 'These are the last photographs that were taken of Magda. I think Magda would have liked you to have one each.'

Julianna still looked to Wiktor for permission. He nodded. She left her chair and went to the end of the table. Sensing her diffidence, Helena moved back to give her more room. Julianna studied the photographs for a full five minutes before picking up a snapshot of Magda that had been taken with Father O'Brien at the last Sunday school Christmas party. Magda was leaning over a group of smiling children, who were all looking up at her as she cut into an iced sponge cake.

315

'Choose one for me, Julianna.' Maria brushed a tear from a cheek as wrinkled as a winter apple that had been too long in storage.

Julianna's second choice was a picture of Magda arranging Easter flowers in the church. She shuffled the remainder together and returned them to Helena, who replaced them in the box.

'Thank you, Julianna.' Helena pushed the box into her duffle bag. She gazed at the old woman. 'This farmhouse kitchen is exactly how Magda told me it would be. Thank you for allowing me to see it.'

'Goodbye,' Wiktor barked. He held the door open.

Joseph walked through it and Helena followed.

'You won't be back,' Wiktor snapped. It wasn't a question.

'Not here, no.' Helena held out her hand to him but he ignored it.

'I have to get back to my cow.' He stomped off to the cowshed.

Joseph walked Helena to the gate where he had hitched the horse and trap.

She touched his arm. 'Thank you.'

'You didn't receive the warmest of receptions, but at least Wiktor didn't hit you this time.' Joseph untied the reins as the horse continued to crop the long grass at the base of the gatepost. Holding the reins, he climbed on to the trap and held out his hand to Helena. 'Wait. Look behind you.'

She glanced over her shoulder and saw Julianna running out of the house with a parcel.

'For you.' Julianna hurriedly pushed the parcel at Helena. 'Be careful, there is glass inside. Don't open it here.'

'Thank you for whatever it is.' On impulse Helena reached out and hugged her.

'Thank you for this.' Julianna held up the locket. 'Go, quickly, before Wiktor sees us.'

'Goodbye, Julianna. Good health and happiness.' Helena passed the parcel up to Joseph, before taking his hand and climbing up beside him on to the bench seat.

'You can bet your last zloty that it's something she's smuggled out of the house without Wiktor knowing about it,' Joseph said.

Helena lifted the parcel from the floor where Joseph had stowed it. She held it to her nose. 'It smells of cedar and camphor.'

'Intriguing.' Joseph persuaded the horse to turn around, and they started back down the lane. 'Go on, open it.'

'She told me not to.'

'We're not on the farm, she's not here, and curiosity is killing me.'

Helena untied the string around the brown paper. The first thing she lifted out was a framed photograph of Magda. She was sitting on a chair in what looked like a very different yard from the one where she and Ned ate their meals, although the barn doors behind her were the same ones they saw from the landing outside their room.

Just as she'd imagined, there had been a wooden table and chairs on the veranda where Anna stored her crates of empty bottles. And, as Weronika had said, there were tubs of rose bushes around the table.

Magda looked radiant. She was showing off a baby to the camera. The child was wrapped in an intricately worked shawl. Helena lifted up the photograph. Underneath was a tissue-wrapped crocheted shawl, just like the one in the picture. It had obviously been carefully stored as it had only slightly yellowed with age.

'If I had to make a guess, I would say that is Magda with Helena and that is her baby shawl,' said Josef.

'It looks like it. There's something else. Oh my God, I don't believe it.' Helena unfolded another layer of tissue paper to reveal yards and yards of once white, now cream silk.

'A dress?'

'Magda's wedding dress. Look at the stitching and the pin tucks. Julianna really shouldn't have.'

'Yes, she should. Wiktor has boys. Julianna is of an age where she must have given up all hope of marrying, and not only because of Wiktor's attitude to the purity of women. Most of the men of Julianna's generation were slaughtered in the war. Those things belong with you, Helena. Just as you belong in this country. You will stay won't you? I meant what I said earlier about Anna needing you. And you can't ignore the fact that, given the way Magda brought you up, you are more Polish than British. You have no idea how much Poland needs people like you. One-fifth of our population, including all our leaders, thinkers and intellectuals, were killed by the Germans during the war. The cream of our society was completely wiped out. No country can recover from a loss like that in less than twenty years. We need intelligent people to teach our young, to guide them and take us into the future and—'

'Out of Communism?' she suggested.

He looked around and lowered his voice. 'It's not done to say things like that in public.'

'In public?' Helena laughed. 'Joseph, there isn't a soul for miles. I've never seen such flat countryside.'

'There are trees. People could be hiding behind them.'

'You are paranoid.'

'This country would make the most trusting angel paranoid. But seriously, Helena, you can speak, read and write English and Polish. You're a qualified teacher—'

'Josef, I know what I am.'

'What you don't know is how much better we could get to know one another if you stayed.'

'Josef . . .'

'Don't stop me when I am just getting started. I fell in love with you the first time I saw you, when you walked past all those grumpy, disapproving old men sitting in the bar. You looked so cool, so casual, yet I knew what it had cost you to walk in there and face a roomful of strangers. Every muscle in your hands and shoulders was tense. And all I could think of when I looked at you was how much you reminded me of a ray of sunshine pouring through a grimy window. You illuminated the entire room. You were like a shimmering gold icon . . .'

'Josef . . .'

He stopped the horse. Gathering the reins into one hand, he laid his free hand over hers. 'I beg you – stay, and not just for Anna's sake. For mine.'

She gazed into his eyes, darker and more enigmatic than Ned's. She always knew what Ned was thinking; she would only know Josef's thoughts if he voiced them. His looks were more striking than Ned's, and Ned was a handsome man. Black hair and deep blue eyes, as opposed to auburn hair and tawny-brown eyes. Josef was exceptionally attractive, and his white cotton shirt and polyester trousers, which would mark him as old-fashioned and 'square' in the West, only added to his charm. His limited wardrobe had undoubtedly been dictated by what little was stocked in the Communist shops, but it had the effect of making him appear more serious, as if he couldn't spare the time to think about trivia, only the larger questions of life, morality and politics.

He was a sincere and honest young man. He didn't talk, look or act like anyone she had ever met before. If ever there was a man determined to change the world he lived in, it was Josef Dobrow. She had no doubt that he would spend his entire life working for the betterment of Poland, and probably succeed. It was resolute men like Josef who revolutionized society. And she could be part of it . . .

'Helena . . .'

She looked away.

'You haven't heard a word I've said,' he reproached.

'I have, and I've thought about them. You, more than anyone else, has made me realize how Polish I am, and always will be.'

'Then you'll stay?'

A bicycle hurtled towards them from the direction of the square. They sat and watched it draw towards them. Helena withdrew her hand from Josef's.

Ned skidded to a halt alongside the trap. 'I saw you as I cycled into the village. You've been to the Niklas farm?'

'Yes,' Helena said shortly.

'Wasn't that rather foolhardy?'

'Not with Josef to protect me. Wiktor allowed me to talk to Julianna and Maria, and Julianna gave me a present. Some things that had belonged to Magda. I'll show them to you when we get back to the house.'

'I'll look forward to it.' Ned was straining to be his usual polite and charming self, but it was the politeness and charm he usually reserved for strangers, and both he and Helena knew it. 'I left a message for Norbert saying that we wouldn't be far from Anna's whenever he came, and would be packed and ready to travel back to town. Tomorrow if possible; the day after if not.'

Helena touched Josef's arm. 'Can you stop in the square, please? I want to go to the churchyard.'

'I'll come with you,' Ned offered.

'No, thank you,' she refused.

'Then I'll—'

'I want to be alone, Ned. But here.' She pushed the contents of the parcel Julianna had given her into her duffle bag and handed it to him. 'Take this back to our room for me, please. But be careful of the photograph frame; it's old and fragile. I won't be long.'

The usual queue had formed outside the shop by the time Helena walked back to the bar and house. She looked at the counter as she passed by. It was heaped high with pale, greasy sausages that had been rolled into large wheels. People were handing over their ration cards. Women with several children clinging to their skirts were given two wheels, while the older people only warranted a half or a quarter of a wheel.

She smiled and said good day to the queue in general. A few of the women responded and wished her a good day in return. She quickened her step. Josef was right – in some ways she was more Polish than British. How long would it be before she was accepted into the village if she did decide to stay?

She walked through the archway into the yard.

'You finally decided to return. Josef and Ned were wondering if you'd been stolen away by the angels who hover in the clouds above the churchyard.' Anna was sitting at the table under the outside staircase, a pot of coffee and a cup in front of her. She still looked fragile and pale, but slightly stronger.

'I wanted to pay my respects at Magda and Adam's grave again.' Helena pulled out a stool and sat opposite Anna.

'Perhaps you should move into the churchyard,' Anna suggested.

'I wanted to go there one more time so I would remember it.'

'If you want Ned, he is in the bar with Josef. They are probably drowning their sorrows. Neither of them likes having a rival for your affections.'

'How are you feeling now?' Helena deliberately ignored Anna's comment.

'Foolish, weak and not in need of a lecture.' Anna pulled the ashtray towards her, and took out her cigarettes. 'Josef wants you to stay here.'

'Did he tell you that?' Helena asked in surprise.

'He didn't need to. It's written all over his face. Well, I don't want you.'

'Why?' Helena asked.

'Because I like my life the way it is. And you would make me feel uncomfortable in my own house. I daresay Josef told you that I need looking after because he will soon be taking a job in the town and won't be able to spend so much time here. As if I need a nursemaid!'

'He is concerned about you, Anna.'

'I don't need his concern. And I don't need you here because you would be a reminder of things that I have spent most of my life trying to forget. And whatever you may think, you don't belong here.'

'Josef says I do,' Helena said quietly.

'No doubt he told you that he loves you as well.'

'Yes, he did,' Helena admitted.

'It is because he is blinkered, like an old horse that knows the route it has to take so well it no longer needs to open its eyes to look at the road. Josef has only ever seen what he wants to. I know him inside out. He is my child in all but name.'

Helena had to ask the question. 'Then Josef doesn't love me?'

'Josef loves you well enough. Probably more than he loves any woman. But he loves something more – Poland. I have known many men like Josef and I have seen what being relegated to the position of second best has done to their wives and families. Boys like Josef died in their millions during the war. Even Adam Janek, for all his protestations that Magda and Helena were his life, put Poland first, and look where that got him – an early grave with his daughter.

'There was no excuse for a man with his money. He could have taken Magda north when he returned from fighting the German invasion. All he had to do was buy passage to Sweden on a ship out of Gdansk. He, Magda and little Helena could have sat out the war in comfort. Just as Josef could use his contacts to escape to the West, where he could put his brains and his talent to better use than the Communists will ever allow him to do here. But there's no talking sense to him. All he can think about is Poland and fighting to free her from the Soviet yoke – or some other such nonsense. So, to answer your question again: yes, he loves you, but not enough. The question is, do you love him?'

'The Polish part of me does.'

'What kind of an answer is that?' Anna scoffed.

'The only one I can give.'

'Josef would sacrifice everything for Poland – himself, his wife, his unborn children. Not like my Jerzy. He gave his life for Poland, but only because he had no choice. If he'd had money like Adam Janek he would have taken me somewhere quiet and peaceful, away from Poland and the fighting early on in the war. And if he were here now, we would live quietly and leave the politics to the Adam Janeks and Josef Dobrows of this world. You are lucky, Helena. You are living in a time where you can decide how and where to live your life. So, please, make the right choice. For yourself and for me.'

'And Josef?'

'He has his first love, Poland, to console him.'

Helena looked through the archway to the street outside. Thanks to Magda's descriptions she knew this village and its inhabitants almost as well as she knew Pontypridd and its natives. She felt at home here, but the village she knew was Magda's, a place of the past.

After the war Magda had made a brave choice to travel to a strange country where she only knew one person. Helena would never know whether she really intended to marry Bob Parsons. But clearly Magda had felt there was no future in Poland for either of them.

Ned loved her as much as it was possible for one person to love another – of that she was certain. And she had loved him before Magda had died and left her a legacy of doubt about her identity. She suddenly realized Ned was right: nothing had really changed between them. She was what she was: a girl who'd been brought up and educated in Wales to respect her Polish heritage.

The Polish side of her was attracted to Josef, and he loved her, in his way, as much as Ned did. But Anna understood him. Josef loved Poland more. She had no rival for Ned's love. She thought of all he had done for her since Magda's death: postponing their wedding, travelling to a Communist country with her, suffering her moods. She knew there was really no decision for her to make.

'I should go upstairs and start packing,' she said.

Anna finally lit her cigarette. 'Think of me now and again if you must, Helena. But I don't want you to come back. There is nothing for you here. I have Josef; he will take care of me, even from a distance. There are always people he can employ if I become a hopeless invalid. You may send me photographs from time to time.'

'I will,' Helena assured her.

'Especially of your children when you have them.'

'I promise, and I'll also send you food parcels.'

'Not too many. I have more tins in my pantry and clothes in my wardrobe than any other woman in the village. There's no point in making my neighbours even more jealous of me than they already are. But boxes of soap powder are always welcome.'

'I'll remember,' Helena promised.

'And now I will go and make us supper.'

'There is no need—' Helena began.

'Yes, there is. The sausage is not very good but Stefan can cook it while I sit in the kitchen and supervise.'

Helena kissed Anna's cheek.

'My mother used to call kisses between mother and daughter sloppy. They're not so bad.' Anna fell serious. 'My Jerzy loved me. Really loved me. Almost as much as your Ned loves you. Be good to him, Helena. Honest men who love their women more than their causes and themselves are rarer than silver mushrooms. I know because I only ever found one.'

Chapter 22

HELENA CLIMBED the stairs, walked into the attic room and looked around for her duffle bag. She didn't have to look far. Ned had left it on the bed she had slept in every night since their arrival. She opened it, lifted out the photograph of Magda with Helena, and set it on the nightstand.

She stared at it for a long time. Aside from providing a window into another time, another world, there was an ethereal quality about it that reminded her of the Renaissance portraits of the Madonna and child. For the first time she thought about the other Helena as more than just Magda's much-loved and longed-for baby. A little girl who would have developed her own personality had she lived. If Magda had been allowed to bring up both of them, would they have been similar? Would they have argued and fought, as many sisters did? Or would they have been close? Friends as well as siblings. The way Ned was with his sister Rachel, beneath the teasing exterior.

She lifted the shawl from the bed and shook it free from its covering of tissue paper. She spread it carefully over the second bed and stepped back. Only then could she truly appreciate the many hours of a woman's life that had gone into making it. The stitching was perfect, the pattern even more intricate in reality than in the photograph.

She wondered if Magda or her mother had made it. Or even Weronika. Magda had taught her to sew, knit and crochet, but a work of art on the scale of the shawl was beyond her and, she suspected, Magda's expertise. She picked it up and re-folded it meticulously along the creases, re-wrapping each fold in the tissue paper. Perhaps one day it would be used to keep another child warm . . . She suppressed the thought almost before it arose. Her superstitious nature had been a gift from Magda: '*Don't even think about it, Helena, or it won't come true.*'

She lifted the wedding dress from its sheath of paper, and breathed in the scents of camphor and cedar wood. They were stronger than on the shawl. She wondered if they had been packed away in different chests.

She held the dress up in front of her. It was the bridal gown every little girl brought up on the age-old fairy tales of Cinderella and Snow White dreamed of. And it wasn't difficult to visualize Magda's excitement on her wedding day when she wore it in public for the first time. She looked at the stitches again, each one tiny and perfect, and recalled Magda telling her how all the women in her family had helped her to make the gown.

She imagined away her canvas shoes, jeans and T-shirt. Such a gown demanded the finest satin – no kid – court shoes, white silk stockings, a lace veil . . . and she knew, just knew, it would fit her perfectly. She looked down at her feet. Except one.

'It's too short for you.'

She looked in the mirror and saw Ned standing behind her. 'I know. I was just imagining Magda's excitement when she wore it to marry Adam Janek.'

'Were you thinking of lengthening it?'

'No.'

'So you don't have any intention of wearing it on your wedding day?'

She set the gown on the bed and turned to him. 'I have a gown for our wedding day.'

'Our—'

'I know it's irrational, but I've been eaten up with guilt because we were making love when Magda died.'

'And you don't feel guilty any more?'

'A little. But I think loving Adam Janek the way she did, Magda would have understood.'

'She would also have understood that you couldn't be with her every minute of every day,' he agreed.

'Anna told me that you love me.'

'You've known that since the night of the Freshers' ball.'

'Yes,' she said slowly. 'But it's difficult to accept unconditional love when you don't know who you are.'

He looked into her eyes. 'And you know now?'

'I think so.' She stood on tiptoe and kissed him lightly on the lips.

He caught the bottom of the door with his foot and pushed it shut.

'Lock it, Ned.'

'Dinner . . .'

'You're hungry?' she smiled, teasingly, in a way she hadn't done since they had left Bristol.

'No.' His voice was thick with suppressed emotion.

'Then it can wait, Ned. We have some catching up to do.'

He had to ask the question. 'And tomorrow?'

'If Norbert comes, we go home.'

'That is the sweetest thing you've said to me since——'

'Magda died?'

'I didn't mean it that way.'

'I know. Magda left me a legacy I neither wanted nor appreciated until I talked to Anna. What I do with the love she showered on me, and the upbringing she gave me, is my decision. I realize that now.'

'I love you, Helena soon-to-be John.'

'That's one of the changes I need to talk to you about, but not now.' She pulled off her sweater. 'Come to bed.'

'Anna and Josef——'

'Are grown-ups. They'll guess what we're doing.' She unzipped his jeans.

'And when we go home, to Pontypridd?'

'We'll marry, and I'll spend the rest of my life thanking you for helping me to find my way back to you.'

Josef was laying the table in the yard the next morning when Helena ran down the stairs. He set down a coffee pot and a plate of rolls, crossed his arms and gazed at her. The smile she intended to give him died on her lips, and her heart went out to him.

'It wouldn't have worked between us, Josef.'

'So Anna told me – and you.'

'We're from different worlds.'

'You're Polish.'

'Magda brought me up to value the ways of a Poland that was the first casualty of the war. I don't belong in a Soviet state.'

'We need people to fight for Poland's freedom—'

'Not me, Josef. Something else Magda taught me was how to value and live the quiet domestic life. I came here to bury Magda with her beloved Adam. When I arrived I thought I knew who I was and where I came from. I didn't. I have a lot to be grateful to you and Anna for, but it's time for me to move on with Ned.'

Norbert walked into the yard. 'Good morning.'

Helena looked at him in amazement. 'You're early.'

'If you want to go to town, we have to go now, in the next five minutes. I have another two pick-ups today. And you will be pleased to hear that there is a train that leaves at eleven for Warsaw.'

'What about breakfast?'

'You can have a mouthful of coffee while you make yourselves rolls that you can eat in the back of the car.' Norbert glanced up and saw Ned on the landing. 'Bring down your cases.'

'Be with you in one minute.' Ned disappeared inside. He emerged a few seconds later and stacked their cases, bag and his duffle bag on the landing. 'Is there anything else you want up here, Helena?' he asked.

'Nothing, thanks. I have my bag,' she called back.

He glanced back into the room and saw the piles of dollars and zlotys Helena had left on the dressing table beside the chocolates, tins of food and cosmetics. He closed the door, picked up the luggage and went down to the yard.

Anna walked out of the kitchen with two brown paper bags that she handed to Helena. 'Your breakfast.'

Helena hugged her and whispered in her ear, 'How did you contact Norbert to tell him to come here so early this morning?'

'I have my ways.'

As Helena moved back, she noticed the outline of a bottle in Anna's apron pocket.

Anna saw her looking at it. 'That is another reason you should go, and quickly. If I want to drink myself to death I will.'

'Not while I'm around.' Josef wrapped his arm around Anna, slipped his free hand into her pocket and pulled out the bottle of vodka. It was empty.

'You emptied it along with all the others in the house last night,' Anna said.

'You expect me to deny it?'

'No. I kept it for show. Old habits die hard.'

'If I see you drinking in the bar, I'll send you to a health farm,' Josef warned.

'As if you could afford it,' Anna mocked.

Ned held out his hand to Josef. 'Goodbye, Josef. Thank you for your help.'

'Don't you mean I hope I never see you again?'

'Not at all. Call in and see us in Pontypridd anytime you like – maybe in ten years or so? We will have six or seven children by then.'

Josef had the grace to laugh. 'I doubt the Communists will let me go wandering in the West again, but you never know.'

Norbert took the bags and carried them through the archway. Ned shook Anna's hand, took the paper bags from Helena, and followed Norbert.

Josef looked at Helena. 'I'd rather not say goodbye to you.'

'Look after yourself.' She bit her lip as tears pricked the back of her eyes.

'Ned has the girl; he won't begrudge me a kiss.'

Helena expected a peck on the cheek but, very gently, Josef cradled her face in his hands and kissed her full on the mouth, long and lovingly. When he released her, he said, 'That is what you will be missing every day for the rest of your life, Helena Janek.'

'Helena Janek will miss it,' she agreed. 'But Lena John won't.'

'Lena?'

She looked at Anna and saw tears in her eyes.

'Off with you.' Anna pushed her away before wiping her eyes with the back of her hand. 'I hate long goodbyes.'

'We've left some things in our room.'

'Don't worry, Lena, I'll clear up your mess.'

'Goodbye.' Helena knew it would be the last time she would see Anna. She walked through the archway. Ned was waiting for her in the back of the car.

'Well, Helena soon-to-be John?'

'How does Lena soon-to-be John sound to you?' she asked, as Norbert shut the door, climbed into the driving seat and pulled away.

'You want to shorten Helena to Lena?'

'When I was baptized I was given two names of my very own: Lena Matylda.'

'So, no more Magda's daughter?'

'No, Ned. One thing that I have learned in this village is that there is nature and nurture. And both are as important as one another. Magda saved my life, brought me up, cared for me and loved me until her dying day. I will always be Magda's daughter. But there is someone else I want to see before I leave here.' She leaned forward, towards the driving seat. 'Norbert, do you know the shop where Weronika Janek works?'

'Yes.'

'Is it near the railway station?'

'Five minutes away.'

'Can we stop there?'

'For five minutes — no longer if you want to catch the eleven o'clock train.'

'Thank you.' She sat back in her seat, opened her duffle bag, and took out the box of photographs and the two frames she'd packed. She sat and looked at both of them: the one taken on Magda and Adam's wedding day, and the one of Magda sitting in the garden with her newborn baby.

Ned saw her looking at them and wrapped his arm around her shoulder. He didn't need to say anything because he knew what she was thinking.

'I can't possibly take these from you,' Weronika protested when Helena gave her both framed photographs, but she couldn't take her eyes from them.

'They are windows onto another time and another world, Weronika – your and Magda's world, not mine. I have no right to make you wait until I can copy them. Please, keep them.' She kissed Weronika's cheek.

Norbert blasted his horn outside the shop.

'If we are going to catch the eleven o'clock train, I have to go. Come and see us in Britain.'

Weronika followed her outside the shop. 'As soon as I draw my pension and they let me leave the country,' she shouted after Helena in English, clutching the photographs to her chest.

Ned wound down the car window. 'We'll look forward to seeing you, Weronika.'

'My aunt by adoption.' Helena climbed past Norbert, who was holding the passenger seat forward so she could get into the back of the car.

'You haven't much time to spare,' he warned as he pulled out on to the road.

'We'll make it.' Helena smiled at Ned.

'Damn,' Ned cursed. 'I meant to ask Josef if he knew of a good hotel in Warsaw. There's no way I want to stay in the same one again.'

'The Metropol. It's new, it's clean and you can tell them that Vlad sent you,' Norbert said, watching them in the rear-view mirror.

'Vlad?' Ned asked.

'In Warsaw I'm Vlad.' Norbert drew up in front of the station. 'Five minutes to spare.'

Ned pulled out his wallet, but Norbert closed his hand over it. 'I've been paid. Anna must really have wanted to get rid of you two.'

Chapter 23

RONNIE RONCONI moved to the end of the receiving line at the wedding reception, shook hands with Ned and kissed Helena's cheek. 'Congratulations. Ned, you look like the cat who's stolen all the cream from the dairy and the mice to garnish it. My commiserations, Helena; a cracker like you could have done better.'

'It's too late to give Helena advice. I have the certificate, signed and safe.' Ned patted the breast pocket of his suit before wrapping his arm around Helena's shoulders.

The blue and silver ballroom in the New Inn was packed with friends and Ned's family, although Alma and Peter Raschenko had so enthusiastically embraced their roles as Helena's family that Ned had overheard their former student housemate, Alan, ask Peter if he and Helena were first or second cousins.

Ronnie glanced over his shoulder. 'Looks like I'm the last guest.'

Peter left his place next to Helena in the receiving line and went to the door. He glanced outside, turned back and lifted both his thumbs. 'All clear.'

'I think we've earned ourselves a pre-lunch drink after all that handshaking, ladies.' Andrew hailed a waiter and escorted Alma and Bethan towards him.

Peter rejoined Ned and Helena. 'This looks like one of the games of sardines you Ronconis play in your airing cupboards at Christmas,' he said to Ronnie.

'We didn't want to leave anyone out.' Ned hadn't relinquished his hold on Helena since they had left the Catholic church an hour before. Careful to avoid snagging her lace veil, he pulled her even closer to him.

'No one on the original guest list,' Helena clarified. 'I just hope the guests don't mind that we didn't have the big church wedding as originally planned.'

'People prefer wedding receptions to the ceremony. All they want is to see the bride so they can admire her dress, have a good gossip about the other guests' clothes and absent acquaintances, and enjoy free food and drink.' Ronnie Ronconi handed Ned an envelope. 'After the way Helena has gone on – and on and on – about piglets since you returned from Poland, Catrina and Billy wanted to buy you a pair as a wedding present. I thought you might find this more useful. But should you want a piglet . . .'

'No pigs yet, not in a bungalow. But maybe in a few years, when we buy a farm. Thank you.' Helena stood on tip-toe and kissed Ronnie's cheek.

'Ronnie!' Alma waved to attract his attention. 'We need your professional opinion on the relative merits of a Ford Anglia compared to a Morris 1000.'

'Work, work, nothing but work.' Ronnie winked at Helena. 'Save me a dance.'

'Of course.'

'But make it a slow one; none of your jiggery-pokery.'

'As father of the bride for the day, I'll make sure she respects the limitations of a man of your advanced years, Ronnie.' Peter took two glasses of champagne from a waiter and handed them to Ned and Helena before taking another for himself.

'Junior business partners aren't indispensable,' Ronnie teased Peter as he left them.

'You were right about Poland, in every way, Peter.' Ned sipped his champagne. 'But especially about appreciating Pontypridd when we came back. A hot bath never felt so good.'

'No plumbed-in bathrooms in the village?' Peter guessed.

'None,' Ned confirmed.

'I bet there was a lake nearby.'

'And a cold tap in a wash-house,' Ned added.

'Positive luxury. I think you're wanted.' Peter nodded to the top table where the photographer was hovering behind the four-tier wedding cake Magda had chosen.

'Do you mind posing and pretending to cut it now?' the photographer asked Ned and Helena. 'If you do, I won't have to wait until you've finished the wedding breakfast for the real event. That way I can get back to the shop and develop the films this afternoon. Then they'll be ready and in the albums by the time you get back from honeymoon.'

'That's an offer we can't refuse.' Ned led Helena to the table, picked up the long-bladed silver knife and held it over the bottom tier.

Alma saw him. 'Don't cut it,' she warned. 'It's bad luck to slice it before the toast to the bride and groom.'

'Don't worry, we won't.'

Helena laid her hand over Ned's on the knife.

'Look at one another and smile.' The photographer operated his flash gun and camera. 'As soon as the flash has charged, smile at one another, please. Now we'll have the family standing behind.'

Bethan, Andrew, Peter and Alma obediently shuffled into place behind Ned and Helena.

The photographer looked through his lens. 'All of you, this way and smile.'

The smile died on Helena's lips when she thought of Magda, and how much she would have loved playing the part of mother of the bride.

In contrast to their journey out, she and Ned had talked non-stop on their return from Poland. She had suggested that they should keep the secret Magda had been at such pains to conceal from the world, and Ned had agreed. Anna had been right. In every way that mattered, she *was* Magda's daughter. And now, on her wedding day, she missed the woman she had always called Mama more than she would have believed possible.

Ned, his parents, Peter and Alma had worked hard to make the day perfect. But it was Magda's day. She had planned the event down to the smallest detail, from the colour of the table linen to the guests' rose buttonholes and the rose and lily table decorations.

Helena had only agreed to go ahead with Magda's elaborate plans for the wedding reception after talking to Alma. But she had insisted the actual wedding ceremony be small and private, although she had given in to Father O'Brien's pleading that it be held in the church Magda had loved so much.

It had been Father O'Brien and Alma who had finally persuaded her that the best way to honour the woman everyone in Pontypridd still believed was her mother was to marry, just as Magda had planned: wearing the dress Magda had helped her pick out; hosting the reception Magda had organized; and cutting the cake, which had taken Magda two weeks to choose from the baker's catalogue.

The photographer took two more photographs. 'As soon as the flash has re-charged we'll take another couple, just in case.'

'In case of what?' Andrew asked.

'In case of disaster. You never know how they are going to turn out. I had one bride whose eyes were closed in every shot I took.'

'Perhaps she was avoiding looking at her bridegroom,' Peter suggested.

'He couldn't have been as handsome as me,' Ned joked.

'Last one, for luck. And while we're waiting, you did say you wanted five complete albums?' the photographer checked.

'We did,' Ned confirmed.

'Five?' Bethan looked at Ned in surprise. 'One for us, one for you.'

'One for Auntie Alma as a thank you for helping us organize everything.' Helena grasped Alma's hand.

'Darling, I was going to buy one—'

'Our present,' Ned interrupted.

'That still leaves two,' Andrew reminded.

'For my family in Poland,' Helena explained.

'Two? They can't share?' Alma asked.

Helena thought of the angry words Anna had exchanged with Weronika, and how war, bitterness and greed had separated three young girls who had believed their friendship would last a lifetime.

If only Magda, Anna and Weronika could have shared this special day with her and Ned. As it was, all she could do was send Weronika and Anna photographs as mementoes. 'My aunt doesn't live close to the rest of the family, and they don't get on that well.'

'Poles and their tempers.' Peter shook his head. 'Pander to them and you'll encourage them not to share. If you're not careful you'll be packing parcels for Poland for years and years, Helena, just like Magda did.'

Helena glanced at Ned. 'I certainly hope so, Peter.'

Ned gripped her hand. 'And so do I.'

Author's Note

The Nazi organization of Lebensborn (fountain or spring of life) was created by Heinrich Himmler on 12 December 1935 with the aim of reversing the declining birth rate in Germany and also halting abortions, which had reached record levels in Germany after the deaths of so many young men during the First World War. Initially, Lebensborn was a welfare organization that nurtured the wives and children of the SS, as well as racially and biologically 'valuable' families (those the Nazis deemed of Germanic Aryan blood). Lebensborn accommodated mothers who could prove their Aryan pedigree and cared for this select group of mothers and children during pregnancy and infancy in luxury maternity homes.

In 1939, there were 8,000 members of Lebensborn, including 3,500 SS. Lebensborn remained part of the SS Office of Race and Settlement until 1938 when it was transferred to Himmler's Personal staff. Leaders of Lebensborn were SS-Standartenführer Max Sollmann and SS-Oberführer Dr Gregor Ebner.

Lebensborn's maternity homes not only accommodated the wives and mistresses of SS officers. Provided both the woman and the father of her child were 'Aryan', pregnant unmarried women were accepted into Lebensborn and given support away from their families and conservative German society, which frowned upon illegitimacy. To place their women's illegitimate children, Lebensborn opened orphanages and an adoption service. Non-SS members, parents and children were only admitted to Lebensborn after passing a 'medical' examination by an SS doctor to prove their racial superiority.

The first Lebensborn home (Heim Hochland) opened in 1936 in Steinhöring, a village near Munich. The first home outside Germany was opened in Norway in 1941 to assist and support children born to German soldiers and Norwegian women. Approximately 8,000 children were born in Lebensborn homes in Germany, and 8,000 in Norway. Subsequently, Lebensborn established homes in several occupied countries including north-eastern Europe.

When the Nazis invaded Poland in 1939, Lebensborn sanctioned the kidnap of 'racially pure' children, a policy they adopted in all Eastern occupied countries, including Russia and the Ukraine. Thousands of children who matched the Nazis' ideal racial criteria (blond hair, blue or green eyes, long narrow frame and skulls etc) were snatched from their homes, schools, the streets and their families, and transferred to Lebensborn homes and boarding schools to be 'Germanized'. Once the process was complete they were placed for adoption in German families. Older children were told their parents were either dead or had rejected them. Children who failed further 'medical' tests to determine their racial purity, or fought against Germanization, were sent to concentration camps.

No one knows exactly how many children the Nazis kidnapped in Poland and other occupied countries. Historians estimate that between 200,000 and 300,000 children were forcibly seized and taken to Germany from Poland alone. Only 25,000 returned to their families after the war. The SS destroyed the children's original identity papers, and the few Lebensborn records that survived the war had been falsified, making it impossible to determine the children's original nationality or family name. If the children had been taken at an early age, they were unaware of their origins. Some German families became attached to their adopted Lebensborn children and refused to give them up at the end of the war; in many cases, the children themselves declined to return to their original family. Victims of Nazi propaganda, they believed they were German. Further problems were created by the Cold War. German and Allied Occupation authorities were often unwilling to take well-adjusted children from stable families and send them behind the Iron Curtain to Communist Poland.

The Nazis opened brothels for their troops and the SS, and staffed them with girls they enslaved from all the countries they invaded and occupied. But there is no evidence, beyond sensational and inaccurate journalism, that Himmler set up 'Lebensborn breeding centres' or SS 'stud' brothels with the aim of supplying racially pure children. The Nazis were evil, their crimes heinous, numerous and beyond the belief of civilized men and women. Embellishing facts and fictionlizing Nazi crimes only serves to hand ammunition to Neo-Nazis and Holocaust-deniers, who argue, still, that the Nazis are victims of post-war Allied propaganda.

There are numerous internet websites dedicated to recording the post-war and current plight of Lebensborn children; the most heart-breaking bear photographs of elderly men and women, who are still searching for clues to their identity and are hoping that someone, somewhere will recognize a family resemblance, even after sixty years.

Catrin Collier
May 2008